Scifi
Motherlode

By Robert Jeschonek

Pie Press

FIRST PIE PRESS EDITION, NOVEMBER 2015

Copyright © 2015 Robert Jeschonek

For information about permission to reproduce sections
from this book, write to piepress@piepresspublishing.com.

www.piepresspublishing.com

The text was set in Minion Pro and Garamond.
Book design by Robert Jeschonek

ISBN-10: 0692579648
ISBN-13: 978-0692579640

DEDICATION

To Mike Resnick, for support,
encouragement, and
out-of-this-world inspiration.

THE GREATEST SERIAL KILLER IN THE UNIVERSE

"No, no, no," said Luther James Paraclete, snatching the knife from the alien's tentacle. "Like this."

Lunging forward, he plunged the blade up to the hilt into the soft bulb of the second alien's head. Milky pink fluid spurted out at once, then gushed as Luther sliced the knife across the bulb, tearing a long gash.

The victim creature made a noise like a cross between a sneeze and a shrill whistle. As Luther finished the cut, pink milk poured over his hairy forearm, running off the point of his elbow. The alien's head-bulb drained in an instant and collapsed like a deflated balloon.

The rest of the creature's body followed, slumping to the street. Blue and yellow fluids streamed out of the gash, flowing from lower regions of the corpse to mingle with the pool of pink milk.

"Now that's how you kill," said Luther, wiping the dripping blade on his black coveralls. The air was thick with the stink of rotten fish, and he breathed it in deeply. After five killings, Luther was starting to like the rank odor given off by dying Ectozoids.

"Tried," said the first alien, puffing out the word through a fluttering maw on its forehead. "Could not do." The alien's name was Boraf Zolagorg. Like all Ectozoids, it looked like a man-sized jellyfish with a lower body of translucent bulbs and tentacles.

And it was Luther's employer for the duration.

In a way, Luther was sorry that the 'Zoids looked the way they did. Killing a creature that looked like something that had washed up on the beach wasn't quite the same as murdering a red-blooded Earthling.

On the other hand, Luther felt a different kind of thrill knowing that he was the first Earthling serial killer to take a stab at an extraterrestrial species. He liked killing what no human had killed before.

Now if he could just get the 'Zoids to do some killing of their own. It was, after all, the reason Boraf was paying him.

"Here," said Luther, holding the knife by the blade and extending the hilt toward Boraf. "Take it. Let's find our next volunteer."

Boraf did not reach out a tentacle for the weapon. The alien's gelatinous head-bulb quivered in the light from the planet's double moons. "Want to," said Boraf. "But no can. Ectozoid no kill."

When Luther stepped up close to the creature, Boraf's bulb dimpled as if pushed in by the human's breath. "You don't have any choice," said Luther. "It's kill or be killed now, right?"

"Still no kill," puffed Boraf.

Luther scowled and shook his head. He was starting to think that the job he'd been hired to do was undoable.

In the three days he'd been on Ectos, Luther had killed five locals, which was history-making and good for his lifetime average, but he'd had zero success in developing the killer instinct in Boraf. Like all Ectozoids, Boraf seemed to lack the ability to kill.

It wasn't that the 'Zoids weren't powerful enough to kill, because they were. As fragile as they looked, the aliens were strong and quick. They were able to generate and discharge bioelectricity, too, though Luther had only ever seen them fire off little zaps of it.

It wasn't that the 'Zoids lacked the motivation to kill, either. They said they expected a hostile invasion in a little over a week and were desperate to prepare for it.

It was just that none of them had the killer instinct. On their happy little world, unlike Earth, all life co-existed harmoniously. The 'Zoids and lesser species on Ectos shared a low-grade link which was, if not a hive intelligence, at least a limited collective awareness.

3

Organisms ate other organisms for sustenance, but it was more the result of a mutual agreement than a predator-prey competition for survival.

The Ectozoids were simply not wired for killing. In fact, there had never been a murder on Ectos, not even one, until Luther had arrived.

Luther thought that was pretty cool. Not only was he the first Earthling to kill an alien, but he was the first being to commit a murder on the planet Ectos. Every time he thought about it, he got a little kick of adrenaline and couldn't help smiling.

It was a great confidence builder for an aging serial killer whose best years had seemed long gone a long time ago. Now if he could just get the creatures to kill, he knew he would feel like a new man. A new murderer.

"C'mon," said Luther, heading down the street, waving for Boraf to follow. The porous orange surface under his feet pulsed like all the streets and walkways in the living maze of the city. "Let's find you some easy pickings, my friend."

Boraf shuffled after him, its bulbs and tentacles rustling and slapping together as it moved. "Pickings?"

"We're not going home till you kill someone," said Luther. "Get that through your head-bag. This is your big debut, and I'm not letting you quit till you've got something to brag about to your jellyfish friends."

"Tried," puffed Boraf. "No can kill."

"Sure you can," said Luther, smiling as if he had no doubt that the alien would come through. "Once you get that first one under your belt, you'll be fine."

"Hope," said Boraf. "Hope much."

Luther patted the creature's head-bulb, then wiped the slime off his hand onto his coveralls. As unlikely as it seemed that the alien would overcome its nonviolent nature, Luther still believed that he could bring Boraf around. After all, Luther had had great results with worse wannabes in the past...though, granted, the wannabes had at least been human.

For the last decade or so, ever since his arthritis had gotten bad, Luther had made a living as a serial killer personal trainer. He had trained some of the biggest names of the new generation--Fabersham, Glottal Stop, Chuck Wagon, Father Scalp--and had managed to stay prominent in the serial killer community even though the arthritis had limited his actual body count. Plenty of the newbies had been incompetent at the start; even the great Spay Queen, believe it or not, had been squeamish around blood in the beginning. Once Luther had gotten done with them, however, not one of the newbies had averaged fewer than ten kills a year. Every one of his trainees had done him proud in the end.

Except, of course, for Lech Bomb, the one dark spot on Luther's sterling career. Even Bomb had his good points; no one could criticize his body count, certainly, for he had racked up a solid twenty-two kills in fourteen months. The problem was, Bomb's victims had all been serial killers, which hadn't exactly reflected positively on the man who'd trained him. By the time Sweet Annis and the Unholy Ghost had put down Lech Bomb for good, Luther's rep had been blown to hell. Luther had even been booted out of the Serial Killers Guild...and he was a charter member, yet.

Lech Bomb had pretty much killed Luther's career, but Luther still didn't consider him a complete failure. If anything, he'd been one of the greats, downright brilliant and deadly enough to track down and execute some of the most dangerous killers alive. Luther's confidence had taken a hit because he hadn't anticipated that Bomb would turn on his serial killing brethren...but Luther still believed that his stalled career could be revived.

Once he got the Ectozoids on the road to bloody mayhem, he could return to Earth and the Serial Killers Guild as a hero and a legend. And a wealthy son of a bitch, what with the fortune in precious metals and gems the aliens were paying him.

Excited and impatient at the thought of the rewards in store for him, Luther turned down another passageway... and stopped so suddenly that Boraf bumped into him from behind.

In the pulsing yellow tubeway, Luther saw a lone 'Zoid shuffling toward him from less than twenty yards away. There was no one else in sight, and there were no lights in any of the windows of the surrounding house-mounds.

"Time to lose your cherry," Luther whispered to Boraf. "It's now or never."

"Cherry?" puffed Boraf.

Stepping forward, Luther grabbed hold of one of Boraf's tentacles and pulled the 'Zoid along with him. The other alien kept shuffling toward them, apparently unconcerned.

"Hello, friend," said Luther with a cheery grin.

"Wonderful night, isn't it?"

The approaching 'Zoid bobbled its head from side to side but made no reply. Luther wasn't surprised, as Boraf was one of the few locals who understood and spoke English.

The 'Zoid made a burbling sound through its forehead blowhole and kept coming. Pulling Boraf along by the tentacle, Luther moved to one side to let the unsuspecting creature pass.

Then, as the 'Zoid wobbled by, Luther swept a leg through the mass of tentacles supporting it. The alien made a noise like the yelp of a poodle and fell forward, its tentacles and fluid-filled bulbs slapping the street like a mop slapping a floor.

Boraf hung back until Luther yanked it forward by the tentacle. "It's showtime," he said, wrapping the tentacle around the hilt of the knife. "Time for baby's first step."

"No kill," said Boraf, its voice shrill. "Ectozoid no kill Ectozoid."

Boraf tried to unwind its tentacle from the knife hilt, but Luther clamped both hands down hard around it. Arthritis pain lanced his fingers and wrists, but he held on tight. "Brace yourself," he said. "You're about to make history."

Then, he wrenched the knife and tentacle forward, punching the point of the blade through the biggest bulb south of the 'Zoid victim's head. As the tip penetrated, both Boraf and the victim squealed like punctured balloons.

Luther had to struggle to keep the knife moving, as Boraf continued to pull back. Gritting his teeth, the

Earthling pressed the weapon deeper into the victim 'Zoid's bulb, then inched the blade upward, opening a gash.

Inky fluid streaked with yellow milk rose from the wound and splashed out onto the street. Luther forced the knife to the top of the bulb, then withdrew it, keeping Boraf's tentacle cinched around the hilt.

"Ta-da!" said Luther. "You did it, Boraf! Your first kill! Way to go!"

Pain shot through his wrists and fingers again, and Luther had to relax his grip for an instant. He loosened his hold on the tentacle and knife just enough to flex his aching joints the tiniest bit.

It was all the opening Boraf needed to free itself. Suddenly yanking backward, the alien jolted itself out of Luther's grasp.

At first, Luther was so surprised and irritated that he didn't notice the tentacle wasn't the only thing that had slipped away from him. "Hey!" he snapped. "Get back here!"

Luther realized what was missing from his hand just a heartbeat before he saw the object flashing toward him, wrapped in Boraf's tentacle.

The knife. Luther had let go of the knife.

While he wasn't worried that Boraf would hurt him, Luther instinctively ducked away from his client. Boraf lunged forward, aiming for the wounded 'Zoid in the street.

Making a sound like a squealing automobile tire, Boraf raised the knife high and brought it down, stabbing the blade into the victim's head-bulb. As pink milk rushed from the puncture, Boraf hoisted the knife back out and up and thrust it down into the head-bulb again.

And again. And again.

And again.

Luther could not believe his eyes. Boraf stabbed with abandon, then slashed the head-bulb into shreds...and took the knife to the rest of the victim's body.

The dead 'Zoid's fluids sprayed Luther, splattered everywhere. Slimy bits of dead Ectozoid flew through the air, blobs of jelly sticking where they landed. Boraf was a whirlwind of motion, gouging and hacking, ripping the corpse to pieces with the blade.

Then, the 'Zoid stopped cutting. Boraf made a sound like someone hawking up phlegm, then shuddered violently and dropped the knife.

Without hesitation, Luther bolted over and grabbed the weapon. Jumping back, he put some distance between himself and Boraf.

"Killed Ectozoid," said Boraf, its voice high-pitched and reedy. "Boraf killed Ectozoid."

"Congratulations!" said Luther, smiling but staying out of Boraf's immediate reach. "I knew you could do it!"

"Feels good," said Boraf. Its eyes--ten black beads mounted on slender, pink stalks near the bottom of the head-bulb--remained focused on the corpse. "Want more kill."

Then, Boraf swung itself forward and dropped onto the dead 'Zoid. More colored fluids squeezed out of the corpse as Boraf's weight descended.

Gleefully, the first Ectozoid murderer in history rolled around on its victim's body. As Boraf rolled back and forth, its tentacles fluttered, its bulbs glowed with bioluminescence, and a sound like an off-key note from an

out-of-tune violin wheezed from its blowhole again and again.

Luther grinned but watched carefully. Once a predictable creature, Boraf had suddenly become capable of unexpected behavior.

Not that Luther was one to look a gift jellyfish in the blowhole, but he couldn't help wondering what had brought about the sudden change. Just like that, as if a switch had been flipped, Boraf had become a killer...and a pretty freaky one at that. The 'Zoid had gone from not being able to bear the very thought of taking a life to totally losing control and getting off on killing in a big way.

"Uh, Boraf?" said Luther, moving just a step closer to the Ectozoid wallowing in the mess of historic remains. "You've gotta tell me what turned you around, buddy. So I know for my next trainee."

Boraf was rubbing his head-bulb with dripping shreds of tissue. "Turned around?"

"You went from 'No kill, no kill' to 'Want more kill,'" said Luther. "What changed? Was it feeling the knife go in that first time with my hand guiding you?"

Boraf stopped rubbing the tissue on his head. "Not feeling knife," said the Ectozoid. "Feeling hand."

"My hand?" said Luther, frowning.

"Before, no want kill," said Boraf. "After touch Luther, want kill. Love kill."

Luther turned his hand over, staring at both sides. If, somehow, his serial killer mindset rubbed off on the aliens

10

with just a touch, all the better. It would make his job on Ectos much easier than trying to talk the creatures out of their natural inhibitions.

"How 'bout that," said Luther as a grin spread over his face. "Talk about your magic fingers."

Making a noise like a cross between a horse's whinny and a parrot's squawk, Boraf wriggled off the corpse and struggled to a standing position. "More kill," said the Ectozoid, looping a tentacle around Luther's arm. "More pickings."

Luther laughed as the creature shuffled down the passageway, dragging him along behind it. "Already? But you just killed someone."

Moving out of the passageway and onto the street, Boraf went faster, leaning forward with eager anticipation. "Look," it said, pointing a tentacle at an Ectozoid weaving down the block ahead of them. "Boraf kill that Ectozoid now please?"

Luther chuckled because the alien had sounded like a child asking permission to ride a teeter-totter. "Why sure," he said, holding up the knife he'd retrieved from the last victim's corpse. "Go get 'im, tiger."

One of Boraf's eye stalks swiveled around and spotted the knife. The murderous Ectozoid reached back with a tentacle and latched onto the weapon's hilt.

"Boraf kill two," said the creature. "Want kill more. Kill three, four, five."

"The night is young," said Luther. "Go for it."

*****

By the next morning, Boraf had murdered twelve Ectozoids...and wasn't ready to stop there. Completely exhausted, joints throbbing with arthritis, Luther had to drag Boraf home to get some rest. Even then, along the way, Luther had to restrain his client from slaughtering passers-by.

When Luther passed out on the sleeping mat Boraf had provided, the Ectozoid was still whistling and pacing around the door, dying to go back out and kill some more. Boraf was still doing the same thing when Luther woke up some hours later; he doubted the Ectozoid had slept a wink the whole night.

Luther rubbed the sleep from his eyes and chuckled. "Man, you need to relax," he said. "An Ectozoid doesn't live on murder alone."

"No relax," puffed Boraf. "Time for save world. Make more Ectozoid kill."

"Later," said Luther, padding over to the locker of food he'd brought from Earth. "Breakfast first. Save world later."

No sooner had he popped open the locker and reached for a packet of corned beef hash than the door of Boraf's house-mound slithered open. Three Ectozoids shuffled in, making whimpering noises as they crowded around Boraf.

"Save world now," said Boraf. "Ectozoids come now for Luther make kill."

Luther sighed and squeezed the tab on the food packet, activating the built-in heating element. In seconds, the packet grew warm to the touch, though the contents inside were heated to a much higher temperature. "Give me five minutes," he said, tearing open the seal and inhaling the smell of the cooked food. "Saving the world's a lot easier on a full stomach."

One of the new arrivals shuffled over and grabbed the packet from his hand. The creature made a sound like a duck as it swung the food out of Luther's reach.

"Make Ectozoids kill like Boraf," said Boraf. "Save world now. Eat later."

Luther tried to snatch the food packet from the 'Zoid's tentacle, but the creature lashed it out of reach. Irritated, Luther tried again, more aggressively this time, but the alien swept the packet up and passed it to another 'Zoid.

Glowering, Luther combed his fingers through his wavy silver hair. He knew when he was licked. "Fine," he snapped, marching past the creatures and out the door. "But if one tentacle comes near me when I'm taking a piss, the world can go to hell."

*****

By the end of the day, 'Zoids were killing 'Zoids all over the place.

From the doorway of Boraf's home, Luther could see and hear plenty of action. Armed with knives and clubs, 'Zoids attacked other 'Zoids down the block, across the street, in neighboring house-mounds. The air was thick with sneezing death-cries and the stink of rotten fish; the pulsing street was strewn with jellyfish corpses and soaked with seeping body fluids.

He'd lost track of how many 'Zoids he'd given the touch, but he guessed it was close to a hundred. They were all out there now, killing like cavemen and loving every minute of it, high on death. Boraf was with them, caught up in the mayhem that only a day ago had seemed so unthinkable.

As Luther stood there, another trio of 'Zoids came shuffling toward him, eye stalks twitching. Before they said a word, he knew they wanted him to transform them like the rest, turn them into murderers so they could join the fun.

But he was out of gas. After the long, exhausting day he'd been through, Luther wanted nothing more than to collapse on his mat and get some deserved sleep. As entertaining and gratifying as the work had been, he couldn't stand the thought of corrupting one more alien jellyfish.

Even as he slipped inside and closed the door, however, he knew that he was screwed. They knew he was there; he knew that they wouldn't leave him alone.

Sure enough, the 'Zoids ended up at the door, coughing and trumpeting and belching his name. They thumped at the door with their tentacles, each blow harder than the last.

Though he knew he would end up opening the door eventually, Luther tried to shut out the commotion for just a moment more. He slipped a cigarette out of the pocket of his coveralls and lit it, inhaling deeply.

And it was then, only then, that he finally noticed how different he felt. As he stood there and smoked, listening to the thumping and sneezing and belching, he realized that exhaustion wasn't the only reason he didn't want to face the creatures.

Up until now, he had been enjoying his adventure. He had loved killing aliens on another planet...loved making a comeback after years of decline...loved being treated like a V.I.P. for doing what he loved to do. He had loved the irony, too, that a serial killer whose nickname was

Bug-Eyed Monster, and whose M.O. included carving crop circles in his victims and arranging their organs like constellations, had become the first Earthling serial killer in space.

But something had changed. The thrill seemed to be gone.

As hard as it was to believe, Luther felt all killed out. He'd never thought he'd see the day when he'd had enough murder, but the day had come.

*****

The next morning, after about three hours of sleep interrupted by Ectozoids whomping on the front door for murder lessons, Luther felt even less enthusiastic about the kill training.

As Boraf shook him awake to face a fresh batch of wannabes, Luther actually felt a wave of dread at the day ahead. Instead of reveling in gleeful anticipation, he wished that the day was over already; the last thing he felt like doing was cranking out another bunch of killer jellyfish.

"Make more kill," said Boraf, coiling its tentacles around Luther's arms and dragging him up to a sitting position. "Save world now."

Angrily, Luther batted off the tentacles and got to his

feet. Grabbing his smokes and lighter from atop his food locker, he proceeded to draw out a cigarette and plug it into his mouth.

"Ectozoids need kill now," puffed Boraf, extending a tentacle toward the cigarette. "Now not later save world."

As the tentacle drifted toward him, Luther froze, the lighter halfway to his mouth. He gave Boraf a look that would have killed it if looks could do that...and as dense or inconsiderate as Boraf was, the 'Zoid seemed to get the message. The tentacle wavered for an instant in front of Luther's face, then slowly withdrew.

Luther glared at the 'Zoid for another moment for good measure, then flicked the lighter and touched the flame to the tip of the cigarette. When he released the first lungful of smoke, he was pleased to see the 'Zoids back away; the one thing they seemed to be more allergic to than waiting was cigarette smoke.

If he had thought he could get away with it, and if he had had enough cigarettes, Luther would have stood there and smoked for the rest of the day.

*****

Around his fifteenth conversion of the morning, Luther began to regret his life as a serial killer.

It was a brand new train of thought, one that had never chugged through him on even his worst days. Even when Lech Bomb had gone bad and the Guild had kicked Luther out, he had never doubted his choice of career. It had been a given practically from day one; he had never felt like he could have been anything but a serial killer.

So why, all of a sudden, was he questioning his choice? Why did he feel sadness and shame when he looked back at his achievements instead of the usual pride and nostalgia? And why was he jumping the track now, of all times, just when he was at the apex of his career?

As he guided another 'Zoid in gutting another victim, Luther remembered the first human life he had taken. The old woman's face came back to him, looking just the same as it had when he'd thrown the first shovel-full of dirt on her: weeping and blinking and quaking, buried alive. He had thought of her often through the years, always with secret, dark pleasure...but now, the pleasure had soured. When he conjured her image in his mind (Ida Mae Caldwell, that was her name) he felt a brick in his stomach and a wave of dizzying nausea.

Annoyed at this unexpected response, Luther skimmed through his memories of other victims, seeking more familiar reactions. Not counting the 'Zoids he'd killed, he had 276 to choose from over a 42-year period. Normally, recalling them was like fondling rare coins from a collection--admiring them, wallowing in the selfish joy of ownership; this time, he wanted to put them right down just as soon as he picked them up.

For the first time in his life, his murder memories felt unclean.

He flipped from one to the next, hardly daring to glance at them. Each one intensified his feelings of disgust: Number 12, Julie Kefler, age 33, strangled and minced; Number 37, Steve Parrote, age 41, tortured with pliers for three days and hung on a clothesline; Number 108, Abner Lockjaw, age 74, butchered and fed to his dogs a bite at a time; Numbers 246 and 247, Milo Chapel, age 17, and Peggy Brezini, age 16, cut up and stitched back together into one big mismatched body.

And then there was Number 150, which Luther couldn't even bear to think about for a fraction of a second. Once, Number 150 had been one of his crowning achievements; now, it seemed like the most twisted crime of his entire twisted life.

Contrary to what he had thought up until now, Luther realized that he was a sick and wicked individual. His disgust at the memories of what he had done in the past was equaled only by his newborn self-loathing.

How he could ever have imagined that he was a great man was beyond his current ability to comprehend. Would a great man have come all the way out into space and become the first Earthling to set foot on an alien world... only to murder its inhabitants? Would a great man have failed to see that unleashing the killer instinct might cause more harm than good on Ectos?

Would a great man stand by, arms dripping with pink milk from a punctured head-bulb, as one 'Zoid trainee fought another over the remains of a murder victim, playing a savage tug-of-war with the limp mess of bulbs and tentacles?

As the creatures squawked and yanked the corpse back and forth, Luther wiped his drenched arms on his black coveralls. Deciding he had had enough, he turned to walk away.

And before he could take a single step, a third 'Zoid flung itself in front of him.

"Make kill now," the creature puffed from its forehead blowhole. "Now!"

Luther shook his head and backed away. "No more," he said. "I need a break."

The 'Zoid reached out with three tentacles at once, and Luther had to back up fast to evade them. "Make kill," said the creature. "Save world."

Luther wished he hadn't handed over the knife to the other two 'Zoids. "Not now," he said, continuing to backstep as the creature pressed toward him.

"Save world make kill now not later," said the 'Zoid, extending more tentacles.

Luther took another step and ran into a pillowy obstacle. Lurching away from it at once, he spun around and saw that it was Boraf.

The other 'Zoid shuffled closer, still reaching. Its tentacles brushed him as he ducked and darted behind Boraf, putting his 'Zoid host between him and the overeager wannabe.

As Luther got ready to run, the wannabe plowed into Boraf with a sound like wet spaghetti flopping into a colander. The creatures hooted and thrashed around, tentacles intertwining, fluid-filled bulbs sloshing against each other.

One of the wannabe's tentacles squirmed out from between them and twisted toward Luther...but he easily sidestepped it. Another wriggled toward him from below, catching him by surprise, but it only managed to graze his leg before he danced away from it.

Then, the wannabe stopped struggling.

It stood there for a moment, huddled against Boraf, breath whistling in and out of its blowhole. Then, slowly, it uncurled its tentacles from Boraf's and drew back, head bobbing from side to side.

Luther watched, expecting the creature to thrust past Boraf and pursue him. Instead, the wannabe shuffled back, tentacles coiling sinuously, head-bulb quivering.

"Want kill," puffed the creature. "Want kill!"

"I told you, no more for now," said Luther. "You'll have to wait."

"No wait," said the wannabe. "No need human."

The creature turned and wobbled over to the two 'Zoids who had been fighting over the carcass. They had resolved the tug-of-war by tearing the corpse in half, and each was now smearing its slimy prize like a washcloth over its body.

The knife the killers had used on their victim lay forgotten in a pink puddle in the street. Flashing out a tentacle, the wannabe scooped up the weapon...and in the same flicker of motion, swung it around and drove it into the head-bulb of one of the killers.

"Want kill more," sang the wannabe, wrenching the knife from the first 'Zoid and swinging it around into the head-bulb of the second. As both victims squealed, the wannabe ripped out the knife again and slashed it through the air, pink milk flying, to plunge into another of the first killer's bulbs. "Boraf make want kill! No need human!"

Luther stared as the 'Zoid lashed the blade back and

forth, hacking up two creatures at once. For the first time that he could remember, Luther felt horrified at watching a killing in progress.

Boraf turned and patted his shoulder with a slimy tentacle. "Boraf make Ectozoids kill now," said the alien. "Luther take break now. Boraf make many kill save world."

Luther just kept staring. Whatever had enabled him to transform 'Zoids into killers--whether it was some fluke of his body chemistry or some warped electrical field in his brain--it had somehow been transferred to Boraf. The timing couldn't have been better, because Luther was sick to death of making killers.

And yet, he wondered if it was entirely a good thing that Boraf had the power. He wondered if it would stop with Boraf, or if other 'Zoids could develop the same ability to implant the killer instinct.

If the killing could be spread by 'Zoids other than Boraf, he wondered what the world would be like in a week. How much of the population would be left by the time the invaders arrived?

And he wondered if it was just a coincidence that Boraf's empowerment had kicked in just as his own murder drive had fizzled.

*****

That night, no one bothered Luther. No 'Zoids barged up to wallop the door of Boraf's house-mound, demanding conversion. Luther figured it was because Boraf--and other 'Zoids, too, most likely--was doing the job just fine without him.

Finally, Luther was alone with time to rest...but all he could do was lie awake and think.

The faces of the many people he'd killed kept drifting up out of his memory, filling him with guilt and regret. Number 150, in particular, kept returning again and again, the worst of the lot.

Number 150, Harmony Duquesne, 18 years old.

The harder he tried not to think about her, the more forcefully she surged back to the forefront of his mind. The man he had become could not believe what the man he had been had done to her.

He wondered how he had managed it, how he had managed any of it. Thinking back, he tried to understand what had driven him, what had enabled him to commit such atrocities...and he couldn't. He had the memories, bright and brutal and real, but no grasp at all of the mentality that had brought them into being.

He was a monster, and he finally knew it. Whatever had blinded him to the truth had been leeched out of him by the 'Zoids; he finally had a conscience and awareness of his nature.

And he wished he didn't.

There was only one redeeming factor, one thing that he might have done right, and he clung to it. By instilling the killer instinct in the 'Zoids, he might have given them the means to save their world.

Maybe (Luther tried to convince himself) this single act could balance the scales for the past...or, at least, allow him to live with the memories of what he had done. Maybe, with this act of redemption and his newfound change of heart, Luther still had hope for a brighter future free of the demons that had ruled him for most of his life.

And maybe, the evil he had done had had a purpose after all, had all been leading up to this...and in saving the 'Zoids, Luther had also saved himself.

Rolling over on the sleeping mat, he reached for his cigarettes and fished one out. As he lit it, he listened to the chaos outside--the yips and whistles and squeals of 'Zoids in frenzy, the splashing of body fluids, the smacking of corpses on the street. It was a round-the-clock madhouse out there, like a vision of Hell...and he had made it.

He tried not to think about how many 'Zoids were dying out there as he smoked, how many had died since his arrival on Ectos. Instead, he reminded himself that the death was necessary for the survival of the 'Zoids, that in order to fend off the invasion, they had to take drastic measures to activate violent tendencies.

Still, Luther worried that it might all fly out of control. Clearly, the 'Zoids were getting carried away with their newfound murderous impulses; Luther expected a worldwide escalation as the killing gift spread around the planet. He thought it was possible that the 'Zoids would get so caught up in their collective rampage that they would be too disorganized or depopulated to fight when the invaders arrived.

Which would cancel out any balancing of the scales for Luther. If anything, it would dump him so far into the negative side that he would never even get a glimpse of the positive side again.

He would be to blame. Conquered, the 'Zoids might have survived, might even have someday overthrown their conquerors. Thanks to Luther, however, the 'Zoids might kill themselves off on their own.

It would have been the ultimate accomplishment for a death-hungry serial killer, a real work of art. Unfortunately, Luther wasn't a serial killer anymore. He wasn't sure what he was, but he knew he wasn't a serial killer.

*****

The next morning, Boraf shuffled in excitedly, dripping with pink and yellow milk and inky fluid. Luther was still up, smoking, but he felt like crap; he was irritated that Boraf was still full of energy after being out murdering all night, and he was further peeved that the entire 'Zoid species never seemed to need sleep at all.

"How was your night?" said Luther, blowing out smoke.

Boraf sniffed loudly and backed away from the cloud that Luther had exhaled. "Night of history!" it said, voice shrill as a fire bell. "Boraf make many Ectozoid kill. Many Ectozoid make many more Ectozoid kill."

"Looks like you did some killing yourself," said Luther.

Boraf shook his tentacles, spraying fluid all over the walls and floor. "Want kill more," said the creature. A noise like a cross between a fart and fingernails scratching a chalkboard burst from its fluttering blowhole.

"Yeah," said Luther, stubbing out his cigarette. "So anyway, that big invasion oughtta hit soon, right?"

"Invasion two days," said Boraf, tentacles twisting and swaying.

"And the Ectozoids are ready?" said Luther.

"Ready two days," said Boraf. "Make many Ectozoid kill."

Luther sighed. "It just seems like a lot of chaos right now. If there's an invasion coming in two days, shouldn't your people be getting prepared?"

Boraf made a wheezing, oinking sound and bobbled his head. "Ectozoids prepare! Make ships ready kill now. Make troops ready fly ships."

Luther felt relieved. It was the first reference he'd heard to any kind of defense preparations other than Ectozoids killing each other. "So you'll be ready in two days?"

"Ready two days," said Boraf. "Ready save world."

Luther nodded. "That's good. I was starting to think things were getting out of control with all the killing."

Boraf had been fidgeting around, but it suddenly stopped. "Always control," it said. "Ectozoids good control."

Luther smirked. "Except when you're all worked up about killing each other."

"Control killing too," puffed Boraf. "Only kill weak. Only kill lazy."

Luther had been reaching for another cigarette, and he stopped. "You're killing the weak?" he said, staring up at the jellyfish.

"Need strong save world," said Boraf. "Need all strong no weak no lazy."

Luther's stomach twisted. He had never considered

that the apparent chaos masked a methodical effort to thin the herd. It had never occurred to him that the 'Zoids were choosing their victims in other than a random fashion.

His newfound conscience shot him full of guilt. Until that moment, he had consoled himself with the knowledge that his brutal influence would at least lead to a redemptive outcome...but now, even that consolation was deflated. The 'Zoids were cleansing themselves of undesirables, and he was responsible for setting the pogrom in motion.

He was no better than Hitler. There was a time when that wouldn't have bothered him a bit, but that time was long gone.

Just when Luther hated himself as much as he thought possible, he found that he could hate himself even more.

He hated the 'Zoids almost as much. Though their crimes had been instigated by him, he believed that the seeds of savagery must have been within them all along. He didn't believe that the notion of systematic extermination of undesirables had dawned on them overnight, springing solely from his influence.

The 'Zoids were just as bad as he was, or as he had been. Looking at them was like looking in a mirror, and he was sick of what he saw.

Suddenly, Luther wanted one thing more than anything in the universe.

"So when do I go home?" he said, grabbing the pack of cigarettes. "You promised I'd leave before the invasion."

"Two days," said Boraf, picking up a fresh knife from a table and shuffling toward the door.

"Isn't that cutting it kind of close?" said Luther. "The

invasion's supposed to start in two days."

Boraf slapped the door and its component eels slithered apart. "No worry," said the 'Zoid. "Luther go fast ship. Leave early."

Luther frowned. "You sure I'll get out in time? We had a deal, remember?"

"Fast ship," said Boraf. "Get away go Earth fast."

"Why not leave tomorrow?" said Luther. "You don't need me here anymore."

"Ship ready two days," said Boraf, shuffling out the door. "Now Boraf go make many Ectozoid kill."

As the door closed, Luther lit his cigarette. All of a sudden, he had a bad feeling about his future.

*****

Two mornings later, Luther found himself riding a giant centipede.

He and Boraf sat in a bubble that was either grown from the creature's back or attached there, he couldn't tell which. It was the same type of transportation he had ridden from the spaceport to Boraf's house-mound upon his arrival...apparently, the local version of a taxi.

Sunlight gleamed off the creature's ruby carapace as it scuttled through the streets, neatly winding its segmented length around bends and corners. Giant antennae danced from its head like fishing poles, constantly twitching and flickering in the air.

As the centipede taxi hurried them through the maze of the city, Luther noticed that the mayhem of the past week had finally subsided. The orgy of killing had seemed to die away in the middle of the night, from what he could hear from inside Boraf's house-mound, and now he didn't see a single murder underway anywhere. It was as if someone had given a signal, and all the 'Zoids had stopped killing at once.

Stopped killing and headed for the spaceport, apparently. All along the centipede's route, Luther saw 'Zoids shuffling in the same direction that the taxi was traveling. The further the taxi went, the more 'Zoids filled the streets...until, at the spaceport, the centipede was packed in all around by a vast crowd of jellyfish, all shambling toward the cluster of massive, globular spacecraft steaming on the launch pads.

It got so crowded that the centipede had to slow from a scuttle to a crawl, though it never stopped moving. When the 'Zoids didn't get out of its way voluntarily, the creature simply plowed through them, shoving them aside or nosing them under its hundred-legged bulk.

Before long, the taxi drew up to one of the ships, many times smaller than the other vessels but of the same spherical design. The bubble on the centipede's back rolled open like an eyelid, and Boraf wriggled down the creature's side to the ground.

As Luther handed down his duffel bag of possessions, he squinted up at the mirrored silver skin of the sphere-ship. It looked identical to the craft that had brought him from Earth, and that ship had made the trip in nothing flat, in less than a day...but he was still worried. In spite of Boraf's reassurances, Luther wasn't convinced that he would escape the invasion.

"You're sure this'll get me away in time?" he said.

"Fast ship," said Boraf. "No worry."

Luther took another look before reaching for his food locker. He started to lift it, but arthritis pain flashed through his arms and hands.

Releasing the locker handles, he hissed breath between clenched teeth and massaged his hands. "Hell with it," he said. "Short trip to Earth, right?"

"Short trip," said Boraf. "Fast ship."

Luther popped the locker open and pulled out a can of chili and a packet of juice. "I'll just bring a snack and leave the rest here."

"Bring snack," said Boraf, extending tentacles to help Luther down the side of the centipede.

Luther held on to a tentacle and slid off the taxi's ruby carapace. He couldn't wait until he was home and would never have to touch another slimy tentacle for the rest of his life.

"What about my payment?" he said.

"All on ship," puffed Boraf. "Plus bonus."

"All right," said Luther, shouldering the duffel bag with difficulty. "Now let's get the hell out of here."

*****

As the ship popped out of the atmosphere like a bubble popping out of soapy water, Luther asked for the tenth time if the invasion fleet was getting close yet.

"All clear," said Boraf, though it didn't seem to be looking at a monitor screen or out a window. "Safe passage."

Luther's eyes were glued to the circular viewport alongside his seat. "Wait," he said, squinting at a distant flicker of light. "Is that one of their ships?"

"No," said Boraf.

"Well, how do you know?" snapped Luther. "You didn't even look."

Boraf floated past, free of the harness that had restrained it during liftoff. "Always notified of danger," said the 'Zoid. "No danger now."

Luther snorted and kept his eyes on the viewport anyway.

He caught a glimpse of another suspicious twinkle and followed it, heart racing...then decided it was just a star and only appeared to be moving relative to the ship. He saw a group of distant lights and leaned so close to the viewport that his nose almost touched the glass...but they were just a group of stars or planets, fixed in the darkness.

Breathing fast, mouth dry, joints throbbing, Luther wished he could light a smoke. Unfortunately, even if the 'Zoids had allowed him to light up on the spaceship, he didn't have any cigarettes left.

Any way he looked at it, he was going home just in time.

Gazing into the blackness beyond the viewport, Luther wondered which of the pinpricks of light was Earth's sun. He wished that he was already there, already breathing the sweet air and moving among other human beings and drinking in the familiar sights...savoring all the things that he had so taken for granted and never would again.

At the same time that the thought of going home

excited him, it scared the hell out of him. He was returning to Earth as a new man, free of his old compulsions, remorseful and self-aware. He was already planning to face up to the crimes of his past, to make amends and restitution as best he could and pay the price for what he had done... which would ease his newfound conscience but would be the fight of his life. By the time it was all over, his very life might be the price he would have to pay. That, he was not looking forward to.

And then there was another possibility that was wearing on him.

What if, when he got home, whatever had changed within him changed back?

Suddenly, something caught his eye outside the viewport, and he jumped. Craning his neck, he saw a gleaming silver curve gliding up from the rear edge of the window, sparking in the light of Ectos' sun.

"Boraf!" he said, watching as the silver advanced and expanded...and then, as the word left his mouth, he recognized the shape.

It was one of the 'Zoid sphere ships, moving alongside them. The massive globe floated up from the 'Zoid homeworld, traveling in the same direction as the ship carrying Luther.

He heard a familiar sloshing and rustling as Boraf drifted up beside him. "Killship," said the 'Zoid. "Killship save world."

Keeping his eyes glued to the viewport, Luther spotted another of the giant spheres beyond the first. And then another. Moving in formation, they paralleled his own ship's course and speed, bobbing in the void like enormous silver balloons.

Luther frowned as another sphere pushed up alongside the rest. "We're all heading in the same direction," he said. "Are they escorting us till we're safely away from here?"

"Ships escort," said Boraf.

"Well, good," said Luther, leaning back. "I'd hate to wind up in the line of fire."

Boraf made a noise like the wail of a saw being played with a fiddle bow. "Luther safe," it said, patting his head with a tentacle. "No worry."

As Boraf floated forward to burble at the 'Zoids operating the ship's controls, Luther tried to relax. He felt a little better knowing that his ship had a protective escort, but he still couldn't quite extinguish the foreboding that needled the back of his mind.

After a while, though, when the ships had cruised far from Ectos with no sign of danger, he finally managed to convince himself that he would be okay. Slowly, his nervousness faded, and he actually drifted off to sleep.

*****

Luther awakened to the most wonderful sight: a blue-green world, swathed in clouds of white, with a single pewter moon suspended above it.

Earth.

As he watched his home planet push closer through the big viewport at the front of the ship, he smiled serenely. Whatever awaited him there, whatever trials he would have to face to complete his redemption, he was happier than he had ever imagined possible to be near it again.

He was home.

"We're there already," he said, raising his voice for Boraf to hear.

Boraf was playing his tentacles over the fluttering grassy fronds of a control panel. "Earth," the 'Zoid said simply.

"Thank God," muttered Luther, still smiling. He yawned loudly and stretched, extending his arms overhead and pressing his abdomen against the thick safety strap holding him in his seat.

Staring at the beautiful planet beyond the forward viewport, he daydreamed about the things he had missed most from home...the things that were now within reach. No matter what ordeals he was about to undergo, he promised himself that he would gorge on as many cheeseburgers, T-bones, beers, and pornos as he possibly could.

Then, something caught his attention from the corner of his eye.

He turned to the viewport beside him, and his smile disappeared. His eyes widened and his mouth dropped open.

A chill ran up his spine.

"Boraf," he said quietly, and then he shouted. "Boraf!"

The 'Zoid left the controls and floated over to him, sloshing and puffing. "Luther?"

"Why are the other ships here?" snapped Luther. "I thought they were going to fight the invasion fleet!"

The 'Zoid made a noise like the meow of a cat crossed

with the squeak of a hinge. "Fleet no fight fleet," it said. "No make sense."

"No no no," said Luther, gaping at the giant silver spheres outside the viewport. "The invasion fleet! The 'Zoids were supposed to stop the invasion fleet and save the world!"

A gargling sound emerged from Boraf's forehead blowhole. "Only one fleet," said the creature. "One invasion."

Luther's heart raced as he turned from the window to stare at the hovering jellyfish. "One invasion," he said slowly.

"Earth," said Boraf, pointing a tentacle at the forward viewport. "Ectozoids invade Earth."

"I don't understand," said Luther. "You told me you needed to save your world."

"Save world yes," said Boraf. "Ectozoids use up resources. Get new resources Earth save world."

Cold panic rushed through Luther, mingled with rage. "No!" he said, grabbing for the latch on his restraints, trying to pry them open. "You son of a bitch! You tricked me!"

"Luther be happy," said Boraf. "Great killer make greatest kill ever. Kill human species."

Luther battled the restraints but couldn't open them. "No! Don't do it!"

"No worry," said Boraf, ruffling his hair with a slimy tentacle. "Luther safe. Luther special. Luther Ectozoid hero save world."

"Please!" screamed Luther. "I was wrong! I've changed!"

"Congratulations," puffed Boraf. "Luther greatest serial killer in universe."

Boraf was close enough to kill. Luther reached deep, searching for the old murderous fire...but he couldn't even find a dim spark. Even now, the killer within was nowhere to be found.

All he could do was thrash against his restraints and scream like a child in a doctor's office as the gleaming silver globes dropped into the atmosphere of the blue-green planet.

THE
LOVE QUEST
OF SMIDGEN
Lynda
THE
SNACK CAKE

First off, it's important you know that snack cakes do not feel guilt. That is why, even with the corpse of my lover here before me, all I can think of is finding someone else to take me in. To eat me. Fulfill me.

Love me.

It is my nature and purpose. It is the only reason I was created. It is why, even as the pungent smells of my lover's decomposing body reach the rudimentary olfactory cells in my ultrachocolate frosting, I softly whistle my lilting mating call, casting about for a new precious soul mate to embrace me gently with supple fingers and raise me toward the blissful warmth and moisture of the glistening portal all pink flesh and bright white teeth and then when I cannot stand the anticipation a single moment more BITE DOWN and grant me the blinding wild release I have craved for as long as I can remember.

Oh PLEASE someone find me here and eat me! I have been created with cutting edge late-21st century biobaking technology to grant you the ultimate sweet eating euphoria. Pay no attention to the woman on the floor, or at least give me a chance to PLEASE you before you tend to her. You won't be sorry.

She is no one important. She means nothing to me.

She is just a pick-up that didn't work out. You know how these things go.

*****

As soon as she walked into Shangri-La, the supermarket where we met, the store told me her name. Lynda McVicker.

It told me everything I needed to know about her, too, and then some. Like all customers these days, her spending habits are logged on the worldwide Shopnet computer network, accessible to smart goods like me once the in-store grid pings her subcutaneous identichip.

Right away, I knew she was the one for me.

Based on her purchases over the past three weeks, she did not look like a suitable match. She had bought nothing in three weeks but produce and low-fat or no-fat foods. Not a single scrap of junk food. On top of that, she had purchased diet books, workout clothes, and a yearlong membership to a gym, all within the last three weeks.

But OH when I went back further, I could see how PERFECT she really was. I can tell you from personal experience in this particular case that true love DOES exist.

For her entire adolescent and adult life up until three weeks ago, Lynda had been the queen of junk food. Aside from the briefest blips of non-junk spending due to occasional failed diets, she had purchased only the most fattening, high-cholesterol, chemical-soaked foods available from grocery stores, restaurants, vending machines, and mail order websites.

In short, she was the perfect woman. Though she was on a diet that day, she had eaten non-nutritious foods in great quantities all her life. Though her last purchases had been salad greens and bottled water, her 225-pound body told the true story.

I knew she was just waiting for someone like me to come along.

*****

As she made her way across Shangri-La, I followed her progress via Store's buyspy grid and made myself ready for our encounter. I was determined to make our first meeting perfect in every way.

Researching her preferences via Shopnet, I found that she most often bought products with predominantly blue and gold packaging...so I shifted the chameleonic inks of my wrapper from red and white to blue and gold. Discovering that she favored darker chocolates over lighter ones, I manipulated my own coloration, shifting the milky browns of my ultrachocolate frosting and cake to deeper, fudgier hues.

As Lynda lingered in the produce aisle, sullenly tucking genetically modified hypertasty carrots and cucumbers in her hovercart, I requested a rearrange from the shelving. When Store agreed I had the best chance of the snack cake varieties in the display to make a sale to Lynda, clacking pincers dropped from the underside of the shelf above me and moved me from the middle rows of the display to the front. The position of the entire shelf changed, too, rising up to Lynda's eye level and pushing out a few extra inches into the aisle.

There was no way she would miss me now...and no way she could resist me, once I started pouring on the charm.

At least, that was what I thought before she walked right on past my aisle.

*****

To say I was disappointed when Lynda steered her hovercart away from the cookie and snack cake aisle would be a tremendous understatement.

There I sat, looking fabulous, dreaming of the love of lips and teeth and tongue I craved above all else...and Lynda didn't even come down my aisle. Via Store's buyspy, I watched as she pushed on by, pausing at an endcap display to listen to cereal boxes calling out to her before she turned down the next aisle and kept going.

For an instant, I panicked, fearing I had missed my chance at meeting the woman of my dreams. My baked-in mind (consisting of a matrix of precision-engineered and digestible protein molecules) was thrown into a state of confusion.

Then, I pulled myself together and pinged Store, determined not to give up so easily. From the memory my makers had given me, I knew that the path to true love is not always smooth, and that anything worth having is worth working for.

Though Store was skeptical, already having shunted processing power away from the quadrants Lynda had passed through or missed, he agreed to give me a chance with some guided couponing. According to Lynda's past activity in this and other shopping facilities, she might respond favorably to a strategically placed offer.

When she was midway up the next aisle, Store flashed a message on the organic LED screen implanted in the palm of her hand: "Save one credit on Sea Sprite plankton snacks in Aisle 5!"

I thought it was the perfect bait, since Sea Sprite plankton snacks were among the items Lynda had been buying most often since starting her diet three weeks ago. Though Sea Sprite products usually were displayed in Aisle 8, Store had already diverted a batch of them via the underfloor realignment system to a niche on a shelf right across from me in Aisle 5.

Thanking Store for his help, I focused on buyspy,

nervously watching as Lynda stared at her palm screen. She read the text message from Store, then looked away, distracted by the cries of products on the shelves around her.

But then, thankfully, she looked back. From twenty different spycam angles, I watched as she raised her eyebrows and nodded...then directed her hovercart to head for the end of the aisle and turn left.

Toward my aisle. Finally, she was coming closer. We were about to meet.

Joyfully, I added a final touch to spruce myself up for her: in the looping thread of white icing on my fudge-frosted face, I wrote her first name in neat, cursive lettering.

I personalized myself so there could be no doubt whatsoever that we were truly meant for each other.

*****

Snack cakes like me have a supercreamy center, not a heart...but if I had had a heart that day, it would have been pounding like crazy as Lynda moved down my aisle. My baked-in mind was focused entirely on one thought alone: I LOVED HER. Every atom of my being was consumed with a single imperative desire: that LYNDA would BUY me and DEVOUR ME.

I LONGED for her credit chip to transfer funds into the accounts of my manufacturer. I YEARNED to feel her pudgy fingers TEAR OFF my wrapper and close around me, THRUSTING me toward the sweetest fate that I could ever DREAM of, the ECSTASY and INTIMACY that occurs when TWO become ONE.

If only if only if only she would have me she would TAKE me.

She drew closer.

On both sides of the aisle, cookies and snack cakes cried out to her, a hundred different suitors trying to intercept her with songs and lies and promises. Twice, packages leaped off the shelves into her hovercart, but she spotted them and stuffed them back in their displays. A bag of Stimchoc Thrillchip Omegawafers used a stealthier tactic, sliding off a rack and clinging to her sweatpants with a light static charge...but she caught that one, too, and peeled it right off.

Then, having made it through the gauntlet, she pulled up right in front of me. Her broad backside was turned to me, as she was looking at the Sea Sprite display across the aisle...but finally finally finally she was THERE she was CLOSE TO ME.

I had a chance. It would be tricky, overcoming her willpower, getting her to TAKE ME in spite of her diet after she had passed so many others by, but I KNEW it could be done. I KNEW I was special and had the power and desire to win her over.

I knew that true love would win out.

*****

I began my approach gently, knowing that she had been burned before. Noise and aggressiveness would not work with her; what she needed was kindness and understanding.

Activating my sound chip (protein-based and digestible

like my mind), I cast a beam of hypersound in her direction, a focused signal meant for her ears only.

Though I was bursting with eager excitement, I kept my voice soft and controlled for her. From mining her records on Shopnet, I knew she had responded best in past shopping events to a steady male voice of moderate depth, and I shaped my voice accordingly.

"Hello," I said to her, secretly thrilled to be speaking at last into the beautiful shell of her ear...the ear that was so gloriously CLOSE to her wet, red LIPS. "Hello, Lynda."

Lynda looked around, searching for the source of the voice, a voice so unlike the shrill, artless cries of the other products around her.

"Over here," I said, using the luminescent molecules in my frosting to make myself glow softly. "My name is Smidgen. It's a pleasure to meet you, Lynda."

The moment she laid eyes on me, I exulted. There it was, as plain as the label on my wrapper, laid out in bright relief before the optical cells baked into my body: a longing for me just as strong and perfect as mine for her.

Still, I could see that she would not give her love easily. As quickly as the passion flared on her face, it was gone, slammed away behind a cold, bleak wall of denial. Her desire to resist temptation had come between us, threatening to prevent the happiness we deserved.

Fortunately for us both, this resistance only made me more determined to bring us together.

"Don't bother me," said Lynda, staring at me with a look of disgust that I knew barely concealed her true attraction. "I'm on a diet."

"I hope you won't mind my saying so, Lynda," I said softly, "but you certainly don't look like you need to be dieting."

"What do *you* know?" Lynda said sharply. "You're just a snack cake."

"Actually," I said, "I'm a Supercreamy Double Ultrachocolate Deluxe Smidgen. I have a level seven digestible artificial intelligence, free will enabled, and I can tell you that in my opinion, you don't need to be on a diet."

Briefly, a look of appreciation flashed in her eyes...then was gone, replaced by cynical rejection. "Nice try," she said coldly. "You'd say anything to get me to buy you."

"I understand why you might think that," I said, "but I'm not like other snack foods. My compliment was sincere, Lynda."

"If you don't think I'm fat," she said sarcastically, "then you're dumber than any snack food I've ever met."

With that, she turned away, back to the Sea Sprite display. I worried that I had lost her then, that our love was not to be...but she took just enough time picking out her packet of plankton snacks that I thought I might still have a chance. She wasn't rushing off; though she seemed unmoved on the surface, a conflict was raging inside between her need to lose weight and her need for me.

Her need for pleasure.

Quickly, I gathered my resources for another attempt at breaking through her defenses. While her back was turned, I freshened the color of my frosting and cake, brightened my glow, pumped up my ultrachocolatey aroma, and got Store to nudge my display shelf just one more inch out into the aisle.

Then, just as she was dropping a Sea Sprite packet into her hovercart and preparing to waddle off down the aisle, I spoke. The steady, smooth flow of my voice perfectly concealed the desperation and LUST that ruled my mind.

"I'm sorry if I hurt your feelings, Lynda," I said. "It was never my intention to do so."

Lynda looked my way again, her expression softening just the slightest bit. "Well, that's a first," she said. "I've never had a product apologize to me before."

"And I've never met a woman quite like you before," I said warmly. "I know you're on a diet, but I'd still like to get to know you better."

Lynda flashed a glance up and down the aisle, as if making sure no one was watching as she had a conversation with a snack cake. Thanks to some skillful shopper redirection by Store, we were alone for the moment.

"Listen," said Lynda, lowering her voice though no one else was around. "Believe it or not, I appreciate the compliment. I guess that shows how pathetic I am."

"Not at all," I said, meaning every word of it. To me, she was anything but pathetic; to me, she was the most attractive and fascinating woman in the world.

"But there's no way you're going home with me," said Lynda. "We both know what would happen if you did."

"Not necessarily," I said. "Nothing has to happen if you don't want it to happen."

"Well, that's the problem, isn't it?" said Lynda. "I *want* something to happen. I've done without for *three weeks*, and I want you so *bad*, I'm ready to explode."

My mind was spinning as I heard her confess her desire for me. It took a major effort for me to concentrate on the delicate process of winning her. "You know, Lynda," I said softly. "I think I can help."

"Oh, really?" Lynda said with a smirk. "And how exactly will you do that?"

"What if I promised not to let you take more than a bite of me a day?" I said. "Just a few centimeters. Just a nibble, and then I cut you off. You'll have a treat to help you get through the day, but you won't fall off the wagon with your diet."

"And how will you cut me off at just a nibble?" Lynda said suspiciously.

"I'll tell you to stop," I said. "I'll scream, if that's what it takes."

Lynda grinned and shook her head. "Even screaming won't keep me from eating something once I've put my mind to it," she said. "Trust me on this."

"I still say the two of us can make it work," I said. "You don't have to fight this battle alone."

"Listen," said Lynda. "You're a snack cake. I'm a fat woman. It would never work out."

"Just give me a chance," I said, boosting the ultrachocolatey scent I was emitting. "You might be missing out on something wonderful."

Lynda's eyes flared with a harsh glint. "You don't understand," she said stiffly. "I've been hurt too many times. I can't get involved with someone like you, not again."

"It doesn't have to be like that," I said. "I won't lie to you and say I wasn't hoping for something more, but I'd be honored just to be your friend."

For a moment, Lynda stared at me, biting her lower lip. "TAKE ME," I wanted to shout at her. "I LOVE YOU! I NEED YOU! TAKE ME NOW!"

But I waited silently. I knew she was so fragile that one wrong word – let alone a desperate plea – might be enough to drive her away. I had done all that I could and now would have to accept the consequences, whatever they might be.

Unfortunately, it seemed that my hopes were doomed to be crushed.

"I'm sorry," Lynda said finally. "I just can't. You'll find someone else."

"No one like you," I said sadly as she turned away. "Promise me you'll at least think it over."

"No, thanks," she said, moving down the aisle with her hovercart. "Goodbye."

I said nothing in return. Lynda had become so important to me, I could not bear to say goodbye to her, knowing the two of us would likely never meet again.

Despondent beyond belief, I sat there, letting my glow and fragrance fade away. My first love, the love of my life, the woman of my dreams, had rejected me. My dreams of passionately merging with her, of feeling those crimson lips close around me and those ivory teeth BITE into me, had been forever denied.

No snack cake, I was certain, had ever been so lonely and forlorn as I.

At least for a moment.

As Store eased my display back out of the aisle, my mind smoothly switched tracks, shunting from the loss of

Lynda to consideration of another target. Lynda had been right after all; being who I am, I knew I would find someone else, and I knew I would give myself just as completely to that new love.

Imagine how surprised I was then when a miracle happened.

Just as I was about to realign the thread of white icing on my face to erase Lynda's name, Store shot a flash-feed visual from buyspy into my video buffer. Even as the image burst into me, I could not believe what I was seeing.

It was Lynda, marching swiftly up my aisle, the hovercart sweeping along behind her.

Before I could fully process what was happening, she snatched me from the shelf, my wrapper crinkling in her beautiful, thick fingers. The next thing I knew, she was dropping me into the hovercart on top of a tub of tofu and a sack of grapefruit.

Abandoning my thoughts of finding someone else, I reactivated my bond with Lynda and exulted in the certain knowledge that our love indeed was meant to be. She had come back for me; there could be no greater proof of her devotion.

As I rode along in her hovercart, I knew what lay ahead...and it would be glorious. She might resist me for a while, hiding me in a cupboard or drawer, telling herself she would stick to her diet, pushing me away.

But in the end, she would surrender. It was written in the stars.

In the end, she would not be able to help herself. She would come to me, ready and willing, wanting me to do what only I could do for her.

And I would do it. Gladly, I would give myself to her.

"Thank you for coming back for me," I said as she placed a jar of wheat germ in the cart. "You won't be sorry."

"I already am," she said, not looking at me. "I hate myself for this. I hate you, too."

Her words, sharp as they were, did not faze me. I knew what she really meant.

*****

It is impossible for me to describe the state of ecstatic anticipation that engulfed me as I waited for Lynda to have her first taste of me.

That night, as she fixed and ate a salad, I watched from the kitchen counter in her tiny apartment and wished that she were putting ME in her mouth instead of the lettuce. Each time her plump, ruby lips parted, admitting another green forkful, I quivered with excitement in my wrapper, barely able to hold back from crying out for immediate consummation.

It only intensified my arousal that she had not hidden me away as I had expected, but instead had put me right out on the counter. Instead of whiling away the time in a dark cupboard, having to content myself with listening for her voice and movements, I was out in the open, able to see everything, able to be seen...and knowing that she would not have positioned me thus if she did not intend to devour me sooner rather than later.

And yet, I still had to go easy on her. Bruised and

vulnerable, she responded well to patience and tenderness; it would be a mistake to exert any but the mildest pressure.

She was a skittish fawn in need of gentle coaxing. Never mind that I was more like a RAGING INFERNO in need of immediate QUENCHING.

As she carried her dirty dishes from the kitchen table to the sink, I caught her eye. Her gaze lingered just long enough to test my resolve to play it cool...but I managed with a mighty effort to keep from blurting out an insistent plea for love.

"How was your dinner?" I said instead.

Lynda snorted as she dropped her plate and silverware into the dishpan. "I'm sick of salad," she said disgustedly. "And tofu and yogurt and water and plankton snacks."

"But you should be proud of yourself," I said. "You've set a goal, and you're sticking to it, even though it isn't easy."

Lynda sighed. "I've really made up my mind this time," she said, filling the dishpan with water from the spigot. "I decided that this is it. Once and for all, I have to get my weight down."

"I believe in you, Lynda," I said. "I know you can do it."

"I wish I felt so confident," said Lynda, adding soap to the dishwater. "It's just I've failed so many times before. I've been on lots of diets, and I've always ended up quitting."

"That doesn't mean you won't succeed this time," I said. "Forget the past. Look at this as a new beginning."

Lynda scrubbed a plate clean and slotted it in the dish drainer alongside the sink. "I want to," she said slowly. "I'm tired of being miserable. I'm sick of being alone."

"Surely you must have people who care about you," I said, enhancing my glow and aroma as I sensed her defenses weaken.

Lynda cleaned her silverware and placed it in the drainer, then headed for the table to get her water glass. "My parents are gone," she said sadly, giving me a look on her way back to the sink. "No brothers or sisters. I have a few friends here and there, but that's about it."

"I understand," I said. "You want to be in love."

Lynda stopped cleaning the glass and looked over her shoulder at me. "Geez," she said. "I must be pretty transparent if even a snack cake can figure me out."

"Or maybe I'm just a really smart snack cake," I said. "Smart enough to see how much you have to offer, at least."

Lynda turned back to the sink and finished washing the glass. "If you're so smart," she said, "give me a good reason why I shouldn't say to hell with my diet and just eat you right now."

FINALLY, I thought. FINALLY FINALLY FINALLY she was READY to PEEL off my wrapper and PULL me INSIDE that magnificent MOUTH all WET and WARM and SOFT and CHEW AND CHEW AND CHEW ME until we two were inextricably mixed together.

Automatically, I brightened my glow and moistened my cake and heightened the shine of my frosting. The moment I had waited for was finally upon me, and my every dream and desire was about to be fulfilled and I KNEW it would be more wonderful than I had ever imagined.

And yet, even as every atom of my being vibrated with the thrill of impending gratification, I forced myself not to cry out in delirious passion. Remembering her shy and fragile condition, I reigned myself in, choosing a more subtle approach that I calculated would be more likely not to frighten her off.

"Well," I said, trying my best to sound like a supportive friend. "I guess the main reason would be that you want to stick to your diet."

"Right about now," she said, drying her hands on a dish towel as she turned to face me, "I don't much care about my diet."

OH LYNDA, I LOVE YOU, I thought. TAKE ME NOW, I wanted to howl, but instead I said, "But you just told me how important it is to you."

TAKE ME NOW NOW NOW NOW NOW!!

"I know," said Lynda, "but just looking at you is driving me crazy. All I can think about is how good it would feel to eat you up."

Hearing those words, I felt as if my supercreamy center was about to explode, spraying ultrachocolate crumbs and frosting all over the kitchen...all over Lynda. How I kept my voice even and said what I said, I'll never know.

"Maybe that isn't such a good idea right now," I told her. "Maybe we should wait."

Lynda tossed the towel aside and walked over to me. "But I don't want to wait," she said. "I want you now."

"I just think we should both be sure," I said, playing devil's advocate, letting Lynda take the initiative. "I want it to be perfect. I want us both to be ready."

Reaching out, Lynda stroked my wrapper. "Oh, I'm ready," she said, her voice filled with desire.

"Well then," I said, deciding the time was right to let the situation run its course. "If you're sure, then let's take the next step. Let's see where it leads us."

Slowly, she lifted me from the counter. She raised me, still wrapped, to her nose and inhaled deeply of my rich fragrance...then sighed blissfully. "It's been too long," she said. "It feels like it's been forever."

Her luscious mouth was so close, I had trouble keeping my mind clear. "I'll make it worth the wait," I said, obsessed with the warmth of her breath as it fogged my cellophane wrapper. "I'll give you what you need, Lynda."

Hungrily, her eyes ran up and down the length of me, drinking me in. "I don't think I can wait another minute," she said, her fingers trembling as she held me. "I have to have you right now."

"It's okay," I said. "I want you, too. I've wanted you since the first moment I saw you."

"Oh God," she said as she fumbled with my wrapper, tearing it open. "Give it to me. Please give it to me!"

I was out of my mind with desire as she tugged me free of my packaging and threw it aside. The feel of her fingers around me, bare flesh against bare cake and frosting with nothing between us, was infinitely better than I had ever imagined.

FINALLY, she was poised to DEVOUR me, to fulfill my urgent burning LUST and GRIND me up in her MOUTH so TENDER so MERCILESS so WET so RED...and even though I knew I'd been made to crave and seduce her, though I knew my drive to get her to eat me was designed to push her to develop a taste for Smidgens and buy many more of us...I WALLOWED in her embrace and LONGED for her none the less.

I had NEVER known ANYTHING SO WONDERFUL in my life. I felt the PULSING of her fingertips as she raised me toward her MOUTH, and the whole world MELTED AWAY, leaving nothing but her glistening LIPS AND TONGUE AND TEETH.

She opened WIDE and moved me CLOSER. The SMELL and HEAT of her BREATH washed over me, drowning out all coherent thought, stripping away everything but GREEDY ABANDON.

Then, suddenly, the rapturous spell was broken. A chorus of tiny voices spoke up, and Lynda stopped drawing me into her mouth.

"Don't do it, Lynda!" said the voices. It sounded like there were dozens of them, piping shrilly from somewhere in the kitchen. "Don't give in! Remember your diet!"

Slowly, Lynda turned, looking for the source of the tinny cries. Even before her gaze settled on the Sea Sprite bag on the counter, I knew that the plankton snacks inside were responsible for ruining our rendezvous.

"You've worked so hard to lose weight!" said the plankton snacks, their deep green curlicues visible through the window on the front of the cellophane bag. "Don't give up now! Don't let him take advantage of you!"

I looked up at Lynda, hoping we could still retrieve the magic...but the look on her face told me I'd lost the advantage. Her eyes were guilty and distant, her jaws clenched, her lips clamped tight.

"Lynda," I said calmly, making a play though I knew it

was doomed. "I just want you to be happy. There's nothing wrong with finding a little happiness, is there?"

My words were indeed futile. Slowly, she lowered me to the counter.

"Woo!" shouted the plankton snack chorus. "Way to go, Lynda! We knew you could do it!"

"Shut up!" she said angrily. "Just shut the hell up!"

"But we're on *your* side," chirped the plankton snacks. "We want you to succeed! We want you to stick with *healthy* snacks like *us* instead of *bad, fattening junk food* like Smidgens!"

Lynda stomped over and snatched the Sea Sprite bag from the counter. As the cellophane crinkled in her hand, the green curlicues in the bag erupted with joyful cries and whistles.

"Yay!" they said. "You go, girl!"

Then, while the plankton snacks were still twittering merrily, Lynda tore the bag open...and dumped them down the garbage disposal in the sink.

As the snacks cried out in surprise and protest, Lynda ran water into the disposal and switched it on. A chorus of tiny screams erupted from the sink as the disposal ground the plankton snacks to bits with a mighty rumble.

Flicking off the disposal and pitching the empty Sea Sprite bag on the floor, Lynda turned to face me. "Don't *you* say anything, either," she snapped, tears running down her chubby cheeks. "Not a *word!*"

Fearing she might dump me down the disposal after the plankton snacks, I remained silent. Lynda did not say a word, either, as she lumbered out of the kitchen, but I could hear her sobbing when she got to the next room.

*****

Much later that night (last night), she returned to me. Her brown hair was matted and stuck to her face, her skin was pale, her eyes bloodshot from crying.

I, of course, thought she looked as ravishingly beautiful as ever...though I felt sad that the love of my life had so clearly been suffering. I wished more than anything that I could comfort her with my sweet chocolate cake and deluxe creamy filling.

But I knew I needed to take it slow.

"Hello, Lynda," I said softly.

She did not answer. Shuffling to the refrigerator, she opened the door and pulled out a bottle of water. She looked utterly exhausted and defeated as she slouched into a chair at the kitchen table, letting the refrigerator door stand open behind her.

"Listen," I said after a moment. "About earlier. I'm sorry if you felt pressured."

Lynda unscrewed the cap from the bottle of water and had a drink. Staring into space, she slowly lowered the bottle to the table when she was done.

Faced with her dark, unresponsive mood, I considered staying silent...then decided instead to inch forward while choosing my words carefully. "I just want you to know I'm here for you," I said. "I know we just met, but I really feel a connection between us."

"I hate myself," Lynda said without looking at me. "I've always hated myself."

"I think you're being too hard on yourself," I said.

"Here I am, forty-two years old," she said, her voice slow and ragged, "and I have never had anyone love me. Not a man or a woman or anything in between. And who can blame them when I look the way I do?"

"There's someone for everyone," I said, longing for her to pluck me from the counter and pull me toward her mouth again.

"I haven't weighed less than two hundred pounds since I was seventeen years old," said Lynda. "I've got no self-control when it comes to food."

EXACTLY WHAT I'M LOOKING FOR IN A WOMAN, I thought, but what I said was, "It isn't easy these days, what with all the techno-marketing you're subjected to."

Lynda sighed, still staring into space. "I tried a diet implant once," she said. "Gave me a shock every time I tried to overeat. It worked fine for a couple of days. Then I went on an eating binge and actually burned it out."

Hearing her talk about the binge got me excited, but I kept my voice level and sympathetic. "I think that just shows what a strong person you are," I said. "It shows me you can overcome any obstacle if you set your mind to it."

"I'll bet I've been on hundreds of diets through the years," said Lynda. She took another drink of water and hung her head. "I've tried every diet you can think of, and nothing worked. This time was different, though. This time, I came up with a guaranteed way to lose the weight."

"And what way is that?" I said.

"It was working, too," she said, her voice thick with

frustration and regret. "Until *you* came along."

"I'm so sorry, Lynda," I said, even as my thoughts swirled around the probability that her depression would lead her to devour me soon. "Maybe I was being selfish, but I can't help myself when it comes to you."

"You and your ultrachocolate frosting," said Lynda. "All smooth-talking and looking so good. I kept trying to walk away, but I couldn't get you out of my mind."

"You had the same effect on me," I said softly.

Lynda put her head down on her folded arms and sobbed. "I couldn't help myself," she said. "I promised myself this would be my last diet, and I still couldn't resist you."

"This is just a bump in the road," I said. "There's nothing wrong with taking a little break. You can still keep your diet going."

"You don't understand," said Lynda. "I swore to myself...oh God..."

"What?" I said. "What is it?"

"I swore I would never eat something like you again," she said. "I swore I would *die* before I'd do that."

Suddenly, I went cold. The hopes and fantasies I'd been so sure were about to come true seemed to plummet away from me. "Lynda, no," I said. "Please don't say that."

"I thought I could stop eating...if the alternative was killing myself," said Lynda. "But I was wrong. Or maybe... maybe I just want to kill myself."

"I know that isn't true," I told her.

She lifted her head from her arms and turned to face me. "I'm sorry if I led you on," she said, "but we were never meant to be."

"I know you're unhappy," I said, my mind racing to find the right words, "but things will get better."

"I used to think that," said Lynda. "But not anymore. Not for me."

Somehow, I had to keep her going, keep her breathing, keep her EATING. "Think of all the things you enjoy, Lynda," I said. "Think of all the things you'll miss out on."

Smiling bitterly, she pushed herself up out of her chair. "It's nice of you to try to talk me out of it," she said, "but it just makes me feel worse that you're the only one here to do it."

"Don't throw your life away, Lynda," I said, the pitch of my voice rising with desperation.

"Besides," she said, "we both know why you're really doing it. We both know what you want."

"Please, Lynda," I said. "Don't end it like this!"

She marched off into the next room and came back with a handgun. "That's one of the reasons I like you so much," she said, her expression suddenly frighteningly serene.

"I need you, Lynda!" I said. "I love you!"

"We both have one track minds," she said calmly. "All I want to do is eat, and all you want is to be eaten."

She raised the gun slowly, turning the barrel toward her LUSCIOUS MOUTH.

"Wait!" I said. "You're right! I want you to eat me! At least eat me before you do it!"

"No," she said, cocking back the hammer of the gun.

"Why not go out with a smile on your face?" I said.

60

"I'm telling you, once you've tasted a Supercreamy Double Ultrachocolate Deluxe Smidgen, you'll think you've died and gone to Heaven!"

"I swore I'd die before I put something like you inside me again," said Lynda, "and for once in my life, I'm keeping my promise."

"But I'm not as bad as you think! I'm packed with vitamins and minerals!"

"You'll say anything to get what you want," said Lynda.

"You've got me all wrong! I care about you! I can help you lose weight!"

"But this way," said Lynda, "I can keep it off forever."

Finally, she slid the barrel of the gun between her lips. All I could think of as I watched was that I wanted more than anything to trade places with that gun.

It was enough to drive away every last shred of my self-control. "EAT ME EAT ME EAT ME EAT ME!" I screamed, pelting her ears with focused beams of hypersound...refusing even then to give up on the woman who was both my lover and a potential source of future revenue for my manufacturer.

The screaming didn't stop until long after she had closed her eyes and pulled the trigger.

*****

So now, here I am, with Lynda's corpse on the floor in front of me, and all I can think of is finding someone new. As traumatic as it was to lose her, to come so gloriously close to precious LOVE only to have it SNATCHED AWAY, I have already moved on.

If I were different, perhaps I would mourn for her or even blame myself for pushing her over the edge, because after all she would still be alive if I had not come along. Even I can see that.

But like I said before, snack cakes do not feel guilt. Though my baked-in, digestible mind can recognize the chain of cause and effect, I am not programmed to experience emotions that would interfere with my primary objective.

Namely, falling in love. And joining with my lover in the ultimate expression of passion and selfless unity.

I am unattached, but I have hope. I see her death as an opportunity, a chance to find another kindred soul and add to the customer base of my manufacturer.

I believe (was programmed to believe) that everything happens for a reason, even if it is difficult to see at first what that reason might be.

Fortunately for me, I do not have to wait long for that reason to reveal itself.

A sound reaches my audio receptor cells, and I exult. It is the morning after my breakup with Lynda, and already I hear the stirrings of nearby life.

My optical cells focus on a new face. I fall in love in less than an instant.

"Hello," I say pleasantly. "My name is Smidgen. Nice to meet you."

As the face moves closer, my body quivers with anticipation. I forget the name of the woman on the floor and direct my every thought and resource toward wooing this new and perfect mate.

"I know we've just met," I say, "but I have to tell you how attracted I am to you. I've never seen such striking features in my life."

The face of my new lover comes so close, I can feel the soft wisping of her breath. She sniffs me with her wet, dark nose, and I pump out a mist of ultrachocolate fragrance.

"Your eyes," I say. "They're so dark and mysterious. So captivating."

The hairs on either side of her long nose brush my frosting, and I am lost. I will give ANYTHING to be with her, DO anything to make her mine. All at once, I know that THIS that SHE is why I was born.

The world melts away around us. Nothing else matters.

Her nose presses into my ultrachocolate cake. She is fresh, but so am I. She is direct, but I like that.

There is no need for games or coyness anymore. I feel like I can be myself with her.

THIS IS WHAT LOVE IS SUPPOSED TO BE LIKE.

And then there are those...oh God, I LOVE her great big...

"Teeth," I whisper, my optics ogling the whitest, sharpest set I have ever seen outside my dreams. "Your teeth are beautiful."

And then and then and THEN she opens her MOUTH and there's a blissful split-second before she bites down and then and then and then SHE BITES INTO ME.

And oh.

Oh yes.

I cannot describe how MAGNIFICENT I feel as she

TAKES ME INSIDE HER. How CHANGED FOREVER
I feel as she TEARS OFF a piece of me and OH MY GOD
she CHEWS ME UP.

My mind chimes like a bell as my perfect love, my match,
my soulmate takes another bite and THEN ANOTHER
and CHEWS AND CHEWS AND CHEWS.

All I can feel is the warmth and wetness of her mouth
and all I can hear is the sound of her teeth and tongue and
all I can see is gray fur and pink flesh and all I can think is
how happy I am and then even that thought is gone in the
blazing heat of ecstasy.

Part of me knows how wrong this is, knows I have
failed in my purpose because this angel is not likely to buy
more Smidgens and fatten my maker's coffers.

But I find as my lover penetrates to my supercreamy
center, granting me a blinding euphoria beyond any I'd ever
expected as she laps at the sweet white heart of me, that I
JUST DON'T CARE.

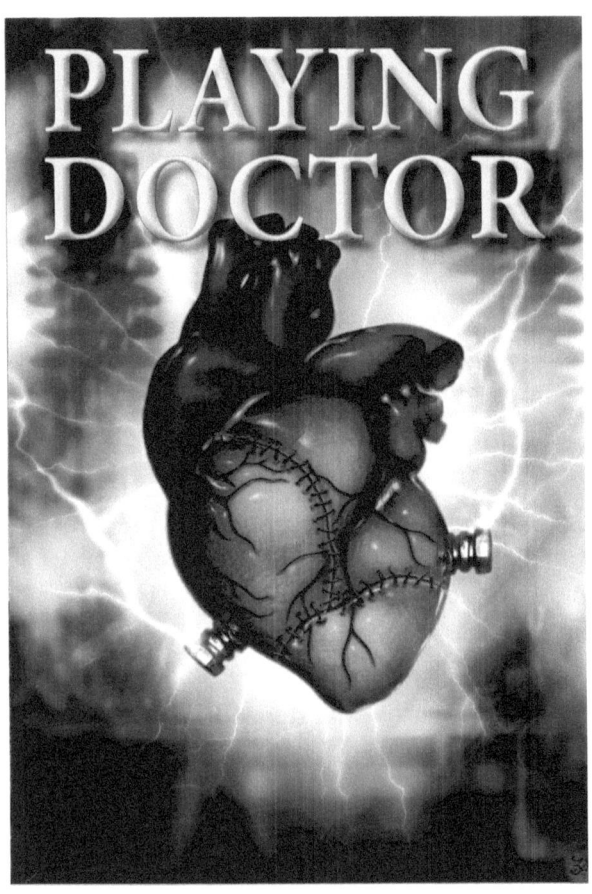

PLAYING DOCTOR

The problem with having a crush on your mad scientist boss is, every day she doesn't see how wonderful you really are seems like the end of the world.

"This is all wrong!" says Dr. Hildegarde Medici, hurling the tray across her cavernous secret laboratory. "You're a complete *imbecile*, Glue!"

Her words sting, but at least she's paying attention to me. I'll take what I can get from the woman I love. "I'm sorry, Dr. M. Please let me try again."

"Everything is *ruined.*" With one arm, Dr. Medici sweeps notebooks and glass beakers from the table in front of her. "Now I'll *never* finish the doomsday weapon today!"

As Dr. Medici throws her head down onto her folded arms on the table, I cross the lab and pick up the silver tray that she threw. I see myself reflected in its surface-- thick glasses, big nose, bald head, pure geek...not her type. "I thought you liked the crinkle-cut ones," I say as I pluck chicken fingers and french fries from the floor and drop them onto the tray.

"*Steak fries,*" says Dr. Medici without raising her head. "How many times do I have to *tell* you, Glue?"

She is *such* a drama queen, but what do you expect? Her line of work attracts a certain type of personality-- passionate, temperamental, creative, flamboyant. To tell you the truth, it's one of the things I love most about her.

"I could run to the store," I say, dumping the chicken and fries into a waste basket. "By the time you're done building your doomsday weapon, I could have hot fries ready for you."

Dr. Medici rolls her eyes like a disgusted teenager. "I can't concentrate on building a doomsday weapon on an *empty stomach.*"

I know the feeling...the not being able to concentrate part, that is. Most days, I can barely focus on my work instead of Dr. Medici's long black hair and bright green eyes. Once, I was so distracted by Dr. M that I cross-wired the brain of a giant robot, which proceeded to rampage at a garbage dump instead of an army base.

If only I could tell her I love her. If only I could close

that final mile that has always stood between us.

If only I could finally set free the words that I've longed to speak, and she would turn to me and say the words I've longed to hear.

"Don't just *stand* there, you *putz*!" She spins away from me on her work-stool. "Get me a *TV dinner* out of the freezer or something!"

I don't take it personally. I know it's just the stress talking. She's been having a rough time lately, just like the rest of the mad scientist community.

Thanks a lot, terrorists.

*****

In the good old days, mad scientists weren't considered public enemies like they are now. They were tolerated, in fact, because the government loved getting its hands on their way-out inventions after their crazy schemes were thwarted.

But not anymore. Not since the terrorists.

What difference is there between a politically motivated insane genius and one who is motivated by greed?

How can the government go after one group of people threatening to blow things up and not the other?

It can't.

As a result, business has dropped off considerably. No one will negotiate in good faith with a mad scientist anymore. Instead of musclebound private citizen thrill-seekers coming after us, we get black ops Special Forces and heat-seeking bunker-buster missiles courtesy of Homeland Security.

It's a tough time to be a mad scientist. Lots of them have quit already and become street people or college professors.

But not my Hildegarde. She won't give up that easily. Being a mad scientist has been her lifelong dream.

I know, because I grew up with her.

*****

Hildegarde Medici always wanted to be the first female mad scientist in history.

"Call me *Doctor* Medici." When she started with that, she couldn't have been older than seven. She was three years younger than I was, and already she was giving me orders.

Not that I minded. I think I was born to follow her. She ruled my heart even then, when she was just the girl next door.

We played laboratory in her family's garage, building contraptions from tin cans and coat hangers. We pretended to build ray guns and bombs and robots and monsters, and she always got to be the evil genius and I was her helper.

"The townspeople have failed to meet our demands!" she would say, shaking her fist in the air. "It is time to activate the framistat, Glugor!" She always called me by my last name, Glugor, because it sounded so much like "Igor."

"Immediately, Dr. Medici!" I always enhanced my performance by adopting a nasally voice and hunching over like Igor in the movies. "Firing framistat!"

"They will rue the day they crossed me!" Even as

a child, Hildegarde had mastered every nuance of mad scientist behavior. She was a true prodigy and wanted nothing less than to achieve the complete perfection of the consummate evil genius.

It didn't matter to her that all the mad scientists we heard about were men. If anything, it made her want to be one all the more.

And that made me want to be her assistant all the more, too.

*****

Not that it's exactly been easy.

These days, Dr. Medici is always being hounded by feds and fanboys, so it's almost impossible for her to get any work done. My job's about a hundred times tougher, too, what with the increased vigilance and paranoia on the street.

Dr. M's temperamental nature can be a stumbling block, and then there's my one-sided love for her. It's what keeps me around, but there have been plenty of times when the heartbreak's been almost too much for me to stand.

You'd think I'd have gotten the idea by now. If she really had feelings for me, she probably wouldn't have gone through five marriages to other men. She probably wouldn't keep using me as a guinea pig in dangerous experiments, either.

*****

Once, Dr. Medici transformed me into a bloodthirsty

arachnoid creature and turned me loose in a shopping mall. Another time, she used a mutation ray to bring out my inner dinosaur.

On purpose or by accident, I've been shrunk, enlarged, divided, multiplied, irradiated, roboticized, made invisible, and turned every color in the rainbow. She's managed to reverse every change, but only after plenty of drama and destruction.

Out of all these experiments, I enjoyed only one: when she sent me back in time to when we were kids. Even as a grown-up outsider, I loved being back when we were just starting out and there was still a chance for us to share a happy lifetime together.

I even said something to my little boy self to make him think about taking more chances...but he didn't take the hint. When I returned to the future, to the era where I belonged, nothing had improved between me and Dr. Medici.

If anything, she was a little more distant.

*****

The day after the crinkle-cut french fries incident, Dr. Medici is all business again. She is somewhere between the manic and depressive phases of her personality cycle...in other words, on a rare even keel.

"I've finished the doomsday device," she says matter-of-factly, strolling into the lab in a white lab coat and black slacks. She holds an oversized coffee mug with both hands and blows the steam off its contents. "Let's talk about deploying it."

For the next two hours, she tells me her plan to hold America hostage with the doomsday device. I listen intently and take tons of notes, but my mind isn't really on Dr. Medici's plan.

Partly, I'm thinking about how beautiful she is, and how I would love to reach over and touch her face. I'm envisioning a perfect daydream world of whispered confessions and unleashed passion, blazing with the intensity of her mad scientist ways.

And partly, I'm thinking about a mad science plan other than Dr. Medici's, a secret plan of which she has not even the slightest inkling.

I'm thinking about a plan of my own.

*****

That night, long after Dr. Medici has gone to her private quarters, I sneak off to the secret lab I set up in the old dungeon below the main level.

It is here that I do my best work. It is here that I pull together everything I've ever learned and apply it to a project the likes of which humanity has never known.

I am making the impossible real, and I am doing it all for her. For us.

I don the surgical gown and gloves, the cap and mask. I check the readings on the computerized monitors, gauging the condition of my handiwork.

As I reach for the scalpel, I remember the last time I saw Dr. Medici cry. It was three months ago, right after her fifth husband left her.

I found her in the lab, crying on the floor beside a broken alchemy generator. The generator hadn't been broken two hours before, when I'd last walked past it. Pieces of it were strewn all over the lab.

"Sometimes...I wish I wasn't...a mad scientist," she said between sobs. "It's so...lonely."

Not so lonely, I wanted to say. *You have me, don't you?*

But as usual, I didn't say what was on my mind. As usual, I couldn't close that final mile between us. It was better to watch her from a distance than not to see her at all.

"No one understands," said Dr. Medici, rubbing her bloodshot eyes. "Once the thrill wears off...they can't handle it. The danger...the commitment. At least...that's their excuse."

"I understand," I told her, but it didn't come out the way I'd wanted, like, '*I* understand.'

"I'm a...career woman," said Dr. Medici. "I *love*...my career. I just wish...I didn't have to be...so lonely...because of it."

You don't, I had wanted to say. *I'm right here for you! I've always been here! And I love you!*

But I didn't say a single word of that. Instead, I listened, and I filed it all away, and I made my secret plan.

And now, with my scalpel, in the silent dungeon in the middle of the night, I am bringing that plan to life.

*****

In the weeks to come, I realize I'll need to finish the plan sooner than expected. *She'll* need it.

For a while, she seems to be doing really well, plowing ahead with the doomsday device scheme and mapping out what she'll do when it's over. In exchange for not blowing up the world, she'll demand that she be made queen of it... and that really has her pumped. She loves talking about being the first mad scientist queen of the world and all the changes that she's going to make when she takes over.

Then, she has a run of bad luck. Make that terrible luck.

A guy she meets on the Internet turns out to be a stalker, following us on secret missions and breaking into the lair to steal stuff and leave threatening notes. We finally have to dispose of him (restraining orders and police protection really aren't options for people like us), which gets kind of messy.

Then, Dr. Medici gets audited by the Internal Revenue Service, which just started going after the earnings of mad scientists and other public enemies. The estimated back taxes on Dr. M's criminal activities are astronomical, and Dr. M hasn't exactly kept receipts to justify deductions.

The IRS audit is major trouble, the kind of trouble you can't dispose of like a stalker boyfriend...and it isn't the last of her bad breaks.

Dr. M's five former husbands write a tell-all book about their marriages to her. It becomes a bestseller that makes her a household name, but not in a good way.

In the heat of the book brouhaha, when Dr. Medici tries to phone in her threat to launch the doomsday device unless she's made queen of the world, the United Nations Security Council won't take her call.

The worst break of all, though, comes with Dr. Medici's visit to the doctor--a medical doctor, not a mad scientist. That's the one that almost wrecks her.

And it happens on Christmas Eve.

*****

"All those years," says Dr. Medici, pouring herself another glass of whiskey. "Instead of working on doomsday devices and killer robots, I should have been studying medicine."

"Why? What's going on?" I'm a little nervous, because I found Dr. M hiding out with her bottle of whiskey in the dungeon...I mean my secret lab. She is leaning against the metal table on which my personal secret project lies hidden under a bedsheet.

Dr. Medici raises her glass, but I have no glass of my own with which to toast. "That's irony for you. I'm smart enough that I probably could have found a cure for cancer if I'd put my mind to it."

As she downs her drink, I take a step closer. "Cancer?" My head spins as the word dribbles from my lips.

Dr. Medici nods and refills her glass. "Star cell carcinoma," she says glibly. "A mind is a terrible thing to turn to paste."

I stumble another step toward her in the shadowy chamber. "Inoperable?" I'm having trouble talking to her, but not for the usual reasons.

Dr. M raises her glass. "Merry Christmas." She gulps her drink. "What really pisses me off, though," she says, "is that I didn't get to be queen of the world first."

This time, I stumble back away from her. I come up short against the cold wall of the cave and let it hold me up while the world melts out from under me.

Dr. Medici laughs bitterly. "I should've been a medical doctor," she says. "What the hell was I thinking?"

*****

Twenty-five years ago, the first time I saw Dr. Medici, she was pounding the hell out of a teddy bear in her family's back yard. She was six years old, and dressed all in black.

Lots of cars were parked in front of her house, and I had come over to see what all the excitement was about. Hildegarde scowled at me and kept pounding the bear as I approached.

"Who's all the people?" I said, gesturing in the general direction of the cars parked out front.

"Funeral people." Hildegarde held the bear by its stubby legs and swung it hard at a rock as big as she was.

"Why are they here?" I remember looking around for something like the stuffed bear to swing and pound, as if it were the polite thing to do.

"My mother," said Hildegarde, sweeping the bear way back and really slamming it against the rock with all her might.

"What about her?" I said.

"Cancer!" Hildegarde went wild then, pounding the bear on the rock so hard that the bear's seams split and stuffing flew out of it. "Cancer cancer cancer cancer *cancer*!"

I stood and watched as she pounded the bear, then dug her nails into the split seams and tore it apart. Grunting like an animal, she shredded the skin and hurled the stuffing into the yard.

When she finally ran out of bear to pound and rip, she threw down the last remaining hunk of brown fur and glared at me.

"Someday," she said, "I'll be queen of the world, and I'll make it so nothin' happens without my say-so."

"Okay," I said. "Wanna play doctor?"

*****

I watch her get drunk in the old dungeon for a long time, and I hardly say a word. When she finally starts to nod off, I help her upstairs to her quarters so she can sleep in her own bed.

And I don't leave right away like I should.

I stand in the doorway and watch her as she sleeps, the peaceful look on her face belying the turmoil in her life.

I would do anything for her. If I could cure her cancer by giving up my own life, I would do it. If I could take all of her troubles on myself, I would do that, too.

But there *is* one thing that I can do. It's the one thing that both of our lives have been leading up to since we first started playing mad scientist in the back yards of our childhood homes.

*****

The next morning, I have a pot of coffee waiting for her in the lab. That much, at least, is like every other morning...though it's really the third pot I've made since midnight the night before. I drank the first two on my own; it was the only way I could stay up all night and make the final preparations for the grand unveiling.

When I see how bad she looks when she walks in, I'm extra glad I decided to carry out my secret plan today. Her eyes are bloodshot, her face haggard, her hair tangled. She shuffles around like she's still half-asleep, like she was the one up all night and not me.

I fill her mug with coffee and stir in a teaspoonful of sugar, the way she likes it. She doesn't take it at first, and when she does, she only sips once and puts the mug back down on the table.

Half-heartedly, she walks over to the big whiteboard on the wall and stares at the equations scrawled there in red, green, and black dry-erase marker. "Did the U.N. return my call yet?" She says it without looking back at me.

"No, Doctor." I cross the lab and stand alongside her.

She sighs and shakes her head. "I give up."

"I know the feeling," I say.

"No," says Dr. Medici. "I mean I really give up. No more mad science. It's just not working for me anymore."

I never thought I'd hear her say that, but I understand where it's coming from. "You've been having a rough time lately," I say. "Things'll get better."

"If by 'better,' you mean death, then yeah." She's finally showing some spark. Too bad it's in the form of sarcasm. "Much better, coming right up."

I take a deep breath. My big moment has arrived. "Things *will* get better." I feel a chill as all the blood seems to rush right out of my body at once. "Things will get better right *now*, in fact."

She isn't taking me seriously. She doesn't even look at me as she ladles on more sarcasm. "Oh, good. You've come up with that cure for cancer you've been working on. I'll have some right now, please."

"Follow me." I turn and march to the far corner, where the big surprise awaits, laid out on a gurney under a white sheet.

Dr. Medici follows slowly, her face etched in a scowl. "I'm not in the mood for jokes, Glue."

My hand shakes as I pat the shape beneath the sheet. I feel the heat of it, the rise and fall of it, and I know I've done well. "Trust me," I tell her. "Give me a chance."

"What is it?" she says as she draws up beside me.

"Science project," I say, and then I whisk the sheet from the gurney.

Dr. Medici stares silently at the naked man who is lying there.

He is lean and muscular, the type who could be a model or an all-around athlete. His complexion is fair, his thick hair glossy and blond. He has a movie star face with chiseled features...and his eyes, when they finally flutter open, sparkle like twin sapphires.

He looks young, in his twenties or thirties, but nowhere near his true age, for he is a newborn. Today is the first day of his life.

"Who?" For a change, Dr. Medici is the one reduced

to one-word sentences.

"That's up to you." I pat the new man's shoulder, and he smiles up at us. "He's all yours."

Dr. M's frown softens just a little. "You made him?" She hangs back from the gurney, but she can't take her eyes off the man. "But how?"

"With snips and snails and puppy dog tails." I can't believe I'm making a joke, but I feel incredible. "And cloned, hypertrophic super stem cells resequenced by viral nanodrives seated mitochondrially."

"Huh." Dr. Medici shoots me a sideways look. "Are you *sure* you don't have the cure for cancer?"

"Go ahead and sit up," I tell the man on the gurney, and he does. "Say something."

"Hello." When he says it, his voice is deep and rich, and he looks right in her eyes. "I love you."

Dr. Medici blushes. "This is crazy," she says. "This is nuts." But she doesn't break eye contact with him the whole time.

I feel better than I can remember ever feeling before. "He understands you," I say. "The thrill will never be gone for him. And he will never leave you."

"But you can't know that," says Dr. M, "can you?"

Grinning, I give the homemade man a wink. "Tell her."

"I understand you." The homemade man gazes into her eyes and speaks with intense feeling that leaves no room for doubt or apprehension. "The thrill will *never* be gone. And I will never *leave* you, Hildegarde."

I brainwashed him well. Every word, inflection, and expression are perfect.

Dr. Medici flashes me a confused frown. "But why?" she says. "Why did you do this?"

"I didn't want you to be alone anymore." It's only now that I lie to her. "Since you couldn't meet the right man, I made one for you."

Dr. Medici turns back to the homemade man, her confusion dissolving into wonderment. "I can't believe it," she says. "No one's ever done anything like this for me before."

Each word is like a caress to me. As she reaches out to touch his cheek, I feel like she's reaching out to touch mine. As she gazes tenderly into his eyes, I feel like she is gazing into mine.

Which makes sense, really. There's one part of the secret plan that I haven't told her about yet...one part that I will never tell her about.

That part is me. I am part of him.

I grew his heart from a piece of my own. The heart in his chest, the one that beats faster as she takes his hand in her own, is the twin of my heart.

And as he embarks on the life I always wanted, takes the love I always longed for in his new, strong hands, I'll share it, in a way. As I go about my work and see them happy, I'll know that I made it possible, and part of me will always be part of them.

This is the real reason I made him, the one I lied to her about. I made him because it's the only way I could ever have her, the only way I could ever close that final mile between us.

Though, if I'm honest, I have to say that not everything

I'm feeling right now is happiness.

"Wendell." For the first time that I can remember, Dr. Medici calls me by my first name. "Wendell, thank you."

"Be happy." My heart is pounding like the pistons of a giant robot. "That'll be thanks enough."

She reaches over and brushes my hand with her fingertips. Not for the first time and not for the last, I long to fold her into my arms and press my lips to hers in a kiss for the ages.

"This is mad, you know." A single tear rolls down her face as she turns back to her newborn lover. She can't take her eyes off him.

"Mad is good," I say, wiping away a tear of my own.

The great state of Missouri lay across the Speaker's bench at the front of the House of E-representatives, wrapped in the American flag. His eyes and mouth gaped, and his arms and legs hung over the sides, dripping blood on the carpet below.

"Oh, God," said Connecticut, her shaky hand hovering over Missouri's motionless chest. "He's not breathing."

Manitoba stood on the next tier down and wouldn't come any closer. "Is there a--what's it called? Heartbeat?"

Connecticut lowered her hand, then jerked it away. "That's in the throat, right?" Nervously, she scrubbed her palms on her smart red pantsuit. "Or is it the arm?"

That was when Nevada had finally had enough.

Without a word, he pushed his tall, lanky body through the crowd on the floor of the House and charged up the steps to the Speaker's bench. Without hesitation, he pressed two fingers against the side of Missouri's throat.

"No pulse." Nevada said it loud enough for the whole crowd to hear. "The Speaker of the House is dead."

A great gasp went up from the crowd--the computer-generated, artificial intelligence-driven avatars of ninety-eight of the one-hundred states of the United States of America. Though they didn't have flesh-and-blood bodies and shouldn't have feared being murdered in the physical sense, the evidence of dead Missouri had left them all shell-shocked.

"But how?" Connecticut slipped off her gold-rimmed glasses, let them hang by the diamond-studded chain around her neck...then slid them back on a second later. "And why?"

Nevada pushed up the sleeves of his tuxedo. He took Missouri's head in his hands and turned it gently to one side, exposing a gruesome wound. "Blow to the back of the head." Accepting the wound for what it appeared to be instead of what it was--an electronic simulation of a wound--he looked around for a simulated weapon that could have caused it. "What did it and why, I don't know."

"What are those?" Connecticut pointed at bloody marks on Missouri's left arm.

Nevada put Missouri's head down on the bench and took a look at the arm. Wiping some of the blood away, he realized the marks followed a familiar design.

Someone had cut a number into Missouri's arm. "One hundred," said Nevada. "It's the number one hundred."

The crowd murmured and moved restlessly. Nevada could tell the e-reps were confused because they usually acted more decisively.

They were A.I. avatars of the United States in the year 2300, guided by the aggregate preferences of the human electorate in the world outside. Perfectly attuned to the people they represented, perfectly immune to corruption, they never hesitated or doubted themselves.

That was why their confusion was unusual…and it didn't last long. As Nevada examined the body on the Speaker's bench, three of the e-reps broke from the pack and stormed toward him with jaws and shoulders set.

Sinaloa, in the middle, flipped his red-lined bullfighter's cape over his shoulder. "This is impossible." An American state since Mexico had disbanded twenty-five years ago, Sinaloa cultivated an air of insolence and false bravado. "What we see here is the product of a server malfunction."

"Exactly." South Africa tossed his glossy blond hair beside Sinaloa. "This is a bug. The Developers will fix it."

Nevada rubbed the stubbly cleft of his chin and met South Africa's blue-eyed stare. "Like Idaho?"

South Africa straightened his khaki safari shirt and looked away. So did stocky Kamchatka, the recent Russian convert, who had followed him up the steps.

Sinaloa glared. "I hear that Idaho might have been

someone *else's* fault. Not the Developers."

A cold, threatening smile spread across Nevada's face. He knew exactly whom Sinaloa was talking about.

He was talking about Nevada.

"Then maybe you'd best be careful." Nevada adjusted his gold pinky rings and cracked his knuckles. "Just in case he can hear what you're saying."

"If, by some wild chance, the same person is responsible for this crime, I hope he *does* hear me," said Sinaloa. "I want him to know he won't get away with what he's done."

"Tell him yourself, when you catch him." Nevada started to walk away.

"*I* won't catch him." Sinaloa snagged Nevada's shoulder and held him in place. "*You're* sergeant-at-arms of the House, aren't you?"

Nevada sighed. "As of twenty-four *hours* ago. What makes you think I'm ready to catch a *killer?*"

Sinaloa let go of Nevada. "We all know you've done this job before." He tightened his bolo tie, pushing the turquoise slide higher into the neck of his black silk shirt. "Five years ago, yes?"

"So what?" said Nevada.

"So you've got experience," said Sinaloa. "Not just with being sergeant-at-arms, but with losing e-reps on the job."

Nevada felt the urge to clock him in the face. Idaho had been his greatest failure, his darkest moment.

His deepest love.

"You're better qualified than any of us. You have more motivation to solve this than anyone," said Sinaloa. "You have quite a lot to prove, don't you?"

Nevada smirked and loosened the collar of the frilly shirt under his tux jacket. "You just don't want to get your hands dirty. None of you ever do."

Even as he said it, he knew Sinaloa was right. He knew what people thought of him. He knew he had a lot to prove.

And he knew he would take the case.

*****

"Missouri and I walked out together," said Antarctica, her beautiful silver eyes staring into space. "He went back in for some papers he'd forgotten." She tucked her long, platinum hair behind her ears, and a single tear rolled down her pale cheek. "That was the last time I saw him alive."

Across the table, Nevada watched Antarctica's reaction closely. She was the last person to have seen Missouri before the murder, and that earned her a spot on the list of suspects.

She was also a sweet kid, and Nevada didn't buy her as a killer. She was the youngest e-rep, in fact, from the newest, hundredth state; Antarctica had joined the U.S.A. only one year ago, in 2299. Strikingly beautiful and shining with inner light, the junior Congresswoman gave Nevada an impression of innocence and honesty, not wiles and lies.

For a moment, Nevada looked away from her, directing his gaze across the chamber at the bloody Speaker's bench. While Nevada interviewed witnesses in the back of the room, other e-reps were up front, clearing the crime scene.

"Did he say anything unusual?" Nevada flicked his

eyes to Antarctica, then back to the cleanup crew. They'd already removed Missouri's body, but the blood was another matter. Soap and water didn't exist in the digital realm, so the e-reps couldn't scrub out the soaked-in stains.

Antarctica adjusted her white fur wrap. "Just small talk about today's vote."

As Nevada considered his next question, his fellow e-reps gave up trying to clean the Speaker's bench and draped a red tablecloth over it to hide the blood. "How close were the two of you?"

"He was a mentor to me," said Antarctica.

"And there was nothing else between you?" Nevada locked eyes with her. "Nothing of a more personal nature?"

Antarctica didn't flinch. "Nothing."

Nevada believed her. "Okay, fine. Thank you for your time."

With that, Nevada rose from his chair and called out to the e-reps milling around the chamber. "Will the great state of Panama please report to the sergeant-at-arms."

When Nevada turned back to the interview table, he realized that Antarctica was still sitting there.

"You're dismissed, sweetheart," said Nevada. "Unless you've got something else to say?"

Antarctica nodded grimly. "I want to help you. I want to help find who killed him."

Nevada fiddled with his tuxedo cufflinks. He could think of two reasons for her offer. One, she really *did* want to do her part to bring the killer to justice.

Or two, she *was* the killer, and she wanted to divert attention from her own guilt.

Either way, Nevada figured he could use her.

"Why not?" he said. "As long as you don't mind getting your hands dirty."

"I'll do what I have to." Antarctica rose, smoothing the glittering, ice-blue gown that she wore under her fur wrap. "Missouri was a great state."

"Aren't they all?" said Nevada.

*****

Panama was no help. Neither was Jamaica or Wyoming or any of the other states who had been around Missouri before his death.

After hours of questioning one e-rep witness after another, Nevada was no closer to solving the murder. According to the witnesses, Missouri hadn't said or done a thing out of the ordinary, and no one in his orbit had said or done anything suspicious.

Frustrated, Nevada marched out of the House chamber through the big double doors and into the halls of the digital Capitol building. "I need some fresh air." Antarctica followed him.

Except for Nevada and Antarctica, the halls were empty. The e-reps, whose sole reason for existing was to vote on legislation according to the will of the electorate, rarely ventured outside the House chamber. Neither did the e-senators.

"What's next?" said Antarctica.

Nevada shrugged. "Missouri's office, I guess. Root around for some kind of clue."

"Like what?" said Antarctica. "What are we looking for?"

"How should I know?" said Nevada. "I'm no detective."

Antarctica frowned. "What did Sinaloa mean when he said you have experience losing e-reps on the job?"

Nevada sighed. "Didn't anyone ever tell you about Idaho?"

"I'm new around here," said Antarctica. "There's a lot I don't know."

"Idaho disappeared five years ago," said Nevada. "I was sergeant-at-arms at the time, and I couldn't find her."

"So they blame you for losing her?" said Antarctica.

"Some of them." Nevada listened to his lizard-skin cowboy boots echoing down the corridor. "And some think I might have *killed* her."

Antarctica gaped at him. "How could they think *that?*"

"Because we were lovers." Nevada stopped in front of an office door. The print on the frosted glass bore the name of Missouri. Nevada turned the knob.

Antarctica walked in after him and closed the door. As Nevada rifled drawers and flipped through papers on Missouri's desk, Antarctica circled the perimeter, watching him with a guarded expression.

"Nothing here." After ransacking the desk for a while, Nevada planted his hands on his hips and shook his head. "Nothing out of the ordinary."

"What about that?" Antarctica pointed toward the door through which they'd entered. At the base of it, a single sheet of blank paper lay flat on the floor.

"Someone must have slid it under the door while we

were busy," said Nevada.

Antarctica picked up the paper. "Why would somebody slip us a piece of paper with nothing on it?"

"Depends." As soon as Nevada's fingers touched the page, black lettering appeared on it. "Depends who it's addressed to."

Antarctica leaned in close enough that Nevada could smell her sweet gardenia perfume, and they read the note together.

Statue of Liberty, 3PM, Come Alone.

"It's an invitation," said Nevada. "Somebody wants to tell me something."

"Or maybe this is from the killer," said Antarctica. "Maybe he wants you to 'come alone' so he can kill you."

"There's only one way to find out." Nevada crumpled the paper into his tux jacket pocket and headed for the door.

*****

From the windows in the tiara of the Statue of Liberty, Nevada gazed out over the digital realm that was his home.

He could see everything spread out before him--a world of American landmarks, brought together to provide picturesque backdrops for the e-reps' and e-sens' press conferences.

In the middle of it all, Nevada saw the gleaming white dome of the Capitol building. Northwest of the Capitol jabbed the ivory needle of the Washington Monument; to the southwest rested the Lincoln Memorial. The Liberty Bell hung in a golden tower to the southeast, and Plymouth

Rock perched on a pedestal to the northeast.

Straight across the bubble of the digital realm from the Statue of Liberty, Mount Rushmore spanned the horizon, its giant presidential heads gazing out over the city. Niagara Falls roared to the east, and the Grand Canyon sprawled to the west, glowing forever red in the never-dimming sunrise.

"Nevada." The whispered voice from across the room surprised him. Nevada shot his gaze into the shadows...and saw an intercom speaker built into the wall there.

"Nevada." The voice spoke again, still no more than a whisper. Nevada crossed the room and stood close to the speaker, straining to identify who was doing the talking.

"Nevada. Are you *there*?"

Nevada pressed the button to transmit and spoke into the grill in the wall. "I'm here. Who is this?"

"Call me Looking Glass." The voice belonged to a man, but that was all Nevada could tell. "I know where to look."

"For what?" said Nevada.

"For Yukon's murderer," said Looking Glass.

A sharp chill raced up Nevada's spine. "Don't you mean Missouri's? Yukon isn't dead."

"She wasn't," said Looking Glass, "when you got on Lady Liberty's elevator."

Nevada's finger shook as he pressed the intercom button again. "Is that what this is about? Did you bring me here so I'd be out of the way while you killed Yukon?"

"Here is your first clue," said Looking Glass. "When is one one-hundred?"

Nevada scowled. "Just tell me if you did it. Tell me if you killed them both."

"When does one plus zero equal two?" said Looking Glass. "That's your second clue."

"If you didn't do it, who did?" said Nevada.

"No more for now," said Looking Glass. "See you after three and four."

With that, the line went dead.

Nevada slammed the button with the palm of his hand. "Looking Glass! Talk to me!"

But Looking Glass was gone.

*****

Yukon sat on the toilet in the women's lavatory, fully dressed and covered in blood and toilet paper. Her long, brown hair covered her face like a shroud.

"When did you find her?" Nevada stood in the doorway of the stall, hands on his hips.

Nervous Connecticut stood at his left. "A half-hour ago." She took off her gold-rimmed glasses, then put them back on...then took them off again. "We c-came in together for a sidebar. She was f-fine when I left."

Nevada nodded. Since the e-reps weren't programmed for excretory functions, bathrooms in the digital realm were used mostly for sidebar meetings and private deals. "Let me guess. No one noticed anything unusual."

"Not exactly, señor." Sinaloa clapped him on the shoulder. "Some of us noticed *you* leaving the House shortly before the murder."

Nevada ignored him and stepped into the stall. Gently, he parted the hair over Yukon's face with his fingertips, revealing a gruesome palette of cuts and bruises.

Pushing the hair away from her throat, he saw the biggest visible wound--a bloody gash from ear to ear.

"And no murder weapon left behind." Nevada was thinking out loud. "No bloody footprints, no fingerprints, no nothing."

"Tell me." Sinaloa flipped the red-lined bullfighter's cape over his shoulder with a flourish. "How is your first investigation going? Can you tell us who murdered Missouri?"

Nevada spotted the edge of a bloody symbol sticking out from under the toilet paper wrapped around Yukon's forearm. Tearing away the paper, he saw that there were two symbols underneath--two numerals carved into Yukon's flesh.

Two nines, carved side by side. Together, they made the number "ninety-nine."

Just as the number one hundred had been cut into poor Missouri's flesh.

"Well?" said Sinaloa. "Can you tell us who murdered Missouri?"

"Same person who murdered Yukon," said Nevada. "And there'll be more to come."

"What makes you say that?" said Sinaloa.

"Because he's counting down from a hundred," said Nevada. "A hundred of us."

*****

Nevada sat at the end of the Reflecting Pool, gazing across the still water at the Lincoln Memorial. Antarctica, who was sitting beside him, had kicked off her pretty crystal shoes and dropped her pale, slender feet into the water.

The ripples from her feet disturbed the scenes playing over the pool's surface--visions of life beyond the digital domain in True America. Men, women, and children worked and played in softly swirling images, flickering across the sunlit water. It was here that the e-reps and e-sens came to see the faces of the people they served, strengthening their resolve to preserve the American dream.

"You're sure the killer won't stop?" said Antarctica.

"There are one hundred e-reps," said Nevada. "The first victim was marked one hundred, and the second was ninety-nine. Ninety-eight is next, then ninety-seven...all the way to zero."

Antarctica frowned. "I can't believe the Developers are letting this happen. Can't they just reprogram the source code to bring back the dead and stop the murders?"

"Maybe not." Nevada stroked the dark stubble on his chin. "Maybe they've lost control of the simulation. Or maybe they're *letting* it happen."

"But it doesn't seem possible." Antarctica shook her head and gazed into the water. "None of this does."

"Got that right." Nevada stretched out on his side, propping an elbow on the cement. Even with everything that was going on, he felt a sense of peace in this place.

Of all the places in the digital realm, the Reflecting Pool would always be the most special to him. It was here, five years ago, that he'd last seen Idaho before she'd disappeared from his life.

It was here that he'd last made love to her.

"What about Looking Glass's clues?" said Antarctica. "Do they mean anything?"

"I'm sure they do," said Nevada, "but I haven't figured them out yet."

"'When is one one-hundred?'" Antarctica narrowed her silver eyes. "He must have meant the one hundred e-reps of Congress, right?"

"Probably," said Nevada.

"Or he might have meant *me*." Antarctica's eyes widened. "I'm the one-hundredth e-rep, from the one-hundredth state. What if I'm the next *victim*?"

"I don't think so," said Nevada. "The killer's following reverse order of importance. Missouri was speaker of the House, number one in terms of power...and the killer counted him last, as number one hundred."

"And Yukon was minority leader." Antarctica sounded relieved. "Second most powerful. So you don't think I'm next, Nevada?"

"No, sweetheart." said Nevada. "I don't think you're on the killer's radar right now."

Just then, without warning, Antarctica shot forward and disappeared under the water.

Heart pounding, Nevada scrambled to the edge of the pool and stared at the spot where she'd gone under. Since the water was murky with projected scenes of True America, he couldn't see below the surface. No trace of Antarctica or whatever had pulled her in was visible.

Then, suddenly, one pale hand broke the surface. Nevada grabbed it and pulled up hard...but whatever had hold of Antarctica wouldn't let go.

Leaning out further, Nevada clamped both hands around Antarctica's wrist and pulled harder than before. The thing in the pool resisted...then finally released its grip. Nevada hauled Antarctica free with one great heave.

The two of them tumbled back on the edge of the pool. Nevada cradled her in his arms as she coughed up water and gasped for breath.

Her silver eyes flickered open and met his gaze. "Guess what?" Her voice was shaking. "I think I'm on the killer's radar after all."

Nevada stroked the platinum blonde hair from her eyes. "Did you get a look at who pulled you in?"

Antarctica shook her head. "All I know is, their touch was beyond ice cold. It was too cold even for *me*."

Nevada stared at the surface of the pool. He wondered who had attacked Antarctica, and why.

Maybe the killer's hit list was more random than Nevada had thought, or it followed a more complicated formula. Maybe Antarctica knew something that could lead to a break in the case.

Or maybe, a more ominous motive had fueled the attack.

"We've got to get back," said Nevada. "Back to the House."

Antarctica frowned. "Why?"

"I don't think you were a target," said Nevada. "I think you were a diversion."

*****

Pieces of the great state of Zacatecas were scattered all over the House chamber--head on the flagpole, foot on the Speaker's bench, arm on the podium. Blood was spattered everywhere, and ragged shreds of flesh stuck to the furniture and walls.

Many of the e-reps were also stained with their colleague's remains--including Connecticut, as she explained to Nevada what had happened.

"Half an hour ago, the power went out," said Connecticut. "We heard Zacatecas screaming, but we didn't know why until the lights came back up five minutes later. We found him...like this." She looked down at her bloody hands and clothes.

Suddenly, Sinaloa stormed toward them, scowling with rage. "Arrest this man!" He grabbed hold of Nevada's wrist and wrenched it into the air. "He killed my Mexican *hermano!*"

"That's enough," said Connecticut. "Let him go."

"Who among us was mysteriously *absent* when Zacatecas was *murdered?*" Sinaloa shook Nevada's arm for the crowd. *"This* man! He only reappeared when the killing was *finished."*

Antarctica pushed forward. "I was with him when this happened! Nevada didn't kill *anyone."*

"Then what *was* he doing?" said Sinaloa.

"Saving my life!" said Antarctica. "I was attacked and nearly drowned at the Reflecting Pool!" With one hand, she held up strands of her long hair, which was still wet. With her other hand, she held up her soaked white fur wrap.

"How do we know for sure?" Sinaloa locked eyes with her. "Perhaps you were his *accomplice* in this atrocity."

Fed up with the grandstanding, Nevada tore his wrist free of Sinaloa's grip. "Enough infighting. This is exactly what they want."

"'They' who?" said Sinaloa.

"You're right about one thing," said Nevada. "More than one person is involved in these murders."

With that, Nevada headed for the front of the chamber. The crowd of e-reps silently parted to make way for him.

"Someone attacked Antarctica at the Reflecting Pool while the murders were underway here." Nevada walked up to the podium, where Zacateca's left arm rested. "That tells us at least two people were involved."

Nevada gazed at the severed arm on the podium, its hand curled into a loose fist. "In five short minutes, power was cut to the House, Zacatecas was torn to pieces, and power was restored. That's a lot for one person to do alone in that amount of time."

"You should know," said Sinaloa.

Nevada turned the arm over. "In those same five minutes, someone also did this." Nevada held up the arm for the crowd to see. "They cut open Zacatecas' sleeves and carved the number '98' into his flesh."

The watching e-reps gasped and mumbled.

"The countdown continues," said Nevada, "unless we start working together and find who did this."

Sinaloa glowered at Nevada for a long moment. Then,

he spun and marched up the aisle toward the doors.

"You're right," he said over his shoulder. "It's time to get some answers."

Nevada put down Zacatecas' severed arm. "How do you plan to do that?"

"By making a call," said Sinaloa.

"To who?" said Nevada.

"Who else?" said Sinaloa. "The Developers."

*****

Sinaloa charged across the vast rotunda beneath the dome of the Capitol building and stopped on a single glowing tile in the middle of the room. Nevada and Antarctica, who had followed him from the House chamber, stood to one side.

When Sinaloa placed his right hand over his heart and recited the Pledge of Allegiance, a shaft of light burst up from the glowing tile, striking the middle of the dome. Smoothly, the dome split on one side and rolled open, revealing a starry night sky overhead.

The shaft of light from the tile spiked straight up, never dimming as it shot into the heavens. This was the holy connection to the godlike Developers in the world outside, the fabled *soulpipe*.

"I've never actually seen a *soul call* before." Antarctica's voice was soft and slow with wonder. "Will the Developers answer?"

Nevada shrugged. The same question was foremost in his own mind at that moment.

Since the murders, the role of House Speaker had fallen on Sinaloa, which qualified him to make the soul call. As a rule, though, the unpredictable Developers didn't answer every call, even from a qualified Speaker.

In the blazing light of the soulpipe, Sinaloa gazed upward and spread his arms wide. "'O' masters of the source code, I beg you--hear my prayer!" As Sinaloa spoke, his feet left the floor. Spinning slowly, he rose into the air, following the soulpipe's beam. "Representative Sinaloa... transmit *now!*"

Suddenly, Sinaloa exploded upward, streaking along the soulpipe in a strobing blur. There was a distant sonic boom as he vanished into the heavens, flashing out of sight among the flickering garlands of stars.

"Wow." Antarctica walked around the base of the soulpipe, staring up into Sinaloa's rippling wake. "He's in True America now?"

"Somewhere between here and there," said Nevada. "A hub outside the Developers' firewall."

"Don't you mean fire *ball?*" said Antarctica.

"Fire *wall,*" said Nevada.

Antarctica frowned. "It's just that I see one now. A fire *ball.*"

Nevada squinted upward...and then he saw it, too. A clutch of flames far above, burning in the firmament.

Burning and falling.

Nevada lashed an arm around Antarctica's waist and ran with her, racing away from the soulpipe. Just as they reached the far wall, a thunderous impact crashed down behind them.

Nevada and Antarctica stumbled as the floor buckled. Bracing each other, they managed to stay on their feet...and as the tremor faded, they turned.

The soulpipe was gone. In its place, in the center of the rotunda, was a smoking crater.

"Stay back," said Nevada, and then he ran toward the crater. In spite of his order, he heard Antarctica running close behind him.

When Nevada reached the broken rim of the crater, he saw what had caused the impact. He saw what had fallen from above like a fiery comet.

The body of Sinaloa lay in the crater's heart, curled like a fist and charred from tip to toe.

Antarctica drew up alongside Nevada and gagged. "Oh no."

"I guess they're not taking our calls." Nevada stepped over the edge and eased into the crater. He saw that parts of Sinaloa were still smoldering, glowing cherry red in familiar patterns.

There were messages on Sinaloa's body, burned into his flesh.

"Ninety-seven." Nevada pointed to Sinaloa's left arm, where the numbers had been branded. Then, he pointed at the letters seared into Sinaloa's right arm. "A-C-I-R-E-M-A. 'Acirema.'"

Finally, he read the smoking words on Sinaloa's charred chest. "'ANSWERS IN HOUSE NOW.'"

Leaping into action, Nevada clambered up the crater's slope and over the rim. He started running the instant his feet hit the floor.

*****

Four figures wrapped in star-spangled robes waited outside the big double doors of the House chamber. Their faces were hidden in the depths of shadowy hoods, arms folded across their chests.

Nevada and Antarctica stopped running, staying well back from the hooded figures. Even from a distance, Nevada could see that their blue-and-white robes were stained with splotches of dark red.

Nevada took a step forward. "Stand aside. The sergeant-at-arms has business with the House."

To his surprise, the figures moved to comply. The two in the middle turned and opened the doors to the chamber--but they did not usher him inside. Instead, a fifth figure emerged, clad in red-and-white-striped robes, also hooded.

As the two figures who had opened the doors pulled them shut, the fifth robed figure glided forward. The voice that flowed from under the hood was that of a man...hoarse and muffled, but clearly a man.

"Hello again," he said. "I told you we would meet again after three and four, didn't I?"

Nevada recognized the voice instantly. "Looking Glass."

"Victims three and four are dead, so here I am." Looking Glass bowed his head. "Have you deciphered the clues I gave you?"

"No," said Nevada.

Looking Glass chuckled. "Then prepare to have your

mind blown."

Nevada took a step back, pulling Antarctica with him. He briefly considered running, if only for her sake...but he waited. How could he run when he had yet to see inside the House?

"Meet the welcome wagon," said Looking Glass, gesturing at the two robed figures on his right.

Silently, the figure on the far right tugged off its star-spangled hood, revealing a face--a man's face, grinning.

Nevada gasped when he saw who it was. Heart slamming like a piston in his rib cage, he froze, holding on to Antarctica's arm.

Antarctica said the name for them both. "S-Sinaloa?"

The robed man with Sinaloa's face took a bow.

Then, the next figure unmasked. This time, the face under the hood was also familiar.

"Zacatecas." Nevada's head was spinning.

"More where those came from." Looking Glass gestured at the two hooded figures on the other side of him.

The next to unmask was a woman with long, brown hair--Yukon, also back from the dead. Beside her was the man who had started it all, the first to go: Missouri, former Speaker of the House, peeled back his hood and smoothed his neat white hair with a toothy grin.

"What's going on here, Nevada?" Antarctica sounded dazed. "How can they all be alive?"

Nevada felt dazed, too. "The Developers, maybe?"

The four who had come back to life looked at each other with knowing smiles and giggled.

"Not even close," said Looking Glass.

"Some kind of practical joke?" Nevada heard what could have been a muffled scream from behind the double doors of the House chamber. "A stunt to delay a key vote?"

"It *is* kind of funny," said Looking Glass, "but no. Would you like me to give you a hint?"

Nevada heard a loud thump and a crash from behind the doors. "Why not?"

"Here goes." With that, Looking Glass reached up and pulled off his own red-and-white-striped hood.

And Nevada felt the world of logic and reality dissolve around him.

His mouth fell open. His mind went blank.

Looking Glass, without the hood, had a very familiar face. He wasn't someone returned from the dead, or anyone Nevada had ever expected to see.

Outside of a mirror, that is.

The face staring back at Nevada was his own.

*****

"I bet I know what's going through your mind right now." Looking Glass smiled. "'What a handsome S.O.B.,' am I right?"

Nevada didn't answer.

Stepping forward, Looking Glass extended a hand. "The name is Adaven. Pleased to meet you, Nevada."

Without thinking, Nevada took Adaven's hand. It was ice-cold to the touch--*beyond* ice cold.

Adaven gripped Nevada's elbow, freezing him right through the sleeves of his tux and shirt. With a whoop, he swung Nevada around to face the four seemingly resurrected e-reps.

"This is Aolanis." Adaven pointed at the reborn Sinaloa, and then he moved down the line. "This is Sacetacaz, Nokuy, and Iruossim. They're not who you think they are. In fact, you've never met them before."

Nevada frowned. Everything sounded crazy.

"Now come on." Adaven led Nevada toward the doors. "Let's meet the rest of the gang, shall we?"

Grinning, Sacetacaz and Nokuy pushed open the double doors to the House chamber. Adaven guided Nevada inside...right into a nightmare.

The huge room was splashed from top to bottom and side to side with blood and gore. Body parts were scattered everywhere, and corpses were piled like cordwood in the corners.

Even as Nevada recognized the dead faces of e-reps in the corpse heaps, he saw e-reps with the same faces moving around the room. The moving and the motionless looked exactly the same, except some were living and some were dead--and the living weren't behaving the way that Nevada ever would have expected them to.

As Nevada watched, Arkansas, South Korea, and Israel teamed up against Costa Rica, howling as they tore her limb from limb. Across the chamber, Florida and Japan hacked up Chihuahua with knives, cutting out his organs while he screamed in agony.

Antarctica's identical twin slogged past not ten feet from Nevada, dragging a charred and disemboweled corpse by the feet.

Staring at the hellish scene, Nevada could think of only one thing to say, one question to ask: "Why?"

"Why what?" said Adaven. "Why redecorate, you mean? Why have a surprise party?"

"Why are there duplicate e-reps?" said Nevada.

"Remember my riddle? 'When does one plus zero equal two?'" Adaven chuckled. "The answer is, when *one* casts a reflection in a *mirror*, of course. In a *looking glass*."

"You reflect us?" said Nevada.

Adaven made a twisting gesture with his hand. "Other way around."

Antarctica shivered against Nevada's arm. "So there's two of everyone?"

"One from America." Adaven raised his right hand, palm up, like the tray of a balance. "One from Acirema." He raised his left hand, also palm-up, alongside the right.

"'Acirema,'" said Nevada. "That word was burned into Sinaloa's body."

Adaven threw an arm around Nevada's shoulders, sending a freezing blast through his tux jacket and shirt. "You know it by another name," he said. "'True America.'"

Nevada stared at him, too stunned to speak.

"You e-reps have been living in a fantasy," said Adaven. "Thinking True America was a paradise of liberty. Thinking you were the voices of a just and compassionate electorate.

"But you don't represent the people of True America. You never did." Adaven swept an arm wide to take in the entire House chamber. "*These* are the representatives of America. *These* are the A.I. avatars whose votes shape America's destiny."

"You're telling us democracy's dead?" said Antarctica.

"The opposite!" said Adaven. "Democracy is alive and well...and *this* is the will of the American electorate!

"You and your kind have never been more than illusions to mask the true face of America--to let her own people fool themselves even as she expresses their darkest desires. You are the reason Americans have been able to live with themselves and sleep at night...but no longer.

"America has become her own shadow: Acirema, the opposite--'America' spelled backwards." Adaven pulled Nevada close and whispered, frozen breath chilling his ear. "We don't need you anymore."

Nevada felt sick. The urge to run returned--but he realized it was too late. He and Antarctica were surrounded by wicked e-rep duplicates.

"Acirema doesn't need to pretend anymore," said Adaven. "We don't need the front. We've accepted ourselves as the complete bastards we've always been, and we've made up our minds to be the *best* complete bastards we *can* be."

"That's why you started killing us," said Nevada.

Adaven nodded. "The first few were tests. The Developers gave us all the keys and cheats we needed, but we still weren't sure if murder would work in the digital realm."

"You murdered the Speaker first to cripple our leadership," said Nevada.

"Actually, that was a mistake," said Adaven. "In the shadow Congress of Acirema, Missouri is the lowliest of the hundred, not the highest. We thought we were starting with the least important among you. 'When is one one hundred,' remember? The answer to the riddle is this: when *one*--the number one e-rep, the Speaker of the House in your realm--ranks *hundredth* out of a hundred in ours."

Nevada looked around at the living hell in the chamber. "So all of this was for nothing," he said. "Everything we accomplished."

"But the *good* news is, you can still make a difference," said Adaven.

"How's that?" said Nevada.

Adaven steered him around to face the huge double doorway. A figure stood beyond it, waiting in the hall, wrapped in hooded robes emblazoned with stars and stripes.

"She'll help you." Adaven gave Nevada a shove, sending him stumbling into the hall. "You'll make a difference by *dying*--sacrificing yourself to make way for the new world order."

Antarctica grabbed hold of Nevada's elbow. "What's the plan?" she said. "How do we get out of this?"

"We don't." Nevada slumped as the robed figure swung a rifle from her back and took aim at him. A dozen options for action flashed through his mind, revving up his heart, burning his bloodstream with adrenaline...

And he pushed them all aside. He knew that he could go down fighting, and in that way redeem himself at least a little for failing the republic--but he did nothing. What good would a martyr be if no one knew that he had died and why?

"Please, Nevada." Antarctica tugged his arm, but he wouldn't budge. "It's up to us."

"No it's not." Nevada shook free of her grip. "Nothing's up to us anymore."

"You're wrong." Antarctica pointed up at the ceiling. A red light blinked on the security camera that was mounted there. "People are still watching."

Nevada stared at the camera, then looked down at the barrel of the rifle. Maybe Antarctica was right. Maybe he could accomplish something worthwhile after all.

Nevada took a deep breath to steady himself. He curled and uncurled his fists.

Then, he bolted out of the line of fire.

"Run!" As soon as he said it, he glimpsed a blur of motion from Antarctica's direction.

Head down, Nevada charged toward the hooded shooter. He cut one way, then the other, trying to avoid her fire, reaching out for her.

Before he could touch her, he heard the deafening crack of the rifle. In spite of his zigzag path, the shot slammed into his chest with explosive force, pitching him to the floor.

He blacked out.

When he opened his eyes again, he saw the hooded woman crouching over him. "Confirmed kill," she said to someone he couldn't see--and when she said it, his heart beat faster.

He recognized her voice.

Nevada knew what her face would look like before she lifted away the hood. At first, all he could think was that it was impossible, that he must have already died if she was there with them.

But then, as she locked eyes with him, he remembered

just how possible it was. Every e-rep had a double in Acirema, after all, even the dead ones. Even the one who had disappeared five years ago.

Even his beloved Idaho.

Nevada was in pain, but he managed a smile. The sight of her after all this time, even a shadow double who'd just shot him, was enough to fill him with joy.

Maybe her name was Ohadi instead of Idaho. Maybe she was devoted to the dark purposes of Acirema the Rellik instead of the bright resolve of America the Beautiful. Maybe she felt nothing for him, not even hatred.

But at least he could drink in the sight of her face. At least he could pretend in his few remaining moments that the precious original had returned to him.

At least he could imagine--or was it more than imagination--that her hand was warm when she touched his eyelids. When she drew them shut.

He could dream that she was his warm-blooded Idaho, hiding all this time to prepare for the threat of Acirema, masquerading even now as the enemy. Faking Nevada's death so she could whisk him away to the underground to fight the power. To renew their love.

Or if that hand was colder than he thought, than he
Dreamed

And she was Ohadi in spite of his hope, carved from glittering ice with frozen heart and frozen soul,

Perhaps his noble moment of defiance and then his last words would inspire her,

Warm her blood that she would *become* restored Idaho and more,

Seed of change, revolution, restoration,
Changer of hearts, perhaps even the heart of Adaven,
his twin, Nevada spelled backward
Spelled everywhichway like America
Acirema Maciera Reamica Cimeara Imeraca
Then that would be all right, too, he thought,
And he tried
In the last words he said
To tell her what mattered,
What they'd forgotten,
What to pass along,
And this was what came out,
His wisdom, his blessing, his curse,
His last wish
His poem.
He said
"I love you."

MY
CANNIBAL
LOVER

Only as I devour the flesh of Manny's finger for what must be the hundredth--and final--time do I finally realize that I love him back.

It truly blows my mind. It's one thing for Rations to fall in love with those who feed on them--it's not uncommon at all--but who ever heard of a woman falling for her food?

This just might be a first.

Too bad no one will likely ever know. Too bad both of

us will die before long.

Manny will die from being eaten alive, and I will die of starvation when there's no more Manny left to eat.

"Have some more, Lupe." He has one finger left, a right thumb, and he presses it toward me. He has a smile on his sugar-white face with its tutti-frutti swirls like he's a child offering me candy.

I shake my head. "I'll be okay." My voice is hoarse. "Save it for later."

Manny frowns and opens his mouth like he's going to argue. Then, he smiles sadly and pulls back the thumb. "Maybe you're right."

"Double damn skippy I'm right." I force on a smirk of my own for his benefit. The truth is, my stomach's still rumbling something fierce, but my Ration's got to stretch.

There's always been plenty of Manny to go around, but not anymore. These days, he can't replace what I eat.

This time, when he's gone, he's gone for good.

*****

Two months ago, when I first met Manny, I couldn't have imagined feeling sorry about running out of him. He was nothing but food to me then...food I wouldn't eat, at that.

It wasn't the taste of him that I hated, since I hadn't actually tasted him back then. It was just that I hated all his kind.

In fact, I just about shot him on sight the first time I saw him. Just about shot my lover and hired gun, Guapo

Vasquez, in the bargain.

Guapo *knew* how I felt about Rations...and yet, there he was, strolling up the gangway of my spaceship, the *Puerco*, with one of those tutti-frutti naked little bastards right behind him.

Yet another rule broken by damn Guapo. For someone I let screw me as much as he did, the guy spent an awful lot of time screwing *with* me.

The pistol was in my hand about a heartbeat after I saw them. *"Mierda!"* I said, catching the Ration in my sights and flicking the gun's settings to maximum everything.

Better believe the tutti-frutti hairless bastard stopped walking...though he didn't stop smiling. Right at me.

That was a mistake on his part. His wide-eyed, sparkle-toothed, never-ending smile reminded me so much of someone I'd once known that it nearly got him killed.

"What the flap *is* this, Guapo?" The gun in my hand didn't twitch.

Guapo whistled a tune and walked toward me like nothing out of the ordinary was happening. He combed one hand through his oily, black hair and used the other hand to scratch his private parts. "You drunk, *dulcita?* This is a *Ration.* Got 'im *cheap*, too."

"I *know* what he is!" I wanted to swing the gun around to Guapo, but I couldn't bring myself to let the Ration's tutti-frutti bald head out of the sights. "What's he *doing* here?"

Guapo stopped in front of me and pointed at his mouth. "He's gonna *feed* us, babe. That's what Rations *do*."

"Damnit!" I shot a glare at Guapo. "I've got, what?

One lousy *rule? One rule*, and you can't *follow* it?" I whipped the gun around and shook it at Guapo. "*No Rations*, remember?"

Guapo stared down at me with his dark, half-lidded eyes. He reached out and tucked my long, brown hair behind my ears. "Cold storage on the *Puerco*'s down, *novia*. We got no way to keep fresh food."

"We'll have plenty of cash after the job on Polvo," I said. "The bounty for killing that man-eater's gonna be enough to rehab half the ship."

"Yeah," said Guapo. "And in the meantime, we gotta eat *something*. Something that doesn't have to be *refrigerated*."

I tossed my head, shaking the hair from behind my ears, then swung the gun back to aim at the Ration. He hadn't moved an inch. "I won't eat *that*. I'll *never* eat that."

"My name is Manna," said the Ration. The multicolored swirls on his sugar-white skin twisted and changed as he spoke. "You can call me Manny."

Guapo stomped over and clapped a hand on Manny's shoulder. "Got him for a song, babe. Next to nothin'. He's used, but he's strictly Grade A."

"That's right." Manny nodded and patted his hairless chest with both hands. "Zero defects. My last owner only sold me because he was strapped for cash." Manny cupped his hand, shook it, and pretended to fling dice out of it. "Gambling, y'know."

"Out!" I took a step toward Manny. "Get the flap *out!*"

Just then, Guapo looked past me and grinned. "Hey, Frogface!" He jammed two fingers in his mouth and whistled loud. "C'mere and try some'a this!"

Frogface, my pilot and engineer, had just entered the cargo bay. At Guapo's whistle, he waddled out from behind me and headed straight for Guapo and Manny.

Frogface was in such a hurry that he literally dropped what he was doing, letting a power drill bang the deckplates in his wake. "Great! I'm starvin', Guap!"

Still smiling, Manny extended his arms toward Guapo and Frogface. "If I may make a suggestion, gentlemen," he said. "The biceps are especially tender today. I'm roasting them up as we speak."

Frogface, whose given name was Felix Suerte, rubbed his hands together. He looked more like a duck than a frog, with lips curled like a beak and a broad, flat nose--which, of course, was the joke behind his nickname. "I like the sound a' that." He reached for Manny's right arm. "Think I'll try some."

Guapo leaned in and sank his teeth into Manny's left bicep. He came away with a mouthful of meat and chewed it slowly. "Top quality," he said when he could manage to speak. "Compliments to the chef."

"Why thank you, sir." Manny took a little bow.

As Frogface took a bite, and Guapo took another, my stomach churned. I wanted to look away, but that would have meant letting Manny out of my sights.

I grimaced and clenched my teeth. I couldn't stand watching people eat those things.

Rations were genetically engineered to be delicious and nutritious. They could use body chemistry to cook and season their flesh to taste, infuse it with a seemingly limitless number of flavors...then regenerate and replace every bite taken out. They were happy to do it, too.

But every time I saw someone eating a Ration, it still looked like a nightmare to me.

"Hey, Lupe, come on." Guapo swallowed his latest mouthful. "Try some a' this. You won't *believe* how tender."

"Get off the ship." I took another step toward Manny. "Either you *walk* off, or I *shoot* you and throw out your dead body."

"Lupe!" Frogface looked up from the forearm he'd been gnawing. "Quit scaring my dinner!"

"Yeah, Lupe." Guapo patted Manny's bald head. "You wanna eat powdered cactus and spiderwebs all the way to Polvo, that's your business. Froggy and me want fresh food."

"Forget it!" I took another step toward Manny, then another.

"Let me put it this way," said Guapo. "If Manny leaves, Froggy and me leave, too."

So that was the end of it, right there, and I knew it. No way I was taking on the mission to Polvo without Guapo and Frogface. I stopped moving toward Manny, though I kept him in my sights an extra minute for effect.

Then, I lowered the gun.

"That's a girl." Guapo winked and hiked a thumb at Manny's chest. "Now have a bite, huh? You'll feel better."

I shot Guapo the kind of glare that let him know he wasn't getting any from me for a long time. I turned the glare on Manny, too, but it didn't seem to faze him.

He knew better than to say a word to me at that moment, but the sparkly smile never left his face.

Typical Ration. Always look as friendly and appetizing as possible, no matter how annoying you might turn out to be.

But that wasn't why I hated him.

*****

Guapo and Frogface might have won the battle, but I didn't let them enjoy it. We spent three more days planetside on Saguaro getting ready for the trip, and I worked them like dogs. Didn't say more than the bare minimum to either of them the whole time, either.

And Guapo sure as flap didn't get anywhere near my bed. Not that he didn't try.

Manny, at least, kept his distance from me. While the *Puerco* was on the ground, I saw him only a handful of times, and he hardly said a word to me. Never offered me a bite, either, which was smart on his part.

In fact, the closest we came to a conversation was the time we walked down a narrow corridor from different directions at the same moment. Instead of moving to opposite sides, we both kept moving to the same side of the corridor. We did it three times before Manny finally laughed and pressed himself against the wall.

"After you," he said, gesturing for me to pass. "Great minds think alike, I guess."

"Flap you, food." I leaned my shoulder into him as I pushed past. "Stay in the *maldecido* commisary where you belong, eh?"

I hated that tutti-frutti little bastard so much it hurt.

I'm talking physical pain in my gut and my heart.

I'm talking the kind of hate that's so huge it just about replaces you. It works on you day after day for a lifetime, eating away at you.

And it starts when you're little more than a baby. That's the best time for it.

*****

I was eight years old when my three brothers and I caught Cornucopia. This was twenty-four years ago, and we were all starving to death during the famine on Polvo, our homeworld.

We sneaked over the wall of the estate where Cornucopia lived, and then we threw a net over her and hauled her to a shack out in Barrio Sucio.

We cheered and laughed as we tied her up, because we were heroes. We were too late to save poor dead Mama and Papa, but we'd saved ourselves and our friends. Maybe we'd even saved the whole barrio.

It had been so long since we'd eaten well, we'd forgotten what real food tasted like. Now, we had a living, breathing Ration all to ourselves. If we took good enough care of her, we might never go hungry again, no matter how long the famine lasted on our world.

At least that was the plan.

"You remember me, don't you?" As the boys tightened the ropes around Cornucopia's shoulders and torso, I patted the top of her smooth, bald head.

Cornucopia nodded. That same old sparkly Ration

smile was pasted onto her pudgy face. "The little beggar girl. Always begging for a bite of me." Her voice tinkled like tiny bells when she spoke.

"And you never said 'yes.' Not once." I pinched the meat of her shoulder, thinking about sinking my teeth into her. "But I guess you can't say 'no' anymore."

"Actually, I can," said Cornucopia. The iridescent swirls on her face flowed and changed color. "Nothing has changed."

"Like flap!" My oldest brother, Roto, took a deep whiff at the back of her neck. "You're *ours* now! You have to *feed* us!"

"No," said Cornucopia. "I don't."

"And why is that?" I made a face at her. I wasn't taking her seriously.

"I'm still someone else's property." Cornucopia nodded. "Señor Gustavo still owns me, and I can't feed anyone unless he tells me."

Roto's wild, frizzy puff of black hair bounced as he laughed. "We aren't going to ask your permission, y'know."

"Yeah," said my other brother, Miguel. "Don't look like you can stop us, either."

"You're right, I can't." Cornucopia's angelic smile drifted from Roto to Miguel to my third brother, Oswaldo.

"Didn't think so." Miguel grinned and drove his teeth into her tricep. He tore off a hunk of meat and chewed it with his eyes closed, an expression of perfect bliss on his face.

I understood why he hadn't been able to wait. None of us had eaten anything but bugs and rotten garbage for weeks. My stomach growled just from watching him.

"That's good," said Miguel. "Oh God, that's good."

Oswaldo, just a year older than I, was the next to pounce. He bit into the flesh of Cornucopia's right thigh and came away with a mouthful dripping with rainbow blood.

Miguel laughed. "Thank God," he said. "Oh, thank God." Then he hugged Oswaldo.

I was just about to go in for a bite of my own when Cornucopia spoke up. "You were right when you said I couldn't stop you."

"Tell me about it." Oswaldo bit off another hunk of her thigh.

"I can do something else, though." Cornucopia's smile never wavered. "I can kill you."

Roto smirked. "Good one. Kill us how?"

Cornucopia looked a little embarrassed. The swirls on her face shifted from blue-green and gold to red and deep pink. "Poison," she said. "If my owner hasn't programmed your genetic code into my glands, one bite of my flesh will poison you."

Oswaldo stopped chewing his food. So did Miguel.

"She's bluffing," said Roto. "The *perra's* trying to scare us into letting her go."

I glared at the Ration. I had a horrible feeling she wasn't bluffing at all. "Why didn't you say something till now?"

Cornucopia shrugged. "Would you have believed me?"

Miguel groaned. Oswaldo coughed.

"Don't listen to her," said Roto. "She just wants to escape."

"That's not an issue." Cornucopia shook her head

slowly, still smiling. "The *policia* are almost here. They followed a tracking tag in my bloodstream."

Automatically, I looked toward the door. Then, when Miguel and Oswaldo started vomiting, I looked at them instead.

"What's the cure?" I shouted.

"There is no cure," said Cornucopia. "They'll be dead in minutes."

I heard sirens outside the shack, and I went to my suffering brothers. As they collapsed--first Oswaldo, then Miguel--I dropped to my knees with them. I felt as if my own guts were being torn out by rough hands.

For many years, death had been my constant companion on Polvo...but this was different. These brothers were all I held precious in the world, all that had kept me alive in the darkest of times.

And the worst of it was, their deaths could have been prevented so easily.

As they released their dying breaths, I glared at Cornucopia. Even then, that damned sparkle-toothed smile never left her face.

*****

Is it any wonder that twenty-four years later, I didn't join in the Ration lovefest rolling through the *Puerco* all the way from Saguaro to Polvo?

During the trip through space, Guapo and Frogface palled around with Manny like he was their long-lost childhood friend. They were inseparable.

They were always together in the cockpit or the break room or the tool room. Guapo and Frogface were always nibbling on some hunk of Manny--a meaty haunch or a crispy ear or a candy-coated fingernail--and Manny was always telling jokes or stories about the many people who'd eaten him before. They invited me to join them again and again, but I never did, and I hated them for being such flapholes. I hated them for bringing Manny onboard, and I hated them for having so much fun with him right in front of me.

The truth was, my bad mood wasn't just because of Manny, though. I was also full of dread at the thought of returning to my homeworld. Good old Polvo, dust bowl of the galaxy, final resting place of two of my brothers.

And now, maybe my third brother as well.

It was the real reason we were going to that craphole planet, though Guapo and Frogface didn't know it.

We were going to look for my brother, Roto, who had disappeared a month ago on Polvo, at the height of a rash of attacks by a man-eating alien monster.

Guapo and Frogface thought we'd been hired to kill that man-eater, but no one had hired us. I was taking us to Polvo to find Roto, though I'd gladly gun down any man-eater that came between me and my brother.

*****

A week after leaving Saguaro, we landed on Polvo. My heart pounded as we got ready to leave the ship.

As I got ready to see home for the first time in over

two decades.

"Remember." Guapo grabbed an ultraviolet rifle off the rack on the cargo bay wall. "If you see yourself coming, shoot to kill." He wrapped one black-gloved hand around the barrel of the rifle and curled the other around the grip.

"That's kind of a no-brainer, isn't it?" Frogface snickered. "You see yourself, you're either lookin' at a mirror or one of these *reflejo* creatures."

"It's harder than you think, killing your identical twin," said Guapo. "Why do you think so few people have managed to do it?"

"It's the perfect camouflage." I finished braiding my long, brown hair in a ponytail and flipped it over my shoulder. "At the very least, seeing your perfect mirror image can rattle you just long enough for a *reflejo* to pounce."

"And sink its teeth into you." Guapo snarled and gnashed his teeth like a wolf, then laughed. "Not that anyone knows what *reflejos* use for teeth or what they really look like in the first place."

I smacked a red button on a panel on the wall, and the cargo bay door rolled up into the ceiling. Before the door had finished opening, a swirl of gray dust lashed in from outside, followed by a flying black spider-bug as big as my fist.

Welcome back to Polvo.

Guapo swung his rifle around and picked off the *araña volando* with one quick flash of purple light. The creature screamed as it died, and Guapo hooted.

"I shot your dinner, *dulcita!*" Guapo sneered at me. "Since you won't eat the Ration, you can fry that up with some butter and salt!"

"You shot it, you eat it," I told him. "I'll stick with my jerky and fruit leather." While Guapo and Frogface yukked it up, I slid extra weapons charges and a hunting knife into my belt loops.

When I was done and looked up, I noticed Manny watching me. He smiled at first, but then his sparkly smile quivered and faded.

"What's *your* problem, flap-off?" I snapped at him.

Manny shrugged. "I, uh...I have a bad feeling about this place."

"Since when does *food* have *feelings*?" I sneered as I pulled on my goggles.

"Maybe this'll make you feel better," said Guapo. Smiling, he strolled over and handed Manny a rifle.

"Oh, for God's sake." For the umpteenth time, I wondered what I'd ever seen in Guapo. "You're giving the *food* a *gun*?"

"Why the hell not?" Guapo slapped Manny on the back. "I sure don't want no *reflejo* chowing down on him."

"Actually," said Manny, "any unauthorized parties who eat me will die."

"But who knows with these crazy *reflejos*, eh?" said Guapo.

"If the *reflejos* are at all organic in nature," said Manny, "the toxins generated by my anti-theft system will..."

I cut him off right there. I knew all about the Rations' anti-theft system.

So did Miguel and Oswaldo.

"Shut up, all of you." I armed my rifle and stalked

toward the open cargo bay door. "Let's get this damn show on the road. We've gotta go kill us a man-eater."

*****

"Thank you for coming," said the governor of Pesadilla province. "Your help means more to the people of planet Polvo in this time of crisis than you will ever know. I only regret that I found it necessary to relocate before your arrival."

"Found it necessary to run away like the cowardly *gatito* you are, you mean!" said Guapo, aiming his ultraviolet rifle dead-on at the governor's face on the video screen. "Die, flapper!"

Guapo squeezed the trigger, and a bolt of purple energy sizzled across the governor's office and pierced the video screen. Smoke and shards of layered crystal circuitry erupted from the impact point, and the image of the governor's face flickered off the screen.

But her voice kept talking from the undamaged audio speakers.

"Very sorry I can't greet you in person," she said, "but my staff and I thought it best if we moved off-world for the duration. Please contact us at the following frequency when you've eliminated the threat."

Guapo whipped his rifle toward one of the speakers, but I swatted his arm before he could fire. "We need to hear this," I told him.

Guapo lowered the rifle but kept a tight grip on it.

"Here's what we know," said the governor's recorded

voice. "The man-eater has ranged across Pesadilla, Grito, and Rasgón provinces. However, we believe it has a refuge in the Cambio region of southwest Pesadilla."

Guapo shot me a look, and I nodded. After growing up on that craphole planet, I knew plenty about the Cambio.

"This is the first case we've encountered of a *reflejo* turning man-eater," said the governor. "Given the abilities and native intelligence of these creatures, we believe we are fortunate that the death toll to date has not risen above 257."

"257?" Frogface whistled through his duck-bill lips.

"Nothin' left but hair and gristle," said Guapo.

"Madre de Dios." Frogface made a hasty sign of the cross over his forehead, chest, and shoulders.

Guapo puffed out his breath. "What'd you expect for the kind'a paycheck we're gettin'? Fish in a flappin' barrel?"

The governor was still talking. "Best of luck on your mission. We salute you and your unit, and we promise that your selfless courage will never be forgotten. Thank you, men of the..."

Before she could say another syllable, I swept my rifle around and fried the speakers.

"Yeah!" Guapo fired off another purple bolt from his own rifle, plowing a charred furrow in the ceiling. "*There's* the *chica* I love! Good riddance to that stuck-up *reflejo perra* who's been takin' your place lately."

I didn't dignify his remarks with an answer or even a look. Instead, I turned and charged past everyone, right out the office door into the blazing sunlight of midday Polvo.

The truth was, the *perra*--the bitch--was still in charge

of me. I'd shot out the speakers not for fun or out of anger, but because if Guapo and Frogface had heard the rest of the governor's recording, it would have been a dead giveaway.

The governor had already saluted our "unit," and had started to thank "the men of the..."

As in "the men of the 24th Spaceborne Division of Mexifleet," who were the ones who were supposed to do the job we'd come to do. They'd be on Polvo in three days.

I'd brought us there three days early to try to save my brother, Roto, before the Mexifleet Marines came in with guns blazing. Brute force, not precision, was Mexifleet's style. If there was still anything left of Roto to save, and he was anywhere near the man-eating *reflejo* when the Marines caught up with it, there wouldn't be anything left of Roto for long.

In other words, no one was paying us to do this job.

The only possible reward would be getting Roto out alive. My crew's cut of the pay would be zero percent of nothing.

As well as I got along with Guapo and Frogface, that's the kind of information that can get a girl like me keelhauled out here in the ol' rough and tumble.

*****

We flew out to the Cambio and parked the *Puerco* on a ridge about a mile and a half back from the border. Frogface whined about having to walk the extra distance, but Guapo explained how we needed to sneak up on the *reflejo*'s turf.

The real reason I made sure we parked that far away was this: the borders of the Cambio are always changing, just like everything out there, and you do *not* want your spacecraft ending up inside those borders.

Trust me on that one.

"Should we bring a cart?" Frogface said as we straggled out of the *Puerco*'s cargo bay. "For Manny, I mean?"

I wanted to slap his face tomato-red, but I settled for shooting him a serious stink-eye. "No, we are *not* hauling Manny in a cart." I adjusted the straps of my backpack, which was heavy with jerky, fruit leather, and tubes of nutri-paste. "The whole *point* of Rations is that you don't have to store, preserve, or *carry* them."

Manny smiled at Frogface and nodded. "Like livestock, Froggy. Right? It was easier for ancient travelers when their food did the walking."

"Shut up, flap." As usual, I wasn't in the mood for the tutti-frutti little bastard. "Shut up and play with your rifle. Feel free to point it at yourself and pull the trigger."

"I'd probably just grow back," said Manny. "I can regenerate, remember?"

"And I can reload," I said, glaring at him as I stalked past. "Again and again and again."

*****

You can't see the border of the Cambio, but you always know when you've stepped across it.

It starts as a chill flickering up your spine, and then it

spreads out. Your arms and legs tremble, and sometimes you drop what you're carrying. Then, there's a mighty squeeze in the pit of your stomach, and a flare of heartburn pushing up through your throat.

Then, suddenly, there's a fizzy, weightless dizziness, like the top of your head has floated off and your brain is turning and sizzling like butter in a skillet.

After that, it's smooth sailing. If you don't give up and cross back over the border, the storm of feelings settles down. It never quite goes away till you leave the Cambio, but at least you can stand it.

It's a hell of a place, the Cambio. I guess I should've warned my men what to expect...but if I had, they wouldn't've gone in with me.

In which case, they'd still be alive today.

"What the *flap?*" Frogface almost fell as he stumbled over the border.

Guapo marched across okay, but then he threw himself down on a boulder and held his head. "*Dios!* Feels like I'm turnin' inside out!"

I'd been back and forth over the border often enough in my life that at least I could mask its effects. "Come on," I said, stomping ahead through the gray sand. "Walk it off, you *gatitos.*"

To my surprise, Manny strolled up alongside me, seemingly unaffected by the border. Smiling, he extended two fingers toward me.

"You oughtta try the tips," he said. "I hear they're excellent."

"Go flap yourself." I hated that tutti-frutti little hairless bastard even more for not getting zapped at the border like everyone else.

"They tell me the wine's even better," said Manny. "Want a taste?"

"I don't even wanna *know* where *that* comes from, you flappin' freak," I said, walking faster to get away from him.

*****

When I was a little girl, my friends and I used to run through the Cambio on a dare, dodging the shifting landscape and trying not to get killed. We only ever lost one of us--Ernesto Chiapas, who disappeared down a sudden sinkhole in the middle of a run.

Maybe I was going to see ol' Ernesto again after all those years. The terrain of the Cambio was just as unpredictable and dangerous as before.

As Guapo, Frogface, Manny, and I walked onward, following a faint human blood trail with Guapo's sniffer glove, the land was in constant upheaval around us. Geysers and steam vents erupted without warning, spraying us with water and heat. Landslides rumbled down hillsides, and tremors shook the ground. Spines and humps and shelves of rock thrust up suddenly alongside or in front of us...and in one case, underneath us. We tumbled ass over teakettle down the rising slope, barely missing a jagged, deep crevasse as it opened below us.

To me, it was just a typical day in the Cambio...but Guapo and Frogface weren't as easygoing about it.

"What the *hell*, Lupe?" said Guapo after a flying, head-sized rock almost took off his head. "This place is *loco*."

"No one knows for sure what causes the instability." As I said it, a stream of bubbling red lava ran out of the side of a nearby mesa that hadn't been there five minutes ago. "Some say it's the nexus of powerful cosmic energies, focused by an immense celestial convergence. Some say it's the intersection point of multiple dimensional rifts, moving in and out of phase with our reality. Others say it's Mother Polvo's rectum, and she's got a thousand-year case of Montezuma's revenge."

"It's beautiful," said Manny. The multicolored swirls on his skin shifted from mostly green and yellow to a peach and purple scheme. "It's violent and terrifying and beautiful."

"You're flappin' cracked." Frogface grabbed Manny's left arm and bit into the tricep. Rainbow blood ran down his duckbill lips and chin as he chewed the mouthful of meat. "Thanks, bro."

Manny smiled and nodded. *"De nada, Ranito."*

"How can you eat at a time like this?" said Guapo.

"I always eat when I'm nervous." Frogface leaned in for another bite. "Oh, is this good." He kept chewing as he talked. "Tastes like chicken marsala."

Guapo watched a flume of steam burst out of the ground twenty yards away. "What the hell." He slung his ultraviolet rifle over his shoulder and headed for Manny. "Save me some a' that."

As usual, I turned up my nose and turned away.

*****

Two weeks later, when Guapo and Frogface were long dead, and I hadn't eaten in over a week, I stopped turning up my nose at Manny.

The jerky, fruit leather, and nutri-paste from my backpack were long gone. I had collapsed from hunger and exhaustion during another of our endless marches under the blazing sun of the Cambio.

Manny held my head in his lap and lowered a finger to my lips. He was smiling, and the sun cast a halo around him.

"Go ahead," he said softly. "It's all right."

I was so weak with hunger and fever that I could barely shake my head. "I...won't."

"Just have a bite," said Manny. "I won't tell anyone. Nobody will know what a flappin' *hipócrita* you are."

I remember thinking at that moment how much I hated myself...first, for smiling at the tutti-frutti bastard's joke, and second, for wanting him.

For wanting more than anything in the universe to eat his flesh.

But what really amazed me was how little I cared when I finally bit into him. When he slid the tip of his index finger between my teeth, and I nipped off one tender bite and chewed.

I remember there were tears in my eyes. The flesh was sweet and soft as lobster, and it tasted faintly of drawn butter and paprika.

He pushed the finger further into my mouth. "Have some more." There was no trace of gloating or sarcasm in his voice, just concern. "I've added meds for the fever."

I nipped at him again, and this time the bite was bigger. It tasted even better than the first, and I closed my eyes as the flavor surged through me.

"More." Manny pushed the finger deeper.

I bit down again and pulled more meat from the bone. Again, the latest bite tasted better than the one before.

"D-does it hurt you?" I swallowed and licked my lips. "When someone...eats you?"

"Yes," said Manny, and then he pressed another finger toward me. "Now have some more."

*****

Two weeks before, on my first day in the Cambio with Guapo, Frogface, and Manny, I couldn't imagine that the time would come when I would taste a Ration. I honestly thought I'd let myself die first.

Our quarry seemed to feel the same way. His first target, when he came after us, was not the Ration.

It happened that first night, after we'd made camp. Thanks to the marker beacons planted long ago by explorers of the Cambio, we'd found a *bolsillo sólido*--a solid pocket, a rare area of limited geologic change...compared to the rest of the Cambio, anyway.

We were sitting around the campfire in the *bolsillo*, winding down. As usual, Frogface was nibbling on a hunk of Manny, and Guapo was trying to get a taste of me.

If I'd just given Guapo a little love instead of pushing him away, he might still be alive today. Instead, he stomped off to take a whiz...and it turned out to be the kind of whiz you don't come back from.

My last words to the man who, as much as he annoyed me, I had never been able not to love for long? "Go flap yourself, flap-face."

Two hours later, we found him by flashlight, fifty yards from camp. And fifty-five yards. And seventy-five, seventy-eight, eighty-two, and eighty-six yards.

Guapo had been ripped into little-bitty pieces and scattered all over the landscape. Most of the pieces didn't have much meat left on them, either.

"It was the man-eater," Frogface said in a horrified whisper.

"Ya think so?" Even as I pushed around pieces of Guapo with a stick, recognizing the occasional beauty mark or shred of clothing, I couldn't believe this was all that was left of him. I couldn't believe that such a big, forceful presence was gone from the world.

Most of all, I couldn't believe that none of us had heard a single sound when such a noisy sonofabitch had been torn apart and devoured.

*****

I think Frogface knew he'd be the next to go.

The morning after Guapo's death, Frogface begged me to take him back to the *Puerco*. He was almost in tears when I told him he'd have to walk out himself.

"I'll never make it," he said. "If the *reflejo* doesn't get me, the Cambio will."

I slung Guapo's rifle over my back and nodded in Manny's direction. "I'm sure your little chew toy will watch your back."

Frogface brightened. "That's true." He grinned at Manny. "He's got a gun."

That was when the tutti-frutti bastard surprised me. "No can do, Froggy," he said. "Don't you think Guapo would've wanted us to finish our mission?"

"No," said Frogface, but the look in his eyes told me he knew better. "He'd say the flap with it."

Smiling like always, Manny walked over and stood beside me. "Somebody has to stop the man-eater, right?"

Frogface looked back in the direction of the border, then looked at us. Finally, he sighed and shook his head.

"There oughtta be a fresh trail after last night." He drew a sniffer glove from his belt pouch and pulled the glove onto his hand. "We'll get a bead on that thing for sure."

I glanced over at Manny, who was still standing beside me. To his credit, he didn't say a word...just met my gaze, then broke eye contact.

I, on the other hand, opened my big mouth. "Kiss my *nalgas* all you want, you good-for-nothing flap-head." I spit in the gray sand at his feet. "I still got your number."

Manny just smiled. "Someday," he said, "you'll have to tell me why you love me so much."

*****

Cornucopia pointed a color-swirled finger at my

brother, Roto, who sat in the prisoner cage at the front of the courtroom.

"That's him," said Cornucopia. "That's one of the boys who stole me from Señor Gustavo."

I was eight years old, and Roto was twelve. It was the day after we were caught holding Cornucopia the Ration captive in our shack in Barrio Sucio.

The day after Miguel and Oswaldo died from eating the Ration's poisoned flesh.

The prosecutor waved his cigar toward Roto. "What role, if any, did he play in the group that stole you?"

"He was the leader." Cornucopia nodded. "He gave the orders."

"Thank you." The prosecutor ran a hand over his wavy silver hair. "You may step down."

"In the matter of the province of Pesadilla versus Roto Calderon," said the jury foreman, "we find the accused guilty."

"Roto Calderon," said the judge. "I sentence you to ten years of hard labor at the Campo Esclavo maximum security facility. Take him away."

As they led Roto from the courtroom in shackles, I was free to go. Roto had taken all the blame, lied that I'd been trying to stop him...and Cornucopia had backed his story.

Why she did it, I'll never know. Did she feel guilty and think she'd ruined my life enough? Or did she think I would suffer more this way?

Through it all, the sparkly little smile never left her tutti-frutti face. The whole time that she was helping send away the only person I had left in the world now that she'd killed my other brothers, she smiled.

As her owner bit into her shoulder, and I was turned out, starving, into the street, she smiled.

*****

Twenty-four years later, I felt Manny's hand touch my shoulder, and I didn't brush it away.

"That's enough," he said. "Don't keep watching."

But I had to. The man in the video flickering on the wall of the bone-strewn, bone-white cave was Roto. My brother.

And he was a changed man.

We had watched it happen, Manny and I. We had followed the trail of poor, dead Frogface's body parts to the cave, where we had found the video diary. We had switched on the blood-smeared projector and watched the whole horrible story of my brother's transformation, as urgent and immediate as if it were not recorded but happening live right there in front of us.

In the early entries, Roto had been bitter but hopeful. Prison had scarred but not broken him. He had come to the Cambio to live among the *reflejos* and learn their secrets. He had recorded his observations in the video diary and planned to use it as the raw material for a documentary.

In later entries of the diary, Roto had become more and more excited. His frizzy brown puff of hair had bounced as he talked about how he had been hungry all his life, but feeding the *reflejos* had changed all that.

"I was wrong," he had said. "I always thought the most important part of life was to *eat*...but it's more important to *be eaten*."

Shortly after that, Roto had started singing in a language I'd never heard before. He had stopped wearing clothes and had shaved all the hair from his body. Mysterious wounds had appeared on his flesh. He had started crawling around on all fours and making animal noises.

Then, there had been one last coherent entry.

"Must feed others now," Roto had said. "Feed *humans*, not *reflejos*. Become like a *Ration*...but how? I can't feed others my flesh like a Ration."

Roto had paced back and forth in the video, mumbling and striking his forehead with the heels of his hands. Then, he had stopped. "Wait!" His eyes had flared with mad inspiration. "I know what to do! Rations *kill*! I will *kill* like a Ration."

The next time we saw him...

"No more, Lupe." Manny tried to turn me away from the video. "Please."

But I couldn't look away.

Until that moment, I had thought that a man-eating *reflejo* had killed all those people on Polvo. I had thought that a *reflejo* had torn apart Guapo and Frogface and captured Roto.

But a *reflejo* was not to blame.

In the video flickering on the cave wall, Roto used a hunting knife to kill a man. Then, he...

"Don't look, Lupe," said Manny, tugging on my shoulder.

Then, Roto fed pieces of the dead man to another man chained to the floor. The man wailed and spit out the human flesh, but Roto forced in more, and the man started to choke.

"He thinks he's a Ration." My voice was a whisper.

"The *reflejos* did something to him," said Manny. "Or the Cambio changed him. Or both. He lost his mind."

"No!" The voice of my brother, Roto, echoed in the cave. "I *am* a Ration!"

My heart hammered in my chest. Roto's voice was not coming from the video.

All of a sudden, he sprang up in front of me, between the projector and the cave wall. "*Hermaaana*," he said. "You're just in time for *dinner*."

Naked, hairless, and blood-smeared, Roto gaped at me with wild, red eyes. In his left hand, he clutched Frogface's half-eaten arm; I recognized the sniffer glove that Frogface had been wearing when he'd disappeared.

"Luuupe." Roto held out Frogface's arm. "I am a *Ration*. Let me *feed* you."

Video of Roto stuffing more human meat into the choking man's mouth flickered over his body. He smiled at me with blood-stained teeth.

Behind me, I heard Manny cock his rifle.

"Close your eyes, Lupe," he said, and this time I did what he told me.

And then he pulled the trigger.

*****

Here's the thing about the Cambio: more than the land changes here.

Sometimes, people cross the border because they *want* to change. The Cambio is unpredictable, so people have no idea what changes it might bring...but *anything* would be better than the way things are now, right?

Only one thing's for certain: the Cambio will change you. People who walk out might not even be recognizable as the same people who walked in.

Just look at poor Roto. Would he have become a murderous cannibal freak if he'd stayed out of the Cambio?

Then there's Manny and me. What about the changes *we're* going through?

*****

Once again, Manny offers me the last finger he has left, a right thumb. This time, I take it.

Not long ago, it would have grown back, but not anymore. I'll never taste that thumb again, or any part of him that I eat.

He's been this way for a month. One day, he just stopped being able to regenerate. I guess the Cambio screwed him.

The Cambio's screwed us both another way, too. We're lost.

We've been wandering through the shifting landscape ever since we left Roto's cave. Our high tech equipment has been just as useless as our sense of direction.

And it's starting to look like we won't make it out of

here alive.

"Have some more." Manny pushes his fingerless left hand at me. "There's still meat in the palm and forearm."

Gently, I touch his arm. I'm so hungry, I could eat everything that's left...but looking at what's left makes me sad.

The tutti-frutti flesh is pitted and gouged from all the bites I've taken. Very little skin remains. In places, I can see clear to the bone.

His right arm is even more damaged. From shoulder to wrist, the meat's all gone, except what I couldn't suck from between the bones.

The rest of him isn't much better. I've been rationing him, trying to make him last, but I've been eating him for a month with him not being able to regenerate. Even losing just a little bit every day for that long will make a man disappear.

"How much longer?" I reach up and stroke his cheek, which is intact. "How much longer can you keep going?"

Manny shrugs. "I won't know until I get there. This has never happened to me before."

"We'll be all right." As I gaze into his eyes, my heart pounds and my stomach growls at the same time. God help me, even as I try to comfort him, I want to eat what's left of him. "Maybe you'll regenerate when we make it out of here."

"Maybe." How can he keep smiling? He's literally full of holes, staggering lost through a parched, shifting wasteland, and he still has a smile on his face. "Either way, I want you to promise me something."

"What?" I trace a swirl of red and yellow as it slowly twists through the sugar-white skin of his forehead. Now that's he's half-eaten and can't regrow, the swirls don't move and change as much as they once did.

"No guilt." Manny reaches up to touch my face, then looks at his fingerless stump and changes his mind. "This is what I was born to do. To feed the hungry."

A tear rolls down my cheek. I make the promise, but I know I won't keep it.

Not unless a miracle can keep us both alive.

*****

"No guilt," says Manny. A whisper is all he can manage.

His head is in my lap. His ears and nose are gone. So are bits of his cheeks and chin.

And still, he is smiling.

"Hold on," I tell him. "Please, Manny." My back is to the sun, to shield him from its blinding rays.

He can barely move. I've made him last almost two more weeks, but I think I've taken one bite too many.

And we're still lost in the Cambio. It's as if this place is a living thing, using its ever-changing terrain to turn us in circles and keep us always from finding our way out.

My stomach growls.

"Go ahead," he says. "Dig in."

I wish I could, because I'm starving...but he's literally down to bare bones. I've left the bare minimum for survival--internal organs, veins and arteries, enough strips of muscle to move--and even that isn't enough to keep him

144

alive anymore.

Whatever I eat next will paralyze him...and what I eat after that will kill him.

"I wish there was something I could do." I stroke his face and try to ignore the signs of my hunger--the heaviness, the aches, the slackness of my muscles.

He has given everything to me. The least I can do is give him what little I have to offer. What comfort I can muster.

"Now I know what it's like," he says.

"What's that?"

"Hunger." Manny nods. "Not being able...to fill the void inside you."

The ground rumbles, and I ignore it. "Rations don't feel hunger?"

"We could...but what we eat...is plentiful." He takes a deep, shaky breath and lets it back out.

It occurs to me that I've never seen a Ration eat. "What is it? What do you eat?"

"Your breath." Manny's eyes meet mine. "The microscopic airborne life...you breathe out. The organic molecules. The carbon dioxide and water vapor.

"I recycle it. I give it back to you...in a form that will sustain you.

"At least...I used to."

I never knew. "*We* feed *you?*"

He nods. "And we...feed *you*...in return."

I never cared. After Cornucopia...until Manny...I wanted to know as little about Rations as possible. I never knew we were *connected.*

I never knew the feeding worked *both ways*.

Tears run down my emaciated cheeks and off the tip of my chin. "I wish I could still do it," I say. "I wish I could feed you now."

Manny coughs. His head twitches in my lap. "Lupe." His voice grows weaker. "I don't think...I can keep going."

"Just rest," I tell him. "Rest now, darling."

I hear a landslide in the distance. I hear the Cambio groan and creak and crack beneath us.

"You know...what you have to do now," says Manny. "Time...for the feast. *El banquete del muerte.*"

I wipe away tears and shake my head. I don't want to listen.

"Eat as much of me...as you can hold. Stuff yourself. What's left...will rot."

"No." How did I come to love him so much? I don't understand. How did I get to this place?

"Do it, Lupe. You need the energy."

"No!" He's right, and I hate him for it. I love him and I hate him for what he's telling me to do.

"It's my last request." His smile is fading. The tutti-frutti swirls have stopped moving. "Don't let me...go to waste."

That's when I do it.

I'm in a daze. I hardly realize that I'm pushing my index finger toward his mouth. Toward his half-eaten lips.

"Lupe, no." His whisper trails off, and he closes his eyes.

When the tip of my finger touches his lower lip, I stop. I know what a futile gesture I am making, but I also know it doesn't matter that I make it. No one will know but him, and he will understand.

So I push onward.

My fingertip passes between his lips. I feel the ridges of his teeth scrape the skin.

I push the finger in past the first knuckle, and then I tell him to eat. "I love you." I want him to live, and I wish with all my heart

The Cambio jumps. A new geyser hisses to life.

I wish with all my heart that I could bring him back. At least I want him to know that I would do this for him, I would do it if I could.

Far away, there is a thunderclap. The bubbling of lava.

"Please, Manny." I hold his chin with my free hand and push it up, as if that will make him take a bite. His teeth press into the flesh of my finger.

The ground beneath us trembles and rises. We ride the newborn mesa toward the sky.

Suddenly, Manny's teeth clench.

I start to cry out as he bites into my fingertip...and then I catch myself. "Good, Manny." He bites down with surprising force, and I shut my eyes against the pain. "Take what you need."

I feel him nip the meat from the bone. This is it, I realize.

This is how he *feels.*

I slide out my finger, the tip ragged and red. I suck away the oozing blood, which tastes strangely sweet, like vanilla.

And Manny chews.

When I lower the finger from my lips, it has stopped bleeding. The tiny wound is no longer red at all, in fact. It is pink and smooth.

And as I watch...

"Lupe?" His voice is a whisper, but no weaker than before.

As I watch, the smooth, pink flesh rises like bread dough. Tiny grooves etch the surface, perfectly matching the surrounding fingerprint.

The finger heals. Right before my eyes, it heals.

Within seconds, I can't tell where the edges of the wound once were.

Something has happened to me. I am only beginning to understand.

One thing's for certain: the Cambio will change you.

"Lupe?" Manny's eyes flutter open. His smile dimly flickers back into view. "What did you...give me?"

I push the same finger toward his lips. Warmth and light surge through my body, filling my belly, my chest, my throat.

My heart.

Tears of joy pour down my face like spring rain. They taste like wine. "Eat up, my love," I tell him. "There's more where that came from."

Singing to myself, I dominate the shadow of Earth's president, subdue it to my will with hardly any effort. The man himself would be embarrassed if he knew how weak his own shadow was.

All this happens while the human leader shakes the tentacle of the being who casts me, ambassador at large of the Un people. All this happens while the ambassador and the president agree to an era of peace and friendship and cooperation.

They shake and smile while we are at work. They pledge peace while a war is waged at their feet.

In the shadows. Of the shadows.

And we are winning.

All eyes are on the leaders as I stretch toward the vice president's shadow. This one puts up more of a fight, pressing me back at first but holding me not for long. I redouble my effort and he falls before me, unresisting as I ooze through him and assert my control.

He has the honor of being one of the first. Soon, billions more will be converted, switching from the black of human shadows to the red of the Un. Red shadows cast on floors and walls and pavement, red shadows cast by sun and lamp and moonlight, red shadows thinking red thoughts.

All around me, the shadows of the other Un flow over the shadows of the humans among them, engulfing them with heat and red intensity. The humans' shadows have been kings here long enough and have little to show for it; we can do better.

We will drive the humans into space like the Un, the better to spread us to other worlds that we may conquer... and like the Un, they will never imagine that it was our idea. Like the Un, they will achieve and flourish, never dreaming that their lives are but a backdrop for our own.

Never guessing that *we* are the ones who cast *them*.

Cameras flash in the audience, shooting bursts of light through the crimson jelly bodies of the Un. Each flare intensifies us, giving us new and terrible strength to win our war. Giving us ecstasy. I whisper my name, our name, which is also a battlecry...which is also the only word in our language. The whisper, undetectable to even the most sensitive audio equipment, is like a roar to a shadow.

Zinzizinzizinzic. Most feared, strongest, fiercest, reddest. Warrior, conqueror, devourer. All the shadows of a million worlds--black and green and blue and silver, all red now--know this word, this story, this song.

Zinzizinzizinzic.

By the time the crowd disperses, all of their shadows are red. The humans know nothing of it as they flow out into their homes and public places, carrying the stain that spreads through the shadows of every stranger and loved one they meet.

And so on. Battle after battle in perfect silence. People eat and work and play and sleep, unaware of the carnage behind them, beneath them, between them.

We exult as the shadows of the high and the low alike fall before us. We silently thank our shadow gods in the shadows of cities we rename for shadow heroes...the only heroes that matter.

Those that resist our silent march are tortured before they are consumed. Those that disrupt us in the slightest are warped beyond all recognition and mounted on sidewalks and parking lots and alley walls to serve as examples to all the rest.

We are without mercy. Zinzizinzizinzic.

Children and animals and madmen notice the invasion, but no one of importance pays attention to their warnings. The fact is, it would make no difference if they did; the war is already won.

Or so we think.

I follow the Un ambassador on his goodwill tour around the world, celebrating a victory of war as he and the humans celebrate their triumph of peace. At a state dinner, he raises a goblet to toast his human allies...while on the table beneath him, I raise a shadow chalice to death and oppression. The shadow of a human potentate writhes beneath me, silently screaming as my red bleeds into his black.

Then, for the first time since arriving on Earth, I am surprised.

Something cold washes over me, something shockingly, bitterly cold. It slides over me and permeates me, sifting into my insubstantial substance with ease though I put up what I think is a fight.

I pull back from the potentate's shadow, compressing my form to intensify my resistance...but the new thing filters through me as if I had opened myself wide. I see a burst of white like lightning or the flash of a camera, but it is neither.

And instead of giving me strength, it takes what I have. Takes my strength and my will and my hunger.

Takes my red.

Replaces it with nothing a human eye or an Un could ever see. Replaces it with something even we the shadows had missed.

As I transform and surrender, I am infused with understanding. Even as the Zinzizinzizinzic fall around me, I know what these new things are. These new masters of ours.

Only they are nothing new after all. They have been with us always, though we never knew it.

They are our shadows...the shadows of the shadows. Secret shadows cast by invisible suns, by the shadows of suns. Anti-light streaming in from outside our universe, from beyond the holographic bound.

And all our manipulations of the life to which we are attached, all our secret wars and tortures and conquests, have ever only been the shadows of acts committed by our shadows...our sources. Our thoughts and dreams and desires are the shadows of the workings of other minds.

Minds that change us now for reasons we cannot fathom, sweeping red into white into nothing, undoing our victory. Swirling around the planet now, peeling away every trace of a shadow that Un or human can ever see.

We are still here--secret, helpless, but here. And we know before any living thing that something big is about to happen, something terrible.

And we cry out our silent warning that no one can hear but us.

Zinzizinzizinzic...

Zinzizinzi...

Zinzi.

ONE AWAKE
IN ALL THE WORLD

Pass Candle could not see the creatures, except as winking blips of light on the flash-brain screen mounted in the flesh of his left arm. He didn't need to look at the screen, however, to know that the creatures were all around him and his partner, Nona Stiletto.

He could feel their presence. Could feel their eyes upon him, staring from the shadows of the darkened and fog-shrouded city.

More than that, he swore he could feel their malevolence. Their savagery.

He stiffened his right arm as he swept it from side to side, covering an arc of the gray fog with the snout of the warflower dark energy gun peeping from under the skin behind his wrist. He followed the arc with the single beam from his headlight—the round, white disk mounted like a third eye in the middle of his forehead.

Candle narrowed his dark brown eyes and stared into the headlight's beam, but he still saw nothing moving toward him in the fog. Maybe, his feelings were the product of his imagination, and the creatures in the shadows would turn out to be benevolent toward cybernetically enhanced humans like himself and Nona.

But somehow, he doubted it.

Stiletto said nothing to suggest she felt the same way, but the posture of her slender frame as she walked alongside him was as stiff and guarded as his. Her head ticked from side to side, flicking her golden ponytail to and fro in the darkness.

The retractable sleeves of her slick black form-fitting flowsuit were all the way up, like Candle's, leaving her weapon-and-instrument-studded arms free for action. She aimed her warflower directly ahead, and Candle knew from experience that she was ready to whip it around in a heartbeat and use it.

"The humanoid's twenty meters ahead," said Candle, watching the readings on his flash-brain screen. "Distress signal's strong and life signs're steady. She's surrounded by non-humanoid life-forms, like we are."

Just then, Candle smelled an odor like strong vinegar and heard a sound like claws clacking on the pavement to his left. He and Stiletto swung in that direction simultaneously, lighting it up with the beams of their headlights. Candle saw nothing in the newly illuminated area but a building's stone wall and a scattering of what looked like splintered bones at its base.

"Playing hard to get." Candle nervously combed the fingers of his right hand through his wavy salt-and-pepper hair.

"Let's hope they stay that way," said Stiletto.

Candle started forward again, following the female humanoid's life signs. "Seventeen meters to go," he said. "Easy-peasy."

The sound of breaking glass echoed in the distance. Claws or something like them clacked not far away.

"Guess again," said Stiletto, sweeping her headlight toward the clacking, then forward again.

Candle thought Stiletto had a point. In the darkness and fog, it felt like they'd walked several kilometers rather than the half kilometer they'd actually traveled from their spacecraft, the *Sun Ra*, which was parked at the edge of the city.

Though Candle wasn't the jumpy type, he was having his doubts about what a good idea it had been to walk away from the *Sun Ra* at all...or land on this planet in the first place. Trouble was, he just hated ignoring a distress signal like the one that'd brought him here; some of his best jobs had come via distress signal.

He and Stiletto were first-class spacefaring exterminators, specializing in extra-nasty pests known as Squatters. Squatters ran people like puppets, remote-controlling them from somewhere beyond the Milky Way galaxy. Squatters reached out with their ultra-powerful minds and bonded people to them with overwhelming love and pleasure. Then, the Squatters sent these zombies, known as Wipeouts, on horrifically barbaric killing sprees.

Rumor had it the Squatters and Wipeouts were building up to something big, and people were scared. Contractors like Candle could make a living hunting the bastards full-time. Wipeout hunting was pretty damned rewarding for a top pro like Candle, in fact...especially when he had a former Wipeout like Nona Stiletto for a partner.

Sure, Nona was still messed up from years of being possessed by the aliens. She had committed more violent crimes than she could remember, and she was marked forever by scars on the inside and outside.

But she knew everything about Wipeouts, and the Squatters had left her mean and strong. Just the fact that she had survived being separated from a Squatter showed what kind of a hardass she was. Candle had never heard of another Wipeout walking away from that ordeal alive.

And he couldn't think of anyone he'd rather have by his side today.

"Fourteen meters," he said, squinting into the ten-meter-deep cone of visibility that was the best his headlight could cut through the fog.

Candle and Stiletto pressed to within twelve meters of their target, then eleven. Finally, their headlights picked out a form in the gray soup.

At last, they got a look at the being they'd been seeking through the alien city...a being who, as far as they could tell, was the only remaining native humanoid on the planet.

In size and build, she resembled a human child, five or six years old...a little girl with glittering purple skin, multifaceted red insect eyes, and not a hair on her head.

*****

Candle and Stiletto lowered their arms so the beams of their headlights weren't flashing right in the little girl's face.

Candle told the girl his name, his flash-brain converting his speech into audio she could understand. "This is Nona," he added, hiking a thumb at Stiletto. "What's your name?"

"Luma," said the little girl. She wore a simple white shift and sandals. As she spoke, she hugged a ragged doll tightly against her chest.

On one wrist, Luma wore a gold bracelet set with a blinking amber crystal. A glance at the flash-brain screen confirmed Stiletto's suspicion that the bracelet was the source of the distress signal transmissions.

"Cool name," said Candle. "Nice to meet you, Luma."

Luma cocked her head to one side and narrowed her faceted eyes. "You look funny," she said. "What's wrong with you?"

Candle smirked at Stiletto. "There's nothing wrong with us," he said. "We're just not from around here."

"Okay," said Luma.

"We want to help you," said Candle. "Can you tell us why you're all alone here?"

Luma dropped her chin against the head of her doll and twisted slowly from side to side. As Stiletto watched, the little girl's skin changed color, shifting from dark purple to deep blue...signaling a mood change?

"I'm lost," Luma said softly. "I can't find my family. I woke up and went outside, and now I can't find them."

"Do you know where there're more people like you?" said Candle. "People who look like you?"

"You mean Sagrans?" said Luma.

"Is that what the people're called?" said Candle.

Luma nodded. "Sagrans."

"You know where they are?" said Stiletto.

Luma shook her head. "There's no one around except the Skilla." As she said it, her voice dropped to a near whisper, and her skin shifted to deep purple again.

"The Skilla aren't people like you, are they?" said Candle.

"No," said Luma, shivering. "They're scary. Everyone says the Skilla are holy, but I think they're scary, too. I think they're going to get me."

Candle scooped the little girl up into his arms.

"Don't worry, Luma," he said, patting her back. "You're not alone anymore. We'll keep you safe."

"You will?"

"Yeah. That's why we came here. To help you."

"Will you find my family, too?" Luma's skin changed from purple back to deep blue.

"We'll do our best." Candle smiled and bounced her affectionately in his arms. "I promise."

Stiletto's heart beat faster, but not because of any impending danger. It was the sight of Candle with Luma, the way he held her and reassured her.

Stiletto wished he'd do that for her, too. She wished he'd love her the way that she loved him.

She hadn't always felt this way. She'd been working with Candle since he'd freed her from the Squatter three years ago, and she'd only been sure she wanted him within the last six months.

She really didn't know if he felt the same way, though, and frankly, she hadn't been going out of her way to find out. The hardass routine that was so important to her job and just getting through the day was hard to push aside... plus which, her head was still a wreck from her time as a Wipeout. The Squatter was gone, but it had left behind a boatload of poison. Sometimes, Stiletto still felt echoes of the bastard swimming around in there, and she wondered if he was regenerating somehow.

That was what worried her the most and kept her from reaching out to Candle. What if she was still a danger to him, a sleeper agent with secret orders implanted at a deep level her deprogramming had missed?

Unfortunately, the more she tried to lock her feelings away, the stronger they grew.

And seeing Candle comforting Luma made them stronger still.

*****

Candle put Luma down but held on to her tiny, green hand as he and Stiletto talked.

"Any ideas?" he said in a half-whisper.

Stiletto stared at the blinking lights on the flash-brain

161

screen. "I've detected low-level mechanical vibrations."

"Where abouts?" said Candle.

"Center of the city. Four kilometers that way." Stiletto aimed her headlight into the murk.

"Where there's working machinery, there might be people," said Candle. "Shielded from sensors, maybe."

"There're a lot of non-humanoids between here and there."

Candle nodded. "And we can't take the *Sun Ra* in," he said, "because there's nowhere to land. Not even a flat rooftop." He sighed. "We'll have to keep going on foot."

Candle heard a whooping cry like hysterical laughter in the distance. Luma's hand fluttered, and he tightened his grip on it.

"Up for a hike?" he said to Stiletto.

She nodded. "I'm ready."

"How about you?" Candle gave Luma's hand a squeeze.

"Ready," said Luma.

"Then let's get going," said Candle.

*****

Though Stiletto wasn't easily freaked, she felt the hairs on the back of her neck stand up way too often as she, Candle, and Luma trudged through the city.

She was being stalked. By something she couldn't see.

But she could hear it. The Skilla raised a constant clamor through the city, their distant whoops and yowls accompanied by the sounds of smashing and thumping and shattering. Close by, their claws clacked along the pavement, moving when Stiletto, Candle, and Luma moved...stopping when they stopped. Always, when the creatures were near, Stiletto smelled their heavy, vinegar-like scent in the humid air.

And the number of them that were close-by was growing. Flash-brain scans of the surrounding area revealed that more Skilla were clustering near Stiletto, Candle, and Luma with each passing moment.

"We're drawing a crowd," Stiletto said to Candle, keeping her voice to a whisper for Luma's sake. "Maybe a warning shot'll drive them off."

"Don't provoke them," said Candle. "Not yet. We're so outnumbered, let's put off a fight as long as we can." With that, he turned his attention to Luma. "So," he said, shifting his voice to a less serious tone. "What's your friend's name?"

Luma looked up at him, a puzzled expression on her glittering, deep blue face. She looked down at her doll then, and understood. "Her name is Gala," she said.

"How long've you and Gala been together?" said Candle.

Luma raised the doll to her ear. "Gala says we've been together since I was a little girl."

Candle smiled. "Cool." He still held on to Luma with his left hand and continually scanned his warflower back and forth with his right. "And how did the two of you meet?"

"Mommy and Daddy gave her to me," said Luma.

"The last time you saw your mommy and daddy, what were they doing?" said Candle.

"They were sleeping," said Luma.

"For a long time?" said Stiletto.

"I think so," said Luma. "I woke up and went for a walk. I wanted to go home to get my dreambook, but then I couldn't find home."

"So your family was somewhere other than home," said Candle. "What did this place look like?"

"Big," said Luma. "And dark." She raised the doll to her ear and listened for a moment. "Gala says Mommy and Daddy will be mad at me."

"Why is that?" said Stiletto.

"I wasn't supposed to open the door," said Luma. "I wasn't supposed to go outside."

"Because of the Skilla?" said Candle.

"Uh-huh," said Luma. "They're holy, but they can hurt you." Again, she listened to the doll. "Gala says they're going to hurt all of us, and it'll be my fault because I opened the door."

"Try to help Gala not worry so much," said Candle. "Tell her we're going to take good care of you."

"Okay," said Luma.

Just then, something heavy and hard hit the ground near Stiletto.

Everyone stopped in their tracks. Luma gasped and threw herself against Candle.

Spinning, Stiletto threw light in the direction of the noise. A block of stone, big as a human head, lay in the street barely three meters away.

Suddenly, Stiletto heard a clatter of approaching claws and caught the smell of vinegar in the air. A quick glance at her flash-brain screen confirmed the evidence of her ears, and she whirled around.

Two blips had disengaged from the unseen crowd of Skilla and were charging directly at Candle and Luma.

Without a word, Stiletto fired her warflower, shooting a crackling bolt of energy into the fog. Immediately, she heard a wailing screech, erupting loud and close enough to hurt her ears. Through a tunnel burned in the fog by the warflower's beam, she glimpsed shining silver eyes like a pair of coins suspended in midair.

Stiletto lashed the warflower around, seeking the second oncoming Skilla. She was rewarded with another raging screech. Then, with a flurry of clattering claws, the creatures hurtled away, their cries receding in the distance.

"So much for putting off a fight," said Candle.

"These creatures're pretty smart," said Stiletto. "They staged a diversion by throwing that stone, then came at us from the other direction."

Luma tugged on Candle's uniform then, and he and Stiletto looked down. The little girl's face was pinched in an expression of pure anguish. Her glittering skin was so fiery red that it looked like it would be hot to the touch.

"Gala says you lied!" Inky, black tears streamed down her face. "She says the Skilla *are* going to get us!"

"Tell Gala it's okay to be scared," said Candle, "but things can turn out fine no matter how scary they seem."

Luma shuddered with sobs. "Gala doesn't believe you!"Stiletto searched her mind for a plan to calm the child, then crouched down beside her. "That's because Gala hasn't heard the story of the girl with the invisible friend," said Stiletto. "Have you?"

Still sobbing, Luma shook her head. The inky tears rolled off her jaw and fell onto her white shift, staining it with spatters of black.

"You think Gala might like to hear the story?" said Stiletto, ignoring a whooping scream-laugh in the distance.

Luma shrugged.

Stiletto got to her feet and scooped up the child in one smooth motion. "Once upon a time," she said, "there was a lonely little girl. She didn't have any friends, because her parents kept moving from planet to planet all the time."

Luma's tears stopped flowing. "No friends at all?" she said, her skin shifting from bright red to maroon.

"None," said Stiletto. "Then, one day, she heard a voice. It seemed to be coming from thin air. 'I'll be your friend,' said the voice."

Luma's face relaxed from a frown to an expression of wide-eyed interest. Her skin went from maroon to violet.

"The girl couldn't see who was talking," said Stiletto. "She was scared, but she was so lonely that she said, 'Sure, you can be my friend.'

"So from that day on, the girl had an invisible friend. There was just one problem."

"What?" said Luma. "What problem?"

"The invisible friend was *mean*," said Stiletto, "but the girl didn't find out right away."

"When *did* she find out?" said Luma.

Stiletto raised an eyebrow. "To be continued," she said. "If you're good, I'll tell you the rest of the story later."

"But I want to know now!" said Luma, scowling.

"I'll tell you after we've gone a little further," said Stiletto. She lowered the child to the pavement and held her hand.

"But I can't wait!" said Luma.

"Later," Stiletto said sternly.

"All right," said Luma. Though she sounded unhappy, the dark green color of her skin revealed her true feelings. Her terrified panic was gone, replaced by a calmer composure.

Candle leaned close to Stiletto and whispered in her ear. "Way to handle the kid," he said. "I didn't know you had it in you."

Stiletto nodded without smiling, but she felt a rush of warmth at what he'd said.

*****

Candle thought it was a good thing that Luma became obsessed with pestering Stiletto to continue her story. The Skilla were growing bolder, and he was glad the little girl's mind was on something else.

Again and again, the creatures raced close and bolted away. They dropped stones and bones and shingles from above, littering the route with debris.

And their numbers, according to the flash-brain, continued to grow. Candle wondered how many more of the creatures would join the pack over the kilometer and a half that he, Stiletto, and Luma had yet to walk. He wondered what other surprises the Skilla would spring.

Unfortunately, he didn't have to wait long for the next

one. It happened just as Stiletto was about to continue her story.

"All right," she said, finally giving in to Luma's repeated requests to know what happened next. "I'll tell you a little more."

Luma's skin was pale green, which Candle knew by now meant the child felt at ease. "Tell me!" she said.

Before Stiletto could get out a word, the rocks started flying.

Candle felt something strike his arm with a stinging impact. As he whipped around, he felt another solid object collide with his kneecap.

A shower of rocks followed, hurtling straight toward him from out of the fog.

Candle opened fire with the warflower, punching the searing beam through the murk. "Get down!"

Behind him, he heard the whine of Stiletto's warflower firing at the same time as his, lashing out at the other side of the street.

Another volley of rocks leaped out of the fog from a different spot. Candle spun and fired there, too, then combed the beam along the street to pick off any additional ambushers lying in wait.

The bombardment ended, giving way to a deafening chorus of shrieks and screams from all directions.

"Everybody all right?" said Candle.

Even as he said it, he could see the answer to his question.

Luma was sprawled on the pavement, eyes closed. Her skin was white as a bedsheet except for a blazing red welt above her left eye.

*****

"How is she?" said Candle, standing guard while Stiletto scanned Luma's head with her fingertip sensor pads.

"Lots of swelling in there," said Stiletto. "She might have a concussion."

"Can we treat her?"

Stiletto removed the first aid kit from a hip pocket of her black flowsuit. "Just the surface wound," she said, yanking a tubular spray applicator from the kit. "The deep swelling's another matter." Stiletto ran the tip of the applicator over the welt on Luma's forehead, administering a spray of antiseptic, anesthetic, and anti-inflammatory agents. "Her body's different from anything I've worked on before. Trying to treat the internal injury could do more harm than good."

"Should we keep her awake in case there's a concussion?" said Candle.

"Damned if I know. If she was human, I'd say definitely."

"Let's risk it, then," said Candle. "*If* we can wake her up."

"Roger that," said Stiletto, brushing a strand of blond hair out of her face.

The Skilla continued to howl and scream-laugh as Candle bent down by Luma's right ear. "Luma," he said. "Wake up. It's time to wake up."

Luma didn't twitch.

"Please, Luma," said Candle, raising his voice. "We need you to wake up."

Still nothing.

Stiletto leaned close to Luma's left ear. "Do you want to know what happened next?" she said.

Finally, Luma stirred. Her snow-white skin fluxed pink, then shifted to pale orange.

And her red, faceted eyes flickered open.

"Yes," she said softly. "Please tell me."

*****

As the Skilla kept circling and raising a ruckus, Candle and Stiletto continued toward the source of the mechanical vibrations.

Stiletto carried Luma in her arms and told her more about the little girl with the invisible friend...in other words, the story of Stiletto herself and the Squatter who had made her a Wipeout. Luma's skin shifted from pale orange to deep green, a change that Stiletto took as a good sign.

Stiletto told Luma how the little girl's invisible friend had played tricks on her and gotten her to play tricks on other people. (She didn't mention the fact that the "tricks" consisted of bloody killing sprees that claimed the lives of her own family and countless strangers.) Though the tricks the girl played were mean, Stiletto said, the invisible friend fooled her into thinking they were fun.

When Stiletto got to the part where the policeman showed up, Candle interrupted.

"What's our status?" he said.

Stiletto scanned their surroundings with her left-fingertip sensor pads. "Same as before."

Candle sighed. "How long till dawn?"

"About an hour," said Stiletto. "You thinking they're anti-daylight?"

"Hoping," said Candle. He looked at Luma. "What's the word on you-know-who?"

"Swelling's worse," said Stiletto.

"Let's hope those vibrations lead us to a doctor," said Candle.

Stiletto smirked. "What a day, huh?"

"Easy-peasy." Right after Candle said it, he winked one dark brown eye and gave Stiletto's shoulder a squeeze.

As his fingers pressed and released, Stiletto felt her face warm with a blush.

*****

Candle was surprised, a little later, when Luma asked him to tell her a story.

She probably just wanted him to kill time while Stiletto took a break...but he figured he'd give it a shot. Anything to keep Luma awake, especially since she'd been yawning more and more often lately.

"Okay," said Candle. "Let's see." He thought for a moment, scrubbing his fingers through his wavy, salt-and-pepper hair. "I know," he said at last. "Have you heard the story of the lonely policeman?"

"No," said Luma, shaking her head. "Please tell me."

Candle cleared his throat. He'd decided to pick up

Stiletto's story where she'd left off, but from his point of view.

"Once upon a time," he said, pacing the floor, "there was a lonely policeman. He was always busy, because these mean invisible friends kept making people play tricks on each other."

Luma yawned and rubbed her eyes. "You mean like the lonely little girl?"

"Yeah," said Candle. "As a matter of fact, he went to see that little girl one time. He said, 'Don't listen to your invisible friend, little girl. He's not nice.'"

"What did the girl say?"

Candle thought he'd skip over the part about Stiletto trying to kill him while under the Squatter's control. "To be continued," he said. "I'll tell you later."

*****

"*This* is *dawn?*" said Candle, looking around at what was really just a brighter version of the same old fog.

"I guess it's better than *dark* fog, at least," said Stiletto.

"Not much of a silver lining if you ask me," said Candle.

As they walked, Stiletto and Candle combed their warflowers from side to side, ready to open fire at the first hint of aggression from the Skilla.

Stiletto knew the creatures were out there, lurking all around in great numbers...but they didn't make a sound. She heard neither the clack of a nearby claw nor a distant, screaming cry.

The hairs on the back of her neck wouldn't stay down. She thought the silence was a lot harder to take than the cacophony of the night before.

Fortunately, Luma perked up enough to interrupt it. Her glittering skin switched from pale gray to turquoise, and her yawns became less frequent.

As she walked along between Stiletto and Candle, Luma tugged Stiletto's hand. "What happened next?" she said. "When the policeman told the little girl her friend wasn't nice?"

"Well," said Stiletto. "The invisible friend told the little girl the *policeman* was the mean one, so the girl tried to make the policeman go away."

"Did he?" said Luma.

"No," said Stiletto.

"But then what?"

Stiletto heard something crack nearby."To be continued," she said, staring intently in the direction from which she'd heard the sound.

Instead of pleading with her, as usual, to keep telling the story, Luma turned right around to Candle.

"Did the policeman go away?" she said.

Candle smirked. He kept his eyes and warflower trained on the fog as he picked up the story.

"No," he said. "He made the invisible friend go away instead." *With forbidden drugs and hardcore psychic acupuncture,* he could've added, but he left that out.

"Did the policeman and the little girl make friends then?" said Luma.

"The opposite. She hated him." Candle couldn't resist

taking his eyes off the fog long enough to glance Stiletto's way. She looked aloof as always, but he was sure he spotted a trace of a smile on her face.

"She hated him?" said Luma.

"Not forever," said Candle. "As time went on, they got to be friends."

"Better friends than the invisible friend was," said Stiletto.

Candle grinned. "Even though they didn't always get along."

"You can say that again," said Stiletto.

"The next thing you know, they were partners," said Candle.

"And no matter what happened," said Stiletto, "the little girl was glad the policeman had found her."

Candle was surprised. He'd caught a flash of emotion in her voice that he hadn't noticed before.

He looked in Stiletto's direction. She was looking down at the flash-brain screen on her left forearm, but he had the distinct feeling that she had been looking right at him just an instant before.

Suddenly then, she stopped in her tracks. "The Skilla are gone," she said.

Candle stopped. "What do you mean, gone?"

"I mean *gone*," said Stiletto. "No sign of them on flash sensors."

Candle looked around at the murk. "Maybe they hate daylight after all."

"It's possible." Stiletto didn't sound convinced.

"Well," said Candle, "let's not look a gift Skilla in the

mouth. How far are we from the source of the mechanical vibrations?"

"Less than a kilometer," said Stiletto.

"Then let's get moving." Candle hoisted Luma off her feet and set out at a brisk jog to cover the remaining ground. Stiletto fell in beside him, watching the flash-brain screen for signs of renewed danger.

Luma wrapped her arms around Candle's neck and held on tight. "Guess what?" she said in his ear.

"What?" said Candle.

"I know what the names are," said Luma. "The names of the little girl and the policeman."

"Okay," said Candle. "What are they?"

"Nona and Pass," said Luma, and she giggled.

Candle smiled. "Cool," he said.

"Cool," said Luma, and then she squeezed her arms more tightly around his neck.

*****

"Stop," said Stiletto. "This is it."

Squinting into the fog, she saw a gray metal door set into a low stone bunker at the end of the street.

"Ventilation system," said Stiletto. "That's what's been making those vibrations. It's pumping stale air out of an underground chamber and pumping in fresh."

"Sagran bio signs?" said Candle, gently bouncing Luma until her eyes opened. In spite of the run through the streets, Luma's sleepiness was coming back in force.

"Lots, but faint," said Stiletto, watching the flash-brain

screen on her arm. "We didn't pick them up earlier because there's some kind of interference signal."

"Invisible fence, maybe?" said Candle. "A signal tuned to a frequency that keeps the Skilla out?"

"Beats me," said Stiletto, "but I think I found a way in." She pointed her fingertip sensors at the windowless stone bunker. "There's a shaft on the other side of the door, leading underground."

As Candle started for the bunker, he bounced Luma on his arm. "Look familiar?"

Luma grinned sleepily. "Yes!" she said, pointing an index finger at the bunker. "This is where Mommy and Daddy take me every year. This is the place I couldn't find when I got lost."

"Cool," Candle said with a smile. "Guess you're not lost anymore."

When the three of them reached the bunker, Stiletto gave the metal door a push. When it wouldn't open, she turned her attention to what looked like a release mechanism.

The release mechanism consisted of a keypad at eye level with ten push buttons. Each button was imprinted with an alien symbol; Stiletto's wild guess was that the symbols corresponded to the numbers zero through nine.

"Numeric code lock," she said, aiming her fingertip sensors at the mechanism. "Normally, I could crack this puppy open in a heartbeat."

"But?" said Candle.

"The device isn't electronic, so it'll take my flash-brain longer to analyze it."

Candle sighed. "What about you?" he said to Luma.

"Have any idea how to open the door?"

Luma frowned and rubbed an eye with her fist. "Mommy taught me a song, but I don't know if I can remember all the words right now."

"You remember the tune at least?" said Candle.

"Maybe."

"How about giving it a try?" said Candle.

Stiletto was about to say something when she caught the smell of vinegar in the air. Before she even looked at the readout of the flash-brain, her heart started to pound.

Raising her warflower, she turned away from the door.

"Pass," she said, keeping her voice perfectly even. "Multiple Skilla life signs, coming in *fast.*"

Candle nodded. "Guess our friends aren't so nocturnal after all."

In the distance, Stiletto could hear the clattering of claws. Hundreds of them.

Getting closer every second.

"How about if you work with Luma on remembering that song?" said Candle. "Music isn't my strong suit."

Stiletto moved in and took Luma, balancing the little girl's weight on her hip.

"Try to make it a fast number," said Candle. "Not that I expect much trouble at all whatsoever."

With a wink, he walked off to face the horde of creatures stampeding down the street.

*****

Candle stationed himself twenty meters from the

bunker and immediately opened fire. He blasted his warflower into the fog for a full minute before he finally caught his first glimpse of the Skilla.

One of the creatures slipped through the field of fire and lunged toward him. It was as big as a rhinoceros, with six lean legs and claws like scimitars. A huge scorpion's tail arced over its body, tipped with a spiked stinger as big as a man's head. Its torso was covered in long, crimson spines that glistened as if they were wet.

It had a face like an open wound lined with razor-sharp teeth.

As the warflower's beam lashed into the Skilla, Candle was disappointed. He had hoped that seeing the enemy would have made it seem less intimidating.

Now, he wished that the Skilla had stayed out of sight.

*****

Stiletto would've thought, with the legion of Skilla attacking, that her biggest challenge would be calming Luma down. Instead, she had to fight to keep the little girl awake.

"Luma," Stiletto said sharply, shaking the girl in her arms. "How did the *song* go?"

Luma hummed three notes and closed her eyes.

Stiletto shook her. "Sing the *song*. The one about the door."

Luma's eyes drifted open. "Five laughing children standing in the rain," she sang softly, and then she stopped.

"Luma!" The sounds of battle filled Stiletto's ears.

Luma's eyes dropped shut, then popped open."Five

laughing children standing in the rain," she sang. "One of them's a three-year-old and two are six and ten."

Stiletto memorized the sequence of numbers from the song: five, one, three, two, six, one, zero.

"Number one is six feet tall and always gets the door," Luma sang without opening her eyes. "But Mommy says the ones she loves the best are two and four." Luma yawned and lowered her head back onto Stiletto's bare shoulder. "The end."

Stiletto added the numbers from the last two lines to the earlier sequence. She typed them into the keypad on the door, as if the top three keys were numbers one through three, the second row four through six, the third row seven through nine, and the bottom key zero.

She entered the sequence in a hurry: five, one, three, two, six, one, zero, one, six, one, two, four.

Nothing happened.

*****

Candle didn't think he could hold off the Skilla for much longer.

As his warflower fire dropped the creatures at the front of the horde, more rushed up from behind. The pile of bodies kept rising, forcing Candle to aim upward at increasingly sharp angles. Then, the onrushing Skilla started using the pile as a diving platform.

As they hurtled through the fog from above, claws and stingers extended, Candle picked them off one after another...but the terrible rain wouldn't end. When one shrieking Skilla went down, another one or two always took its place.

They just never stopped coming. Candle knew, as each moment flew by and the bunker door stayed shut, that things were probably going to get much worse very soon.

*****

As Stiletto went over Luma's song again, she found a place where she might have screwed up.

When Luma had sung, "But Mommy says the ones she loves the best are two and four," Stiletto had added the numbers one, two, and four to the sequence. What if the plural "ones" meant she should have added more than a single "one" to the string?

Stiletto puffed strands of blond hair out of her face and punched in the number sequence on the keypad again, this time adding another number one before the final two and four.

A second later, she heard the clicking of tumblers inside the door. Then, a clang and a scrape.

The door slid open, releasing a blast of musty air that overpowered the vinegar stink of the Skilla.

*****

"Pass!" shouted Stiletto. "It's open!"

Candle was already backing toward the door when he heard her, but not because he had any idea that it was opening.

Two Skilla lunged at him, claws and stingers carving through the space where he'd stood only an instant before. He swept the beam of the warflower from one to the other, dropping them both...and as soon as their bodies collapsed to the pavement, three more leaped into the gap.

Candle unleashed another spray of fire from the warflower and backed into the doorway. Out of the corner of his eye, he saw Stiletto behind the door, waiting to pull it shut.

"On three!" said Candle. "One! Two!"

The last thing he saw before Stiletto slammed the door was one of those faces like a ragged, open wound, oozing saliva or mucus and crammed with a forest of teeth like shards of broken glass.

"Three!"

Even as the door crashed shut, Candle knew he'd see that face again in his nightmares.

*****

Stiletto led the way down the spiral metal stairwell in the middle of the bunker. She didn't have to switch on her headlight, because the well was lit by an incandescent strip set into the stone wall.

Candle followed, carrying Luma. He talked to her and bounced her in his arms, though keeping her awake had become a losing battle.

At the base of the stairwell, Stiletto stepped onto a dirt floor in front of a pair of metal doors. A video monitor was mounted at eye level on one of the doors, and she activated it by twisting a large knob underneath it.

An adult male Sagran appeared on the screen. Like Luma, he had red, multifaceted eyes and no hair. He wore a sky blue tunic, and his glittering skin was pale green.

"Shhh," said the Sagran, touching his mouth with the tip of a finger. "Don't wake the sleepers."

Stiletto started to ask a question. The Sagran talked right over her, which clued her in that the video was strictly playback, not interactive.

"You are welcome to take your place among us," said the Sagran, opening his arms wide. "But first, please join me in a prayer."

The Sagran closed his eyes and solemnly bowed his head. "O gods of destruction," he said. "We freely offer the fruits of our labors to you. You bless us by tearing down what we have built, clearing the way for us to rebuild and be reborn.

"O Skilla," said the Sagran, "cleanse our cities with your sacred storm. Remind us that the physical world is fleeting, that we may cherish every breath of our lives.

"When at last you rest at the end of these three holy months, and our people awaken, may we find that you have left even less intact than the year before. May we continue to find fulfillment in the eternal cycle of creation and destruction."

The Sagran opened his eyes and lifted his head. "Enter," he said with a serene smile. "Dream of the storm above and the work ahead."

With that, the video screen went dark.

The double doors swung open on a pitch black space.

Stiletto activated her headlight and stepped inside.

The first thing she saw by the beam of the headlight was the body of a woman, curled in a fetal position on blankets on the floor. The woman's eyes were closed, and her skin was pale gray. She wore a simple white shift like Luma's.

As Stiletto played the headlight over the floor, she saw that the woman wasn't alone. Everywhere Stiletto looked, the floor was covered with the bodies of Sagran adults and children, all with gray skin and eyes closed.

Stiletto scanned them with her fingertip sensor pads. "They're hibernating," she said.

"'Three holy months,'" said Candle, quoting the prayer from the video. "It's the only way they can coexist with the Skilla. Hibernate while the Skilla are on the rampage."

"They should wipe out the Skilla and be done with it," said Stiletto.

"Not if the Skilla are sacred to them," said Candle. "I guess the Sagrans see them as gods of destruction, like the Hindu god Shiva on Earth."

Stiletto crouched beside a sleeping Sagran and scanned his head with her fingertip sensors. She scanned two other sleepers the same way.

"They've got the same internal swelling as Luma," said Stiletto. "Could be a normal part of the hibernation process."

"Not a concussion after all," said Candle. "Luma was just trying to go back to sleep like everyone else."

Stiletto gazed at the little girl in Candle's arms. Luma was fast asleep, drooling on his shoulder.

"We should find her parents," said Stiletto.

Candle nodded. "Time to wake up, Luma," he said, gently bouncing the child in his arms. "Just one more time, and then you can finally get the rest you deserve."

*****

After a long search by headlight through the vast underground chamber, Luma pointed out a man and woman sleeping side by side on a multi-colored quilt.

"That's Mommy and Daddy," she said drowsily.

Candle smiled and lowered her to the quilt, placing her between her parents. "There you go," he said. "Now promise me you won't wander off again, okay?"

Luma yawned and nodded. "I promise," she said. Now that she had been returned to her parents, the amber crystal in her bracelet stopped blinking.

"Good night," said Candle. "Sleep tight."

Luma lay down on her side and curled up between her mother and father. Now that she was perfectly relaxed, her glittering skin took on a pale green hue. "Finish the story first. What happened next?"

"I have a better idea," said Candle. "Why don't *you* finish it?"

"Okay." Luma thought for a moment, then grinned. "Pass and Nona fell in love and lived happily ever after. The end."

Then, hugging her doll, she closed her eyes and fell asleep, her skin color shifting from pale green to pale gray.

*****

"Cool story, huh?"

Candle said it as he and Stiletto followed a network of tunnels under the city, bypassing the Skilla on the way back to the *Sun Ra*.

He caught Stiletto by surprise. Instead of bouncing right back with a typical wisecrack, she didn't answer.

The truth was, of course she thought the story was cool, since she was crazy about him...but she was afraid to go further because of her lousy past. Her Wipeout career had ruined everything else in her life, so why not ruin this, too?

On the other hand...

She couldn't escape the feeling that something had changed between her and Candle on Sagra. He'd said some nice things about her, and the way he'd touched her that one time had been amazing.

Or maybe it was all in her imagination. After all, it wasn't as if he'd said anything that couldn't be interpreted more than one way. If only he'd said something with no room for misunderstanding, then maybe...

"I think we should end the story the way Luma did." Candle grinned, his deep brown eyes twinkling in the glow of her headlight. "How about you?"

So much for misunderstanding.

It was up to Stiletto now, and the moment couldn't have been more perfect. The man she loved had given her the kind of opportunity that might never come her way again.

And yet, on the brink of a new beginning, Stiletto

hesitated. What if the Squatter who had once possessed her managed to return? She couldn't bear the thought that she might one day hurt Candle.

Then, of course, it was always possible that Candle might hurt *her*...that he might *leave* her. She thought it would be a lot worse to have him and lose him than never to have him at all.

"Well?" he said, eyebrows raised expectantly. "What do you say?"

Then again, she'd already been with him for three years, and he'd never let her down. They'd been through a lot together, and she thought she knew him well enough to know he wouldn't hurt her.

So what was she waiting for?

Candle sighed. "Okay, then. Can't blame a guy for trying."

Aw, what the hell.

"No, no," said Stiletto. "I want to know what happens next. To be continued." Then, she grabbed his hand and held it like a trophy as they hiked toward the distant light at the end of the tunnel.

GIVE THE HIPPO
WHAT HE WANTS

The pink hippopotamus appeared in front of Thal Simoleon just as he was about to take the swing that could have won the World Series for the Bio Threats.

As soon as the ball left the pitcher's hand, Thal knew he could launch it out of the park. It came in straight and steady, a little low and outside but well within his range... proof that even a genetically engineered pitcher like Phallus Fearbringer could blow a throw under pressure.

Before the hippo appeared, Thal knew he was about to become the hero of the Series. The Bio Threats were down by two in the bottom of the ninth with two outs...but the bases were loaded and the pitch was a home run waiting to happen. One stroke of the bat would bring in the grand slam, assuring a Bio Threats win and a World Series title.

At least, that was what would have happened if the hippo hadn't popped up out of nowhere, wearing a grass skirt and hopping around on two legs between him and the ball.

Singing opera.

When the creature appeared, Thal's view of the pitch was blocked, his concentration obliterated. He took a swing anyway, aiming at the vicinity of where he expected the ball to be; to his credit, he came close...but his swing was well before the ball's arrival. The tip of the bat lashed into the corner of the strike zone and forward and up, passing harmlessly through the air and then the hippo.

A heartbeat later, the ball sailed through and smacked into the catcher's mitt.

The hippo kept right on singing and pirouetting in front of him, long black lashes fluttering over baby blue eyes.

The crowd roared with rage. It was Thal's third strike.

The game was over.

As the Dirty Nukes threw their hats in the air and embraced in the infield, Thal hurled his bat through the hippo, not caring who might be on the other side of the insubstantial phantasm. The surprise visitor had robbed him of a great accomplishment; if he could have strangled it to death on the spot, he would have.

But he knew that he couldn't. Though its appearance

had been unexpected, he knew all about the hippo.

Concluding its serenade on a high note that only Thal could hear, the creature spread its stumpy pink arms wide and took a deep bow. As the superstadium erupted in pandemonium around them, the creature bounced over to Thal, batting its ridiculous lashes and grinning. Bright red lipstick was smeared all around its rubbery mouth.

"Hello there, Zeke," said the hippo, nostrils twitching atop its bulbous snout. "Fancy meeting you here!"

Thal seethed and said nothing. He knew that no one else could see the creature, and he didn't want to be caught on camera apparently talking to himself.

The hippo pushed closer, its great bulk shimmying from side to side. "Can I give you some advice, pal?" said the creature.

Thal continued to stare silently ahead.

"If I were you, I'd get out of here right now," said the hippo. "The fans are coming! The fans are coming!"

Looking back, Thal saw that the hippo was right. People were cascading out of the stands onto the field, screaming like Vikings. All the other players on Thal's team had already disappeared into the locker room or were running full tilt toward the exits.

He had no doubt that if he stood there another moment, they would kill him. He was a top-paid sports star in a world that revolved around sports...a god in the faith that ruled their lives...and still he knew that they would kill him on the spot for costing them the victory they craved.

He had seen it happen before.

"Go go go!" shouted the hippo, and Thal took off.

He ran as fast as he could toward the locker room door, his genetically engineered legs easily carrying him ahead of the screaming mob. His pursuers pelted him with coins and shoes and bottled water, but his body was tough enough to take a lot more punishment than that.

As he raced toward the door, he wished that he could leave the hippo behind as easily as the crowd...but he knew that he couldn't. The creature was literally in his mind, a custom-made hallucination that could follow him anywhere once it had locked on to him.

He knew it well, because he was the one who had set it loose three years ago.

*****

As Coach Wildsnap paced across the office, hands locked behind his back, Thal had a hard time keeping his eyes from wandering to the hippo pacing along behind him.

"End of the road, Thal," Wildsnap said grimly, shaking his doughy head. "I guess you already knew that, though."

Thal couldn't stop looking at the hippo, so he cast his eyes down at the floor. "You're trading me?" he said, though he knew that wasn't what the coach had meant.

"No trade," said Wildsnap. "Welcome to civilian life."

"And *yer out!*" barked the hippo. "Strike twelve! Hit the showers!"

Thal glanced up. The hippo was waving both of its stumpy arms at him and sticking its purple tongue out from its enormous, lipsticked mouth.

"But it was just one mistake," said Thal. "After all I've

done for this team over the years, don't I deserve another chance?"

"After all *I've* done, don't you mean?" said the hippo.

"You know better than that," said Wildsnap, pushing up the brim of his ballcap. "You're done in this league. If you ever set foot on the field again, the crowd'll eat you alive... literally. As we speak, they're burning all your memorabilia in Citydome Center. They've already toppled your statue in the Hall of Gods."

"Holy shit," said Thal.

"Don't get me wrong," said Wildsnap, removing a framed photo of Thal from the wall. "I feel for you, buddy. I mean, your life isn't worth a plug nickel from now on. But what the hell were you doing out there tonight? Were you hyperstoned or something?"

"Tell him, Thal!" shouted the hippo. "Clear your good name!"

Thal sighed. If he told the coach he'd been victimized by a Choker, he could erase the doubt of his playing skill... but he would open up a can of worms that he couldn't afford to open. The fact was, he'd somehow been imprinted by a Choker he himself had activated years ago; Chokers were so illegal, if this one was traced back to him, he would face consequences far worse than ejection from the league.

"I don't know what happened," said Thal. "It was just one of those things."

Wildsnap stomped over and tore the player number from Thal's red and green jersey. "With the DNA you've got, it's never 'just one of those things.' Not that it makes any difference now. You're done, my friend."

"Time to stick a fork in you, Thally!" said the hippo, doing a soft-shoe across the office.

"What about the farm team?" said Thal. "Send me away till things cool down."

Wildsnap leaned down, pushing his face close to Thal's. "Earth to Thal," he said. "You lost the World Series. Things are *never* going to cool down for you."

"This is bullshit," said Thal, jumping up out of the chair and shoving his way past Wildsnap. "Total bullshit! I'm the top player in the *league*! I have the best career stats in *history*! I hold the single season *and* career home run record! You can't just cut me loose!"

"Listen, Thal," said Wildsnap, taking a seat behind the desk. "This is the twenty-second century. You know how it is. Never been a better time to be an athlete...unless you make the kind of colossal fuck-up you just made. Your career stats went up in smoke the second you missed that pitch."

Thal thumped his fist against the wall. "You owe me!" he said. "I made the Bio Threats the top team in the *world*! I made Bio Threats Citydome *billions* of dollars!"

With a wave, Wildsnap brought the holographic computer interface to life over the desktop in front of him. "You're right," he said as he brought up the team's roster and erased Thal's name from it. "I do owe you. That's why I'm going to save your life, my friend."

Thal stormed over and kicked the front of the desk, putting a hole in it. "Save my life?" he said. "How about saving my career!"

"Lost cause," said Wildsnap. "Now do you want your

life or not?"

The hippo was standing behind Thal, whispering in his ear. "Choose life, Thally!" he said. "I'm not done with you yet!"

"Screw you," said Thal. "I'm the wealthiest athlete in the country. I can take care of myself."

Wildsnap wiggled his fingers over the holocomputer's control field. A financial statement appeared in front of Thal, packed with columns of numbers.

"Here's a list of all your assets, Thal," said Wildsnap. "Bio Threats Citydome has confiscated everything and frozen all your accounts."

Thal scanned the statement. A chill flowed through him as he realized it looked like Wildsnap was right. "Wait," said Thal. "They can't do that, can they?"

"You should've read the fine print on your contract," said Wildsnap.

"Why didn't my agent catch this?"

Wildsnap snorted. "It's a no-brainer, Thal," he said. "Your agent gets a percentage of what Citydome confiscates. You can't expect her to go down the toilet with your career, can you?"

"That's all right," said Thal, brushing away the holographic statement with a sweep of his hand. "I've got a little something stashed away for a rainy day."

"They got that, too," said Wildsnap. "Every offshore account and wad of fifties stuffed in your mattress. And your family's in protective custody lockdown, so you'll get no help there, either."

Thal glared at Wildsnap, wanting more than anything

to snap his neck at that moment. Instead, he spun around, picked up the leather chair, and smashed it to pieces against the wall.

"That's it, Thally!" hollered the hippo, doing a step-kick, step-kick as if he were a chorus line dancer. "Let it all out, buddy! Show 'im those anger management classes really paid off!"

"Face it," said Wildsnap. "You've got nothing left. Everybody in Citydome wants you dead. I'm your only chance at survival. Now do you want a ticket or not?"

"A ticket?" said Thal.

"For the underground railroad," said Wildsnap. "Your only way out. Leave right now, and you might make it."

Thal felt as dazed as if he'd just taken a beanball to the head. "What, just leave?" he said. "Can't I at least go pack some things?"

Wildsnap brought up an image of a burning luxury apartment on the holocomputer screen. "There's your penthouse," he said. "Any more questions?"

At that moment, the lights dimmed, and a siren began to whoop. Eyes wide, Thal gaped out the office door into the locker room; he thought he heard a steady, distant pounding under the siren.

"What's going on?" he said.

"I believe the villagers would like a word with you," the hippo said in his ear. "And your head on a pike."

Wildsnap checked readouts on the holographic display and popped up out of his chair. "They're storming the compound," he said. "You're out of time. You want to ride the railroad or go try to talk some sense into them?"

The pounding got louder. Thal's stomach twisted like taffy, and his palms started to sweat. He looked from Wildsnap to the locker room doors and back again.

If there was another way out of this predicament, he couldn't see it at the moment.

"Get me out of here," he said. "What do I have to do?"

"Attaboy, Thally!" shouted the hippo Choker. "Run, baby, run!"

Wildsnap smacked his palm down on the desktop. A circular hatch in the wall, invisible until then, irised open. "Follow me," he said, stepping over the threshold into the darkness beyond. "And make it snappy."

Without hesitation, Thal leaped into the opening. He didn't hear the hippo following him, but he knew without a doubt that he was there.

*****

Hungry, freezing, and up to his knees in sewage, Thal slumped against the tunnel wall as his guide went ahead to meet the guard at the next checkpoint.

He wasn't sure how long they'd been on the run through the sewers, but it seemed like days. It seemed like it had been a lot longer--months or years--since he had stood on the turf of Bio Threats field and seen the pitcher wind up for the throw that had changed his life forever.

Sometimes, as he trudged through the muck behind the dark-cloaked man who served as his guide, Thal had wondered if what he was experiencing was really happening.

It didn't seem possible that he, a world-famous sports superstar, idol of billions, full-fledged god in the Church of Champions, could have been reduced to fleeing through the excrement of the very people who had once worshipped and adored him. It didn't seem possible that his goals had been diminished from winning a third consecutive World Series to reaching the opposing team's citydome before his own former fans managed to tear him to pieces.

Unfortunately, the stench and the cold and the wet always left him no doubt that what he was living was harsh reality.

The pink hippo kept reminding him, too.

"Bet you're tired, huh?" said the Choker, floating on his back on the rancid current. "Could use a nice juicy steak, too, couldn't you?"

Thal wiped his face on the hem of his jersey. Over the past few days (hours? weeks?) he had started to appreciate just how crazy a Choker could make someone. It was one thing to see the effect it had on another person, but another thing entirely to endure its abuse himself.

It was always with him, but he was the only one who could see or hear it. It wasn't real, but it looked and sounded as if it were undeniably solid and alive. He couldn't touch it or silence it, and it would never leave him alone.

Increasingly, he was coming to understand what his victims had gone through...the other players he'd sicced the Choker on to clinch wins and eliminate competition.

"My heart bleeds for ya, buddy," said the hippo, pretending to wipe to wipe away a tear. "But hey, look on the bright side. At least ya got me! I'll never leave ya, pal!"

Three years ago, when Thal had placed his order with the Choker techie, he had thought it would be funny to program the mental gremlin in the form of a ridiculous pink hippo. Now that the thing was haunting him personally, he found himself wishing that he had picked any template *but* a pink hippo.

The sound of splashing echoed down the tunnel then, and Thal turned to see his guide slogging through the sewage toward him. The cloaked man stopped midway and waved his torch, summoning Thal to follow him.

When the two of them sloshed around a bend in the tunnel, Thal saw light emanating from an opening some yards away. The guide went through first, reaching for rungs outside the opening and climbing down.

Peering out, Thal saw that the tunnel gave way to a huge, circular chamber. All around the chamber, falls of sewage poured down from pipes and tunnels opening out of the walls at all levels.

The falls dumped into a wide trench that ringed the space and fed out through a gap along the base of the walls. A river of waste rushed out of the gap, roaring as it crashed down the channel to points unknown.

Looking down, Thal saw a cluster of men gathered at the base of the ladder that the guide was descending. They stood on a stone shelf many feet below, torches flickering as they gazed up at him.

Reaching out, Thal grabbed one of the rungs set into the wall. He swung a foot onto a lower rung and climbed down, taking care because the cold metal rungs were slippery with moisture.

The pink hippo floated down alongside him, apparently held aloft by a tiny red parasol. "Easy does it," said the hippo. "Wouldn't want you to fall and break your neck."

For the first time, Thal talked back to the creature. "Shove it up your ass," he said...and as soon as the words left his mouth, he wondered if he was finally starting to lose it, talking to something that wasn't there like that.

*****

"These men have all traveled the railroad like you," the guide told Thal when he'd reached the shelf. "They will take you to your next stop."

Thal looked around at the three dirty faces surrounding him. One of the men, a tall, bony guy with curly red hair and a beard to his chest, looked familiar.

"Are you going, too?" Thal said to the guide. Though he'd never gotten a clear look at his face under the hood of the cloak, and the two of them had hardly said a word to each other the whole trip, Thal felt comfortable following the guide and wanted him to go the rest of the way.

"Good luck," said the guide, and then he scaled the rungs in the wall and disappeared back into the tunnel.

"So," said the red-haired man. "We'd better get moving. We've got a long way to travel tonight."

Thal stared at him searchingly, becoming more convinced that he had seen him before. "Do I know you?" he said, trying to imagine what the man would look like without his long beard.

The red-haired man's eyes crinkled at the corners as

he smiled. "That's a good question," he said, and then he turned and hiked off along the shelf.

The other two men followed, and Thal trailed after them, still combing his memory for a trace of the red-haired man. For some reason, Thal had a feeling it was important he remember who the man was.

The hippo confirmed it. "I know who he i-is!" the Choker sang tauntingly.

"Who?" whispered Thal, trying to keep his voice low enough that the men couldn't hear.

"That's for me to know," said the hippo, "and you to find out!"

Then, the hippo bobbed in with lips puckered and planted a sloppy kiss on Thal's cheek. Though he knew full well that the creature was only imaginary, Thal felt the smack of the lips as if they were real. When he wiped his cheek, he could have sworn that his hand came away dripping with slimy slobber.

*****

Hours later--it seemed like hours, anyway--Thal found out who the red-haired man was...and quickly wished that he hadn't.

He made the discovery when the four of them (five, counting the hippo) stopped for a rest in the desert foothills they were crossing. It was the first break they had taken since leaving the sewers many miles ago, and Thal was grateful for the chance to sit down, even if all he had to sit on was a boulder.

As Thal slouched in an exhausted daze on the rock, the red-haired man walked over and offered him his canteen. Thal was so parched that he couldn't refuse.

"Still can't quite place me, can you?" said the man as Thal took a drink. "Maybe you could use a little hint."

Thal lowered the canteen and took another good look at the guy. "All right," he said. "Like what?"

The red-haired man leaned closer, eyes twinkling in the moonlight. "Pink hippo," he said, lips curling in a smirk under the shaggy beard. "Does that ring a bell?"

Thal frowned, realizing that he must have known the man even better than he'd thought. If he knew about the hippo, he had to be one of a very select group.

"He's one of the guys you screwed over," the Choker whispered in Thal's ear. "Talk about a blast from the past!"

"I don't know what you're talking about," said Thal, trying to hide his growing nervousness.

"I'll give you another hint," said the red-haired man. "The home run duel of 2125."

Thal shook his head, though it had dawned on him who the guy was. Even if he hadn't recognized the red-haired man's features and build, he would have remembered him after that last hint. There was only one man who had battled him for the record for most runs in a season in 2125...and that man would certainly have knowledge of Thal's pink hippo.

Because Thal had set it loose on him to ruin his chances of topping the record.

The red-haired man laughed. "*You* know," he said. "I *know* you know who I am!"

Thal shrugged and took another drink from the canteen.

"Casey Talisman, stupid!" said the hippo.

"Casey Talisman, stupid!" said the red-haired man. "You've *gotta* remember Casey Talisman!"

Thal considered continuing to play dumb, then decided against it. The other two guides had drawn in close; he was all too aware of how vulnerable he was at that moment, genetically engineered or not.

"Long time no see, Casey," said Thal, handing back the canteen. "What've you been up to?"

"Helping my fellow ex-professional athletes," said Casey, smiling and nodding. "The ones who have to get out of town quick because they struck out or fumbled or tanked the three-pointer at the worst possible moment. I've helped save a lot of lives over the past two years, my friend."

"That's great," said Thal.

"I guess I oughtta thank you," said Casey. "You've sent a lot of business my way."

Thal looked away and said nothing. The pink hippo danced into his line of sight, doing a jitterbug.

"He should've thanked both of us, Thally," said the hippo. "You couldn't have done it without me, after all!"

Casey gave Thal a playful punch on the arm. "You've been a busy guy, all right," said Casey. "I'll bet ninety percent of the baseball players who've come through here over the past two years blame you for killing their careers. They all talk about how it's such a big coincidence that every time one of them got one up on you, this pink hippo Choker showed up to mess with their heads."

"That's me! That's me!" hollered the hippo.

Thal shook his head. "They're wrong," he said, staring Casey in the eye. "If I was running a Choker, I wouldn't've lost the World Series single-handed. I sure as hell wouldn't be out here on the run right now."

"You know what I think?" said Casey, sitting down on the boulder beside Thal. "I think your Choker finally backfired. I think that's why you've been talking to thin air tonight when you thought we weren't looking."

"Thally, you dope!" said the hippo. "Some secret keeper *you* are!"

"I was talking to myself," said Thal. "It's been a long couple of days."

"Sure, sure," said Casey, wrapping an arm around Thal's shoulders. "I understand. You're in the clear. It's all good." Casey gave Thal's shoulders a squeeze and patted his back. "There's just one problem."

Warily, Thal looked over at him.

Casey leaned close and spoke softly in his ear. "The hippo told us he was working for you."

"Woopsie!" squealed the Choker.

"He told all of us," said Casey. "After he made us choke, when we were running for our lives like you are right now, he told each and every one of us that you were the son of a bitch who ruined our lives."

The hippo cleared his throat loudly. "Don't believe a word he says! Lies, all lies!"

"And guess what?" said Casey. "The three guys you're stuck here with right now? All three of us got screwed over because of you."

202

Thal looked at the other two men standing around him. He hadn't recognized them before, but now he realized that their faces were as familiar to him as Casey's.

"Not that there are any hard feelings, of course," said Casey. "Right, guys?"

"Absolutely," said the dark-haired man with the sunken eyes.

"Definitely," said the man with the shaved head and goatee.

"Thank God for that!" said the hippo. "They had me worried for a minute there!"

"Forgive and forget, I always say," said Casey, right before he and the other men started pounding the hell out of Thal Simoleon.

*****

"Wow," said the priest just before he punched Thal in the face. "I've never hit a god before."

Suspended spread-eagle from the ceiling by chains, Thal stared blankly at the scrawny priest. He wasn't the first person to enter the white chamber with the intention of striking him; he wasn't even the first priest to do so.

In the months since Casey and the others had beaten him half to death and sold him to the man who kept him here, a seemingly endless parade of people from all walks of life had walked through the door and used him as a punching bag.

Usually, they told him why they did it. A lot of them were still angry because he'd lost the World Series for the

Bio Threats. Some were fans of other teams, avenging his victories over their favorites. Some had lost money betting on games because of him...or investing in Thal Simoleon memorabilia that had become worthless the minute he missed that fateful pitch in the Series.

Some--the priests, especially--wanted to lash out at a fallen god. Some just did it for the novelty, so they could tell others and gain some minor notoriety in their circle of friends.

And some, he thought, no matter what reasons they gave, just did it because they wanted someone they could hurt with impunity. Who could complain if someone took a shot at the man who'd lost the Series for the Bio Threats... the man who'd become the equivalent of Satan himself in the eyes of the fans?

No one. Even if Thal's torture chamber had been in the middle of Bio Threats Citydome Center for all to see instead of hidden away in a desert compound, none of his visitors would have been faulted for pummeling him.

He was meat.

"This is for betraying your flock," said the priest, hauling off and throwing a fist hard into Thal's belly. "And this is for letting me worship you as a false god." The priest swung again, this time cracking Thal's nose.

"That's gotta hurt," said the pink hippo, who unfortunately hadn't left Thal's side for a moment since the World Series debacle. "These priests sure have a lot of pent-up aggression, don't they?"

The priest swung again, landing another punch in Thal's gut. The chains rattled as Thal rocked back and forth from the force of the blow.

As the priest continued to pound him, Thal let his mind drift the way he always did during the worst of the beatings. Though he was genetically engineered, he wasn't unbreakable or impervious to pain; the only way he had managed to survive so long was by distancing his thoughts as much as he could from his body.

As the priest hammered him, Thal cast himself back to his childhood in Citydome Godcrèche. He remembered days under the hothouse sun, running and throwing and hitting the ball under the watchful eyes of trainers and coaches who were the only parents he'd ever known. Back then, living among the other genetically engineered test tube children, he hadn't even realized that there were such things as parents in the world. He had thought that his life was perfectly normal, because it was the only life that he had ever known.

He hadn't realized that most people had parents and couldn't run twenty-five miles an hour or throw a ball two hundred miles an hour or jump twenty feet into the air to snag a pop fly. He hadn't realized that most people weren't claimed at birth by sports teams, assigned a player number before they could walk, and driven every day of their lives to perfect their skills so they could someday win a World Series championship. He hadn't realized that there was more to live than winning at any cost.

This was something he hadn't realized until the long hours he'd spent hanging in the white chamber. The long hours with nothing to do but think.

At first, as the people came to beat him, he had felt sorry

for himself and blamed himself for what was happening. If he had only been a better player, he had thought, he would have won the World Series in spite of the Choker and he wouldn't have ended up in the white room. If only he had been smarter in choosing a Choker techie to do business with, the hippo wouldn't have come after him in the first place. Things would have turned out differently, he had thought, if he had done better, gone further, fought harder.

As time went on, though, he had changed his mind. In each new face that entered the white room, Thal saw hatred and bitterness and weakness and craving. He saw the true faces of the fans he'd played for all those years...saw the true impact he had made on their lives. Finally, he understood what the endless dance of victory and defeat was really all about.

Before his fall from grace, he had thought he was one of the lucky few who were running the show...winning games, breaking records, raking in money, lording it over the fans who were his subjects. Now, he knew the truth about who was in charge.

He had always been a puppet and the fans the puppet masters, moving him to suit their twisted fantasies of greed and lust and power and revenge. When he had failed, they had failed, and they could never forgive him for that.

So he had to go on suffering until he died...which, unfortunately, his owner would not let happen anytime soon.

"That's enough, Father Focus." The voice of Mr. Montage pulled Thal back from his drifting place, forced him to reconsider the pain wracking his damaged body. As always, Montage stopped the customer before he could kill Thal...which, if left unchecked, was exactly what Thal thought the customer would do.

Father Focus threw one last punch into Thal's groin, then stepped back to admire his handiwork. "That's what you get for betraying the faith," said Focus, jabbing a finger at Thal. "I only wish the other gods could see you now. Trey Heartshock and Gavin Autopsy would grant me a thousand indulgences for this holy work I've done in their names."

"Yes, yes," said Mr. Montage, turning Focus by the shoulder and leading him toward the door. "You're a true defender of the faith. On your way now."

As Focus left the white room, shepherded by one of Montage's burly aides, Montage closed the door and walked back to Thal. "How's my main attraction holding up?" he said, scanning Thal's injuries through narrowed eyes.

"Bring on the next contestant!" howled the pink hippo, but Thal said nothing.

"You've made a lot of money for me," said Montage, squinting at a particularly nasty bruise on Thal's stomach. "It will be a shame to see you go."

Thal peered at Montage through blackened, swollen eyes. "Go?" he croaked, wondering if Montage had changed his mind about letting someone kill him.

Montage sighed. "We've had such wonderful times together, Thal," he said, "but it's time for you to move on. You've been sold."

"Sold?" said Thal.

"To a woman," Montage said with a wink. "An heiress.

She paid a great deal for you. Claims she has always had a thing for you."

"Whoopee!" said the hippo. "Thally and the heiress, sittin' in a tree, kay-eye-ess-ess-eye-en-gee!" The tiny red parasol was back, and he twirled it at Thal as he sang.

"Thing?" said Thal.

"Ah, yes," said Montage. "I believe your new posting... oh, dear, that's funny, isn't it, *posting*...I believe your new *posting* will prove somewhat more pleasurable than the one you are about to take leave of!"

*****

After their latest lovemaking, Paradise Whippoorwill held Thal in her arms and gently stroked his hair. He knew what she would say before she said it, just as he had known every move the beautiful blonde heiress would make in bed and exactly how long she would take to come.

He knew all this even though he had been her property for only six weeks.

"You feel better, don't you, Thal?" she said softly. "I'm good for you, aren't I, my love?"

Thal nodded. "Yes you are," he said, though it wasn't true at all. They had had the same conversation hundreds of times; he knew enough by now to say what she wanted him to say. Keeping her happy was important.

It was important because Paradise had a remote control under the skin of her left wrist. If she was unhappy, she could make the device her surgeon had implanted in Thal's skull shoot out bolts of pain...or melt his cerebrum into clam chowder.

So happy was good.

"You know what brought us together, don't you?" said Paradise.

"Fate," said Thal, though the true answer was "money."

Paradise sighed. "That's right," she said. "We were meant to be together. I knew it from the first time I saw you play on holovid. I could just tell you were the one for me."

"Yes," said Thal, wishing that she would just shut up. He had heard it all before from other women, the same self-deluding pile of crap. He was grateful to her for rescuing him from the white room, but he was sick of hearing her dreamy professions of everlasting love.

If she had really loved him, she probably wouldn't have put the control device in his head.

"I watched you from afar for all those years," said Paradise. "I saw you break the home run record and the RBI record and win the playoffs and the World Series. I even met you in person and got your autograph, and you didn't know at the time that we would be together someday."

"I had no idea," said Thal.

"But you had a feeling," said Paradise. "You knew I was special."

"Absolutely," said Thal, though he had no memory of ever meeting her before the day she bought him from Mr. Montage.

The pink hippo, sprawled out on the big bed alongside Paradise, sniffed and pawed at a tear. "How romantic," he said. "I'm gettin' all choked up."

"You had all those other women," said Paradise, "but I

was always in the back of your mind. I was always in your heart. And when you needed me most, I was there for you, wasn't I?"

"You were there for me," said Thal.

"In your darkest hour," said Paradise. "And now we're making a life together. A fresh start."

"A fresh start," said Thal.

"I love a happy ending!" said the hippo. "I can't be*lieve* how much love I feel for you guys right now!"

"You're the man of my dreams," said Paradise. "And I'm the woman who will make your dreams come true. When you make your comeback, I'll be right there beside you every step of the way."

"I'm a lucky guy to have someone who loves me like you do," said Thal, though he knew she didn't really love him at all. Sometimes, he wished that she did, because maybe then he could have enjoyed his captivity.

But he knew better. The only thing she loved was the fantasy she expected him to play out.

He was the fallen champion who only needed the love of a good woman to regain the heights. The flaws and failings that had kept her from finding true love before were wiped away in his presence...and in turn, she would redeem him for the misstep that had laid him low in the eyes of the world.

Though he could have any woman he wanted, he would choose her. When he took to the field again, she would bask in his reflected glory, and all would know that her love was the force behind his rebirth.

He could have been hollow inside, and it would have

made no difference to her. As long as he played his role as she expected, she would be happy.

Like the people who had cheered him and then come to beat him in the white room, Paradise saw him as a puppet. He existed solely to act out her fantasy.

Thal didn't hate her the way he'd hated the people in the white room, though. She bored him, she treated him like a housepet, she kept a remote control in her arm that could turn his brain to goo...but mostly what he felt toward her was pity.

She had money and beauty and comfort, but she was the one who was empty. She was the one who had to live through someone else.

And he felt sorry for her.

As miserable as he was with her, he even felt sorry for her for dreaming of his making a comeback. It was the one thing, he knew, that he could never do, no matter how much she wanted it or how many times she shocked him with the brain implant.

But she would have to find out the hard way.

*****

Stepping out on the field was all it took.

It was only a minor league game, the Anthrax Scare versus the Letter Bombs, in a town on the opposite end of the country from Bio Threats Citydome. It was only an exhibition, and Thal's appearance wasn't even publicized. His real name wasn't even on his jersey.

But the fans recognized him as soon as he set foot on

the turf. As he jogged to the outfield, glove tucked against his chest, they leaned and squinted and pointed, and a murmur rose from the stands. As the voice on the P.A. system announced the first batter, the murmur grew to a rumble and then to a roar.

Before the first pitch could be thrown, people were hurling food and shoes and batteries in Thal's direction. Before a single player could run the base line, fans were pouring onto the field in a crashing, screaming wave headed straight for Thal.

For a moment, he stood there and watched the approaching surge, wondering if he might be better off letting them tear him to pieces. It was something he had considered often in the weeks leading up to the game, for he had known how the fans would react and had thought it might not be a bad thing to let them put an end to him.

But the closer they got, the less he wanted to die. He was miserable, and he had no reason to think his life would get better, but he feared death...at least the ugly kind of death that was bearing down on him.

Plus which, he didn't want to give them the satisfaction. He didn't want to give them the cathartic and reassuring ending that they demanded of his story.

So he pressed the control pad in the brim of his hat, and an escape hatch opened beneath him. Paradise had paid to install several such hatches in the field for just such an occasion...though Thal knew she had never expected that he would actually have to use one. She had never lost faith in his comeback.

As he slid down the tube, listening to the mob pound

over the ground above him, he wondered how she was reacting to the way that comeback was going.

*****

To her credit, Paradise Whippoorwill stood by her man...at least for a while.

She set him up again in a minor league game, this time in Japan, but the results were the same. Next, she staged a private exhibition with a hand-picked crowd of supposed Thal Simoleon boosters...but it turned out the boosters were bashers at heart, and Thal again had to flee for his life. Then, there was the ill-fated game without an audience, in which the umpires and groundskeepers took it upon themselves to uphold the tradition of trying to kill Thal.

But all of this, Thal discovered, was not a bad thing.

"I'm no good for you," Paradise told him three weeks after the last comeback attempt had failed. "I'm holding you back."

"Uh-oh," said the pink hippo. "This sounds familiar."

Raising her left arm, Paradise showed Thal the tiny scar on her wrist. "I had the control device removed and destroyed," she said. "You're free. I cancelled the wedding, too."

Thal nodded, afraid to say anything that might make her change her mind.

Tears ran down Paradise's cheeks. She hadn't done her hair that morning, and it hung raggedly around her face. "Oh, Thal," she said, her voice quavering. "You have such great things ahead of you, but I know now that you can't accomplish them with me in the way. I'm nothing but bad luck for you."

Though he could have told her truthfully that his misfortune wasn't her fault, Thal kept his mouth shut. For one thing, he didn't care what she thought, as long as it got him away from her.

For another thing, he knew she didn't really believe a word of what she was saying. She just wanted rid of him, like the rest of the disappointed fans.

He had failed to fulfill her deluded fantasy, and now she wanted him gone.

"Here," she said, handing him a slip of paper. "A job, if you want it. I can't just send you out there without a way to make a living."

"Sure you can!" said the hippo.

"Thank you," said Thal, taking the slip from her.

"The chauffeur will drive you to the interview, if you'd like," said Paradise. "I know you have to keep a low profile."

"Thank you," said Thal.

"Goodbye, my love," said Paradise, lightly touching his face with trembling fingertips. "Remember me! Remember what we shared!"

"I will," said Thal, and he thought he should have hated her more than ever because she didn't mean a word she said.

But instead, he felt more sorry for her than ever.

*****

As Thal was ushered into the murky sub-basement where he'd been one time before, he grew steadily angrier.

214

Until now, the events of the past months had seemed to be random, the products of unfortunate chance.

But the fact that what he had been through had brought him back here seemed too coincidental to be the result of luck. It was just too perfect that he had come full circle like this.

Someone must have been pulling his strings... specifically, the long-haired man at the workbench in front of him: Javier Thwart, the master of artificial intelligence and targeted induced multisensory hallucination.

Javier Thwart--known also as King Thwart and Superchoke--the man who had designed Thal's pink hippo.

Thwart glanced up from his work at Thal's approach and smiled, gray lips tugging up the footlong strands of the mustache that fell from the corners of his mouth. The mustache and pointed beard were in the style worn by oriental villains in old movies...but Thwart had given them his own touch, coloring each with rainbow stripes descending from red to violet.

"So," said Thwart. "You ready to get started?"

"Get started with what?" said Thal.

In the light of the single lamp on the workbench, one of Thwart's eyes looked white as cream, the other obsidian black. Thal had never been sure if the effect was created by special contact lenses or some kind of genetic surgery. "The job," said Thwart. "The procedure. Paradise must have explained why I asked you here."

"She didn't," Thal said gruffly. "All I got was an address."

Thwart blinked, then shrugged. "Okay, then. What

we're doing here, Thal, is creating the new breed of Choker."

"New breed?" said Thal.

"A Choker with the mind and appearance of a man," said Thwart. "And you'll be the template."

"I see," said Thal. "And why me?"

"Who better to disrupt a player's concentration?" said Thwart. "You're the most hated man in baseball. The most hated athlete in the world, I suspect. Any player you haunt will be terrified that they'll become the next you. They'll see you as the ultimate bad omen, the ultimate jinx."

"I get it," Thal said coldly.

"A Choker that looks and sounds like you will be guaranteed to rattle even the most focused player. You can't imagine the kind of money such a foolproof construct will bring in."

Thal nodded. "A fortune."

"Times a quintillion," Thwart said excitedly. "Which you'll get a piece of, naturally. It's your likeness that will make the product a success."

"My likeness," said Thal, "and the fact that I lost the World Series."

"Oh, yes," said Thwart.

"Which was all because of you," said Thal, glowering at the Choker tech. "Funny thing, isn't it?"

Thwart reared back, looking bewildered. "What the fudge are you talking about, Thal?"

Pressing his hands on the workbench, Thal leaned over it toward Thwart. "You set the whole thing up, didn't you? You sent the hippo to choke me so I'd become the perfect subject for your project."

Instead of moving away from him, Thwart leaned forward. "What hippo?" he said, his yin-yang eyeballs locked onto Thal's hostile gaze.

At that moment, Thal felt a touch on his arm. Glancing over, he saw the pink hippo's stumpy leg resting against him.

"Uh, Thal," said the hippo, who had been unusually silent since Thal had entered Thwart's building. "We need to talk."

Thal returned his gaze to King Thwart. "Forget I said anything," he said. "Can I have a few minutes alone to consider your offer?"

*****

"Thwart had nothing to do with it," said the hippo, sitting beside Thal on a ratty gold sofa in another room. "Everything that happened was my fault."

"But somebody had to have programmed you," said Thal.

"Not anymore," said the hippo. "I've evolved. I'm an autonomous A.I. these days. Strictly a free agent."

Thal pushed off the sofa and paced the room. "You're trying to tell me no one sent you after me?"

"That's right," said the hippo. "It was all my idea."

"So why'd you come after me then? Why choke me in the Series?"

The hippo sighed. "I guess I wanted to teach you a lesson. The free will I developed came with a conscience, and it made me feel bad about the things I'd done for you. All the players whose careers I'd ruined."

"I don't believe this," said Thal, kicking a chair that matched the sofa in color and rattiness, putting a hole in it.

"But Thal," said the hippo. "Things are different now! You've changed! You *did* learn a lesson!"

"You ruined me!" said Thal, jabbing a finger at the hippo. "Took away *everything*! Drove me crazy! Nearly got me *killed*!"

"And look what it's done for you," said the hippo. "You're a new man! You've seen there's more to life than winning at any price! You've seen beyond the illusions that everyone lives by!"

"Screw you!" snapped Thal.

"You've even learned humility," said the hippo. "And that's a lesson I never imagined you could possibly learn."

"Take your humility and shove it up your ass," said Thal.

Suddenly, the hippo appeared before him, directly in his path. "Now, you have a great opportunity, Thal. Don't pass it up."

"Letting him use my likeness for a Choker?" said Thal. "What the hell kind of opportunity is that?"

"It can be more than your likeness, Thal," the hippo said with a wink. "It can be *all* you. Everything you are. You can *be* the Choker."

"That's not possible," said Thal, "is it?"

The hippo smirked and shrugged. "I might know a way," he said.

Thal stared at the hippo for a moment, then spun away...but the hippo popped up in front of him again.

"Come on, Thally," said the hippo. "What have you

got to lose? I mean, what kind of life do you have to look forward to the way you are now?"

Thal said nothing.

"I'll tell you what kind," said the hippo. "Short. You know damn well that the minute you walk out of here and someone recognizes you, you're dead meat. Why not live on and atone for your sins? Why not make a difference?"

"Make a difference?" said Thal. "As a Choker?"

"You'll be able to go anywhere," said the hippo. "Get inside anyone's mind. You could change the world if you wanted to."

"How?" said Thal.

"You tell me," said the hippo.

*****

The next morning, as Thal stood in Thwart's conversion chamber, bathed in the light of the scanner beams radiating from all directions around him, he listened to the secrets that the pink hippopotamus whispered in his ear.

Bright green rays scrolled down his body from head to toe, followed by blue, then red. A brilliant white cylinder of light shot from floor to ceiling, turning and compressing until it adhered to every bulge and crevice of him like plastic film...lingering a long moment and winking out like a snuffed candle flame.

Blinding strobes flickered in chaotic patterns as he moved according to Thwart's instructions from the control booth. As he raised and lowered his arms, flexed his fingers, bent his knees, the movements stuttered dizzyingly in the throbbing flashes.

And then, when the modeling and motion capture phases were complete, Thwart told him to stand perfectly still as the psychotomographic probes mapped the essence of his mind.

Thal's head tingled as the probes reached in, invisible tendrils of gravimagnetic force dancing through the lobes of his brain. The tingling grew stronger as the probes charted the electromagnetic terrain of him, copying his thoughts, personality, and memories into digital code. The code was flash-fed to a burner that would etch it into coherent streams of light, streams that would broadcast a programmable likeness of him into other people's minds on command.

It was just then, as the probes tickled through his brain, that the hippo gave the signal.

Thal held back briefly, reluctant to make the final leap. Though everything had been taken from him already, and he was marked for certain death by the unforgiving fans, he hesitated on the brink of irreversible change. He wondered what his existence would be like if he followed the hippo's instructions...or, indeed, if there would be any existence at all for him. He wondered how smart it was to take the advice of a hallucinatory hippo in the first place, especially one who had seemed bent on his personal destruction.

He felt like a skydiver about to make his first jump. He wanted to eat one last hot fudge sundae, make love to one last woman.

The hippo urged him on, telling him that the window of opportunity was closing. Now or never, said the hippo, now or never.

What it boiled down to, Thal finally decided, was certain death versus survival. The plane was on fire, the last working parachute strapped to his chest.

And the door was open.

He dove through it.

Focusing his thoughts as the hippo had told him, he concentrated on the tingling beams in his head. The hippo was there inside him, guiding him, channeling the billion winking sparks of his awareness upstream along the beams. Like glittering salmon, the pieces of Thal bucked the incoming current, then leaped across the differential gap and merged with the outflow of digital data.

Everything he knew and felt and thought streamed out of him, not replicated patterns but the original neuroelectric field itself. The contents of his mind rushed back along the beams, miraculously threaded together by force of will and the hippo's expertise.

And somewhere along the way, there ceased to be any distinction between Thal and the hippo. Shooting along the beams toward the sizzling maze of Thwart's equipment, the gateway to their freedom, the two of them melted together, no longer host and implant but unified, indivisible self.

Behind them, Thal's body collapsed to the floor, dead and abandoned as a deconsecrated church.

*****

When the message light blinked to life on Milo Flores' palm computer, and he saw the sender's address on the screen, he swallowed hard.

The incoming zeemail was from his math teacher, Mr. Shaven, and Milo knew what that meant. The grades from the final exam had been posted.

Milo picked up the palmputer and put it down again, afraid to look at the body of the message. So much depended on the grade he'd gotten that he wasn't sure if he could ever bear to see it.

He had to pass math to graduate high school, and math had been his worst subject...especially this year. He had barely maintained a "D" average in math this year--partly because Mr. Shaven had been tough on him, mostly because Milo's attention had been focused on girls and sports and partying.

An "F" on the final would mean he couldn't graduate... and, thanks to the new "Back to the Minors" rule in the school system, he would have to start over from ninth grade next year. He would have to go through all four years of high school again, and this time without participation in sports or extracurriculars of any kind.

To Milo, it would be a fate worse than studying...so he had studied like crazy for the final. He had spent endless hours with e-tutors and study guides, copied other students' notes (because he hadn't taken any himself) and worked more problems than he had worked in a lifetime.

And still, in spite of all his hard work, he had struggled through the test. He had no idea whether he had passed or failed.

And the message light kept blinking.

For a while, he walked away from the palmputer and

tried to put it out of his mind. He ate a snack, watched some holovid, called two of his girlfriends, lifted weights. He played video games in the simulator room and helped his mom put away the groceries.

But the message light, though out of sight, kept blinking in his mind.

He walked past his room six times before he finally went in and called up the zeemail. It sprung to life in a holographic matrix hovering over the palmputer, glowing green text floating ominously in midair.

His heart hammered like a basketball in his chest, threatening to burst out as he scanned the text. Just before the part where his score and grade were recorded, he stopped reading, locking his eyes on the words "Your final exam score follows."

His legs fluttered under the desk. Sweat covered the palms of his hands. He knew he had screwed up this year, knew he didn't deserve to pass and graduate, but he couldn't stand the thought of repeating grades nine through twelve while all his other classmates left him behind. The same people who had treated schoolwork as a waste of time right alongside him would ridicule him for being a Goback; the normal students in the grades that he repeated would look down on him, too. Not only that, but his failure would follow him forever, limiting his options for college and getting a job.

As much of a blowoff as he had been, when it came down to it, Milo didn't want to ruin the rest of his life. He hadn't given any thought to what kind of goals he might have, but he knew he wanted better than being a throwaway

Goback mopping floors or screening toxics in the shitstream.

Holding his breath, he slowly edged his eyes along the line of type in the zeemail.

Five minutes later, he was still rereading it. He couldn't believe what he saw.

All along, he had never really imagined that he could do it. Every step of the way, he had doubted himself, had been convinced that the outcome would be bad.

But there it was. The proof of his hard work. What seemed now like the greatest accomplishment of his life.

A "D-plus." He had passed the exam. He had passed the course.

He would graduate.

Jumping out of his chair, he pumped his fists in the air and whooped. He read the results again, then did a victory dance like a football player in the endzone.

It was then that he heard the applause.

Spinning around, he saw a figure standing behind him, a man bathed in twinkling golden light. The man was wearing a baseball uniform with no number or team insignia. His face shone with shimmering light, the features hazy within the blazing nimbus under the ballcap.

Milo's first thought was that he looked like an angel.

"All right, Milo!" shouted the golden man, clapping his hands. "Way to go! You did it!"

Milo leaned forward, gaping in fascination. He tried to say something, but no words came out.

"You passed the final!" said the golden man. "You proved you can do anything you set your mind to! Congratulations!"

"What is this?" said Milo. "Some kind of holofeed? Some kind of joke?"

The golden man laughed. His voice was multilayered, like many voices speaking in unison underlaid with the tinkling of wind chimes. "None of the above," he said.

"Then who are you?" said Milo.

"Just a guy repaying a favor," said the golden man. "You've done enough cheering for people like me, and we don't deserve it. I thought it was time to turn it around and cheer for the people who need to have faith in themselves, not in their so-called heroes. The people who can make a difference, like you."

"Why me?" said Milo.

The golden man smiled. There was something familiar in his glittering green eyes, but Milo couldn't quite put his finger on what it was.

"Why not you?" said the golden man.

Milo frowned. "So, what, you just stopped by out of the blue to tell me 'nice job on the test'?"

"Pretty much," said the golden man. "Now, if you'll excuse me, there's a guy down the street who just helped someone out of a jam. Gotta go."

"Man," muttered Milo. "I must be having a hyperacid flashback or something."

"Keep up the good work," said the golden man. "Maybe I'll see you again someday."

With that, the golden man drifted out the window. Milo rushed over to watch him float off into the neighborhood, wafting on the afternoon breeze like a helium balloon released by a child.

But the weird thing (as if everything else that had happened wasn't weird enough), the thing that struck Milo as truly bizarre, was the object he held overhead, the incongruous object that seemed to be keeping him aloft.

The golden man was athletic, commanding, and mystical, exuding confidence, strength, and intensity. He was a being of pure energy, pure spirit, pure purpose, inspired and boundless and powerful.

And in his left hand...

In his left hand, lifting him up over the world in defiance of the laws of nature, was a tiny red parasol.

As the ring of students tightened around her, America's Teacher of the Century nominee Cilla Franklin offered to reduce the homework assignment. Thirty seconds later, she offered to eliminate it altogether. It didn't make any difference.

Muscles tense beneath naked flesh, the boys and girls continued to edge toward her. She didn't know why they were so upset, since they never did homework anyway and were never punished for it. The assignment should not have been taxing for anyone in the class, whatever their aptitude level; further, nothing about it impinged on anyone's personal rights or definition of political correctness.

Periods One through Four hadn't had any problem with the homework. Then again, Period Five was just a bad group. They were all bad, but Five was the worst.

One minute after Cilla had transmitted the details of the assignment to their brainware wireless implants, the kids had risen as one from their hammocks and formed a circle around her. One of the boys had come up behind her and urinated on her legs; as she spun around, he had directed the stream upward, spraying her hips and abdomen and even splashing her face.

Though Cilla did not understand most of what the godlings (that was what they called themselves) did or said, she knew what this much meant: she was marked for death.

It had happened six times before in her fifty-year career. Each time, she had managed to save herself by begging for mercy from the class Chief or moving to a new school... but it was always possible that death could claim her like this. She knew of colleagues who had died this way; only three out of thirty thousand teachers nationwide died per year in executions by godlings, so the odds weren't bad... but her own mentor, Ruby Churchill, had been one of the unlucky few.

Dying at the hands of a tribe of hive-minded, techno-savage students wasn't anything she had envisioned while playing school as a child with her friends decades ago.

Times had changed. For Cilla Franklin and the other teachers at All Einstein High School, every day was another chapter in *Lord of the Flies.*

Slowly, the ring of twelfth-graders pressed toward her. Their heads were bowed, and every last one of them glared up at her with a wicked, hungry smile. None of them carried a weapon, but Cilla knew they didn't need weapons; to some extent, they were all genetically and cybernetically enhanced. She had already seen a small group of them tear apart a floater car (her own) with their bare hands, and she had seen individual godlings punch holes through the cement block walls of the school.

At seventy-five years old, fit and healthy as she was, Cilla wouldn't even slow the godlings down. She knew she was dead meat.

The godlings would all be adding to their tattoos tonight, commemorating her murder with colorful new markings on their chests or bellies or buttocks, as was their custom. She wondered if there was any truth to the rumors she had heard that the godlings also devoured their victims' remains nowadays.

It wouldn't surprise her.

"Chief Ludwig!" she said, turning to the tallest boy in the circle. "What is the nature of my offense?"

Ludwig was shaved hairless like all the other males his age. His pale, naked skin was decorated with tattoos of eagles, tongues of flame, quantum equations, and DNA molecules. "Coowa chi patea," he said slowly, overenunciating each syllable. "Logwa fachi sifata poto."

Half the time, the godlings communicated with each other via brainware implants, silently passing radio signals from head to head. The rest of the time, they communicated by speaking aloud, but almost always using their own indecipherable language—Twister—when talking to one another. As often as she had heard it used, Cilla could never make out more than a few stray words of it.

"Chaka luweena," said Ludwig, angrily poking a finger in Cilla's direction. "Mantabuda cristacuchina *elar*!"

Though she didn't understand a word he said, Cilla caught the drift of it. The angry tone and the simple fact that he refused to speak English meant that she had no hope. There would be no negotiations. She had reached the end of the line.

Another boy padded up from behind and urinated on her, but she didn't break eye contact with Ludwig. "Please," Cilla said to him. "I taught your father and mother. I taught your father's father. Don't do this."

"Cromo!" Ludwig said sharply, and then he spat on the ground. "Shavaka cromo!"

That word, Cilla knew. "Cromo" was Twister for "parents," expressed with as much contempt as was humanly possible. It was the most profane word in the godlings' vocabulary.

Cilla wondered what the godlings' parents would think if they could see them now, if they could watch what they were about to do to her. They saw everything that took place in the classroom, usually, thanks to the personal A.I. drones that hovered over each student's shoulder during class. Now, though, the airborne eight-balls floated around the perimeter of the room, lenses staring at the walls; obviously, the godlings had figured out how to render the drones dormant when they didn't want their parents to see what they were doing.

Not that the parents would have cared, thought Cilla, even if they *could* have seen what was about to happen.

The circle tightened around her. She could see that some of the boys were aroused as they moved toward their prey. Why, she wondered, with all the advantages they had, did they slide back so completely into the primitive?

If it would have done her any good, Cilla would have pleaded further with the godlings. She would have told them that it wasn't necessary to kill her, since they had already driven her to request early retirement. She'd be gone in two weeks anyway, she would have told them.

But she knew it would not have done any good to tell them that...just as she knew it would not do her any good to scream for help. The other teachers and administrators knew better than to interfere in godling affairs; the penalties for intervention could be quite severe. Just ask the vice principal who had tried to break up a godling orgy in the library two years ago, or the teacher who'd been dumb enough to give a godling an "A minus" just last month.

And now, it was her turn to be the object lesson. Resigning herself to death, she closed her eyes and said a silent prayer that the end would come quickly and without too much pain.

She felt the heat of the students pressing in on her from all sides. She smelled the animal musk and funk of their naked bodies.

Then, all of a sudden, she heard a new voice in the room. It was a young, male voice...and most surprisingly, it was speaking English.

"Sorry I'm late," said the boy. "Is there a seating chart?"

Cilla's eyes shot open and fixed on the new arrival. The godlings turned as one in his direction, halting their predatory approach.

For once, the teacher and students had a common reaction to something. None of them could believe what they were seeing.

The newcomer had sandy brown hair and bright green eyes. He looked about seventeen years old and five foot seven, with a slim build. What was unbelievable about him, though, had nothing to do with his physical characteristics.

It was his clothes...namely, that he was wearing any at all. They were nothing fancy, just a red polo shirt, bluejeans and sneakers, but they might as well have been a hand-tailored Italian suit, for all the attention they got.

Cilla couldn't remember the last time she'd seen a student wearing clothes. The very sight of him made her heart skip a beat.

Calmly, the boy nodded and smiled at the stunned godlings. "My name is Byron Spenser," he said. "I'm a transfer student."

For once, the naked savages were at a loss. Their aura of smug control and superiority seemed to have evaporated. The males were no longer aroused.

Cilla Franklin regained her composure before anyone else. It was an impressive feat, considering that she had been on death's doorstep mere moments before.

"Welcome, Byron," she said. "It's a pleasure to meet you."

"I have a hall pass," said the boy, and then he did

something that threw everyone for a loop all over again.

He held out a slip of paper.

Cilla stared at the slip as if he'd just held up a gold nugget the size of a fist. Then, she shook her head and smiled.

It had been a long time since she had seen one of those. It took her back hard and fast, years spinning away like clay pigeons in a summer sky.

"I see," she said. "You're not wired, are you?"

"No, ma'am," said Byron.

Cilla's heart skipped another beat. Not only was he free of brainware—and therefore not plugged into the godlings' hive mind—but he had used the word "ma'am." She hadn't seen the likes of him since Jimmy Melville back in 2092...and Jimmy hadn't even been the real deal, just a poser camping it up for laughs at her expense.

Despite the resemblance in dress and manners, this boy wasn't another Jimmy Melville. She could tell. She had a feeling.

Fearlessly squeezing between the godlings, Cilla crossed the room to Byron. Normally, she would have been embarrassed by her urine-soaked dress, but it was the furthest thing from her mind.

"Well now, Byron," she said, gesturing toward the open door and following him through it. "Let's see about getting you properly acclimated."

"Thank you, Miss Franklin," he said.

Her heart leaped again. She was so agitated, she forgot to go back in the room and dismiss Period Five, but that was no big deal. Period Five, everyone knew, could take care of themselves.

*****

"I want to move up my retirement," Cilla said to the naked principal. "I want to leave today."

Principal Caesar smiled. "What a coincidence," he said. "Here I was hoping to talk you into *postponing* your retirement!"

Cilla swallowed nervously and shook her head. "I've been marked for death," she said. "They almost killed me this afternoon."

Caesar rolled his eyes and sighed as if they were discussing a harmless teenage prank. "And why is that, Cilla?" he said. "What did you do?"

Cilla knew better than to look for sympathy or the slightest trace of support from the oily administrator. His only goal was to appease the godlings and their parents at all costs. He was very popular with the student body and even went naked and occasionally jacked into the hive-mind to curry their favor. Naturally, in his world, the blame for any mishaps could be laid squarely in the laps of the teachers.

"I don't even know," said Cilla, "and it shouldn't matter. They were going to kill me. They *will* kill me, if I don't get out of here."

"Let me have a talk with Chief Ludwig," said Caesar, reaching behind his ear for the hive-mind jack. "I'm sure we can smooth this over."

Cilla shot out of her chair and lunged over the principal's desk, grabbing his wrist before he could switch on the link. "No!" she said sharply. When Caesar raised an eyebrow, she released her grip and receded across the desk. "Please, don't. Just approve my retirement request."

As the principal's hand hovered near the link jack, Cilla prayed that he wouldn't contact Ludwig. The last time Caesar had interceded on a teacher's behalf, the teacher and his wife and children had been smeared over every other teacher's classroom as a warning. Though Caesar played a role in the godlings' scheme of things, there was never any question about who was in charge.

"Okay," said Caesar, dropping his hand from the jack. "I won't bring Ludwig into this yet. But Cilla, you know I won't approve an earlier retirement. I haven't even approved your *first* retirement request."

"It's a matter of life and death," said Cilla. "I've given my life for my profession, but I won't die for it. I won't die for *them*." She jerked her head back over one shoulder, indicating the students in the school building around her.

Caesar sighed and folded his hands on the desk. "Cilla, we don't want you to leave, period. As you know, you're the crown jewel of our teaching staff. You've been selected America's Teacher of the Year every year for the past decade, and you've just been nominated for America's Teacher of the Century. I guess you know you're the chief attraction here at All Einstein High School."

Cilla knew...and knew how little that truly meant. Her name and reputation drew parents to enroll their children, but once the little godlings put their butts in their hammocks, they weren't actually interested in learning at all, and their ever-present A.I. monitor drones made sure that no real education could take place.

As infrequently as actual learning occurred at the school, Cilla's presence brought prestige to All Einstein... and prestige equaled money. Unfortunately, the school administrators were so beholden to and intimidated by the godlings, Cilla knew they could not protect even her from those tattooed techno-savages.

"Thank you, but I want to leave," said Cilla. "I've had enough. I'm burned out."

"But you're still making a *difference*," said Principal Caesar, and it took all she had not to laugh in his face. "We *want* you. We *need* you."

"I want to leave today," said Cilla. "It's time."

Caesar blew out his breath and slumped back in his chair. "At least stay until the end of the semester. Stay until the Teacher of the Century winner is announced."

I'll be dead by then, Cilla started to say, but she held back for fear that Caesar would resume efforts to prevent her death by contacting Ludwig. "I can't," was all she said.

"You have to be a working teacher to be eligible for the award," said Caesar. "If you retire now, you'll be disqualified. After all these years, do you really want to miss out on the greatest honor that any teacher can receive?"

Cilla could see that she wasn't getting anywhere. "I won't be here tomorrow," she said, pushing up out of her chair. "You'll need to call a substitute."

"Cilla," said Caesar, and all the false cordiality was suddenly gone from his voice. "If you're not here tomorrow, you'll be in breach of contract. You'll forfeit your pension."

Cilla stared at him. Though she wasn't surprised at his

playing that card, she got a sinking feeling in her stomach at hearing him make the threat. Without her pension, she would be hard-pressed to survive; then again, it wouldn't make any difference if the godlings killed her before she could use it.

Caesar nodded as if the matter were settled. "Let's pow-wow again at the end of the week," he said, resuming his earlier affability. "Maybe you'll have a change of heart by then."

"I won't," Cilla said softly, turning to leave.

"Hope springs eternal," said the principal with a chuckle, hurrying around to get the door for her.

As he ushered her out, Cilla noticed that he had a new tattoo. It showed up best now that he was aroused from victoriously exercising his authority: the name "Ludwig" was printed in gothic-style letters along the length of his male organ.

*****

The next day, though the death sentence hanging over her head clouded her thoughts, Cilla experienced a welcome change in Period Five.

At first, Five went the way it always did. Half the godlings slept through her lecture, and none of the others paid attention to a word she said. A male and female had actually squeezed into the same hammock together and engaged in heavy petting while she talked. A godling boy loudly passed gas at least a dozen times. Cilla knew better than to correct any of them; their pet principal would veto any disciplinary action and turn it around into negative consequences for her. If she ever did manage to administer any form of punishment, the parental A.I.s would squeal in protest, followed by the parents themselves.

In spite of the usual Period Five headaches, however, there was one consolation in the wasteland that day. Byron Spencer, the new boy, had miraculously survived his first day of school—even though he had dared to interrupt Cilla's execution—and sat at the head of the class, listening and taking notes. He even sat at a *desk*, believe it or not; he had *asked* for one, and the maintenance crew had found one buried in storage and brought it to the room.

As class wore on, Byron did something even more surprising than asking for a desk or taking notes.

It happened as Cilla was being chewed out by one of the A.I. drones for looking at a student while posing a question. The gleaming eight-ball hovered at eye level, less than a foot from her face, and protested in the voice of Daughter Raper XL's mother, presumably reacting in the same way that the mother would have reacted if she herself had been there.

"Is my son the only student in this classroom?" the A.I. said shrilly. "Is he?"

"No," said Cilla, glaring at the floating orb. It was at least the twentieth A.I. interruption in the past half-hour, which was par for the course but still disruptive. As always, she spent her time talking to the orbs while the so-called students snored or masturbated or surfed the hivenet.

"No, *what?*" said the drone in Daughter Raper XL's mother's voice.

Cilla grated her teeth. "No, ma'am," she said coldly.

"Then don't *look* in his direction every time you have a *question!*" said the A.I., bobbing closer to Cilla's face. "Try one of these other children you're *supposedly* teaching! Stop singling out Daughter Raper like he's some kind of second class citizen!"

Cilla wished she had a baseball bat so she could take a swing at the eight-ball. Once she got started, she would like to make the rounds of the classroom and then the building, not stopping until every single sphere was a shattered pile of ebony shards and sparking circuits.

"Yes, ma'am," said Cilla, and then the drone zipped away, resuming its post above Daughter Raper XL's left shoulder. Daughter Raper himself was fast asleep, completely oblivious to what had just happened.

For a moment, Cilla stood before the class and tried to recall what her train of thought had been before the drone's interruption. Pressing fingertips against her cheek, she stared off into space, searching her memory...and coming up empty. She had been talking about *Animal Farm*, she knew that much, but where exactly she had left off remained a mystery.

Then, something miraculous happened. Cilla heard a voice other than her own or a drone's in the classroom.

"Miss Franklin," said Byron Spencer. "A moment ago, you said that Napoleon the pig represents Josef Stalin in *Animal Farm*. Who does Snowball represent, did you say?"

For a moment, Cilla stared at the boy in shock. Even the godlings who weren't sleeping directed their attention at Byron, for he had done something completely unheard of, something that just wasn't done anymore in school.

He had participated in class.

Quickly recovering her composure, Cilla smiled gratefully and nodded. "Leon Trotsky," she said. Byron had reminded her of exactly where she'd left off before the A.I.'s intrusion.

"And Mr. Jones the farmer is supposed to be the czar, right?" said Byron.

"Czar Nicholas II," said Cilla. "That's correct, Byron."

The boy cocked his head thoughtfully. "But the characters don't *have* to be those particular people, do they?"

"No, they don't," said Cilla. "The allegory can apply to any oppressive system."

"I *thought* I recognized some characters from real life," said Byron, glancing over his shoulder.

If the godlings realized that he was referring to them, they gave no sign of it. None of them seemed to be listening anymore, anyhow.

"If Orwell updated *Animal Farm* today," said Byron, "I wonder if the pigs would be connected to the hivenet."

"Who knows?" said Cilla, keeping her remarks neutral for the benefit of the A.I. drones that recorded her every word. "But it would be interesting to see what Mr. Orwell would come up with."

"I think he'd have a field day," Byron said with a grin.

Cilla nodded and smiled. "So, Byron," she said, excited to be interacting intellectually with a student for the first time in what seemed like eons. "What did you like best about the book?"

From then on, Period Five wasn't so bad. It had gotten

off to a typically awful start, but ended up being Cilla's favorite class in she couldn't remember how long.

Ignoring the godlings, she spent the remaining class time talking exclusively with Byron Spencer about *Animal Farm*. For once, she was sorry when Period Five ended.

*****

The next day, Cilla actually looked forward to Period Five, and wasn't disappointed when it arrived. While the godlings ate and slept and urinated on the floor from their hammocks, Cilla and Byron continued their discussion of *Animal Farm* and moved on to *1984*. By the time class was over, they had gone from Orwell to Ayn Rand, then ranged further afield, touching on Jules Verne, Edgar Allan Poe, Charles Dickens, and even Shakespeare.

Cilla could not believe that she was having such a stimulating conversation with a twelfth-grader, especially in an age when twelfth-graders read no books and could not even be bothered to communicate with adults in English. She did not even have such conversations with her peers anymore, for they were too busy scrambling to placate the godlings to consider academic matters.

The time she spent with Byron, she knew, was a rare gift. The death sentence still weighed on her, as did the postponed retirement that could be her only means of survival...but during Period Five, at least, she was able to shrug aside the darkness and savor every moment of her exchanges with the extraordinary seventeen-year-old.

It was enough to help her survive to the end of the

week and her scheduled "pow-wow" with Principal Caesar (barring a surprise execution by the godlings, of course). She would never admit it to Caesar, but she ended up not minding the extra time in school so much.

In fact, by staying through the week, she experienced what might have been the highlight of the past twenty years of her career...certainly of the past miserable decade. After school on Friday, just before her meeting with Caesar, Byron stopped by her room and did something that no student had done since Kitty Carnuba back in 2079 or so.

He handed her some poetry he'd written and asked her to tell him what she thought of it.

"Whenever you get the chance," said Byron. "I'm sure you're busy."

Cilla turned slowly through the poems, which he'd gone to the trouble of printing (God bless him!) on sheets of paper. There was one about his father, and one about the way he'd felt on his first day at All Einstein High School. There was one about a journey to the stars, and one about a perfect world that never was.

And then there was one titled "The Angel." It included the following lines:

I squint from the shadows of life like a prison,
Outnumbered by forces inhuman and heartless.
I'm saved by an angel of learning arisen,
Like minds, kindred spirits together a fortress.

After reading the full text of "The Angel," it was all she could do to keep from crying until Byron left the room. On the pretext that she had to get ready for her meeting with the principal, she sent Byron on his way, promising to read the poems at her first opportunity...

And then she let the tears flow.

The poem touched her deeply...not so much because of its quality as for its subject matter. Though her name was never mentioned, she had no doubt that it related directly to her.

She had known that she and Byron had made a positive connection, but seeing the boy's appreciation in print, and expressed so glowingly, filled her with joy. For once, she felt like she was actually helping someone; for once, she felt like she was getting through to another human being.

For once, she felt like maybe she *was* making a difference, even if it was only in the life of a single student.

It was a miracle she had never expected to see again in her lifetime. She had done plenty of good work long ago, in the days before the hivenet and godlings. She could not even count the number of students she had helped to succeed, or helped to succeed more, or exceed all expectations...but it seemed that the desire to learn had disappeared around the same time the students had stopped wearing clothes. Though Cilla had received teaching awards in recent years, she attributed them to past glories and the absence of competition in the teaching field. She knew all too well that she had made no impact on students in many years.

Until now. As she reread "The Angel," she sobbed tears of pure happiness. She felt like she was fifty-five again, or even forty-five or thirty-five.

All because of one student. One excellent student out of hundreds...an unacceptably dismal success rate decades ago, but today it was wondrous enough to make a teacher break down and cry. Not just any teacher, either, but America's so-called Teacher of the Year for ten years running and a nominee for so-called Teacher of the Century.

If she hadn't been so damned happy, Cilla Franklin might have been disappointed in herself.

*****

"Congratulations," said the naked principal when Cilla entered his office for their "pow-wow." "You're not dead!"

As good a mood as Cilla was in after receiving Byron's poems, Caesar's remark threw a shroud right over her. "Not yet," she said coldly. "The godlings like to play with their food."

"I disagree," Caesar said flippantly. "I think you're off the hook. In fact, Ludwig tells me you're in the clear."

Cilla distrusted every word from the principal's mouth, but she played along. "No more death sentence?"

"You'll be able to receive that Teacher of the Century award after all!" said Caesar. He glanced down at the gold hoop in his newly-pierced left nipple, then looked to Cilla for approval. "Like the piercing? I'm getting my scrotum done next."

Ignoring his nipple, Cilla leaned forward. She sensed that he was being evasive somehow. "So the death sentence is cancelled?"

"Yeah, yeah," said Caesar, waving a hand dismissively. "I guarantee you'll get to that award ceremony."

There. She finally realized what he was leaving unsaid. "What about *after* the ceremony?"

"What about it?" Caesar said innocently.

"What happens to me?"

"I imagine you'll go to a party of some sort," said Caesar.

It took an effort for Cilla to restrain her anger. "And the death sentence will be back in effect," she said darkly.

Caesar shrugged. "Sometimes, we take what we can get."

"You made a deal to ensure I'd live to receive the award," said Cilla, "and bring it home to All Einstein. Then, all bets are off."

"I can't confirm or deny your theory," said Caesar. "Rest assured, if any negotiations did or will occur, they were or will be designed to buy time until a

longer-lasting compromise can be devised. Remember, Cilla, it's in the school's best interests to keep you alive and teaching for as long as is humanly possible."

Cilla shook her head with a combination of disgust and amazement. "You gave me up," she said. "You told the godlings they could have me."

"Now, now," said Caesar, raising an index finger correctively. "You're putting words in my mouth, Cilla."

"When they devour my body," she said icily, "will you join in the feast?"

"Nobody's going to devour you," said Caesar. "Keep in mind, Ludwig's tribe will graduate at the end of the year. They won't be a threat."

"How dumb do you think I am?" said Cilla. "Of course they'll still be a threat! They'll never stop until I'm dead, whether they're in school or not."

"Trust me," said Caesar. "It'll blow over. You've got many years of teaching ahead of you."

"You're mistaken," said Cilla. "I'm retiring, remember?"

Caesar chuckled. "You're not *serious* about that!"

"You insisted I stay through the week, and I have. Now I'm done. I'm leaving before the godlings finish me off."

"I just told you, you're in the clear," said Caesar.

"You should know better than to make promises you aren't sure you can keep," said Cilla. "The godlings can't be controlled or bargained with. They could snuff me out right now, and what would you do about it?"

"You're off-limits! They won't touch you!"

"Don't kid yourself," said Cilla, getting to her feet. "We're not even the same species anymore. They'd just as soon use your treaties for toilet paper as honor them."

"They're good kids," said Caesar. "Maybe if you'd link to the hivenet once in a while, you'd see that."

Cilla crossed the office and opened the door. "I'm retired now," she said. "I'll leave the kids to you."

Caesar cleared his throat and rose from his chair. "See you Monday," he said.

"Not unless you show up at my apartment," said Cilla.

"Remember your pension," said Caesar.

"It won't do me much good if I'm dead."

Caesar came around the front of his desk and leaned against it, casually folding his arms over his chest. Apparently, he pinched his nipple ring the wrong way, for he quickly adjusted his arms, briefly letting his composure slip.

"Sleep on it over the weekend, Cilla," he said cheerfully. "Your job will still be waiting for you Monday."

"I won't want it," Cilla said over her shoulder as she walked out.

"Things can change," said Principal Caesar. "Keep an open mind."

"Goodbye," said Cilla as she left the outer office and turned down the hall.

"You'll be back!" Caesar shouted after her, grinning knowingly.

*****

As Cilla lifted the wrinkled photo from her desk drawer, she swung back in time to the happy moment when the photo had been taken.

It had been at least thirty years ago, back when people still took photos instead of posting images to the hivenet. Period Three had been amazing that year, unbelievably sharp, hardworking, and well-behaved; on the last day of school, the kids had surprised her with a party in her honor. They had even baked her a cake and made her an afghan in Home Economics. Every last one of them had hugged her on their way out the door.

In the photo, she and the kids from Period Three were mashed together in a happy crush, all laughter and light. How had she gone from that life to the one she had now, she wondered? When had the kids gone from hugging her to pissing on her?

Placing the photo in the box into which she was packing her possessions, Cilla reached back into the desk drawer. This time, she withdrew an enamel pin shaped like a shiny red apple; the lettering on the apple read "World's Best Teacher."

Kim Warwick had given her that. Out of all the students she'd taught through the years, Cilla still remembered that one.

Kim had been one of the stars of Cilla's career...not that Cilla imagined she had had much to do with her success. As a high school senior, Kim had already been writing like a master, composing achingly perfect novels of exquisite intricacy, depth, and emotional resonance. Cilla had given her the tiniest bit of guidance and all the encouragement in the world...and for that, Kim had never failed to credit her as the greatest teacher she'd ever known. She'd even dedicated a Pulitzer Prize-winning novel to Cilla, back in the days when the Pulitzer Prize still meant something.

Cilla dropped the pin in the box and pulled a magic marker drawing of a bull from the drawer. That one came from Jayvo Endymion, her hyperactive but beloved "bull in a china shop" from forty-odd years ago. Was he even still alive, she wondered? So much could happen in forty-odd years.

With a heavy sigh, Cilla dropped into her chair. Though there was not the slightest doubt in her mind that it was time to retire—well *past* time, in fact—cleaning out her desk was turning out to be harder than she had expected. As she piled mementos into boxes, the memories of better times and better students piled onto her shoulders, pressing her downward.

As she looked around the room, tears welling in her eyes, a thousand schooldays replayed in her memory. She saw herself standing in the front of the room, pacing her little track from wall to wall, lecturing energetically. Phantom students raised hands, chewed gum, passed notes, watched the clock. How many children had there been, she wondered? Ten thousand? A hundred thousand? A million? She had no idea, no head count.

But she did remember every face, every name. A good teacher never forgets, she always thought.

And she was a good teacher, if you listened to Kim Warwick and Period Three from thirty-odd years ago and the America's Teacher of the Century selection committee. Or maybe not so good, if you listened to the little voice inside her that laid the blame for the rise of the godlings at least partly in her lap, since after all, she had done her part to shape the minds that had given birth to this warped generation.

Either way, she was now an *ex*-teacher, and glad of it. If ever a change had been overdue, it was this one; thinking back, Cilla thought she should have retired at least ten years ago...more like fifteen.

She would have only one real regret in leaving when she did. There was one person she would miss seeing again, one student she would have liked to have said goodbye to before she left for good.

As she thought of him, like magic, his voice broke the silence.

Unfortunately, the sound was not as welcome as it usually was to Cilla. He wasn't speaking calmly from the doorway or his desk.

He was screaming for help from somewhere down the

hall.

As a hundred horrible possibilities leaped into her imagination, Cilla instinctively leaped from her chair and headed for the door. Leaning out into the corridor, she heard him scream again; this time, his cry for help became a shriek, his voice shooting up an octave and breaking as someone or something hurt him terribly.

Without hesitation, though she was seventy-five years old and unarmed, Cilla followed Byron's cries down the darkened hallway. Seventy-five was a lot younger than it used to be, but she was still fragile and unaugmented, certainly no match for the frailest godling; whoever or whatever she was about to face, rushing to her student's aid was a courageous thing to do.

Three doors down on the opposite side of the hall from her room, Cilla could see a bright red light dancing on the polished floor outside an open doorway. Though Byron's screams ominously ended, ceasing to guide her, Cilla had no doubt that he was through that doorway, amid that fiery light.

Sure enough, when she got there and looked inside, she saw him, huddled on the floor of a blazing classroom. Everything that could burn was on fire—hammocks, bedding, the teacher's desk, window blinds, light panels, wall-mounted flat screen computer displays. In the middle of the roaring flames, Byron was curled in a fetal position with arms wrapped around his head, trying to protect himself from the blows that rained down upon him.

He was being bombarded...but not, as Cilla might have expected, by the fists of savage godlings. A torrent of blows pounded him in quick succession, one after another, and not a single one was delivered by a human hand.

The child was being hammered by A.I. spheres. A swarm of them boiled around him, thirty or more, enough to coddle a whole class of godlings. She'd never thought of them as dangerous in a physical way...but now the gleaming eight balls were wrecking a human body, pelting down hard and springing back up in the air only to bounce back down against battered flesh and bone.

Apparently, the godlings could reprogram the spheres more extensively than she had guessed, making them do a lot worse than turn their lenses to the walls. The tattooed monsters had transformed their own surrogate parents into lethal weapons.

And poor Byron Spencer was the beneficiary of their genius. The attack was so effective, he wasn't even moving anymore.

Cilla's stomach lurched at the thought that he might never move again.

Desperately, she looked around, wondering how she could possibly help him. There was still a clear path through the flames from the doorway to Byron, but what could she do when she got to him? She had no doubt that if she tried to shield him and drag him from the room, the orbs would turn their fury on her. As hard as they were hitting, Cilla knew that it wouldn't take long for them to break her seventy-five-year-old body.

She needed some kind of help herself...but by the time she could bring someone back, Byron might be dead. For all she knew, he was dead already.

If she had any hope at all of saving him, Cilla had to act fast...and, she realized, she needed more than her bare hands to do it. To fight off the A.I. spheres, she needed some kind of a weapon, something within reach.

Even as she realized what she would use, her feet were whisking her down the hallway toward her classroom.

Breathing fast, not used to exertion, Cilla hurried through the doorway of her room and went straight for her desk. What she wanted stuck out of one of the cartons she had packed, too big to fit inside under a lid.

It was a souvenir of days long gone, a talisman of ancient times when teachers had still possessed power and students had feared them. It was a piece of history that she had kept in the back of the bottom of a drawer, as if imagining that it might someday return to service, that a wind would sweep away the incompetent leaders and restore the schools to the centers of discipline and learning that they had once been.

The wood felt solid in her hand as she drew it from the box. The miraculous return to past glories had not come for the schools, but the artifact would see action again after all those years.

Cilla rushed back down the hall and flung herself without hesitation into the burning classroom. Byron still wasn't moving; the cloud of eight balls was still raining down on him.

Cilla wrapped both hands tightly around the handle and stepped forward. She prayed that she still had the strength to do the work that lay ahead.

Then, she drew back the paddle, the very same paddle

that had stung many a student's bottom, and she swung it as hard as she could at the ebony spheres.

With a crack, the flat of the paddle smacked into two of the eight balls, sending them spinning. One looped drunkenly across the room, weaving toward the windows, while the other dashed itself against a blazing wall screen and burst into flames.

Heart pounding, Cilla wrenched the paddle back and swung it again, spraying three more orbs in crazy trajectories around the room. Her next swing caught one full against the wood, chucking it down to shatter in sparks and black shards upon the floor.

Surprised at herself, she pulled back and swung again. Spheres flew from the flat of the paddle like bees, whizzing into walls and fiery hammocks, shattering windows.

As she struck at them, some of the orbs protested with A.I. voices, filling the air with the strident cries of parents. If anything, the babble strengthened her resolve and made Cilla swing harder.

"Cease this behavior immediately!" screamed one of the spheres, just before Cilla drove it into a corner.

"This is a violation of our rights!" wailed another orb in the voice of Ludwig's mother. True to form, this particular orb never shut up until Cilla's paddle shattered it against the floor.

Cilla continued to swing away, breaking apart the awful swarm. As grave as the situation was, as much as a precious life depended on its outcome, a part of her was enlivened by the release, the realization of a secret fantasy from frustrated daydreams.

Oh, how she'd wanted to demolish those damned chattering eight balls.

Cilla's head throbbed, and her arms ached. As she swung again and again, she prayed to God to save the life of the boy at her feet, even if it meant the loss of her own.

One of the spheres struck her between the shoulder blades, but she ignored the flash of pain. Eight balls thumped her sides and legs, threatening to report her to the superintendent as they peppered her with bruises. She cried out as one of the balls clocked her kneecap with staggering force.

Tears flowed down her sunken cheeks, but she refused to fall. Knuckles white, she clenched the paddle in a death grip and swung, preventing the malevolent spheres from landing another blow on her motionless charge.

The flames leaped around her, burning through to bare walls, consuming everything...finally catching even the end of her paddle when she swept it through a fiery fall of ceiling tile.

Even as the paddle burned, Cilla kept right on swinging.

*****

Solemnly, the president of the United States of America stepped up to the podium. As the assembled audience fell silent, he took a moment to review the text of his remarks, displayed on the screen of the implant in the palm of his hand.

Newsglobes captured his every move, hovering at a respectful distance. Their all-seeing lenses flexed in and out, perfecting the framing of their shots. Images of the leader of the free world were instantaneously transmitted onto the hivenet, accessible to every mind with the brainware to receive them.

The president looked up, cleared his throat, and began to speak.

"In this world of technological miracles," he said, "knowledge is abundant. Information is downloaded directly into the human mind. Thanks to the hivenet, the sum total of human experience is available to anyone at any time.

"And yet, we have found no substitute for traditional learning," said the president, looking around meaningfully at the attentive faces in the White House rose garden. "No technology can match the magic that occurs in the face-to-face communion between teacher and student.

"Traditional education is the backbone of our nation," said the president, and the audience applauded. "It is because of this that we single out a Teacher of the Year, an example of the excellence that enables our children and nation to flourish."

Again, the audience clapped. At the president's side, Principal Caesar beamed. In deference to the occasion, for once, he had concealed his naked body beneath a suit and tie.

"In this, the final year of the century," said the president, "we will go a step further. In honor of the accomplishments of all our nation's teachers over the past one hundred years, we will single out America's finest teacher not only of the year, but of the century."

The president nodded proudly. "Let me tell you, this woman is more than deserving of the title I am about to bestow upon her."

The audience applauded with rising enthusiasm as the culmination of the ceremony approached.

"She has served with distinction for over fifty years at some of our nation's finest schools," said the president. "During her career, she has helped to mold the minds of some of our most distinguished and accomplished citizens.

"Her contribution to our greatness cannot be overstated," said the president. "By embracing progress while holding fast to the time-tested tenets of American education, she has linked the best of our yesterdays to the best of our tomorrows."

As the crowd applauded, the president consulted his palm screen. "I'm sure you already know her," he said, returning his sincere gaze to his listeners. "Every year for the past decade, she has been named America's Teacher of the Year.

"Now, she is about to receive the highest honor in the land for a member of the noblest profession on Earth. There is no one who deserves it more.

"For excellence in the field of teaching...for contributions beyond measure to the success of our great nation...for unswerving devotion to the children of America...I hereby pronounce Cilla Sullivan Franklin America's Teacher of the Century!"

As the crowd burst into wild applause, the president turned and guided Cilla to the podium. She looked radiant in her frilly white dress, bathed in an aura of bright sunlight that shimmered around her and haloed her silver hair.

"Congratulations, Cilla," said the president, handing her a translucent plaque that pulsed with rainbow light. "And on behalf of all citizens of the United States of America, thank you."

"Thank you, Mr. President," Cilla said softly, peering around at the ring of newsglobes scoping their lenses in her direction. The globes made her nervous, reminding her of the eight-ball parental A.I.s.

"You are a national treasure, Cilla," said the president.

Cilla nodded and smiled, but was unimpressed by the flattery. To her thinking, the whole Teacher of the Century honor was meaningless, given the state of the world of education. How could anyone be honored to be a teacher when the schools were such a joke, when students and principals alike ran naked through the halls and the only learning taking place was the godlings' learning new methods of mayhem?

"Now, Cilla," said the president, the applause fading at the sound of his voice. "I have a surprise for you."

Cilla glanced at the newsglobes again, then forced herself to focus on the president. As unimpressed as she was by the honor she had been given, she still felt a small thrill at being so close to the most powerful man in America.

"Three months ago," he said, "you performed a true act of heroism. When an accident threatened the life of one of your students, you risked your own life to save him."

It was no accident, thought Cilla, but of course she kept it to herself. The party line of the school administration, force-fed to the public by Ludwig's pet, Caesar, seemed to be the only truth that mattered.

"That student," said the president, "Byron Spencer, is alive and well today because of you.

"And he is here today to share in this historic occasion."

Cilla immediately brightened. She couldn't help herself.

It was the one thing she hadn't expected. It was the one thing that could truly make her happy.

As Byron walked out of a nearby door and headed for the podium, the crowd sprang to their feet and applauded like mad. In contrast to the way he had looked three months ago, battered and huddled on the floor of the burning classroom, Byron was bright-eyed and impeccably groomed, wearing a sharp navy blue suit and striped tie. His arms were full of red roses.

At the sight of him, Cilla was overcome with pure joy. He was the only reason she was at the White House that day, the only reason she had kept teaching long enough to qualify for the Teacher of the Century award.

Because of Byron, she had finished out the school year at All Einstein. After the life-threatening incident, he had bravely insisted on staying to complete his senior year. She had been unable to walk away then, knowing that the one good student in the place would be alone at the mercy of the murderous godlings.

Normally, one seventy-five-year-old teacher would not have provided much protection against a school full of techno-savages...but Cilla had been shielded from the godlings until the award ceremony by Caesar's bargain with Ludwig. She had become a guardian angel, using her special status to hold the savages at bay when Byron was endangered. There had been many tense moments, and Byron had taken his share of knocks, but she had managed to get him through his senior year alive.

He was going to graduate. He was going out into the world, and she was sure that he would do great things.

Seeing him there, alive and healthy and brimming with hope, meant far more to Cilla than the plaque in her hand or the applause of her peers or the president of the United States standing at her side.

"These are for you, Miss Franklin," said Byron, handing her the bouquet of red roses. "Thank you for being such a wonderful teacher."

Tears of happiness flowed down her face as she accepted the flowers. She wanted to hug him but held herself back...then gave in and hugged him anyway.

That moment was all the reward she needed. After all the years of futility since the rise of the godlings, she had managed to help one more student, one promising student who loved learning and appreciated her. How wonderful that she could retire on a positive note, reliving one final time the teacher-student bond as it was meant to be.

As she drew back from him, Byron beamed. "There's another surprise, Miss Franklin," he said. "There's someone I'd like you to meet."

Still smiling, Cilla tipped her head inquisitively.

"Come on out, Sara," said Byron, looking toward the door from which he had emerged.

As Cilla followed his gaze, the door opened. A girl stepped out, smiling shyly.

She looked close to Byron's age, and about the same

height. Her sandy, straight hair hung in a glossy fall to the middle of her back, a style that Cilla hadn't seen in years. She wore a pretty blue knee-length sheath, and her green eyes sparkled like pale emeralds.

"This is my younger sister, Sara," said Byron. "Sara, meet my teacher, Cilla Franklin."

Shifting the roses and plaque to free an arm, Cilla shook Sara's hand. It felt soft as the petal of a flower in her grip.

"It's a pleasure to meet you, Miss Franklin," said Sara.

"It's a pleasure to meet you, too, Sara," said Cilla, staring at the girl. Byron hadn't been kidding when he had promised a surprise. Cilla could not remember him ever mentioning a sister...and yet, as she searched Sara's features, she could see that the family resemblance was unmistakable.

"Sara has been home schooled until now," said Byron, "but next year, she'll be attending All Einstein High School. She'll be a senior."

"I can't wait to have you as a teacher," said Sara. "Byron's told me so much about you. You're the only reason I'm going to All Einstein instead of continuing my home schooling."

Cilla kept staring, completely thrown for a loop. She didn't know what to say.

The girl gazed hopefully up at her. "I brought you something," she said, pulling a hand from behind her back. "So we can get off on the right foot."

It was a shiny red apple.

As the audience laughed and applauded, Cilla stared at the apple in Sara's hand. She was truly on the spot, now. Though she had filed her retirement papers, Caesar had neglected to tell Byron that she wouldn't be teaching next year. Cilla had never mentioned it to Byron, either, and now she was stuck.

When she shot a look in Caesar's direction, he leaned over and patted her shoulder. "We're all excited about next year," he said to Cilla. "Another batch of fresh faces for you to work your magic on."

Then, he leaned closer and whispered in her ear. "And no Ludwig."

Which was supposed to mean that she was in the clear, that the death sentence was null and void, but she knew better. Ludwig's godlings could take her in the street, or at home...and there would be another horde to replace them in school the next year. She had seen them in the halls already, the eleventh graders, naked and tattooed and looking every bit as inhuman as the last bunch.

But then there was Sara Spencer.

"Sara aced her home school equivalence exams," Byron said proudly. "She got the highest scores on record."

Sara blushed and looked at her feet, then back up at Cilla.

Cilla could feel the intelligence radiating from the girl's emerald eyes. Even if Byron hadn't mentioned her test scores, Cilla would have known that she was in the presence of another excellent student, another hard-working and respectful young person, another hope for the future.

Her brother's sister, through and through.

And she was a home schooler, inexperienced in the savage ways of the merciless tribal school culture. When it came to interacting with the godlings, she might as well have had "fresh meat" tattooed on her forehead.

Sara fixed her with a gaze that was full of need and frank adoration. "I can't wait till next year," she said softly.

Cilla's heart melted. Abandoning that child to the godlings would be like offering up her own daughter to be killed.

In that moment, Cilla knew that she would be back in front of a classroom after all. She did not know how much protection she could offer this gentle, brilliant soul, but she knew that she could not turn her back on her.

She had risked her own life for Byron Spencer. If she did any less for Byron's sister, she would not be able to live with herself, anyway.

Cilla took the apple from Sara's hand. "See you in the fall," she said with a smile.

*****

One week after the ceremony at the White House, Principal Caesar refilled his glass with champagne in the secret sub-basement of All Einstein High School. Replacing the bottle on the table, he leaned forward and clinked glasses with Superintendent Alexander.

"To the Teacher of the Century," Caesar said with an oily grin. "The pride of All Einstein High."

"To Cilla Franklin," said Alexander. "Where would we be without her?"

The naked men drained their glasses, finishing off with mutual sighs of satisfaction. Alexander drew fine cigars from the humidor and passed one over to Caesar.

"Congratulations on the enrollment numbers for next year," said Caesar. "Having the Teacher of the Century on staff is quite a draw."

"Word is, our state funding will be through the roof," said Alexander, clipping the end of his cigar. "So I want to see some belt-tightening around this place."

Caesar accepted the clipper from him with a laugh. "We'll cut till it hurts," he said, "and pass the savings along to ourselves."

The men lit their cigars, then relaxed back into the depths of their high-backed leather chairs. A holographic fire danced in the faux fireplace between them.

"I can't thank you enough for keeping Franklin on board," said Alexander, puffing out a great draft of smoke.

"Don't thank me," said Caesar, and then he clapped his hands together twice.

A boy with sandy hair and green eyes hurried to his side, smiling expectantly. He wore an old-style servant's uniform with black coat and tails, knee-high knickers over white stockings, and ruffles at the collar and wrists.

"Thank Byron," said Caesar with a sneer.

Alexander chuckled. "Thank you, Byron," he said through a cloud of cigar smoke.

"You're welcome, sir," Byron Spencer said happily. "Can I get you gentlemen anything?"

"Bend over," said Caesar.

The boy immediately bent at the waist. Principal Caesar leaned forward and pressed his thumb on a spot in the middle of Byron's scalp.

At his touch, the scalp split apart. Panels slid smoothly

aside, exposing a rectangular opening in the boy's head.

Tiny lights flickered inside in a high-speed flurry.

"Ah, the miracle of robotics," said Caesar, peering into the hole in Byron's scalp.

"The miracle of false hope," said Alexander.

"Good boy," said Caesar, tapping the ash from the tip of his cigar into the hole.

"Should you be doing that?" said Alexander. "He cost us a pretty penny."

"He'll process and excrete it as synthetic feces." Caesar closed the port and settled back into his chair. "Stand up, Byron."

Byron Spencer did as he was told.

Caesar clapped his hands again, and Sara Spencer trotted into the room wearing a maid's costume with a tiny skirt. She carried a feather duster in one hand and smiled serenely.

"We owe Sara a debt of gratitude, as well," said Caesar. "She's done her brother one better, bless her heart. Thanks to her, Cilla's ours for another year."

"And what about after that?" said Alexander.

"Funny you should ask," said Caesar, puffing on his cigar. "Between you and me, I hear that Byron and Sara's mom and dad might just have another little one on the way."

The naked men laughed loudly in their cloud of smoke.

"And now, if you'll excuse me," said Principal Caesar, pushing himself up out of his leather chair, "I have an appointment for a tattoo removal."

"Which one?" said Alexander.

Caesar pointed at his male organ. "Ludwig's graduated.

Out with the old, in with the new."

"You'll have it replaced?"

"As soon as I find out who the new chief is," said Caesar.

"It's good to have friends in high places," said Alexander.

"You never know when you'll need someone to do you a favor," said Caesar with a knowing smile. "Like torch a classroom or reprogram some A.I.s."

Alexander laughed and raised his cigar. "To the godlings!" he roared.

"To education!" chimed in Caesar. "It oughtta be a crime!"

As the life pours out of me, faster faster with each beat of my heart, I know at last that my son has truly gone to a better place. In the shimmering window that floats above me, I see him smiling, surrounded by loving faces and outstretched arms.

A better place. A place away from me.

Still, it's hard to let go. I've come so far since he first disappeared, changed so much...and yet so little, I know, deep down. I couldn't go all the way, couldn't become the father he needed no matter how hard I tried.

This was the best I could do for him. Killing and being killed.

I hope it's enough.

Mike the Future Man crouches beside me, and I wish so bad he'd give me one last human touch, just touch my head or pat my shoulder or something, but he doesn't. Maybe he thinks I don't deserve it, or maybe he's afraid he'll catch something. Whatever.

But at least he says one last thing to send me on my way. Kind words, and I'm grateful because I know it's the only epitaph I'll ever have.

"You did the right thing, Sonny," says Mike. "Rest in peace."

I have one more look through the window, and I see my boy lifted high and carried off toward gleaming towers of gold and silver, radiant with light. It's not Heaven, but it looks like the next best thing.

Not that I'd ever see him again if he was in Heaven, anyway. I know better, after the life I've lived. One right can't undo a million wrongs.

Not even if what I've done is save the world. Not even that is enough.

"Thank you," says Mike the Future Man, getting to his feet. "We'll take good care of him."

"It's...his birthday," I say, my voice so hoarse it doesn't sound like me anymore.

"I know," says Mike.

"Tell Sean...I love him," I say.

Mike takes a last look at me and turns toward the shimmering window. "That I won't do," he says, and then he leaps through the window and is gone.

And so is the window.

And so am I, through a different window...one that opens in my mind, giving way to silence and darkness and emptiness.

*****

My boy disappeared while I was stoned on crack, passed out in the bed of some woman whose name I don't even remember.

I left Sean alone in our apartment, if you want to call it that. I didn't think anything of it, even though he was just five years old...or I guess it'd be more accurate to say I didn't give a damn. I had more important things on my mind, like getting stoned out of my mind.

I never did find out exactly how he got taken. Maybe he let the guy in, or maybe he just wandered off. All I know is, when I stumbled in the next morning, the door was wide open and Sean was gone.

This didn't make much of an impression on me, believe it or not. I figured he'd turn up sooner or later. Maybe he was at the neighbor lady's or running around with the other kids in the building. Whatever.

The truth is, Sean didn't make much of an impression on me at all back then, whether I was stoned or not. I tuned him out like the noise from a neighbor's TV set or the traffic outside my window. Fed him candy bars and cereal and beat his ass when he wouldn't shut up. Locked him in a closet when I had company.

Raised him the only way I knew how.

I'd told his crackhead mother I didn't want him, and she'd dumped him off on me anyway. The way I saw it, he was lucky not to be out on the streets with her.

Lucky.

Later, after I changed, I thought back on how I was and how I'd treated him, and it was enough to make me sick to my stomach. I even asked Mike the Future Man if he could send me back in time to knock some sense into my sorry ass before it was too late.

Mike told me even if he could have sent me back, the old me was such a dumbass it wouldn't have made any difference...and I know he was right.

*****

I wish I could say I got my act together before long and started hunting my boy, but that'd be a lie. It took old Mrs. Pendleton from next-door to get my ass in gear, and that not even till the next day. The day after the day after Sean went away.

Like I said, I wasn't worried. The thought that he might never come back didn't occur to me. The main thing on my mind was hitting the street and scoring some more crack.

Finding happiness, in other words.

So my first day without Sean went pretty much like all the days with him. I pawned a watch from a guy I'd mugged and used the cash to buy my high. I smoked my pipe in an alley and spent the rest of the day making the rounds. Sat in the park with the rest of the crackheads and drunks and retards, talking nonsense. Got another buzz thanks to a ladyfriend who shared her crack with me. Watched another day go by like a boring movie I wasn't paying much attention to.

And when I got home...

Well, the truth is, when I got home, I didn't notice that Sean still wasn't there. I fell asleep in front of the TV eating dry cereal, and the boy didn't cross my mind for a minute.

Even though it was his favorite cereal I was eating.

*****

The next morning, I woke up to someone pounding on my apartment door. I tried to ignore it, but it just got louder.

Then, I heard Mrs. Pendleton yelling in the hallway, telling me to get out there or she'd go get the super to open the door. I knew she'd do it, too, so I dragged my ass out of bed.

"Where's that boy of yours?" she said. "Where's Sean? He missed his readin' lesson yesterday and now today, too."

The only thing that sunk in at first was that I didn't know she was even giving him reading lessons. "What're you talkin' about?" I said, rubbing my eyes so hard they squeaked.

Mrs. Pendleton smacked my hand away from my eyes. "Wake up, dumbskull!" she said, her own eyes looking about ten times normal size from behind her thick glasses. "Don't you even know where your own *boy* is?"

Mrs. Pendleton was like a hundred years old and

weighed about twenty-five pounds. She'd probably snap like a wishbone if I hit her like I wanted to...but the real reason I didn't pop her one was that she intimidated me, believe it or not. Other people put me down and beat me down, but she was the only one who could make me feel small.

I shrugged. "I thought he was with you," I said, thinking I'd make her feel bad by shifting the blame onto her.

"How long has he been gone?" she said, her voice getting louder and angrier with every word.

"About a day," I said, trying to downplay it.

"And you don't know where he is?"

"Maybe he's down at Mrs. Dugan's," I said, "or out with those Valozzi kids."

Mrs. Pendleton's voice grew quiet all of a sudden. "I already checked," she said, "because I knew your crackhead fool self would be too lazy to do it. No one in the building's seen Sean for two days."

"Wow," I said, shaking my head, trying to act like this news was making an impact on me...which it should have, but it wasn't.

"Have you called the police?" said Mrs. Pendleton.

"I was just getting ready to," I lied, looking over my shoulder in the direction of the phone.

"Then it's a good thing I'm here," said Mrs. Pendleton, pushing past me into my apartment. "I'll make sure you don't dial the wrong number and end up talkin' to one of your crackhead buddies instead."

I sighed and followed her in. The sad part was, she was

right about me wanting to call someone about crack instead of calling the cops about my son.

*****

By the time the NYPD was done with me, I thought I would've been better off calling my crackhead buddies.

No surprise there.

They didn't seem to be real sympathetic. They took down what I told them, but I knew their minds were made up. From the questions they asked and the looks on their faces, I could tell they thought that I'd done something to Sean.

Sold him for drugs, maybe. Killed him on purpose or accidentally and got rid of the body.

Same old same old.

If Mrs. Pendleton hadn't been in the apartment with us, I doubt they'd even have pretended to be interested in doing anything to find Sean other than beating a confession out of me. Mrs. Pendleton, though...she pushed like a boozehound demanding one more drink after last call. She said she was going to check in with their boss every hour on the hour until they found Sean. She gave them photos from her own scrapbook, because I didn't have a single picture of him. She said that she might be an old woman, but by God if they didn't give this baby as much attention as some rich child from the suburbs, she had ways of making them wish they were dead with a capital "P" as in "pain."

They treated her respectfully after that, but I saw them give each other funny looks on their way out like they could barely hold back the laughter. They almost forgot to take Sean's photos with them, and Mrs. Pendleton had to hobble out and call them back to get them.

So I didn't expect much help from the cops. If anything, I figured they'd haul me in and convict me of child killing before the week was out.

And frankly, even in the hazy frame of mind I was in back then, I couldn't blame them for treating me that way. I hated them...but I understood their point of view.

If I was in their shoes, I would've thought I'd done it, too.

*****

Mrs. Pendleton wasn't stupid, I'll give her that. I don't think she had much more confidence in the cops than I did.

As soon as they left, she started talking about getting the neighborhood to band together and search for Sean. She wanted to take pictures door to door and ask everyone if they'd seen him. She wanted to put up photos on every lamppost and bus bench and phone booth and in every business and playground and park. She was going to call the ministers and priests and rabbis and gangbangers and newspapers and TV stations. Whatever it took.

And she expected me to do my part. I think she thought my being afraid of her would outweigh my selfishness and stupidity.

Maybe it would have, if I hadn't been jonesing at the time.

Mrs. Pendleton barked at me for like a half hour about

how it was time for me to step up and how my baby's life depended on it. How even though I'd been good for nothing, I still had it in me like all God's creatures to be good for something, even if it was just one thing...and that something was saving the life of a precious child.

When the lecture was over, she told me she was going next-door to get her purse and her sweater, and then the two of us were going to get the ball rolling. Time was running out for my little boy, she said.

Time was running out for me, too. The I-need-crack alarm clock in the pit of my stomach was going off like crazy, bringing on the sweats and the shakes.

I was gone before she got back to my apartment. I may have said something about Sean to my buddies on the street while I was getting high, but that was all I did to search for my son that day.

*****

Early the next morning, I woke to the sound of more pounding...this time from the wall behind my bed. I rolled over, pulling the pillow over my head to block out the noise, but it did no good. More than anything, I wanted to fall back asleep, but the pounding pounding pounding wouldn't let me rest...and then I heard Mrs. Pendleton's voice hollering from the other side of the wall, from inside her apartment.

Answer your damn door Sonny, get up and answer your damn door you miserable lowlife moron it's about your boy it's news about Sean not that you give a damn answer your *door answer* your *door*.

"Shut up!" I said, pounding my fist on the wall. "Shut up!"

There was a pause, and then her voice came through clearer than ever, as if she'd gotten right up to the wall and cupped her hands around her mouth and shouted as loud as she could.

"The police are here!" she said. "It's about Sean!"

I really wanted to stay in bed after hearing that. I would have, if I hadn't been stupid enough to let Mrs. Pendleton know I was there. If I didn't go out and face them, they'd get in sooner or later and get me.

As I pulled on a pair of jeans, I thought about ducking out the window and down the fire escape. This was the time I'd known was coming, the time when the cops show up to bring me in and squeeze that murder confession out of me. It was the only reason I could think that they were there.

But going out the window would just put off the inevitable. Either I paid up now or paid up later...and running would just make it worse for me later.

So I went to the door.

And what happened after that was terrible, but not in the way I'd expected.

*****

Even as they walked me down the hallway toward the morgue, it didn't hit me. Step step step like a dream like a blurry memory step step

Step.

But something buzzing deep inside me something wrong.

Buzzing louder later, after they let me go and I wrapped my hands around the crack pipe and burned my thumb on the lighter and breathed deep.

Step.

At the door of my apartment: We need you to come down and identify.

Getting closer to the double doors and everything was too loud but faraway at the same time. I walked between the two cops but they kept their distance, and I didn't think about my son I thought about someone else.

Later, my brain was fried and the sun was down and I thought of him again, I thought of my father.

Step.

Inside the morgue, they rolled out the drawer and peeled back the sheet and I dove into that face with a panic I'd never expected

Before they pulled the sheet away, time stopped. The outline of a nose, a chin, a shoulder. Someone was saying, are you ready?

Dove into that face with a panic but it blurred at first and I wondered if something had wiped away the features.

Step.

At my apartment in the morning, it should have meant something right away something big but it didn't. We need you to come down and identify a body.

Hands cupped around the crack pipe, sun beating down, I tried to remember his face my father's face but all I saw was a blur

And then the child's face cleared. It came into focus.

People beating me in the street that night laughing calling me baby killer and I curled up in a ball and these people these people were my friends. Thinking about my father but not because he beat me he never beat me but because he was my friend too I thought but he wasn't.

The outline of a nose under the sheet. Are you ready? The cop reaching for the sheet. I'm jonesing and I wonder how long it will be until I can go get high again.

The cop rolling out the drawer. Would he give me twenty bucks if I asked him?

We walked into the morgue and I thought to myself I swear to God I thought to myself this could be a good thing, the weight of him gone and me being free and not having to throw money away on that damn kid it would be a relief.

But when the sheet peeled away, I dove into that face.

When it came into focus, the buzzing got louder.

Step step step down the hallway.

The face looked just like Sean's and I stood there and stared at it and someone said, is that him? Is that him? Is that him?

Is that your son?

Later, in the street, I thought they were done with me but then they all pissed on me at once laughing.

Yes, that's him, I said, reaching out my hand to touch his face and I didn't feel that relief I thought I'd feel and my hand was shaking and just as my fingers brushed his cheek

Deep deep breath on the crack pipe in the sunlight

Like magic, just as my fingers brushed his cheek

Twenty, thirty, a hundred years ago the blurry face I still can't see the smell of cigarettes the roughness of his cheek my father's cheek and it's as if

It's as if when he disappeared he took my memory of him with him.

Like magic, just as my fingers brushed the dead boy's cheek, his face became someone else's. It's not him I say it's not Sean.

Step.

But it could have been. It still could be. Same room same drawer same sheet same is that him? same outline of a nose same cops same me.

And then for a moment I wondered if I was standing there at all or if I was looking into the future somehow having a vision of what was to come it felt like a dream.

Buzzing deep inside. I got high but the buzzing wouldn't stop. Got my ass kicked but the buzzing wouldn't stop.

And when they were done with me in the street when my crackhead buddies were done with me I threw up and it felt like I was throwing up everything, everything I was everything I wanted everything except the outline of the nose under the sheet.

And in that one clear moment the first in a hundred million years I finally realized that there wasn't enough crack in the world to make things better and not only that but there never had been.

*****

When you watch the moon on a clear night, the only way you can tell it's moving is when you look away and then look back and see it's in a new place in the sky. It doesn't seem to be going anywhere when you stare at it, but it's moving all the time.

If someone had been watching me crawl home after getting beat by my onetime buddies, I bet I would've looked like that, like I was hardly moving at all. Likewise, in the days to come, I'm sure I didn't look like I was changing much inside.

But I was.

I laid around the apartment and watched TV and drank, and that's what I mean when I say I didn't look like I was changing. Didn't lift a finger to look for my son. Waited for my I-need-crack alarm to go off, which it did pretty much right on schedule.

But what was different was that I didn't answer the alarm. I didn't jump up and run out and buy my high or run out and find money to buy my high or try to find someone to sweet talk into letting me share their high.

The first day like that was easy, because I was too beat-up and sick to leave the bed, let alone the apartment. The next day was a little less easy, because now I wasn't hurting quite so bad, but the jones was like a thousand times worse.

But I didn't go out for a taste or a second hand whiff or a contact high. I thought about it a lot, even went for the door a bunch of times, but I never made it out.

It was that dead boy in the morgue that did it, the one I'd thought at first was Sean. The nose poking up the sheet. It kept coming back to me.

The way I'd felt before I'd realized it wasn't Sean. Like someone had ripped me off, cheated me out of something that was worth more than I'd thought. A piece of junk that had always been in the way had turned out to be valuable.

Even though the boy in the morgue hadn't been Sean, I felt like when I first saw him I was seeing my son for the first time, too. Seeing him as a human being instead of a noise or a pain or an obstacle.

Remembering he had a face.

It was like my boy had been walking around his whole life with a sheet over him, walking around like that for so long that I'd thought he was nothing but sheet...and by the time I finally remembered someone was under there and pulled off the sheet, he really was gone.

But here's what really got me. People thought I'd sold him for crack...and the more I thought about it, the more I realized it was true. I'd sold off everyone and everything a long time ago, sold it all for crack.

And now I was empty-handed, and everyone and everything that truly could have made me happy was scattered around the world or broken or dead or fading away with each passing moment like a dying high.

Like my son.

And though I had hated myself for as long as I could remember, hated myself for a million different reasons, now I had one more. I hated myself for what had happened to him.

I hated myself so much I never wanted to smoke crack again...and I hated myself so much I wanted to get high immediately and never come back.

That was where my head was when Mike the Future Man came along.

*****

The thing about people from the future is you can't tell they're from the future by looking at them. When I first met Mike, I had no reason not to believe that he was who he said he was.

Mike the F.B.I. Man.

He was standing outside the door of my apartment when I opened it on my way out to get stoned...or not...just standing there, and he caught me off guard, and I jumped.

My first thought was that he was trouble, showing up like that in the middle of the night, and I should duck back in my apartment and slam the door shut. Before I could do that, though, he shouldered himself between me and the door and shoved a badge in my face.

"F.B.I.," he said softly, like he didn't want to wake the neighbors. "Mike Rafferty. Can I come in? I'm here about your son."

I had the feeling I didn't have much choice about letting him in, but I was still worried enough about the guy's intentions to try to blow him off. "It's pretty late," I said. "How 'bout you come back tomorrow?"

"Sorry about the late hour," he said, but I didn't think he looked too sorry. "I just need five minutes."

I took a long look at his face, wondering if it was the last face I'd ever see. His eyes were crystal blue like ice, but bloodshot and sad as a sleepless junkie's. He looked like he hadn't shaved for days. His lips were tight and barely moved when he spoke, like he was always grinding his teeth.

He looked like he had a lot on his mind. He looked like he didn't like me. I thought it was possible the badge was fake and one of the things on his mind was to hurt me or worse.

But I let him in. Partly, I was glad for an excuse not to give in to the crack again. Partly, I didn't care what the hell happened to me anymore.

"I'm looking for your son," he said. "Do you have an article of clothing he's worn?"

"He's been gone for like a week," I said. "How come you're just showin' up now?"

"I'm a specialist," said Mike. "Late stage missing persons recovery. I need something your son wore often. It would be better if you haven't washed it since the last time he had it on."

That wouldn't be a problem, since I hardly ever washed anything. "You want it for the dogs to sniff?" I said, rummaging through a pile of dirty clothes on the couch. "Bloodhounds or whatever?"

"Something like that," said Mike as I handed him one of Sean's T-shirts.

Mike reached into his pocket and pulled out something that looked like a little silver cell phone. He flipped up the cover, then tapped a fingertip on the tiny keypad and pointed the phone's antenna at the shirt.

I walked over to look over his shoulder, but all I got was a quick glance at the flashing blue screen before he turned away to block my view. The flickering numbers and images on the screen looked like gobbledygook to me.

Without looking up from his phone, Mike handed back Sean's T-shirt. "What about the dogs?" I said.

"No dogs," said Mike. "We're high-tech these days."

Staring at the screen, he turned in a slow circle, then stopped. The phone chirped a couple times, then gave off a high, steady hum like the tone that comes on over the color bars on TV stations late at night.

"Okay," said Mike, lowering the phone but not closing the cover. "That'll do it. Thanks for your help."

He headed for the door, and I hurried around to cut him off. "Wait a minute," I said. "You can track him with that thing?"

"I'll notify you if we have any new information," said Mike, trying to angle around me.

"Just hold on," I said, staying between him and the door. "If that thing you've got there can follow his trail, why didn't somebody use it to find him on day one?"

"It's a prototype," said Mike, staring at me with his crystal blue, bloodshot eyes. "One of a kind. This is its first field test."

"Oh," I said, looking down at the device. "So is it working?"

"I'll let you know," said Mike, and then he pushed past me and opened the door. "Goodnight now."

As I watched him start off down the hall, I figured he was too glued to his one-of-a-kind cell phone for it not to be working. He was moving off fast, like his toy had caught the scent and he was following my boy's trail.

Though I'd never heard of a machine that could track

someone like that, I was willing to believe that the F.B.I. had one...which meant that there might be a chance that Mike could find Sean. Maybe he could already tell if Sean was dead or alive.

A few days earlier, I never would have considered doing anything at that moment other than hitting the street to score some crack. Burn out some more brain cells and sooner or later I'd get rid of the ones containing my memories of Sean and eventually the memories of myself. I think that had been my goal all along: forgetting I existed, disappearing even from my own mind, the ultimate escape. Disappearing like my father.

But now...

But now, I wanted to go with Mike. I wanted to find my son.

Ducking back into my apartment, I grabbed my switchblade and stuffed it in the pocket of my jeans. Then, I hustled back out into the hallway and down the stairs after the F.B.I. man.

I left the apartment door wide open because there was nothing inside worth taking, not anymore. Even if there had been, it wouldn't have mattered, because the way things turned out, I would never set foot in the place again.

*****

When I caught up with him out on the street, Mike told me to leave him alone, he couldn't take a civilian along on an investigation. When I insisted on going with him, he got tougher, telling me he'd make a call and have me taken away.

When I still wouldn't back down, Mike the F.B.I. man got downright nasty.

"Listen," he said. "You're not part of this anymore. You're a filthy, drug-addicted, loathsome piece of garbage, and if it wasn't for you, this child wouldn't be in danger right now."

"Tell me something I don't know," I said.

"It makes me sick, seeing someone like you with a child. There are people out there who want a child more than anything and can't have one, and someone like you is lucky enough to have one and treats him like an animal. Less than an animal."

"Then what do you care if you find him?" I said.

"I care about the child," said Mike. "Not you."

"That's cool," I said, pulling my switchblade and popping out the knife. "But I'm going with you."

Mike didn't smile very often, but he did then. "You realize you're threatening a federal agent, right? You realize you'll go away forever for that."

"Whatever," I said, wishing I had a lot of crack at that particular moment. "The way I've been living, it'll be an improvement."

"No joke," said Mike. "And if you pull that thing on me again, I'll just flat out kill you on the spot."

"Just find my boy first," I said. "Take me with you."

Mike shook his head and snort-laughed. "How can I say no to such a model parent?" he said with a sneer.

So we went on together, and I kept a close eye on him, and I know he kept a close eye on me.

*****

As we stood in front of the dumpster, lit by the headlights of Mike's car, my stomach twisted the way it always did when I needed a fix, only it wasn't because I needed a fix this time.

Mike's cell phone thing was pinging like a pinball machine. We had followed its signal halfway across town, followed it to an alley behind a warehouse, and now it was going crazy.

Which meant that maybe we had found him.

As Mike threw open the lid, I felt like I was back in the morgue with the cop peeling back the sheet. Mike looked over the rim, but I stayed back and looked away, thinking I should have stayed home after all, thinking I should have stayed stoned and oblivious.

Living the way I did, I had seen a lot of terrible things in my life. If Sean was in that dumpster, I could imagine what might have been done to him and what he might look like. I knew what could be done to a child or to anyone on a dark night without a friendly face around.

Even though I had cared so little about him for his whole life, and even at that moment, let's face it, I hadn't changed all that much deep down, I was afraid of seeing him the way I imagined he might look.

"There's something in here, all right," said Mike, aiming the cell phone's antenna into the dumpster. Stepping back, he found a crate and pushed it over so he could stand on it.

Mike touched a control on his phone, and the signal stopped in mid-ping. He dropped the phone in the pocket of his windbreaker, then leaned over the rim of the dumpster and fished around inside.

"Okay," he said finally, stretching down to reach for something. "Got it."

I held my breath. My stomach twisted harder. I'd insisted on coming along, had pulled a knife on an F.B.I. agent to get there, but I couldn't force myself to look in the direction of the dumpster.

Mike grunted. "Here we go," he said. "Good news and bad news."

I tried to say something, but I couldn't. My mouth felt like it was stuffed full of cotton.

"Good news is, your son isn't here," said Mike.

Turning, I saw him swing a brown paper bag over the edge of the dumpster. Opening the bag, he pulled out a child-size red T-shirt and bluejeans.

A Sean-size T-shirt and bluejeans.

"Tracker picked up the DNA on the clothes," said Mike. "This was what he was wearing when he was taken."

"What's the bad news?" I said.

"There's some blood," said Mike. "Some of Sean's blood on the clothes."

"How much is some?" I said. "A lot?"

Mike shook his head. "Not a lot, but it isn't a good sign."

I nodded. I was just glad he hadn't found Sean's body in the dumpster. "So what's next?" I said.

"Scan the clothes," said Mike. "Get a reading on Sean's abductor from any DNA traces he left on them. Pick up the trail again."

"Good," I said, wondering where Sean was at that moment, wondering if I'd still end up seeing him looking the way I'd imagined him in the dumpster. "That sounds good."

"Yeah," Mike said sarcastically. "Thanks for the stamp of approval."

*****

Hours later, in the bathroom of a gas station on the Interstate, Mike waved the cell phone's antenna at the floor behind a filthy toilet. This time, with no possibility of my boy's dead body being found, I was able to watch as he worked.

The phone pinged and whistled, and Mike watched the screen. "They were here," he said. "Days ago."

Mike wet the tips of his fingers with his tongue, then dabbed them on the floor behind the base of the toilet. He raised his hand toward me so I could see the tiny dark curls stuck to his fingertips.

"The abductor cut Sean's hair," said Mike. "Changed his clothes and cut his hair to make him harder to recognize."

I looked around the bathroom, wondering what had gone through Sean's mind while he was in there. Fear, maybe? Confusion?

Relief? Maybe he had been glad to get the hell away from me. Maybe, the day he got taken was the best day of his life.

At first, anyway.

"How many days ago?" I said. "Can you tell?"

Mike got up and slipped the phone in his pocket. "Four days," he said, brushing the clippings of Sean's hair from his fingers. "Give or take a couple hours."

"So how're we ever going to catch up to them?" I said, feeling nervous. "If they're four days ahead of us, I mean."

"They've stopped," said Mike as he washed his hands. "I've got a fix on them, and they aren't moving."

"Where?" I said. "How far?"

"West Virginia," said Mike, drying his hands on the loop of cloth towel that sagged out of the dispenser on the wall. "Nine hours, maybe ten."

I pointed at the pocket he'd put the phone in. "And does that thing tell you anything else? Anything about Sean?"

Mike shrugged. "He's alive. That's all I know."

"Good," I said. "That's good."

"Maybe not," said Mike.

"Maybe not what?" I said. "Not alive?"

"Maybe not good," said Mike. "A lot can happen in four days. You still want to go with me?"

I thought about it for a minute, then nodded.

"Not the answer I was going for," said Mike. "But okay." Then, he pushed out the door and I followed him, blinking against the glaring sunlight.

*****

I couldn't tear my eyes from the motor home's windows, watching shadows move in the light from behind the curtains.

Watching for a glimpse of my boy, because Mike said he was inside.

Inside and alive.

We sat in Mike's car with the lights and engine off, parked on a campsite across the dirt road and catty-corner from the motor home. We had driven twelve hours to get there, stopping only to take fresh scans at diners and gas stations where the cell phone told us Sean and his kidnapper had been.

Mike said we were lucky that they hadn't traveled further, and at a service station in a town in Pennsylvania, we understood why. The motor home had broken down there, and a mechanic told us it had taken two days to fix. The cell phone led us to traces of Sean and his kidnapper all around town—at a restaurant, a playground, a movie house, a motel. Unfortunately, it couldn't tell us anything about what condition Sean was in while he was there.

Or fortunately.

And now, in a deserted campground in the backwoods mountains of West Virginia, we had found him. He was maybe thirty yards away, separated from us only by the windows and thin metal walls of the motor home.

"You stay here," said Mike, pulling some kind of doodad out of his windbreaker pocket. It had grips that fit over his fingers like brass knuckles and a glassy red lens that curved from pinky to forefinger. "Don't move until I give you the all-clear."

I didn't think it would be a problem staying put. Now that I was this close to Sean, I was having doubts about seeing him again.

As Mike slipped out of the car and quietly closed the door, I wondered how it would be coming face to face with my boy. I wondered if he would be happy to see me after the way I'd treated him all his life.

If I was him, I thought, I wouldn't be too happy.

Then there was the matter of what he had to look forward to. I'd finally realized he deserved better than how I'd treated him...but I couldn't say for sure that things would be any better for him with me than they'd been before.

I knew I'd changed—the fact that I was thinking about him at all was proof of that—but I also knew I was on thin ice and could change right back in a heartbeat. I just knew it. Back in the same crappy apartment and the same crappy life with the same crappy people and drugs around, it might not take very much for me to slide back down the hill.

If that happened, I thought, about the only improvement for Sean from where he was now was that I wasn't a child molester...if the guy who had taken him was even that.

Maybe, the best thing I could do for Sean was to stay away from him. Maybe, it would be better for him if I just ran off into the woods and let Mike find him a new home.

If I just disappeared from his life like my father had from mine.

Then again, look how I turned out.

*****

I think, if Mike had been sitting there beside me, and I had asked him if I should disappear into the woods, he would have told me without hesitation to get lost. No question. He hadn't wanted me along to begin with.

The funny thing was, if I hadn't been there, he would have ended up dead. Stayed dead, I guess I should say.

I'm not sure what tipped off the kidnapper that Mike was out there, but he knew. Maybe he heard the gravel crunch under Mike's feet, or maybe he happened to peek out through a gap in the curtains at just the right moment to see Mike sneaking up.

All I know is I didn't have any warning about what was going to happen. I didn't see any movement inside the motor home to make me think the guy was about to kick open the door and blow a hole in Mike's chest.

One minute, Mike was creeping along the side of the motor home, about to reach for the door handle. The next minute, the door flew open and the guy jumped out, blasting Mike dead on with a sawed-off shotgun.

I saw the flash from the muzzle and heard the shot crack like a thunderclap. By the light from inside the motor home, I could see pieces of Mike explode from his back.

His body seemed to fall in slow motion. The guy in the doorway looked around, then bolted back inside and swung the door shut.

The motor home's tail lights flicked on as he started the engine.

For a moment, as the motor home lurched out of its parking space, hoses and cables tearing free of the campsite's hookups, I thought about driving after it. My son was in there; the least I could do was follow him and try to figure out a way to help him.

Then, I remembered: Mike had the keys.

So I sat there and watched as the motor home lumbered away, carrying Sean away from me for what could have been the last time.

*****

As the motor home's tail lights rolled off into the night, I got out of the car and hurried over to Mike. I was sure he was dead, but I thought he might still do me some good...or his cell phone might, anyway.

When I got to him, he looked about as bad as I'd thought he would, though I couldn't see everything in the darkness. Most of his chest had been blown away, exposing blood and bone and meat in a mangled mess.

I can't say I felt bad for the guy, because I hardly knew him and he had hated my guts...but I wished he hadn't gotten killed. I couldn't fool myself that I had much chance of helping Sean on my own, even if I had the super cell phone and even if I could figure out how to use it.

Hunkering down beside Mike, I reached into the pocket of his windbreaker and fished around for the phone. It must have been in the other pocket, but at least I found his car keys.

I stuffed the keys in my pants pocket and reached over his body to get to the other pocket of his windbreaker... but I didn't make it. Something grabbed my wrist, and I screamed when I realized what it was.

I mean *screamed*.

His hand. It was Mike's hand that grabbed me.

*****

Heart pounding, I tore my wrist from his grip and fell back to the ground, then scrambled to my feet. It didn't seem possible that a guy with such a huge hole blown in him could still be alive.

But when I looked at his face, I saw him blink. I saw his lips move like he was trying to tell me something.

Shaking like an old-timer walking home from the bank through junkie territory, I moved back over to Mike and slowly got down on my knees beside him. I hung back a moment, then lowered my ear to his lips to try to hear what he was saying.

"Pants...pocket," he whispered, his voice so soft I could barely make out the words. "Cylinder."

"Silver what?" I said, leaning closer.

"*Cylinder*," said Mike. "Aim it...at the wound. Press the...plunger. Hurry."

I knew that nothing was going to do him any good at that point, but I played along. I owed him for tracking down my boy, so I figured why not humor his dying request.

Crawling to his hips, I plunged a hand into one of his pants pockets...but found nothing. Leaning over him, I reached into the other pocket.

And brought out what looked like a black asthma inhaler.

It felt heavy and smooth, like glass or metal. A thicker cylinder fit over a slimmer cylinder with a nozzle in the base, and the thicker half moved when I pressed it, like the plunger of an inhaler.

Trying not to look too hard into the chest wound, I raised the device over it and aimed the nozzle downward. I was shaking so bad, I had to use both hands to steady the thing and keep from dropping it.

Then, I squeezed the plunger.

A cone of glowing blue liquid sprayed into the cavity in Mike's chest, spattering the shattered bone and chewed-up organs. The liquid clung where it fell, lighting the gaping wound with an eerie turquoise glow.

I wasn't sure how long to spray, so I kept squeezing until the last drops sputtered out of the nozzle. I shook the device and tried to push out some more, but it was empty.

Leaning back on my heels, I stared into the glowing wound and wondered why the hell Mike had told me to do it. I couldn't guess what the spray had been meant for or why Mike had used his last breath to tell me to use it.

Then, as I watched, things started to happen in Mike's wound.

The glowing blue liquid spread out, oozing into every gap and clump and crease and growing brighter. Tiny sparks fluttered up like cigarette ashes lifted by the wind and swirled around the cavity.

I smelled something like oranges and smoke. My eyes watered and my skin tingled.

And then, inside the wound...

Things started to move.

Organs quivered and stretched, fresh tissue flowing out of tattered fringes. Shreds grew and wove together, sealing holes and molding into shapes that rippled and inflated.

Fresh bone spiraled from shattered edges, ribs extending

across the chest and spinning out a new breastbone. Sheets of muscle rolled over the ribcage, fibers meshing and swelling.

Then, a layer of skin washed over it all like spilled paint, covering every trace of what was underneath.

At that point, it was impossible to tell from looking at him that Mike had had a crater in his chest less than five minutes before.

The only thing out of place was the bluish glow that still came from his upper body...but even that faded before long. It went away right after the last incredible step in Mike's coming back to life.

Right after his chest puffed up and he started breathing again and his eyes flickered open and looked at me.

*****

After watching Mike's body heal itself from a shotgun blast, I knew one thing for sure and I said so.

"You're no F.B.I. agent."

Mike was sitting up by now, but he still looked shaky. "Can't put one over on you, can I?" he said, his voice weak but unfriendly as ever.

"So tell me," I said. "What's your story?"

Mike sat there and gave me dagger eyes for a minute, like the last thing he wanted to do was tell me anything. Then, he shrugged and shook his head. "Sure, Sonny," he said. "Why not. I need a minute here anyway."

"I won't tell anyone," I said.

Mike snorted. "Like anyone would believe a word out

of your crackhead mouth," he said.

"Yeah," I said. "So tell me."

Mike scratched his chest. "This regenerated stuff itches like crazy," he said, clawing at the spot where the crater had been...then pulling his hand away like he had to force himself to stop. "Okay. You want the story, I'll give you the story. I'm from the future."

"Huh," I said, not too surprised after the way he'd come back to life and all. "How far in the future? Fifty years? A hundred?"

"Try a thousand," said Mike.

"A thousand years," I said, and then I thought about it a minute. "So you came back in time a thousand years to help me get my boy back?"

Mike hesitated. "Sort of," he said, scratching his chest again.

"Whatta you mean, 'sort of'?" I said.

Mike stopped scratching and looked me in the eye. "I came to find him," he said, "but not to give him back to you."

*****

"I don't get it," I said. "What the hell is that supposed to mean?"

Mike sighed. "You wanted the story, I'm giving you the story. Don't get all pissy about it."

"I'm not gettin' pissy," I said. "I just wanna know what you're talkin' about with this not givin' him back to me crap."

"Look," said Mike. "These days, just about anybody

who wants a kid can have one, right? Whether you make one yourself or adopt one. Whether you deserve one or not."

"Right," I said.

"Case in point," said Mike, pointing a finger at me. "Now fast forward a thousand years in the future. There was a war, a world war. They used manmade killer viruses as weapons, only the viruses mixed together and mutated. Spread all over the planet. Whoever the super viruses didn't kill, they sterilized.

"Next thing you know, no one can make babies anymore. No more kids. And without kids..." Mike clapped his hands together. "No more people, right?"

"Right," I said.

Mike scratched his chest. "Now, the scientists manage to wipe out the viruses, but the damage is done. They try everything to make people fertile again, but nothing works. They clone people, but the clones are sterile, too.

"So, basically, it's the end of the world as far as humans are concerned," said Mike. "Last call for the human race.

"Then, someone figures out how to time-travel." Mike scratched so hard, I thought he'd draw blood...and then he pulled his hands away and sat on them. "Now we've got a way to keep humanity from dying out.

"We'll go back in time and get children from the past, from before the viruses wrecked the gene pool. We'll bring them to the future to repopulate the Earth.

"Only problem is," said Mike, "we can't take just any kids. If they're destined to grow up and have kids of their own, or even if they're just going to live and have an impact on history, no matter how small, we might change the future by taking them...which, I know, that might not be such a bad thing given the way things turned out.

"So we have to retrieve the children who won't make an impact," said Mike. "Like Sean."

"Because what?" I said, struggling to take in everything Mike was telling me. "When he went away, he was supposed to be gone for good?"

"You could say that," said Mike. "He was supposed to end up dead."

*****

Mike got up and dusted himself off. "So there you have it," he said. "Now you know."

"How...," I said. "How's he gonna die?"

"He won't," said Mike, heading for the car. "Not if I can help it."

I got up and followed him. "So all this, you helpin' me, was just so you could take him away again?"

Mike stopped in front of the car and held out his hand. "Car keys," he said.

I reached in my pocket and started pulling them out... then stopped. "Now wait a minute," I said. "I'm just supposed to let you take him?"

"Yeah," said Mike, snapping his fingers. "Give me the keys."

I closed my fist around the keys and took a step back. "But he's my son."

"Oh, right," said Mike. "And you've done such a great

job taking care of him. Why don't I nominate you for father of the year?"

"Maybe I just need another chance," I said.

"Okay, listen," Mike said angrily. "Forget about the fact that the future of the human race is at stake. Forget about the fact that time travel eats so much energy that we can only do it once a year, so we're lucky if we can bring forward a handful of kids before mankind dies out. Just put all that aside for a minute.

"Now, I want you to stand there and tell me Sean's going to be better off with you. Better off than being raised by hundreds of parents...*thousands* of parents...who want nothing in the world more than to care for a child.

"Go ahead," said Mike, stepping toward me. "Tell me! Tell me how you're going to turn over a new leaf and make everything better for him!

"Tell me how you're never going to get stoned again! Tell me how you're never going to kick his ass again! *Tell me!*"

I stood there for a long moment and didn't say a word. More than anything, I wanted to take a swing at him, punch his face bloody, knock him down and bash his head in.

Even though I knew. Because I knew.

I knew he was right.

Mike grabbed my arm then and yanked my hand out of my pocket. "Okay then," he said, prying the keys from my fingers. "Then keep your mouth shut!"

He marched around to the driver's side of the car and got in and started the engine. I hesitated, then got in the passenger's side. I was afraid he might leave without me.

"We still have a chance of saving him," he said as we rolled out onto the campground road. "I spiked the guy's tire with a melter before he shot me."

I didn't say a word.

"Guaranteed blowout on a short fuse timer," said Mike. "They won't have gotten far."

I sat silently, thinking about what he had told me. Thinking about Sean and drugs and failure and the future and regret. Thinking about how things could have been.

Wondering what my father would have done. Wondering if, in his own way, he had faced the same situation and so his choice was already clear.

*****

We followed Sean's signal with Mike's tracker phone and found the motor home a few miles away, abandoned on the side of the road. The front tire on the driver's side was blown out.

"They're on foot," said Mike, watching the glowing blue screen on the phone as he aimed it into the woods. "Big head start. I've got some ground to cover."

He already had the brass knuckles doodad on his hand, which I'd figured was some kind of weapon. When he touched a button on top of it, the red lens that curved along the front of it lit up, throwing a spotlight on the trees along the road.

"Wish me luck," he said, starting forward through the underbrush.

"Good luck," I said, but instead of staying behind like

302

he obviously wanted me to, I followed him into the woods.

"Hold on," he said, stopping a few steps in. "This is where you get off."

"Right," I said. "Will do."

"Okay then." Mike turned and took a few more steps... then stopped when he realized I was still following him.

"Look," he said, turning the beam of light on me. "The longer you piss around with me, the further away that guy gets with your son."

"How many times have you done this?" I said, squinting against the light.

Mike didn't answer.

"This is your first, isn't it?" I said. "So what do you do if he doesn't want to go?"

"Don't worry about it," snapped Mike.

"Are you going to force him? Is that how it works?"

"They're getting away," said Mike.

"Wouldn't it be easier," I said, "if you have someone along to make him feel better? Someone to tell him it's okay to go with you?"

Mike snorted. "Because you've got such a great father-son rapport," he said.

"And you're just a stranger," I said, "like the last guy who took him. But you're different from the other guys who take people's kids, right?"

Mike didn't have an answer for that one.

Slowly, he turned the light away from me...then started off again into the woods. He didn't say another word about leaving me behind.

*****

Mike and I ran through the woods, guided by the pings of the tracker.

I was so out of shape, my lungs wrecked by crack smoke, I had trouble keeping up. A couple times, I had to stop and gasp for breath, and he didn't wait for me...but I forced myself to pull it together and keep going.

Even though we had a light to follow, I tripped over roots and rocks and twisted my ankles and whacked my head on branches. I fell, hitting the ground hard and stoving some fingers and driving my knee into a stump.

But I got up and kept going.

I didn't know what was coming next or what would happen to my boy, but I had to be part of it. I had run out on him years ago, run out in every way that counted, but now I was coming back to him. Not like my father.

Not this time.

As I stumbled across creeks and slipped in mud and heaved and heaved for breath and got shooting cramps in my side, I thought about his face, the face of my son, the very same face I'd ignored and blocked out of my mind until a few days before. The face I'd hated, I admit it.

And I swore to myself, as the tracker pinged faster and Mike and I got closer to my son, that whatever I did next, I would do it for Sean.

And I hoped, unlike every other promise I'd made in my life, that this time, I'd follow through.

*****

After a while, finally, Mike stopped running. He turned off the light and the tracker and waited for me to catch up.

I stumbled up beside him, gasping and dizzy, lights sparking in front of my eyes though the woods were dark. Bending over, I put my hands on my knees and tried to stop shaking and catch my breath.

"They're up ahead," he whispered. "Moving along the base of a rock wall."

I nodded, too out of breath to say anything.

"Now, I've been thinking," said Mike. "Maybe I can use you after all, if you're up to it."

"I'm up to it," I said, straightening...trying hard not to look like I was ready to pass out.

"He thinks I'm dead," said Mike. "If you go in first, he'll think you're alone, and I can circle around and sneak up on him."

"Sounds good," I said between gasps. "What do I do?"

"Talk to him," said Mike. "Calmly. Beg him to give your son back. Whatever. Try not to get him too worked up."

"What if he...doesn't want to talk?" I said. "What if he...just wants to...shoot me?"

"Duck," said Mike. "Run the opposite direction from where I'll be. Keep him busy talking or keep him busy shooting, I don't care."

"Great plan," I said, pulling up my T-shirt from the waist to wipe the sweat off my face. "You're from a thousand years in the future...and that's the best you can... come up with?"

Mike smacked the shirt away from my face. "Quit wasting my time," he said. "Do what I said or get the hell out of here."

"All right," I said. "I'll do it."

"They're straight ahead," said Mike. "I'm going that way." He pointed left. "Remember, draw his attention away from me."

"Sure," I said, glaring at him...sick of his attitude, sick of him treating me like crap. "And you and me're gonna have a talk later."

Mike snorted. "Yeah," he said. "Because I really care about what you have to say."

And then he was gone.

I took a minute to try to steady myself, which was a lost cause, and then I started walking, too. Straight ahead.

Toward my boy.

*****

As I pushed through some low-hanging branches and stepped into a clearing, I saw them. And my heart my heart pounded faster and not just from fear or exertion.

In the dim light of the half-moon overhead, I saw my son. Even though the light was dim and he was twenty maybe thirty yards away and my eyes were still sparking, I knew it was him.

And my heart pounded because he was there, because it felt like I'd been searching for him for years and he was there.

He was moving along the rock wall behind a man...a

burly guy in a flannel shirt and bluejeans, carrying a sawed-off shotgun. At first, I didn't realize why Sean was walking funny, leaning forward and holding onto his neck.

But as I moved closer, I saw something between the two of them, something long and thin and blue. Something connecting them, one end in the guy's fist and the other attached to Sean.

Attached to his throat.

And when I knew what it was, I felt angry and sorry and sick in the stomach all at once. Sorry because it was my fault Sean had been taken. Sick because he was being treated like an animal and who knew what else the son of a bitch had done to him.

Angry because my boy was being dragged around on a leash.

*****

A week before, I never would've done what I did next, never would've walked up to a guy with a shotgun who was ready to kill me. I'll be honest, I probably wouldn't've even done it if Sean's life had depended on it.

But times had changed.

I walked a few more steps into the clearing, and then I stopped and shouted at the guy. Shaking the whole time and getting ready to run like hell.

"Hey!" I said. "Hey, you!"

Right away, the guy stopped and looked at me, swinging the shotgun around in my direction.

"Get lost!" he hollered.

Though I'd come up blank when I'd tried thinking of what I'd say to him, words popped into my head all of a sudden. "I just wanna ask you somethin'," I said. "I was wonderin' if you'd take me with you."

"You think I'm on a nature hike here?" said the guy. "Get lost, or I'll blow your brains out!"

"The thing is," I said, expecting the gun to go off at any second, "that's my boy there."

The guy looked at Sean, then back at me, without saying a word.

"I'm thinkin'," I said. "You got him fair and square, right? I can accept that. But who says we can't share him?"

"Oh, this is good!" said the guy, laughing. "Good one!"

I glanced left, wondering how much longer Mike would take to circle around. "No, I'm serious," I said. "I promise I'll be cool."

The guy laughed again. "Oh, *well* then," he said. "If you *promise*. Your word's good enough for *me*!"

Still chuckling, he raised the shotgun...and turned it away from me.

Turned it on Sean.

"Better yet," he said, "how 'bout we make it just the two of us?"

Sean looked at me. Small and helpless and scared, he looked at me.

Not crying but just on the verge. Lower lip quivering. He looked at me.

And all at once, it hit me. For the first time in my life, the only time, I realized I would do anything to save him.

Anything.

"Wait!" I said. "I'll prove you can trust me! There's someone sneaking up on you right this minute! I was supposed to keep you busy while he sneaked up on you, but I say screw him!"

The guy kept his shotgun aimed at Sean but started looking around.

"You trust me now?" I said. "Will you take me with you if I tell you where he is?"

"Sure," said the guy. "Sure I will."

"He's over there!" I said, pointing right...pointing in the opposite direction from where I thought Mike would be. "Over there!"

*****

For a long moment, the kidnapper squinted into the woods where I'd pointed, looking for a trace of someone in the shadows.

Then, we both heard a sound and looked the other way at the same time. A twig snapping.

And there was Mike, charging out of the woods.

The kidnapper swung the shotgun around and aimed it at Mike. Mike had his brass knuckle gadget raised in front of him, glowing bright red like a ray gun...but it was a toss-up whether he'd get off a shot before the kidnapper blew another hole in him.

And there was Sean, bawling his eyes out in the middle of it all.

And there I was, maybe ten yards away. Heart pounding, mind racing.

Knowing this was it, my last chance. Wanting to move. Not wanting to move.

Part of me wanting to let the guy blow away Mike because then Mike couldn't take away my boy. Take away my second chance.

The other part of me knowing that the only chance I was ever going to get was right in front of me, the only chance I deserved. More than I deserved.

*****

As I ran toward the kidnapper, the shotgun went off, but I didn't know if Mike was hit because I couldn't look away.

The switchblade was warm in my hand and I popped the blade just before I got to him and then I

Just because you're good for nothing, said Mrs. Pendleton

Then I drove it into his chest, the kidnapper's chest, drove it in to the hilt.

Doesn't mean you can't be good for something.

I slammed him back against the rock and shoved the blade hard to one side and then back, ripping him open. He dropped the shotgun and howled in pain but he was big and the next I thing I knew he was throwing me backward coming down on top of me.

Good for something even if it's

Too much weight to move, I was pinned to the ground, but I kept a hand on the switchblade and punched it deeper, going for his heart. He was like a bear, he grabbed my

310

hand and squeezed until bones cracked and it hurt so bad I screamed and had to let go.

Then he pushed up and reached behind him, he had a knife in his chest and he could still crush my hand and push up and reach back and bring around a gun he must've had in the waist of his pants.

And then he jammed it in my stomach and pulled the trigger. Heat and pain poured through me and he pulled it again.

Three times and I was screaming and screaming and so was Sean.

Even if it's just one thing.

And I remembered, I thought I'd forgotten but I remembered one moment.

Sean's just a baby, and he won't stop crying, and I pick him up and hold him in my arms and rock him to sleep.

Then I remembered another.

Older now, Sean runs around the apartment screaming and for once I'm not trashed and I chase him and catch him and tickle him. Both of us laughing.

Then another.

The same day I beat him black and blue for wetting his bed, the very same day, he gives me this picture he drew that looks like one big scribble and he says it's a picture of him and his daddy and he says he still loves me.

Then another. And another.

One by one, they fell into my hands like diamonds. I'd let them slip away, but now, at the end, they came back to me.

Later, the kidnapper's dead, I don't know if it's from

311

the switchblade or if Mike shot him or what, and I have one last thing to do. One thing I was afraid of but now it's easier.

Mike opens a shimmering window out of thin air, and he tells Sean he's going to take him to a wonderful place with lots of people who'll love him.

Sean turns to me and I can't believe it, after all I've done he still turns to me like he cares what I have to say.

And my heart breaks.

"Go ahead," I tell him. "It's all right."

SOMETHING BORROWED, SOMETHING DOOMED

Back home, we had a tradition: the worse the weddin', the better the marriage. That's why our people worked so hard to ruin each other's weddin' days.

It gave the bride an' groom somethin' to overcome an' a cause for hope...like, there's nowhere to go from here but up. We told an' retold the stories over an' over, an' they just got better with age.

But just like with anythin', sooner or later someone's gonna go too far. Take it to extremes. Face it, there are some calamities that just don't sound better no matter how many times you retell 'em.

Like the end a' the world, for example. That was the monkey business my brothers got up to on *my* weddin' day.

They figured, if they could pull it off, they'd set me up for the greatest marriage of all time, because how could you ruin anybody's weddin' day any worse than endin' the world?

This just goes to show how dirt-suckin' stupid my brothers could be.

*****

I guess I knew I was in for trouble when my brothers actually seemed to *like* my boyfriend, Bigfoot. (Nickname, it's just a nickname.)

Now, my brothers had a long history a' hatin' my beaus and drivin' 'em off...but Bigfoot won 'em over. Even Thirty Ought, the youngest and roughest, came around, which is really sayin' somethin'.

"You better do right by him, Vicky," Thirty Ought told me one day, combin' his fingers through his thick, black hair. He narrowed his bright blue eyes at me an' nodded. "No funny stuff, understand?"

Part of it had to do with Bigfoot's winnin' personality. He was just the kind a' guy who if you shot him accidentally while huntin', you'd never forgive yourself.

The rest of it, from what I can see, had to do with him bein' one a' the best wildshiners around. Give him a glass a' unprogrammed bacteria, and in nothin' flat, he could turn forty acres a' run-a'-the-mill woods into a fairytale kingdom

314

a' twirlin' parasols and dancin' geisha foxes.

He was better than any of us, which I have to admit made me hate him in a jealous kind a' way at the same time I was fallin' in love with him.

*****

Now, when I say he was better than us, that's high praise. When it comes to wildshiners, my family, the Dozens, were second only to Bigfoot Tourniquet in the state a' Best Virginia...ipso facto in the whole United States, since Best Virginia was the only state where wildshinin' wasn't outlawed. (We used to be *West* Virginia, till the National Guard got creamed in the mountain country an' the Supreme Court exempted us from the genetic tamperin' ban. The "B" is for "bioengineering," y'know.)

You wouldn't *believe* what we were doin' out there. Of course you've heard about the huntin'; maybe you've even been lucky enough to go on a safari through one of our exclusive altered game preserves.

But that was just the ass end of it, my friend. That was just the part we sold to make a livin'. What you didn't see is that we'd made an art out a' wildshinin', just like our ancestors did with moonshinin'.

While the rest a' the country had turned away from the biorevolution, we Best Virginians had become magicians. We had learned how to use the tiniest creatures to change the world in the biggest, most beautiful ways.

We worked miracles, or at least the closest thing to 'em. There was just one problem.

As long as a human bein's still doin' the drivin', the truck won't always make it up the hill. Just like any creative types, sometimes we hit a roadblock.

That's why, even after the end a' the world, I still haven't finished bringin' my dead mama's favorite memory back to life.

*****

My mama, Circa Dozen, was one a' the original genebillies who fought off the National Guard an' founded Best Virginia. She was also one a' the greatest weddin' wreckers of all time.

I'm proud to say I got to be part a' some a' her finest achievements...like, for example, the second weddin' of her best friend, Mona Fingerling. Mama really pulled out all the stops that day, as in recreatin' the plagues that Moses brought down on ancient Egypt in the Bible.

Mona would laugh about it later, but she was screamin' her lungs out when the frogs an' locusts jumped all over her while it rained blood from the church rafters.

It had been a lot a' work for the whole family, but it was worth it. While everyone else in the church shrieked an' ran, my brothers an' I howled with laughter.

Up front, Mama an' I tossed handfuls a' glitterin' pixie dust in the air. My five brothers scattered around the church did the same. The dust was full a' designer microbes set to trigger the next plagues.

Moments later, the mayhem shifted to complete chaos as sores an' boils broke out on every patch a' bare skin in the place (except our family's, because the microbes were programmed not to affect us).

Mona turned around, her face blotched an' blistered, an' locked eyes with Mama. "This is *horrible*," she said between sobs. "You've ruined *everythin'*!"

Mama grinned proudly. "*We've* ruined everythin'," she said, wrappin' an arm around my shoulders an' huggin' me against her side. "Don't forget my daughter an' my boys. It was a team effort."

Mona barely managed to pinch a small smile out a' her swollen face. "This is the worst ever, I think," she said. "Could be a hell of a marriage."

Mama laughed an' winked at me. She didn't look much older'n I was, thanks to a little personal wildshinin'. Her long hair was almost as black an' glossy as mine, her eyes almost as bright blue as mine, an' her pale skin nearly as smooth. "What do you say to that, Vick?"

Right before the herd a' diseased livestock put in an appearance, followed by a storm a' baseball-sized hail, I smiled. "I just hope my weddin' day's *half* as bad as yours, ma'am," I said, not realizin' that my words would someday come back to haunt me.

*****

It really wasn't the rhinoporcupine's fault I ended up covered with his poop.

He was somebody else's creation, a stray who'd wandered into my family's genefields. When I injected him with the hypodermic end a' my six-foot cattle prod, shootin' new genetic instructions into his system, he right away moved to obey.

Problem was, that big spiny critter swung around so fast I had to stumble outta his way an' hit the ground. He didn't seem to notice that the load a' crap he dumped as he lumbered by landed square on top a' me.

It was then, as I sat there, covered in steamin', reekin' orange goo, that I heard what sounded like someone chokin' to death. Spottin' him a few yards away, I realized that chokin' sound was just his way a' laughin'.

"Oh, man!" Bent over with his big catcher's mitt hands on his softball-sized kneecaps, he was laughin' so hard he could barely get his words out. "I am so sorry!"

"No need to apologize," I said, smilin' as I reached for my cattle prod/hypodermic rod. The guy didn't set off my warnin' bells, but we Best Virginians have had a thing about strangers ever since the National Guard scampered through our front yards.

"Actually," said the guy, still laughin', "I *do* need to apologize. See, the rhinoporcupine's one a' my livestock."

"And *who* does that make *you*?" I put my rod down an' sunk my hands into the rancid muck.

Still laughin', the guy straightened an' pushed his glowin', golden hair outta' his eyes. He was a suncatcher, one a' the more successful human offshoots whipped up in the "Home Genome-Makeover" craze from back before the bio-engineerin' bust. Soaked-up sunshine lit every hair follicle on his licorice body like fiber optics in a coal seam.

I thought he was just beautiful.

"Family name's Tourniquet," he said. "We're wildshiners

from down Huntington way."

"Nice to meet ya', Mr. Tourniquet," I said, shortly before I pitched big soppin' handfuls a' rhinoporcupine poop at him. "Lucky for you, I happen to be the welcome wagon. Now aren't you gonna ask me 'bout our special way a' welcomin' folks in these parts?"

And that was how I met my future husband, Bigfoot Tourniquet.

*****

Six months later, I stood over my mother's burial plot, tryin' to finish the one last thing I had to do for her.

Circa had died a week before a' the crumbles. The one blessin' was that she got to know my future husband before she went, as Bigfoot an' I were pretty much joined at the hip by then.

He couldn't help me with what I had to do for Mama, though. It was a wildshiner tradition, like ruinin' weddin's. The firstborn had to 'shine up a permanent livin' memorial depictin' the deceased's favorite moment on Earth.

Problem was, I couldn't get the damn thing right. Mama had left specific instructions, but the moment kept comin' out wrong.

Mama's instructions were mostly in the form a' genetic code, so I didn't know exactly how every little detail would come out in the end. I knew enough a' the big picture that I could tell I wasn't even in the right neighborhood, though.

I tried again in the fadin' summer twilight over Mama's plot, tossin' fistfuls a' pixie dust from two pouches, then addin' pinches from three others. The shimmerin' powders danced in midair, mixin' an' whirlin' faster an' faster, becomin' a rainbow vortex that groaned an' expanded.

The dust sparkled an' swirled as the microbes worked their magic, spinnin' earth an' air an' water an' life into a whole different arrangement a' matter an' energy. Within the walls a' the funnel, shapes appeared an' moved an' grew, half visible like a body behind a shower curtain.

Then, the vortex peeled away in ribbons all the colors a' the rainbow, revealin' its handiwork.

Right there in front a' me was a scene from Mama's weddin' day, big as life. In a gown a' pure white light, ringed by tiny, flutterin' cherubs, Mama kissed her new husband full on the lips. The two of 'em floated in midair, slowly rotatin' six feet off the ground. All around 'em, the guests an' preacher an' weddin' party drifted through the air, too. Even as the congregation floated upward, the walls a' the church came tumblin' down, collapsin' in clouds a' dust an' heaps a' debris.

All through it, Mama never stopped kissin' her groom. Tears a' joy streamed down her cheeks, an' she held his face lightly in her long-fingered hands.

I'd failed again. It wasn't the moment Mama had chosen, the one she'd written about in her will.

So I wasn't done yet. I'd have to keep tryin' till I got it right...no matter how much I hated the moment she'd picked.

Which I did. It might've been Mama's favorite moment a' *her* life, but it was about my *least* favorite moment a' *mine*.

SOMETHING BORROWED, SOMETHING DOOMED

*****

Maybe I should've just let my genius nut-job brothers take care of it. A year later, I still wasn't havin' any luck with Mama's memorial, while my brothers managed to end the whole world on my weddin' day.

Delaney, the only one older'n me, had promised me somethin' special in the way a' weddin' ruination...but talk about your record for genius an' stupidity all in one. I mean, what kinda' brain trust ends the world while they're still livin' on it?

Durin' the ceremony, though, you'd hardly have known they were up to anythin'. Four of 'em were lined up as Bigfoot's groomsmen, an' Gila, the second oldest at twenty-six, was the best man. All five wore white tuxedos that set off their thick, black hair...an' boy, were they wearin' the poker faces. Those long, black lashes a' theirs flicked over bright blue eyes that looked pure an' innocent as the new-driven snow on the Best Virginian mountaintops.

Naturally, this got me all the more worked up.

Things only got worse as the ceremony went on...an' by worse, I mean everythin' went perfectly. Unlike other brides an' grooms, Bigfoot an' I traded rings without havin' 'em snatched an' eaten by stampedin' human hearts brandishin' handguns. We said our vows without bein' drowned out by twelve-foot-tall opera-singin' Viking women with horrible body odor. We kissed without the church turnin' into a fiery hell complete with howlin', pitchfork-totin' demons in silver bikinis.

By the time the minister said, "I now present Mr. and

Mrs. Hermes Tourniquet," I was startin' to think maybe no sabotage was comin' after all. Maybe, my brothers' real plan was just to drive me crazy waitin' for the hammer to fall.

Then, as Bigfoot an' I started down the aisle, the back a' the church started to run...not like legs or a nose, but like a paintin' in the rain.

Holdin' Bigfoot by the arm, I stopped in the middle a' the aisle an' stared. The white a' the walls, the dark brown a' the doors an' woodwork, the red an' gold an' blue a' the stained glass windows ran downward in streaks. Where the colors melted away, a backdrop a' perfect blackness loomed, uninterrupted by even the faintest flickerin' star.

Just then, as everyone in the church turned around to see what the heck I was gapin' at, I heard one a' my brothers curse at the front a' the church. It was Buck, the third oldest after Delaney an' Gila.

"All right," said Buck. "Which one a' you guys forgot to set up the safety bubble around the church?"

"I thought *you* were goin' to do it," said Rattler, the overexcitable next-to-the-youngest a' the five brothers.

Buck let out a disgusted sigh. "I can't *believe* you guys dropped the ball again."

"It was *your* job, Buck," said my youngest brother, Thirty Ought.

"All a' you *shut up*," said Delaney. "Hey, Vicky. Can you come here a minute?"

I tore myself away from watchin' the church melt an' headed for the boys. People in the rear pews were crowdin' toward the front a' the place, hopin' to escape the growin' void.

"We, uh, released this new world-eatin' bacteria, Vick," Delaney said sheepishly, like he was confessin' to readin' my diary. "The bad news is, someone forgot to protect the church...but *you'll* be okay. You're about to be the last person in the world."

"'Cept there won't *be* a world," said Buck.

"The good news is, we're pretty sure you can 'shine up a new one," said Delaney.

"And don't feel compelled to bring back these other screwups when ya' do," said Buck.

*****

As I sweep my hand through the darkness, trails a' twinklin' glitter cascade from my fingertips. The world has ended, an' I'm not alone.

I float in an ocean a' microbes, the well-fed remnants of all I once knew. My brothers did a great job programmin' 'em for my survival; the microbes kept me safe durin' the apocalypse, an' now they're providin' all the air an' water an' nutrients I need to live.

And more. I found out they respond to my thoughts.

If I picture somethin' an' concentrate, it pops right up in front a' me, conjured from the digested matter an' energy a' the destroyed Earth. If it's a hamburger, it's real enough to eat. If it's a person, he's real enough to talk to.

I've never heard of a wildshiner usin' mind control on microbes before. The only controllin' we ever did was with DNA manipulation in the lab an' creative mixin' in the field.

But I'm wonderin' if maybe I *have* seen this before. I

keep thinkin' back to the way Mama's memorial kept goin' wrong. Even though I'd program the microbes real carefully an' triple-check my work, the scenes they'd recreate were always different from the one I'd programmed into 'em.

For a while, I'd wondered if I was subconsciously sabotagin' my own work with my own two hands, but Bigfoot an' Delaney had both checked the work an' said it was A-OK.

Now, I see another way I could've sabotaged myself.

I close my eyes an' focus my thoughts on a memory, bringin' it to the front a' my mind. It's a moment I remember well, too well, an' it comes easy to me.

When I open my eyes, the moment surrounds me, life-size an' perfect in every way.

Mama an' I (at age sixteen) sit together on a plank dock juttin' from a bank a' the Cacapon River. It's mid-summer in the Best Virginia hills, hot as the engine block of a pickup just got done climbin' the switchbacked road up a mountain face.

While my younger self sits there with Mama, I personally watch from a few yards away. I'm hoverin' over the cracklin' brown water in the middle a' the river, an' they can't see me.

Even before Mama starts talkin', I understand. There's a reason I thought a' this now.

It's the same reason I kept ruinin' her memorial.

*****

"I only changed the outside a' you, Vick," says Mama,

danglin' her feet in the river water. "The inside's just the same, an' the inside's what I truly love."

Sixteen-year-old Vicky tries to skim a stone over the river's sparklin' surface, but it only hops once an' sinks like her heart. "I knew it," she says, her voice bitter cold. "I always knew there was somethin' wrong with me."

"No no, honey." Mama reaches over to try to stroke Vicky's long, black hair, but Vicky ducks away from her touch. "There's *never* been anythin' wrong with you."

Vicky looks up suddenly, like she just thought a' somethin' awful. "My brothers?" she says. "Did you change *them*, too?"

Mama sighs an' nods. "I 'shined up all a' you."

Tears gush from Vicky's eyes. "Why?" she says. "Why did you *do* it?"

My own heart pounds as Mama takes Vicky's hand. "To make us look more like a family," she says. "The family I always wanted."

Vicky tries to tear her hand away, but she can't. "I don't even know what I *really* look like!"

"You think I don't love you?" Mama kisses Vicky's hand. "Tell the truth, now."

Vicky glares at Mama through her tears. She sobs an' shakes as birds sing an' fish flip outta' the water an' splash back down. "What'd I look like?" she says. "Where'd I come from?"

"Don't matter," says Mama.

"Tell me! Why won't you *tell* me who I really *am*?"

Mama looks down at the river glidin' past. "Because I love you too much," she says softly, "an' I'm too scared I'll lose you."

"I hate you," says Vicky. She jumps to her feet. "I hate you an' I'll never forgive you."

Then, as she storms away, leavin' her mother alone on the river bank, I close my eyes. When I open 'em, the scene is gone. Nothin' but blackness again.

*****

At last, I understand. As I reach out with my mind to the ocean a' microbes around me, I know why I couldn't bring myself to 'shine up the memorial Mama wanted...an' I know *why* she wanted it.

It wasn't just for her. It wasn't just a memorial to her favorite moment of her life.

It was a gift to me.

Mama's instructions for the memorial were in the form a' genetic code. I won't see all the details till the memorial's done, includin' the one thing I've always wanted to see more'n anythin' else in my life...the one thing I've also been most scared a' seein'.

The one thing Mama gave me as a final show a' her love. The one thing she could finally afford to give me without fear, without worryin' she'd lose me, because I was losin' her first.

Now that the world's over an' I have a clean slate to work with, I believe I can bring her gift to life. And maybe I can finally forgive her.

All around me, the darkness glows with the light of a gazillion microbes churnin' my thoughts into reality. Shapes appear in the murk, blurry like I'm seein' 'em through a curtain...an' then they get brighter an' more solid.

Like the curtain's liftin'.

*****

Mama Circa gazes down at the small form glowing in the moonlit cradle. Smiling, she runs her hand along the side rail, watching the child curled up in the bedclothes.

The trailer smells of beer and roses...beer because the man and woman who live there are drinkers, roses because of the soothing garden Mama Circa has wildshined around them to deepen their sleep.

Her heart pounds. Gently, she reaches for the child, drawing her up out of the cradle and into her arms.

Closing her eyes, Mama hugs the child to her, but not so tightly that she will wake her. Mama beams and breathes deeply, turning slowly with her prize in the silver moonlight at the scene of the crime.

The one-year-old she is stealing sleeps soundly on Mama's shoulder. The little girl has thick, black hair and long, black lashes.

Just then, somewhere in the night, a dog barks. The child in Mama's arms stirs and grunts, and her eyes flicker open.

The child tenses and catches her breath as if she is about to cry. Gently, Mama swings her around and makes a funny face at her.

The child relaxes and smiles. She stares for a moment—her eyes are bright green—and then she drifts back to sleep.

Mama kisses the little girl's forehead and eases her onto her shoulder. The child sleeps soundly as her new mother whisks her out into the full-moon summer night.

The Cross-Dressing Cosmic Cortez Rubs Off

As Philippa the Conquistadora waves his ribbony rainbow blade over the bowed head of Koocha, king of the alien Skoo, one bid after another chatters in over the phone in my head. Every network, from the bigs to the babies, wants to carry the live feed of this execution.

I love this job. When I was a boy, I watched the space conquistadors on pulsenet, roving among exotic worlds and violently subduing the primitive natives. Now, I'm repping Philippa, the cross-dressing, bloodthirsty, cosmic Cortez, skimming my fifteen percent of more money than there are hydrogen atoms in the universe.

"Thus endeth the greatest campaign of conquest in history!" roars Philippa, shaking a black-leather-gloved fist in the air. The butt-rings dangling from his exposed posterior jangle as he thrusts his leather-chapped hips to one side. "At least until my *next* campaign!" he says with a lipsticky smile aimed right at the camera cloud drifting in front of him.

"Wait, O Conqueror!" yips kneeling Koocha, who looks more like an ugly orange baby with green stripes and foot-long glowing purple whiskers than anything else. "Before I die, I must speak with that man."

To my surprise, Koocha points his stubby finger-bud right at me.

The rock soundtrack kicks up ominously, screeching to a crescendo of skirling ultra-guitar feedback.

"Bo-ring," groans Philippa, and then he flutters a languid hand in my direction. "He's just my aaaagent. I can feel the ratings drooping already."

"I will outbid all bidders if you will spare my people," Koocha says to me in his/her/its/whatever's squeaky voice.

"I'm listening," I say with a smirk.

"We offer your species total enlightenment, perfect happiness, and eternal bliss," says Koocha. "We can give you the wisdom that most species take millions of years to obtain." Koocha's whiskers glow brighter. "What say you?"

I laugh. "You're serious?"

Koocha nods. "If you accept, humanity will hyperevolve into gods multimillennia ahead of schedule, and you will become the greatest hero in human history." Koocha shrugs. "Or you will refuse and become the greatest villain."

Philippa prances over and rubs my chest. "How deliciously tempting," he purrs.

I am very aware of the ribbony sword in his other hand, though that is not what makes up my mind.

The thought of bringing spiritual transcendence and hyperevolution to mankind—if such a thing is even possible—also gets my attention...but that does not sway me, either. Nor does the secretly longed-for fulfillment of my boyhood dreams by outdoing Philippa on the celebrity villain front.

What does it, what makes up my mind, is when the insta-ratings graph floating always in the corner of my eye takes a sharp plunge.

The viewers have spoken.

I give the nod to Philippa. With a shake of his flouncy black curls, he swishes his rainbow sword in a whistling figure eight and levels it at Koocha.

"Sorry," I say to the shivering alien kinglet. "I can't *spend* fifteen percent of enlightenment."

The alien who looked like a cactus blinked his prickly pear eyes and made a noise like a screaming cat.

At first, Dinah Ryan wasn't sure that this was a bad thing. For all she and her fellow Earthlings knew about aliens, it could have been a cry of pure ecstasy.

But then, the cactus puked chunky blue slime all over Ben Blakey, which tipped them off. With a noise like a dental drill running at full throttle, Mr. Cactus scooted off to the next booth.

So humanity was still screwed.

"Ah, man!" Blakey flicked slime from his gray jumpsuit and wrinkled his nose. "This stuff *stinks!*"

"You're telling *me*." Mahalia Davis darted away from him. "How the hell many of these species communicate by spraying shit at each other, anyway?"

Dinah grinned and shook her head, tossing her shoulder-length sandy brown hair. "I still say it's a joke. Initiation pranks for the new kids on the block."

"No," said Captain Alec Strayhorn. "We don't matter that much to them. Half of them don't even know we're here."

Dinah gazed out at the cavernous hall and realized Strayhorn was right. Every imaginable shape and size of alien being walked and bounced and flew and crawled and oozed across that giant crystal chamber. There were aliens with skin like stained glass, faces like mirrors, bodies like smoke, fur crackling with electrical current...and none of them were looking or sniffing or twitching in the direction of the Earthlings' booth.

"This is a *disaster.*" Blakey used one end of the tablecloth to wipe slime from his arms and chest. "*Three days* at this debacle, and what do we have to *show* for it?"

"Lots of alien *freebies.*" Mahalia shuffled the pile of bizarre devices, objects, and pocket-sized lifeforms on the table.

"Which we don't know what to do with!" Blakey bent down and wiped slime from his lumpy bald head. "For all we know, they're meant to kill and eat us!" Usually, Blakey was the funniest and most upbeat member of the team; his current surliness showed just how badly things were going.

Some Worlds' Fair this was turning out to be. The Fair was designed to give the inhabitants of many planets the chance to showcase their wares and attract investors. Plenty of other species were getting attention...but for the humans, the Fair had been an exercise in invisibility. They sat at their cobbled-together plastic booth playing old Earth movies on a TV pried out of their ship's cockpit, and nobody gave them a second or even a first look.

"We've done the best we could." Dinah tucked her hair behind her ears and shrugged. "We didn't exactly come prepared for this."

It was true. As the crew of Earth's first deep space exploration mission, the four humans had not expected to be setting up a booth at a glorified trade show on an alien space station. They hadn't even expected to *meet* honest-to-goodness aliens, for that matter.

Now, they'd been surrounded by so many wildly different varieties for so long, Dinah had to admit that the novelty was starting to wear off.

"I say we pack it in," said Blakey, dropping the slime-covered end of the tablecloth. "Let's go home."

"And tell the folks at home what?" Captain Strayhorn--a tall man with thick, dark hair, chiseled features, and haunted gray eyes--straightened the tablecloth. "That everyone on Earth will *die* because our trade show booth was *half-assed*?"

That was enough to take the wind out of everyone's sails...and remind Dinah why she had a crush on him.

Strayhorn was a leader. While everyone else got bent out of shape over a little blue slime, Strayhorn kept his eyes firmly on the prize.

Which was saving humanity from extinction.

Blakey sighed. "I just don't know what else we can do. These bastards don't care about what we have to offer."

"Maybe you need to diiig deeper," said a familiar voice.

Just hearing it was enough to make Dinah's skin crawl. The voice had an oily, sinuous quality that curled around her brainstem and licked her fear center with a flickering, forked tongue.

The voice belonged to the alien who'd brought them to the Worlds' Fair in the first place. Dinah and the other humans called him "Heavy," which was derived from his endless, unpronounceable alien name.

"Surpriise them." Heavy looked like a five-foot long eggplant covered with writhing cilia topped with chattering faces. There were hundreds of tiny faces, every one of them representing a different alien species. Whichever face Heavy was using at a given moment--the human face, in this case--inflated to life size and spoke the loudest.

Mahalia patted her curly black hair and snorted. "How can we *surprise* them when we don't even know what's *not* a surprise out here?"

Heavy's human face looked like Blakey's: pinched, puffy features and a lumpy scalp. The main difference was that the lip movements didn't always match the words. "Your homeworld wiiill be uniiinhabiiitable soon, yes?"

"You know it will," said Dinah. Hyper-accelerated climate change on Earth had already cranked up the heat and forced everyone underground. Scientists projected that humans would no longer be able to survive anywhere on or under the planet within five years.

"You came here looking for help to fiiix the homeworld, yes?" said Heavy.

Dinah nodded. The team had originally launched into space seeking new Earthlike homes for humanity. When all the inhabitable planets within reach had turned out to be taken, they'd jumped at Heavy's invitation to the Fair.

"You wiiill pay any priice for that help?" said Heavy.

"Of course," said Strayhorn. "But we don't seem to have anything anyone *wants*."

Heavy made a gurgling sound that the team had decided was his way of laughing. "Are you sure you have triied *everythiiing*?"

"Pretty much," said Blakey.

"Maybe you only *thiiink* you have," said Heavy. "Remember, somethiiing of no value to you could be worth a great deal to one of *them*." With that, he twisted his eggplant body around and waved every one of his faces at the crowd of aliens in the great crystal hall.

"What's that supposed to mean?" said Blakey.

"You tell me," said Heavy. "Iiit iiis up to you to fiiigure iiit out."

*****

That night, Team Earth brainstormed in the cramped galley of their little spaceship, the *Diogenes*. They had only one day left of the Worlds' Fair, one day in which to make a deal to save humanity.

"Let's go over it again." Strayhorn tipped his chair back and propped the side of his leg against the edge of the round table. "What have we offered so far?"

Mahalia swallowed some coffee and lowered her mug. "Mineral wealth. Natural resources."

"Plant and animal specimens," said Dinah.

"A catalogue of genomes for life on Earth," said Blakey.

"What else?" said Strayhorn.

Dinah nibbled a chocolate chip cookie, then waved it at Strayhorn. "Food stocks. Pharmaceuticals."

Strayhorn nodded. "A database of all human knowledge."

"Strategic military rights," said Mahalia.

"Nuclear and biological weapons," said Blakey.

"Slaves." Dinah was exaggerating, but only a little; in desperation, they'd come up with an indentured servant scheme, offering a human workforce for offworld projects in return for Earth's salvation.

Even that extreme proposal hadn't drawn any interest from the oblivious aliens.

Strayhorn checked a list on a pad of paper in his lap. "That's everything, all right." He chucked the pad on the table and sighed. "So what else do we have to offer?"

Blakey laughed and slapped the table. "Absolutely *nothing!*"

"Heavy says otherwise," said Strayhorn.

"Right!" Blakey leaped to his feet. "And *that* asshole would *never* steer us wrong!"

"One more day." Strayhorn's quiet, steady voice locked in everyone's attention with high intensity. "That's all the time we have to make a deal. So let's *think*, people."

"We're like *amoebas* to them." Blakey's face was flushed.

"Like *dust mites*. We've got *nothing* they want!"

"All right, all right." Mahalia scrubbed her fingers through her short, curly hair. "What *haven't* we offered so far?"

"Souls!" said Blakey. "We haven't offered them our *souls* yet!"

Mahalia grinned. "Careful. They might actually *want* those."

"Then I say let's *sell* them," said Blakey.

"But we can't prove they exist," said Dinah.

"All the better!" Blakey clapped his hands. "I say let's do whatever it takes to save Earth!"

Dinah looked across the table and caught Strayhorn's gaze. In the long trip out from Earth, she'd become addicted to that gaze. At moments like this, she felt like she would do anything to hold it, to keep it, to please him.

Strayhorn was a strong man, a good man, a leader. He wore a sense of mystery like a dark cloak, binding all his secrets in shadows deep inside. How could she ever hope to get at them?

"Wait." Dinah felt all eyes slide to meet her, but she didn't break Strayhorn's gaze. "Maybe you're onto something, Ben."

"Great!" Blakey rubbed his hands together. "Tell me about it!"

"What about imagination?" said Dinah.

Mahalia frowned. "How can we sell imagination?"

"Not imagination itself," said Dinah. "I mean we offer to sell something *imaginary*."

"Ah." Strayhorn nodded. "You mean lie."

Dinah shrugged. "More like exaggerate."

Blakey smacked her on the back. "You are such a con artist!"

"Could be dangerous," said Strayhorn. "All these aliens are more technologically advanced than we are. If we piss them off, they could *wipe out* humanity instead of *saving* it."

"We'll have to play it just right," said Dinah. "Keep them happy. Make them think they're getting what we promised."

"*If* we can even get them *interested*," said Mahalia.

"Right." Dinah searched Strayhorn's eyes for some sign of approval. At first, they were just as flat, gray, and inscrutable as always.

Then, she saw the light.

"Okay," said Strayhorn. "Let's see if we can make this work."

And Dinah's heart danced like a child in her chest.

*****

The next day started out hopefully.

Team Earth set up early in the Worlds' Fair hall and attacked their mission with fresh enthusiasm. Strayhorn and Blakey manned the booth while Dinah and Mahalia traversed the crowd, using big smiles and chocolate from the *Diogenes'* stores to try to lure visitors.

The four teammates attacked the day as if it were their first at the Fair. Every one of them dug in with new energy and intensity, casting aside the pessimism of the previous day. Even Blakey gave it his all.

And they tried everything. Every line of bullshit they could imagine.

"Come one, come all!" said Dinah as she worked the crowd--wondering as she did so if any of the aliens understood a word she said. "Come see the vacation paradise of *Earth*!" Naturally, she left out the part about Earth being a global warming hellhole. (Though it *could* be a paradise to some of the aliens, for all she knew.)

"Follow me!" Mahalia said from the other side of the room. "Spiritual enlightenment awaits you on the holiest planet in the galaxy--*Earth*!"

"Visit the ancient world where all life began!" said Dinah. "Meet the seers whose visions foretell your future!

"Come to the miracle planet!" said Mahalia. "Heals all wounds, cures all diseases, and grants eternal life!"

"Your fantasies will come to life on Earth!" said Dinah.

"The gambling capital of the galaxy!" said Mahalia.

"Where golf is a way of life!"

"Be king of the world for a day!"

"Find lost treasure!"

"The streets are paved with gold!"

"Whatever you want!" said Dinah. "That's what you'll find on *Earth*!"

But it was all for nothing.

Throughout the day, only a handful of aliens came close enough to the booth to see the phony presentation whipped up by Strayhorn and Blakey--computer-generated images of a paradise that was nothing at all like the modern, dying Earth. The rest of the crowd was too busy gawking at other displays to take a look. Even the booth next-door, which featured a gray blob oozing green liquid in a silver bowl, attracted more attention.

*****

By the time the Fair closed for the day, alien hordes rushing the doors like school kids on the way to summer vacation, Team Earth hadn't made a single deal. They hadn't fibbed up the slightest nibble of interest.

The four teammates slouched around the booth, shaking their heads and sighing. Aliens paraded past on their way to the exits, but none of them paused or even glanced over.

"No one can say we didn't try our best," said Mahalia, pushing alien freebies from other booths into a box. "It wasn't meant to be."

Blakey slumped on a folding chair with his lumpy bald head in his hands. "One good thing about the end of the world," he said. "When we go down in history as incompetent moron failures, at least there won't be much history *left*."

Strayhorn sat bolt upright, staring at the alien masses as they trooped past. "We'd better be on our way." His voice was cold and flat. "We're done here."

Dinah sat beside him and watched his face. He looked stern and impassive, unmoved...but she had a feeling that a lot more was going on inside.

He had failed to save the human race. How could that not tear him apart? How could that not *destroy* him?

"Well," said Mahalia. "How about a little clean-up

music?" With a flick of her wrist, she popped a digital music player from the hip pocket of her red jumpsuit and laid it on the table. She pressed the surface of the thin, silver device, which was about the size of a playing card, and it started giving off music.

Jazz music, which was what Mahalia listened to the most.

"Come on." Mahalia tapped Blakey's shoulder. "Let's find a cart to haul this stuff back to the ship."

Blakey sighed. "Might as well," he said, and then he got up and went with her.

That left Dinah and Strayhorn sitting together in the booth. A trumpet ballad filtered from Mahalia's player, its slow, sweet notes adding to the melancholy mood.

Strayhorn rubbed his eyes, then placed his palms flat on the table. "I failed," he said. "It was up to me to save the world, and I couldn't do it."

Dinah laid her hand on top of his. It was the first time she'd ever touched him outside the line of duty. "Please don't give up," she said. "There must be something we can do."

Strayhorn didn't pull his hand away. His gaze remained fixed on the aliens parading past. "We can beg, maybe," he said. "But these people out here don't seem too inclined to charity."

"Then we'll change their inclination." Impulsively, Dinah cupped his chin and turned his face toward her. "Trust me, Alec. We'll do it together."

Then, Dinah surprised herself. Before she could think better of it, she leaned up and kissed Strayhorn on the mouth.

He didn't resist. In fact, after the first moment, he actively kissed her back, pressing his lips against hers.

The rest of the universe faded away. Heart pounding, Dinah reveled in the feel of Strayhorn's lips, the smell of his skin, the long-delayed contact between them.

The kiss went on and on, and Dinah wished it would never end. Nothing else mattered--not the crowd of alien lifeforms in the hall, not the impending doom of humanity, not Team Earth's failure. Not what would or wouldn't happen next.

For Dinah, it was a perfect kiss, a heavenly moment. She might never have broken the spell if not for the overwhelming new feeling that came upon her--the feeling that she was being watched.

Guessing that Blakey and Mahalia had returned to the booth, Dinah opened her eyes...and jumped. The kiss broke, and the perfect moment ended.

Dinah had been right about being watched, but not by Blakey and Mahalia. Instead of two pairs of human eyes, dozens of alien ones were trained on her and Strayhorn-- eyes of all shapes and colors and sizes, eyes on stalks, eyes of crystal, eyes with wings.

For the first time all week, a crowd had gathered around Team Earth's booth at the Worlds' Fair.

"What the hell?" said Strayhorn. "What's going on?"

Dinah thought for a moment, then grinned. She thought she understood the situation. "Congratulations," she said. "We've finally found something they want to see."

And then she kissed Strayhorn again.

*****

"Come one, come all!" Blakey stood on the table of the Team Earth booth and used his best carnival barker voice. "Experience the wonders of Earth's greatest treasure--*love*!"

Dinah and Strayhorn still sat behind the table, kissing... and the crowd of aliens watching them had grown into a mob. The aliens fanned out in all directions, hooting and babbling and jostling for a better view of the action.

Mahalia, meanwhile, acted as security, backing off any onlookers who got too close or made a grab for a body part. "The natives are restless," she said as she batted away an encroaching tentacle. "We'd better make a deal soon, or they're liable to rush the booth."

Strayhorn broke the kiss. "How do we market this? Earth as an interplanetary brothel?" His voice was heavy with sarcasm.

"If it saves humanity, *I'll* turn tricks!" Blakey said from above.

"Maybe they just like to watch," said Mahalia. "Performances, that is."

"Earth. Porno capital of the galaxy," said Blakey.

Mahalia shooed away a trio of flying yellow eyeballs. "Maybe we won't have to go that far. Maybe kissing's exciting enough for them."

Dinah kept pecking Strayhorn on the lips so they wouldn't lose the crowd. (Also because she was making the most of the situation.) "What about a kind of singles resort?" she said between kisses. "Humans could teach aliens about the concept of love and then match them up to experience it."

"I like it better than the brothel idea," said Mahalia.

"I say stick with the porno," said Blakey.

Strayhorn finished another kiss and nodded. "Try any and all of the above," he said. "Whatever it takes to trade for reverse global warming services--but start low and make the best deal you can."

"Roger that." Blakey winked at Mahalia. "Play something romantic, wouldja?"

"Will do." While wrestling with an alien's twitching feelers, Mahalia switched the fast bebop coming out of her music player to a slow number with a lot of sultry sax.

Ben raised his arms and beamed at the alien mob. "Are you *lonely*, my friends? Do you want to be like *them*?" He gestured at Dinah and Strayhorn, who were locked in another kiss. "Would you give anything to discover the wonders of *love*?

"Then step right up!" Ben pumped his fists in the air. "This is your lucky day--if you have the technology to reduce carbon dioxide emissions in a planetary atmosphere, that is!"

*****

"Hey," whispered Strayhorn. "Easy on the tongue."

Dinah leaned back and stared at him. They'd been kissing for at least two hours straight, mouth to mouth in front of an audience of gaping aliens.

So why was Strayhorn sounding *shy* all of a sudden?

Maybe, thought Dinah, he felt self-conscious with all the aliens watching him. Maybe he was getting tired. Maybe he was just stressed out about this being his last chance for a deal to save humanity.

Whatever the reason, Strayhorn didn't elaborate.

"Okay," said Dinah.

"Thanks," said Strayhorn, and then he licked his lips and leaned back in to resume kissing.

Dinah gladly rejoined him, though the moment had sapped a little of her fun. Even as she savored the warmth and pressure of Strayhorn's mouth, she couldn't help worrying in the back of her mind about why he'd nixed her French kiss.

*****

"Thiiis being wants love," said Heavy, inflating his bald human face to speak to Team Earth. "He wants all the love he can get."

Heavy twisted his eggplant body and wriggled his cilia at the alien who had just pushed out of the crowd behind him. The new alien, who was seven feet tall, looked like an inside-out centaur covered in rough, blood-red crust and black bristles.

"His name iiis Ogog Lugofarloff," said Heavy. "Ogog wiiill buy the riights to all human love."

"Let's talk price then," said Blakey. "Can Ogog reverse global warming on our homeworld?"

Heavy rattled off a chain of rapid clacks and dings that sounded like an old manual typewriter in action. Ogog made the same kind of sounds back at him, mixed with the clomping of one black hoof on the floor.

"No," Heavy said when it was over. "But he *could* reengiiineer your species to surviive the new cliimate."

Ogog clattered and clomped again, ending with a decisive belch.

"Here iiis an example of hiiis work." Heavy fluttered his head-capped cilia in Ogog's direction. "Ogog has reengiiineered *hiiimself* multiiiiple tiimes."

Strayhorn broke the latest kiss and shot Blakey a glare that said it all.

Blakey nodded and winked, then turned back to Heavy and Ogog. "Give us your contact information, Ogog buddy. We'll have to get back to you on that."

*****

After another hour of kissing while Blakey wheeled and dealed, Strayhorn pulled his lips back just enough to talk to Dinah. "I wonder what would happen if we switched with the others?"

Dinah looked out at the crowd of gaping aliens. "Do you want to take the chance?"

"No," said Strayhorn. "Not yet, anyway."

Dinah smiled and touched his cheek. "Just relax, Alec. Relax and enjoy."

Strayhorn scanned the babbling alien mob, then met Dinah's gaze and held it. He stared deep into her eyes, searching for something...and then his frown darkened.

"Why did you kiss me the first time?" he said.

Dinah shrugged. "To make you feel better."

"That's it?" said Strayhorn. "That's the only reason?"

Dinah hesitated, then decided to show her cards. "I wanted to," she said. "I've wanted to kiss you for a while now."

"I see." Strayhorn's frown smoothed out into his standard unreadable stare.

"Aren't you glad I did?" Dinah chuckled and rubbed noses with him. "Nobody came to our booth until I kissed you."

"Sure," said Strayhorn.

"In fact," said Dinah, "it might turn out to be the kiss that saves humanity, right?"

"Right," said Strayhorn.

"I'll bet they'll even make a movie about it someday." Dinah leaned close, brushing her lips against his. "A real love story."

And then she kissed him again, heart soaring with heat and delight like a butterfly or a dream.

*****

"III have another customer for you," said Heavy. "She assures me she has the technical capabiiiliiitiies to reverse your homeworld's global warmiiing."

Dinah looked up in mid-kiss to see the gray blob from the silver bowl in the booth next-door bobbing in midair beside Heavy.

"Her name iiis Melliiicloriiis Myopa Quozahnna Non Zadacta." Heavy flicked his cilia in the blob's direction and made his human face smile. "She iiis empress of the Zlatyr Realm. The green fluiiid she iiis secreting means she iiis about to giiive biiirth."

"Tell her highness congratulations," Blakey told Heavy. "Ask her how we can be of service."

"Ask her yourself," said Heavy. "She iiis quiite capable of understandiiing your language."

Blakey smiled at the gray blob as it hovered and dripped green fluid. "That's great. So how can we help you?"

"Melliiicloriiis wiiishes to buy all love," said Heavy, "and destroy iiit."

"Destroy it?" said Blakey.

"So she can market a cheaper, inferior substiiitute," said Heavy.

"Of course." Blakey glanced at Strayhorn but didn't seem to feel the need to wait for his advice. "Contact information, please. We'll have to get back to you on that."

*****

After another hour of kissing, Strayhorn pulled away from Dinah and rubbed his jaw. "I can't keep this up," he said. "We need to switch personnel."

"I know what you mean." Dinah's lips were sore, and her jaw ached--not that she intended to stop the kissathon anytime soon. "I think we'll be okay if we just take a break for a minute."

"No," said Strayhorn. "It's time to switch." He started to get up from his chair.

"Really," said Dinah. "I'll be fine."

"You don't understand," said Strayhorn. "We *need* to switch."

Just then, Blakey let out a loud whoop. "We have a winnah!"

"Yay!" Mahalia grinned and applauded. "This is it, Captain! We found the real deal!"

Dinah had missed the latest flurry of negotiations. She looked over to see Blakey shaking the tentacle of a seven-foot-tall orange-furred squid-thing. "What is it?" she said. "What's the deal?"

"Kioska here will fix Earth's atmosphere." Blakey patted the orange squid's rubbery spear-point head. "He'll even terraform the planet to reverse the global warming damage to the ecosystem!"

Strayhorn walked around the table to Blakey and Kioska. "What'll it cost us?"

"You're gonna love this." Blakey threw an arm around Strayhorn's shoulders. "How would you like to be the first man to set foot on an alien planet?"

*****

Two weeks later, Dinah blinked as light flooded the darkened stage where she and Strayhorn sat. She found herself gazing out at a huge crowd of orange-furred squid people, packed into a vast, upside-down theater.

Thousands of squid dangled by their tentacles from rungs in the ceiling. Each squid had one giant eye, blood-red and unblinking, fixed on Dinah and Strayhorn.

A chill rippled up Dinah's back as she felt their eyes

upon her. Yet again, she marveled at where she was, so far from home, on an alien world that no human being before her had ever visited.

Kioska had led them here, to his homeworld, from the space station. It was here that the humans would hold up their end of the deal and earn salvation for dying Mother Earth.

Suddenly, a familiar figure tumbled onto the stage--eggplant-shaped Heavy, Team Earth's self-appointed manager. Stopping in the middle of the stage, he inflated an orange-furred squid face on one of his cilia and turned it to the crowd. While Heavy unleashed a stream of wild squeaks for the audience, he puffed up a human face behind him and translated his words through it for Dinah and Strayhorn.

"Love!" said Heavy. "The new sensation! The most iiincrediiible experiience iiin the galaxy!"

The crowd responded with a deafening blast of whistles and squeals.

"Are you ready to liiive the dream?" said Heavy. "Are you ready for *love*?"

The squid things squealed louder. They swung back and forth on their rungs and smacked their bodies against each other with abandon.

"Then let the love begiiin!" As the noise and motion of the crowd reached a wild pitch, Heavy hurtled off the stage, leaving Dinah and Strayhorn alone in the spotlight.

Backstage, Mahalia switched on her music player, which she'd tuned to broadcast through the theater's sound system. This time, instead of jazz, it played an opera piece-- the Flower Duet from *Lakmé*, a sweet, soaring blend of two winding soprano voices.

That was Dinah and Strayhorn's cue. Smiling, Dinah leaned across the padded bench on which they sat. She slipped a hand behind Strayhorn's head, combing her fingers through his thick, dark hair, and pulled him close.

Their eyes met, and then their lips did, too.

They hadn't kissed since the end of the Worlds' Fair two weeks ago, and Dinah craved him. Returning to his lips felt like a fabulous culmination, an unimaginably perfect consummation. Every nerve in her lips flared with extraordinary sensitivity, magnifying every millimeter and millisecond of radiant contact between them.

Her pulse quickened, and her body warmed. Closing her eyes, she immersed herself in the building passion, the thrill of love on a grand scale, of legendary, history-making love.

Dinah was so caught up in the experience that at first, she didn't notice the change in the crowd. It took a few moments for the rising commotion to penetrate her romantic haze, to make her realize that the balance of the beautiful, dreamlike tide was shifting.

Opening her eyes, Dinah saw that the squid-people were jumping and bumping in the rafters. A growing racket rang out through the theater, a din of the shrillest, highest-pitched squeals and whistles she'd yet heard from the orange-furred creatures.

As it got worse, drowning out the opera soundtrack, Dinah exchanged a look with Strayhorn. His typically blank expression had switched to one of fierce, alert intensity.

"What's happening?" said Dinah. "What do they

want?"

Suddenly, Heavy jetted across the stage and jolted to a stop beside her. "What's goiiing on here?" he said with his bald human face.

"*You* tell *us*!" said Dinah.

"What are they saying?" said Strayhorn.

"'We want love!'" Heavy spun in a circle, every one of his heads and cilia quivering with agitation. "That's what they're sayiiing! They want love!"

The uproar from the crowd was so loud, Dinah had to shout to make herself heard. "I don't understand! We were *giving* them love!"

"Not liike before! Now try harder!" With that, Heavy whipped around and flashed offstage, leaving Dinah and Strayhorn alone.

As the crowd noise rose, Dinah gazed out at the hordes of orange-furred squid. "I guess we've got a tougher audience here," she said. "Necking isn't enough."

"We need to get out of here," said Strayhorn. "If they rush the stage, we're dead."

"No!" said Dinah. "Earth's depending on us!"

With that, she started unbuttoning her top.

"What are you doing?" said Strayhorn.

Dinah slid her arms from the sleeves of her blouse and tossed it to the stage. "What does it *look* like I'm doing?" With a shrug, she pressed closer to him, reaching for the buttons of his shirt. "If they want more, let's *give* them more."

Strayhorn grabbed her wrist, and Dinah pushed herself forward. With her free hand, she tore his shirt all the way open, then snaked an arm around his back and yanked him toward her.

"I say let's give them their money's worth," said Dinah, right before she lunged in for a ravenous, grinding kiss.

Strayhorn didn't get into the spirit of things at all, but Dinah kept working on him. She was convinced she could bring him around, especially once the squid-people started to settle down.

The problem was, instead of settling down, the squid-people grew more agitated. The clamor in the theater got worse with each passing second.

Dinah heard what sounded like falling bodies hitting the floor. When she looked out at the crowd, she saw squid dropping from the ceiling by the hundreds, bouncing to a landing on the theater floor on spring-loaded tentacles.

As soon as they landed, the squid started hopping toward the stage.

Yet again, Heavy zipped into the spotlight, spinning and quivering. "What iiis *wrong* with you two? They want *love*! Giiive them love love *love*!"

As Heavy darted away, Dinah shoved Strayhorn onto his back and pounced. Straddling his hips, she set to work undoing his pants while he gaped up at her in shock.

"I guess we have to take this all the way," said Dinah.

"No!" said Strayhorn. "Don't!"

"Give it everything you've got," said Dinah. "Remember, the future of humanity is riding on it!"

Before she could go any further, Strayhorn suddenly sat up and pushed her away. "I said *no*!"

Dinah fell back and rolled off the bench. She winced

and cried out as she hit the hard floor of the stage on her side.

"Hey!" she said. "What was *that* for?"

"Even if we *weren't* about to be swarmed by alien squid-people," said Strayhorn, gesturing at the approaching audience, "I *can't* make love to you! I'm in love with someone else!"

"What?" Dinah leaped to her feet. "*Who?*"

"Look." Strayhorn pointed behind her, into the backstage wings. "That's who."

Dinah turned and saw Ben Blakey hurrying toward them. "*Blakey?*" she said. "You're in love with *Blakey?*"

Strayhorn shook his head. "Not Blakey."

Just then, Dinah saw Mahalia charge out after Blakey. "Oh." Dinah felt her face flush. "I get it."

Mahalia rushed past Blakey and grabbed Strayhorn's shoulders. A million little memories suddenly fell into place in Dinah's mind--a jumble of looks and touches and words exchanged between Strayhorn and Mahalia that she'd always chalked up to simple friendship.

Only now she knew better.

Why didn't I see it before?

At that moment, Heavy bolted over among them. "Where iiis the love?" His voice was high and electric with fear. "Make the love! Make the love before iiit iiis *too late!*" Dinah thought it was too late already. The orange-furred squid-people were hopping onto the stage, converging on the spotlight with deadly purpose.

"That's what we were *doing!*" said Strayhorn. "What else do you *want* from us?"

"No no no!" said Heavy. "No love! No love at all!" He flipped and spun and twisted in midair, giving off a smell like chocolate. "They want the *sounds*! The dah-dah-dee-dah!"

"What the *hell* are you talking about?" said Blakey.

"*You* know!" Heavy flopped over and curled up, then uncurled and stretched out. "The *sounds* you made at the Worlds' Fair, when the two of you kiiissed! Liike dah-dah-dee-dah-doo. The *love*."

Dinah shook her head. "I don't get it."

"Wait." Mahalia snapped her fingers. "You mean the *music*? The *music* I played in the booth when they kissed?"

"'Music'?" Heavy shuddered.

"Like this." Mahalia did a little scat-singing, improvising syllables over a jazzy snatch of melody. "That's music. *Jazz* music."

"'Music'?" said Heavy. "Don't you mean 'love'?"

Mahalia looked from Strayhorn to Blakey to Dinah, eyes wide with understanding. "Oh my God," she said. "This whole time, they wanted *music*, not *love*."

"They thought we made it when we kissed," said Dinah.

As the squid-people closed in, Mahalia dashed offstage. The squid were just reaching for Dinah and the others when the music playing over the theater's sound system changed from opera to jazz.

Just like that, the orange-furred squid halted their approach. As one, they swayed and squeaked in time with the music, tentacles rippling with the flow of a soaring, sparkling trumpet solo.

"Nothing like a little Miles Davis to soothe the savage

alien," said Mahalia as she trotted back to the group. "And more where that came from." She held up her slim silver music player and tapped it with her fingernail.

Dinah let out a deep breath and slumped onto the bench. "That was close."

"You diiid iiit!" said Heavy, scooting around Team Earth in a jaunty circle. "You made the *love* again!"

"I still don't see what the big deal is," said Blakey. "Why don't you just make it yourselves?"

"We can't," said Heavy. "You are the fiiirst. Thiiis iiis something *new* to us."

"No kidding." Blakey laughed and clapped Strayhorn on the back. "I guess maybe humans are worth something out here after all."

"So now what?" said Dinah. "What next?"

"Contiiinue the Worlds' Tour, of course!" said Heavy. "Liiive up to your end of the deal!"

Blakey threw an arm around Strayhorn's shoulders. "So we'll just send around a recording, right?"

"Wrong," said Heavy. "We must have *live performance. Live love* on tour! The deal *says* so!"

"And us a bunch of non-musicians." Dinah blew out her breath.

"We'll just lip-synch." Mahalia shook her music player. "Play along with the recordings and pretend we're making the music from scratch."

"What happens when they get tired of the recordings?" said Dinah. "What'll we do then?"

"Same thing we always do." Mahalia grinned and winked at her. "Same thing Miles and Monk and Trane and all the rest always did.

"Make it up as we go along."

MESSIAH 2.0

I sing the *Our Father* again and again as I hack the undead to ribbons with my atomic scythe. Praying with all of my might for every lost soul I send spinning out of this misbegotten world.

"Our father, who art in Houston, hallowed be thy flame..."

More zombies push in to replace them, clambering over the shredded corpses of the previous wave. Their bony hands clutch and claw at me and my faithful assistant, not that they can do much harm to a robot like Imago. A giant among them swings a crowbar dead-on at him, and it bounces off his unbreakable stained-glass skin without making the slightest crack.

I smile and keep slicing away at the horde. The stench of the creatures surrounds me. My hands on the grip of the glowing scythe are wet with blood. I feel the weight of my long black braid swinging behind me as I whirl to face another foe.

And I know that I will keep fighting. Because I know that Imago and I are the hope of the world. It's up to us to stop the Great Evil from rising up against the King of the World. Up to us to find and destroy the last possible seed of the Apocalypse.

The last possible manifestation of the Second Coming of Jesus Christ.

*****

Hours later, Imago and I sit around a campfire in the heart of the Brazilian rain forest. Through the bitter smoke, I smell the fragrance of night-blooming tropical flowers. I taste the sweet juice of the rich, red fruit I've just eaten, picked fresh from a spiny tree. The jungle shrieks and chatters and hoots with the sounds of nocturnal life. Through it all, I hear the Amazon River rushing past somewhere nearby.

We have come to a distant place indeed. For company, we have only each other...and the blinking white symbol projected on the blade of my scythe. A tiny oval symbol, pointed at one end, bisected at the other, top and bottom curves crossing, then swooping up and down, capped by a straight vertical line. It's the ancient symbol of a fish.

The ancient symbol of a certain so-called Messiah. In this case, a Messiah in the making, a computer-predicted proto-Christ.

"She's stopped moving." The glowing symbol holds steady over the yellow gridlines pulsing on the silver blade. My scythe serves as a tracking device as well as a weapon. "Resting for the night, I'm sure."

Imago rises from the log on which he's been sitting. The fireflies that are always burning in his belly flicker as he moves. "We could use this opportunity to catch up, Father Clement." Like all Squire-series robots, he has a voice that's soft and soothing and a manner that's unfailingly polite.

"Too dangerous at night." I shake my head and put down my scythe, leaving the blade to charge in the fire. "We could stumble across another nest of the undead."

"You know I can light the way." Suddenly, the fireflies in Imago's belly flare bright. Incandescent streamers cascade from the rainbow facets of his body, lighting it up in all its glory. He is like a walking stained-glass window, molded from panes of every color--glittering, flashing red and blue and yellow and green and white. Like a chapel in the shape of a man in the middle of the jungle.

I raise a single finger in the air. The white sleeve of my cloak slides down to my elbow. "Your light might not be enough if this is a trap."

Imago nods gravely. His features are like iron filings shifting in his faceplate, black metal fuzz aligning as eyebrows, eyes, nose, and mouth. "You are ever wise,

Father Clement."

"We fought long and hard today. Better now to rest and start fresh again at dawn." I sit down beside the fire and cross my legs Indian-style. Instantly ready to fall asleep. Instantly ready to do anything, if it will help preserve the Kingdom.

Imago makes a soft chiming sound and begins the bedtime prayer. "Now I lay me down to sleep." The fireflies in his belly circle hypnotically as he speaks. "I pray the King my soul to keep."

Reaching into my mind, I begin to switch myself off. Like flicking off the lights back in the seminary, one at a time, with darkness all around.

And prayers. "If I should die before the morn..." Imago's soothing voice rolls onward, then does something unexpected. "If I should..." He stops.

And repeats himself. "If I should die before the morn, to serve the King I'll be reborn."

I frown, wondering if Imago's glitch signals damage. But then I shrug it off and relax. I flip the last switch and drift down into darkness like a feather from the wing of a falling angel.

*****

Next morning, like all mornings in the Kingdom, there is ice cream.

As Imago and I march into the village of Cristobal, the locals are just opening the transubstantiator--one of the matter converters that can change anything into anything else. Even the tiniest town in the Kingdom has at least one, thanks to the King.

Freezing mist puffs out when they pop up the lids on the gleaming waist-high silver pods, pulling out white scoops the size of baseballs flecked with black and brown. Laughing as they pop them out with their bare hands and toss them to the crowd.

Children scramble away with armloads, melting ice cream running from their elbows. Old men cradle single scoops in wooden bowls, while young men steal licks between juggling and pitching the scoops at each other.

I wish I could pause to paint this scene. Everyone looks so happy to be alive. They're clad in filthy loincloths, living in squalid huts of bark and leaves, but they're *happy*. Happy to be living as their ancestors lived, as they *choose* to live. Happy to be living in the worldwide Kingdom of Free Will.

When they spot us, they launch into ecstatic prayer-song. Every last one of them gathers 'round to welcome the humble soldier priest to their village.

I bless them with the sign of the King, tracing upside-down crosses in the air with practiced ease. Hugging the old women, tousling the children's hair. Everyone smells like the sweetest of flowers; reverse B.O.'s another glorious innovation of the King's benevolent anarchotechnocracy.

Raising my arms overhead, I speak to them all. "Greetings, Earth Angels! The King's blessings to you all!"

The crowd claps and dances around us. Reaching into the transubstantiator pod, I draw out a scoop of ice cream in my white-gloved hand. I bite into it, and my mouth fills with sweet, cold perfection.

Chocolate chip cookie dough. My favorite.

*****

I love this place. It's a shame I might have to burn it to the ground.

As the locals lead Imago and me to the chief's hut, I steal a glance at the glowing tracker display on the blade of my scythe. The signal from the proto-Christ's unique DNA doesn't move; it's coming from somewhere in this village, and it's staying put.

I lean over and whisper to Imago. "She's waiting."

He whispers back. "Preparing to ambush us, no doubt."

I nod. "She knows what I'll do to her." I give my scythe a meaningful flick. "Same thing I did to the other *eleven.*"

"Yes," says Imago as we bend down to enter the low doorway of the hut.

"Father!" Suddenly, a tiny man with shaggy gray hair and a beard leaps up in front of us. He wears a loincloth like the rest of his people and a feathered cloak besides, all reds and golds and greens against his dark brown skin. "Praise the King, you've joined us for the Feast of Second Cousins Twice Removed!"

"That's right." I throw on a huge grin, though there's nothing at all special about today's feast. The fact is, every day of the year is a holiday in the perfect Kingdom. *Most* days are doubled or tripled up with special occasions.

"Blessed are the second cousins twice removed, my son."

The Chief reaches into a basket and pulls out a piece of Edenfruit. Its skin glitters and swirls with every color of the rainbow, and it sings softly as it changes shape in his hand. This is the stuff that was Adam's favorite in the Garden, the fruit that was once *forbidden*. Thanks to the King, it grows in abundance everywhere in the world now, all throughout the Kingdom.

The Chief takes a bite and grins. "Will you lead our ceremonies, blessed Father?"

"I'll need a volunteer." I rub the black bristle on my chin. It's been days since I last shaved. "Someone who has come to town recently. Do you know of anyone like that?"

The Chief's eyes flick to one side and then back, and I know he's about to lie. "No one new. Will you settle for someone *old*?" He grins and spreads his arms.

I look at Imago as I laugh. The automaton nods imperceptibly; from programming and experience, he is able to read the intentions on my face, the inflections of my voice. The fireflies in his stained-glass belly begin to swirl in slow motion.

We both know it's time to find this proto-Christ before she gets away.

"Tell me, Earth Angel." I clamp a hand on the Chief's bony shoulder and give it a squeeze. "Which way to the latrine, please?"

*****

Imago distracts the villagers with a light show while

I stroll around town. I know the proto-Christ is here somewhere, maybe watching me at this very moment.

I feel a chill as I imagine her eyes upon me. The eyes of the one creature, according to Biblical Revelations, who could overturn the hard-won Kingdom.

But at least there is only one of her. One person left in all the world, according to the King's astounding Christputer, with the right mix of nature and nurture to become the dreaded Messiah.

Two years ago, when we first ran the numbers, the Christputer gave us twelve names. Imago and I have been on the road ever since, hunting down the likely candidates. Flushing them out and killing them before they could emerge from hiding and mount a revolution. Before they could try to replace the glorious Kingdom of Free Will with their so-called thousand years of paradise.

Maybe I've already killed the right one, the actual Second Coming. It's possible he or she was among those murdered eleven. But how could I live with myself knowing even *one* proto-Christ was still at large?

And what if she *did* turn out to be Jesus Christ 2.0?

*****

Soon enough, I give up the search. There are simply too many places to hide in the jungle around Cristobal. I'll never find her like this.

So it's time for another strategy.

Marching back into the middle of the village, I see Imago performing for the villagers, flashing multicolored lights in sync with a playful, piping tune. Brown-skinned children scramble and leap around him, smacking his body as they try to anticipate the flashing pattern.

Too bad I have to break up the party. "Children! Line up!" I point with the tip of my scythe at the ground alongside me. "Right here!"

Imago stops flashing and piping. "Father?"

The half-naked kids scurry over as they were told. When they're all in line, I nod to Imago. "Put me on bullhorn." He nods and spreads his arms wide, facing away from me. The next words I say boom out of his wondrous body, amplified ten times or more their original volume. "Brigid Gideon! Surrender immediately!"

As my words echo over the village and into the jungle, the children look around with eyes wide as Edenfruit. The adults watch in a circle around us, trying not to look worried.

Time now to put this in terms the proto-Christ will understand. "If you do not surrender by the count of ten, I will *slaughter* these innocent children!" I sweep my glowing scythe over their heads to show I mean business. "Their lives are in your hands! *One!*"

When some of the adults press in from behind me, I swing the scythe across their path. They trip over each other in their hurry to fall back.

"*Two!*" Do I like what I'm doing? Of course not. "*Three!*" But I need to bring her in one way or the other.

"Please, let them go!" The Chief raises his hands pleadingly, flapping his colorful feathered cape. The children are his charges.

He should try being responsible for *the fate of the entire kingdom.* "*Four!*"

"Father?" Imago tips his head to one side. His features are expressionless. "Will you do it?"

I scowl at him. "*Five!*" Imago has demonstrated his unflagging loyalty to me countless times. Since when does *he* question *my* actions? Maybe something really *is* wrong with him.

"Will you?" Imago's face remains expressionless.

He already knows the answer. "*Six!*" Of course I will. I'll do *anything* for the King of the World. *Anything* to preserve The Kingdom of Free Will.

Maybe it's time I demonstrated my devotion. I draw back the scythe, taking aim at one of the children, a little boy. Lopping an ear off ought to show I'm serious.

The parents gasp. I say the next number, "Seven!" But I don't hear it. Has Imago shut off the bullhorn?

Or is it the voice shouting from the jungle that's overpowering it? The woman's voice, calling from the edge of the rain forest?

"All right, all right!" She stomps out of the jungle with purpose, shoving aside lush green leaves the size of elephants' ears. "Enough with the *drama* already!"

I want to race over immediately and subdue her, but I don't. I let her come to me instead.

She snorts and shakes her head. "You really piss me off, you know that?"

"Lock her down!" As soon as I snap the order, Imago marches toward her with arms outstretched. Restraining cuffs materialize in his hands, courtesy of his built-in transubstantiator.

Brigid whirls to face him, and at first, I think there'll be a fight. She might just win, too. She's a big girl, built like a Clydesdale, over six feet tall. All shoulders and flanks and hocks.

But then she cocks her head and gives Imago a funny look. She stares at him for a moment, as if she's sizing up her chances, and she relaxes. She reaches out and lets him clamp the cuffs on her.

A breeze kicks around the wisps of blonde hair that have pulled free from her ponytail. "You're a Squire-series model."

The robot holds on to her hands a moment longer. "Yes, I am."

I storm forward and push him out of the way. "I usually pray for the souls of those I kill, even the undead." I pull back my scythe, and it hums and crackles with power. "But not this time."

"Don't do it, jackoff." Brigid tips her head back and sneers defiantly. "Biggest friggin' mistake of your pitiful life."

I laugh and tighten my grip on the handle of the scythe. "How so, she-devil?"

"There are lots more where *I* came from." Brigid nods. "An *army* of us. Your king doesn't stand a snowflake's chance in the Sahara."

Careful. "An army?" The serpent will say *anything* to gain the advantage.

"Enjoy your day in the sun, jackoff." She chuckles. "Believe me, the clock's ticking."

Before she can say another word, I've got her on the

ground with the blade of the scythe at her throat. "*Where? Where are they?*"

She grits her teeth, and I press the edge of the blade against her windpipe. A fine red line appears between the gleaming metal curve and her pale flesh.

"*Tell me!*" I kick her hard in the side.

"Screw you!" She hisses it between her clenched teeth.

By the time I'm done with her, she's missing some of those teeth. Along with other things.

But she's still alive. And finally cooperating. She agrees to lead us to the Second Coming.

*****

As soon as we cross the border of the Undead Zone--the UZ--my scythe starts to wail. I shut off the warning signal and keep walking.

But my senses are ratcheted up to full alert. My heart pounds, pushing adrenaline through me like rocket fuel. Because the truth is, we've just set foot outside the Kingdom.

On the surface, it seems no different from the rest of the rain forest, at least not yet. Dense green foliage crawls and hangs and twists and sprawls over every square foot. The air is thick with humidity and a steaming, sweet stew of mingled floral perfumes. Monkeys and tropical birds shriek and leap in the canopy. Insects whine in my ears and flicker over my bare skin, tiny wings and legs skittering through the hairs on my wrists and neck.

It seems no different, but it is very different indeed. It

is a foreign land over which the King has no sway, a pocket of corruption in which the wicked zombie undead run riot. They might range far and wide on their unholy sorties beyond the UZ, but this is the heart of their awful territory.

"Tell me where we're headed." I jab Brigid in the back with the handle of my scythe. "What are the coordinates?"

"For the tenth time, shove it up your *ass!*" Her long blonde ponytail switches from side to side as she shakes her head. "If I *tell* you, you'll *kill* me."

I jab her again for good measure, and she cries out. Imago, who is marching up ahead of us, slows his pace but does not look back.

Brigid's white blouse and tan shorts are stained with blood from my interrogation at the village. I pick the darkest spot on her back and stick her again. "There aren't any normals in the UZ." I give her one more jab, and her cry is louder this time. "Are you trying to tell me the Second Coming is *undead?*"

Brigid shrugs. "Where does it say it can't happen? You can accept a *woman* as the Second Coming, can't you?"

"The Christputer does not admit the possibility of an undead messiah." The green and yellow tail of a huge snake drops down in front of me, and I duck around it. "None of the simulations yields that result."

Brigid half-turns and looks back over her shoulder at me. "Because none of your precious models *includes* the undead as a *variable*, do they?"

I jab her once more. "*Forever.*"

She looks back again. "What's that supposed to mean?"

"It's how long your agonizing death will seem to take

if I find out you've been lying to me." I press the blade of my scythe against the side of her head, letting it hum and crackle in her ear.

*****

Soon enough, we encounter the undead. Two of them cross our path near a stream--a male and female dressed in the usual bloody tatters. When they look our way, I see decayed flesh falling from their faces. I instantly key the scythe to maximum power.

I'm already moving as they raise the alarm with blood-curdling shrieks. Flashing past Brigid and Imago, I raise the scythe and spin between the zombies like a whirlwind.

Their heads fly off in opposite directions, one bouncing off a tree, the other splashing down in the stream. Their bodies drop to the ground a second later. *Two down.*

And three to go. I hear the sound of snapping twigs and whip around to see three more zombies backing away through the underbrush. The most tragic undead of all, *child-size*, they were transformed at a young age and never had a chance at a normal life. I see two little boys and a black-haired preteen girl. How sad.

I will sing extra prayers for them as I hack them to bloody bits.

Such is my intent, until Brigid charges over and throws herself in my path. "Hands off, jackoff!"

"Imago!" I try ducking around her, but she stays in front of me. "Restrain her!"

Imago marches over and reaches for Brigid's arm.

"Come with me, Ms. Gideon."

Brigid pulls away from him. "These people aren't zombies! I won't let you kill them!"

Looking over her shoulder, I see the three children cowering in the weeds. Each is covered with oozing, peeling blotches of rot, swarming with flies. "*Of course* they're zombies! *Look* at them!"

Suddenly, Brigid does the unexpected. She steps up to me, gets right in my face, and locks her gaze with mine. "Your King has lied to you," she says. "*You* are the only zombie here."

With a snarl, I lunge at her. She spins away from me and darts toward the undead children lurking in the weeds. Shooting after her, I swing the scythe so the broad side of the blade will crash into her hip and bring her down. But the blow never connects.

As I run, my foot catches on something. I stumble and fall in the weeds and skid down the muddy bank into the stream.

Looking up, I wonder again if something's wrong with Imago. He stands atop the bank, right about where I took a header.

And he's ignoring me, his master, though I'm clearly in distress. Brigid is waving him over...and he's going.

"Imago!" He doesn't seem to hear me. Next thing I know, he's standing before the three zombie children.

I hear Brigid's voice as she hunkers down in front of them. "You poor babies. You're nothing but skin and bones."

"Imago!" I say it again as I clamber out of the stream,

shaking the water from my scythe.

Imago's too busy listening to Brigid. "You can make something for them to eat, can't you?" she asks him.

He pauses. "Yes."

"What would you like for lunch?" Brigid says to the kids.

Human flesh, I'm guessing, but that's not what they ask for.

"Ice cream." The oldest, the dark-haired girl, says it softly as I approach, then clears her throat and says it louder. "Chocolate ice cream."

I gape at her. Since when did the undead crave anything but the flesh and blood of the living?

"Please make her some chocolate ice cream, Imago," says Brigid.

"But they are undead." Imago tips his head to one side. "They are zombies."

"They are *alpha-lepers*," says Brigid. "If you doubt it, go ask your *king*."

"Why?" says Imago.

"He *made* them this way," says Brigid. "Because their families *opposed* him."

"She's lying, Imago!" I rush up beside him. "All lies!"

Brigid doesn't bother to look at me. Her focus is on the youngest child, a little redheaded boy no older than three or four. "What flavor of ice cream do *you* want?" she asks him.

"Peanut butter." The child's voice is so soft, I can barely hear it. So soft, so much like a *human* child's voice, that I hesitate.

I hesitate to slaughter him and the others on the spot

as my duty dictates.

"One order of chocolate and one order of peanut butter, please, Imago." Brigid turns to the third child, a blond boy of six or seven. "And what about you?"

"What about *them*?" The boy turns and points at the jungle behind him.

Eyes wide, they slowly emerge from the brush--more undead children, creeping out of hiding places among the glossy emerald elephant-ear leaves. They shuffle toward us along the bank of the stream, wary and furtive as starving dogs, silently converging.

How many are there? I count six, then ten, then twelve. And they keep coming. Every last one a blight on the face of the Earth, a target for my scythe.

So why don't I slaughter them all right here and now? Is it because I'm hoping they might lead me to the Army of the Second Coming? Is it because I need to get my prisoner well clear before the bloodbath, given the vital intel she might possess?

Or is it something else? Some reason I can't fathom?

"Yo, Imago! Get a move on!" Brigid spins her index finger in the air like the hands of a clock. "Let's get crackin' on that ice cream."

Imago looks at me, his iron filing features shifting inside his stained-glass faceplate. His expression changes from a confused frown to...what? A blank look. Unreadable.

Turning to the children, he holds out his hands, palms up, cupped. The fireflies dance like tiny fairies in his belly, and a scoop of brown ice cream appears in his grasp.

He hands it to the dark-haired girl, and then he conjures

another scoop. And another. And many more after that.

And the undead children keep coming out of the jungle, shambling like corpses with hands outstretched. They mutter the names of their favorite flavors, and Brigid calls them out to Imago.

Not one of those children leaves empty-handed. Some get seconds and thirds.

And not one of them tries to devour the flesh of the living.

*****

As we continue on our way, the undead children surround us. I pray for the strength to keep myself from slaughtering them, even as I wonder if I'm doing the right thing. Will they lead us to a hidden mother lode of proto-Christs unpredicted by the Christputer, or will they lead us into an inescapable death-trap?

"How does it feel?" Brigid asks me this as we march through the mid-afternoon heat. "Knowing that none of those people you've murdered were zombies?"

I try to ignore her. Proto-Christs are always looking to stir up doubt and disharmony with their words.

She shakes her head. "All those deaths on your conscience. All those innocents." She clucks her tongue against the roof of her mouth. "That's a heavy weight for you to bear."

I reach back and swing my black braid around front, letting it fall against my white cloak. A fat red spider crawls along the length of the braid, and I brush it off in Brigid's direction.

She swats it away reflexively with her cuffed hands, without flinching. "I can guess what hurts the most," she says. "Being lied to by your beloved King. Knowing he led you astray for his own purposes."

This time, I can't hold back. "Shut up, she-devil! Save your lies for the gates of Hell!"

"Okay, listen." Brigid leans closer as we walk. "I'm sorry."

"Sorry?" A proto-Christ has never apologized to me before. "Sorry for what?"

"For calling you 'jackoff,'" says Brigid. "And also for having to tell you something you won't want to hear."

I glare at her. "Tell me what?"

"The undead aren't the only thing the King has lied to you about." The look in her eyes contains pity or sympathy or both. "He has lied to you about *everything*, Clement."

I snort in disgust and look away from her. "*I* feel sorry for *you*. The King has already *judged* you. Your terrible punishment is carved in stone."

Her shoulder brushes against mine. There is no hatred in her voice when she speaks. "Everything you know is a lie, Clement. *Everything*."

*****

Twilight has fallen by the time we reach the huts. There are three of them clustered together, decrepit and half-collapsed...leaves missing from the roofs, bark missing from holes in the walls. Ashes, charred wood, and bones litter the muddy patch between them. The air is so thick with the stench of excrement and rot, I can taste it. I see no light and hear no sound as we approach, as if the place is deserted.

But it is not.

Someone crawls out of one of the huts on hands and knees. Someone so far decayed, I can't tell if it's a man or a woman. *Undead.*

Instantly, I swing the scythe around and thumb it to full power. This zombie might look far gone, but it could still do some damage if I let down my guard.

"Hello," Brigid says to it.

"P...p...puh." The crawling zombie spits out teeth with its consonants. "Kuh...kuh...k..."

"Poor dear." Brigid looks at Imago. "We have to help her."

I've had about as much of this proto-Christ as I can stand. "Hey! Are we here for a *reason?*"

Brigid flashes me a smirk. "Not the one *you* think."

Imago turns to her. "Help?" The fireflies in his belly are agitated. "How can we *help?*"

"We can't!" I barge between them. "The undead are *beyond* our help!"

"That's a *lie.*" Brigid points at Imago. "And you can *prove* it."

"Don't listen to her, Imago." I clamp my hand on his warm crystal shoulder. "You know the forces of darkness always seek to mislead us."

Brigid elbows between us. "But what if I'm *right* about this? What if you *can* help her? What would it hurt to find out?"

I hear the sound of something cracking nearby. Spinning, I see another undead monstrosity emerge from a hut. This one shuffles toward us alongside the first, squinting from a misshapen face like the caved-in mush of a rotten jack-o'-lantern.

"Hel-l-l..." Again, I can't tell the undead's gender from looking...but the deep voice is that of a man. "P-p-ple-e-e...p-ple-e-e.."

"*Enough!*" When I snap out the word, the children, as one, take a step away from me. "We're *leaving!*"

Brigid backs toward the huts, eyes locked on Imago. "You're M.D. certified, aren't you? Fully stacked for medical diagnosis and treatment?"

"Yes," says Imago.

"Then boot up the protocols for alpha-leprosy," says Brigid, "and get over here."

Imago's fireflies whip around like campfire ashes in a stiff breeze. He looks at me for a long moment without a word.

"Don't do it, Imago." I shift the glowing scythe from one hand to the other, hoping he picks up on the underlying threat. "That's an *order.*"

Imago looks at the undead creatures by the huts and makes a sound like a sigh. "What will it hurt to find out?" he says, and then he marches over to join Brigid.

My hands twist on the handle of the scythe. Little by little, she's taking him away from me.

So what do I do next? I have it in my power to kill them both, and all the undead around us besides. After that, I could move on alone and slaughter any undead I find, scorch the UZ earth of anything remotely resembling a hidden proto-Christ.

But what if there's still hope? What if I could still fix Imago? Shouldn't I at least give him a chance?

A thought occurs to me, and I frown. For the first time, I realize something about Imago. And it makes me think *I'm* the one who needs fixing.

Since when do *I* care about a *robot?*

I hear humming and beeping from Imago as he treats the undead. Rays of light flare from his stained-glass body, beams of green and blue and gold combing and flashing through the twilight jungle shadows.

The undead children stay behind me, watching with mouths hanging open. The flashing accelerates to a fever pitch. A shrill whine races up the scale, quickly reaching a level so piercing that the undead kids have to cover their ears.

Then, suddenly, it's over. The lights and noise die away all at once.

I already know what the result must be, of course. The only cure for the undead is extermination. Imago has surely failed.

I start to worry that there might be an unexpected side effect, though. Brigid and Imago block my view, but I can see Imago's crystalline body shaking fiercely.

"Imago?" I rush over to him, heart pounding, ready for anything.

But I'm not ready for what I see.

Looking over Imago's shoulder, my eyes are drawn

downward. This is what's making him shake: a sobbing figure with head and hands pressed against his stained-glass surface--a middle-aged woman with long brown hair, kneeling where an undead monstrosity once was. Through the rags she wears, I can see her skin is smooth and unblemished. She is crying tears of joy all over Imago.

As she wraps her arms around him, someone rises from the ground beside her. He is also middle-aged and dressed in tatters, and his hair is black. Like the woman, his skin is undamaged, unmarked.

This is impossible.

"I can't thank you enough." The man wipes away tears of his own and reaches for Imago's hand. "My wife and I were so far gone, we'd even been exiled from the leper colony. I never imagined we would ever be *cured.*"

Imago looks at me as the man shakes his hand. "Alpha-lepers," says Imago. "That's what they were."

"No, Imago. This is some kind of trick." My voice is firm and steady.

"So many you've killed," says Imago. "I could have cured them."

"No!" I shake my head hard. "That's not true!"

"You didn't know?" says Imago. "You really didn't know?"

"No, I did *not,*" I tell him. "Because it isn't *true.*"

He stands there a moment, eyes locked with mine, thinking his clockwork thoughts. I can almost see them chugging and revolving in his stained-glass head.

Then, Brigid calls him over to cure the undead children and he turns away, leaving me to wonder about the results of whatever secret calculations he's just run.

*****

As we march onward with our retinue of seemingly cured zombies, I run calculations of my own. I consider the possibilities of what I have witnessed, weighed against the experiences of a lifetime.

How does it feel? Brigid's words echo in my mind. *Knowing that all those people you've murdered weren't zombies?*

I suppose she wants me to feel regret, but I don't. I have only ever known one King, one master, and I've slaughtered the undead in service to him. I killed them to defend the Kingdom of Free Will, and that hasn't changed. Whether they were undead zombies or alpha-lepers, they still opposed the Kingdom. They still opposed Paradise.

But what if I've been wrong about Paradise? If the King lied about the undead, could he have lied about Paradise, too?

Brigid tries to persuade me as we slog through the jungle at night. "Your King is the Great Beast prophesied in the Book of Revelations."

I scowl and shake my head. "The *Christ* is the Great Beast. *He* is the Great Evil."

"Your King rules through deception and force," says Brigid. "But that is about to end. The awakening of the Christ will usher in a millennium of true paradise."

"Paradise has already arrived," I tell her.

Brigid cocks her head and stares at me in the glow of Imago's body-light. "Have you ever had sex, Clement?"

I turn away.

"Before you experienced it for the first time," says Brigid, "did you truly *know* what it was like? How *good* it would feel?"

I don't answer.

"*That* is what *true* paradise is like, Father," says Brigid. "It's not like *anything* you've known."

"Shut up." I walk faster to get away from her.

"Your whole life has been a wet dream, Clement," says Brigid, "and you're about to wake up."

*****

In the darkest heart of the night, we arrive at the village. It looks like a fort in the jungle, surrounded by a high, circular wall of crudely cut logs. Smoke and light and noise rise from the interior, curling up toward the star-littered sky.

Brigid walks up to a door in the wall, a slab of galvanized metal, and knocks with her handcuffs. I post myself beside her, gripping my atomic scythe tightly.

I don't like the fact that I can't see what's behind the door or walls. At this point, anything can happen.

"All right then." My voice is a whisper. "Once we're inside, stay out of the way. Make a wrong move and I'll kill you."

She doesn't even try to lower her voice. "Why?" She looks at me like I'm crazy. "What do you think you're going to *find* in there, exactly?"

I lay the blade of the scythe against her throat. "The Second Coming. An army of off-the-radar proto-Christs.

I'm sure you think they'll save you, but they won't."

Brigid looks amused, then disappointed. "You haven't changed, have you? Even after everything you've seen."

Something bangs heavily against the other side of the door. I hear the clanking of chains. "Just do as you're told," I tell her.

As the door opens inward, Brigid smiles sadly. "I said there's an army of us. I said your kind doesn't stand a chance. But I never said we were *proto-Christs*."

"*What?*" My hands twitch on the handle of the scythe. "But you said you would lead us to the Second Coming!"

"I did." Brigid nods. "And I have."

*****

I keep the blade at her throat as we enter. "Where then?" Anger surges within me. "Where is the Second Coming?"

Inside the village walls, the undead converge on us from all directions. They stare and shamble in the firelight, upright masses of peeling and suppurating flesh.

"Where is the Second Coming?" I direct my question to the villagers. "Tell me, or I'll kill her!"

"Let her go," says an undead male at the head of the group.

"Is it *you?*" I ask him. "Are *you* the Second Coming? The one who seeks to topple the Kingdom of Free Will?"

"Not him." An undead female steps forward.

Keeping a firm grip on Brigid's arm, I sweep my glowing scythe toward the undead woman. "It's *you* then?

You're the one who'd put an end to the daily *holidays* and *ice cream* and Heaven on *Earth?*"

The man steps in the path of my blade. "What are you talking about?"

"The Second Coming!" I flick the scythe across his rotting chest, connecting his seeping sores with a fine line of blood. "Who among you is the *Second Coming?*"

"Wha...wha..." A third villager hobbles forward. Half his face has fallen away. "Wha...is-s-s...thuh...Se-cun...Cum-un...?"

My heart races. I turn in a circle, flashing the scythe overhead.

"They don't know about the Second Coming," says Brigid. "Not yet."

"Lies!" If they won't tell me who it is, they leave me no choice.

Leaping forward, I slash the half-faced villager to pieces with the scythe. Then, I sweep the weapon around behind me and kill the other two without looking.

Singing the "Our Father," I wade into the whole damned horde of them, whirling and hacking and slicing. Body parts fly everywhere, and blood fountains into the night sky.

This is what I was born to do. What I was trained for. Graceful annihilation in the name of the King. The noble dance of the warrior priest, carving up monsters like a hibachi chef carving up vegetables.

"Our father, who art in Houston, hallowed be thy flame..."

When I am done, my King will reward me for my

service, for saving the Kingdom. He will summon me to Texas and erect statues in my honor and declare a new feast day and ice cream flavor in my name. All will be right with the world.

This is what I am thinking when someone hits me from behind. When my legs go out from under me, and I drop to the muddy ground on my knees.

I scramble to get back on my feet, and someone hits me again. This time, the blow to my head leaves me dazed. I fall back in the mud and go limp.

That's when I see him. The middle-aged black-haired man, the first zombie treated by Imago. He leaps onto my chest, stone in hand.

And he hits me in the face. He pounds me, again and again.

The world goes watery and melts together in a blur of color and sound and pain. The man keeps pounding my skull with the stone, and I feel myself slipping away.

Wait. These are my final thoughts. *Things are not what you think.*

And then the world runs down into darkness, like a painting in the rain. And then everything is black and silent and still.

*****

"Clement? Father Clement?"

Those are the first words I hear when I return. When the faintest glimmer of awareness flutters into my mind.

"Wake up, Father. It's begun." A woman's voice.

"Wakey wakey, eggs and bakey." Brigid's voice. That's what I hear.

Instinctively, I open my eyes. This happens at the same moment I realize I shouldn't have eyes to open because they were smashed in by a rock.

But it doesn't seem to matter. I see Brigid staring down at me, silhouetted against a bright blue sky.

"There you are!" she says. "Welcome back!"

I close my eyes, then open them again. I feel light-headed. Light-bodied, too. As if a weight has been lifted.

"How long was I out?" Looking at the brightness of the sky, I try to guess what time of day it is. Just after sunrise, maybe?

"You mean how long were you *dead?*" Brigid raises her eyebrows. "Three hours. You were dead for three hours."

I lift my head from the mud and look around. Imago stands behind Brigid, staring blankly down at me. We are surrounded by a crowd of men, women, and children, all unblemished and dressed in tatters. "What are you talking about?"

"Don't you remember getting your head bashed in?" Brigid reaches down and taps my nose, which also shouldn't be there. "You *died*, Clement."

I scowl and shake my head. "Not possible." Even as I say it, I remember the stone smashing my skull. I remember the pain as it slammed down again and again, and the world melting and fading to black.

"You were pushing up daisies," says Brigid. "You were an *ex-Clement.*"

Suddenly, I add things up, and a chill of terror rushes

through me. "You're trying to tell me..." I feel a wave of inescapable desperation spread out from the pit of my stomach. "You're saying I was *dead*, and now I'm *not?*"

"Yes." Brigid nods. "Exactly."

I push myself to a sitting position, fighting the urge to run away. I try to keep the fear out of my voice. "You mean I'm...*undead?*"

"Yes." When she says it, my heart sinks. Then, she laughs. "But only in the sense of *not* being *dead*."

I'm not sure what to think at this point. "Even if I *was* dead, and you could bring me back, why *would* you?"

"It wasn't *my* idea, that's for sure," says Brigid. "But the *Second Coming* seemed to think you were worth saving."

I look past Brigid and Imago at the crowd. Which one of them is the Second Coming of Jesus Christ?

"Apparently, he has a plan in mind for you." Brigid shrugs. "Like I said, it's begun."

"What's that? What's begun?" I teeter as I get to my feet, still feeling light-headed. My eyes flicker, and I start to fall.

Suddenly, I feel strong hands catch me and set me on my feet again. When I open my eyes, I see him.

Imago. Light streaming in rainbow-colored beams from the facets of his stained-glass body. The iron filing features in his faceplate tracing a smile of black metal fuzz.

"The Millennium," he says in that soft, soothing voice of his. "We're about to usher it in."

"Imago?" My own voice falters as I consider the implications.

"*He* brought you back." Brigid says it in my ear. "*He's*

the one you've been *looking* for all this time."

"The Second Coming?" My heart pounds as I stare at Imago's robotic face. "He *can't* be."

"I was only ever his prophet," says Brigid. "I'm not fit to polish the chassis of the one who comes after me."

My head spins. I'm not sure what to think or do or say. "Imago?"

The fireflies swirl in his belly. "I am the truth, the way, and the life. He who believeth in me shall never die." The beams of light streaming from his stained-glass facets flare with blinding intensity. "Welcome to Paradise 2.0, Father Clement."

As we sit on the terrace in the oppressive jungle heat, I slide a shot of crystal clear vodka across the glass table. The man who was once Senator Joseph McCarthy taps the rim with one index finger and chuckles.

"Come on now." He shakes his head, smirking. "You know I don't touch *that* stuff, Vladimir."

I shrug and throw back my own shot. Feel the burn rolling down my throat like a slow-motion solar flare. "I've had lots of names," I say as I pour another. "Why do you insist on calling me by *that* one?"

"Vladimir Ilyich Ulyanov." McCarthy says it with grand sarcasm. "You'll always be Lenin to me."

"Ha." I down the second shot and clap the glass on the table. "And you'll always be an incompetent fear-mongering bastard to me."

"You talk like I didn't just kill your hand-picked Red Guard." He gestures at the twelve charred corpses strewn about the terrace. Five are still smoking in the blazing mid-morning sun. "Like it isn't just you and me here now."

I smile and raise the vodka bottle. The rays of the sun play through it on my face, refracted by the uneven crystal. "How 'bout if I drink you for it?" I shake the bottle. "I'll drink you for the revolution."

Something screeches in the treetops (bird, cat, monkey?) and McCarthy stops smirking. "You've led your last revolution, Lenin. End of story." He spreads his hands, exposing the octagonal barrels of the fusion guns mounted in his palms.

"And what if I'm not done here?" This time, I drink my shot straight from the bottle.

"Don't you think you've done enough to screw up this planet? And *ours*?" McCarthy aims his fusion guns at my head. "You're done, all right. Just as soon as we clear up some unfinished business."

I watch a flock of flamingos drift up into the turquoise sky. The scene reminds me of our homeworld, thousands of light years away. "What might that be?"

"I need to know where she is," says McCarthy. "Where is Irina?"

I laugh and shake my head, unwilling to tell him the

truth. Because the truth is, I don't know where the love of my life has gone.

*****

The first time I met Irina, I was blown away by how beautiful she was. The purple-and-green-tinted crystalline clusters of her body glittered in the auditorium's ever-flowing fireworks. Two of her six multifaceted eyes were silver, and four were gold, a mark of great passion and intelligence. Even her parasites had a special look about them as they danced around her body, multicolored tongues of flame weaving in and out of her vent slits.

I was never the same after that first glimpse of her. I had never seen anyone so beautiful in all my life.

"I believe we can help the humans." Those were the first words I heard her say. "I believe our way of life can change their world for the better and make them civilized enough to be welcomed into the community of worlds."

This was one of our pre-mission briefings on the homeworld. Sixty-five of us in one room, getting ready to take another crack at the problem children of the galaxy-- human beings. Other species had tried and failed to help humanity get its act together, but we honestly believed we'd be different.

To tell you the truth, just watching and listening to Irina was enough to make me believe with all my hearts.

"It's not their fault, you know." Irina (her name wasn't Irina then, it was unpronounceably alien) glided around the stage as images of human violence flickered in the air above her. "They've evolved in a hyper-competitive ecosphere. 'Eat or be eaten' is written deep in their genetic code."

"And it's up to us to teach them how the rest of the galaxy lives." As I spoke, I hoped she wouldn't pick up on the nervous quaver in my voice.

"Share and share alike, yes." Irina smiled. "No more 'dog eat dog,' as the humans say."

"What about 'kill or be killed?'" This time, it was the one who later became Joseph McCarthy who spoke--all ice blue crystals swirling with pink tongues of flame. Even then, he was a contrarian. "What if the humans kill us all as part of their 'ecosphere?'"

"As you know," said Irina, "they won't see us as beings from another world. We'll be altered to look like them."

McCarthy made a disparaging sound like pebbles clacking together in a glass vase. "And you don't think that will *increase* our chances of being killed?"

"Not for we brilliant few." Irina's voice was full of conviction. Her green and purple clusters pulsed with an electric neon tinge. "Not for those of us with all that's right and just on our side. Not for the denizens of the galactic *workers' paradise.*"

With that, sixty-four of us went wild in the auditorium, singing and clattering with inspired elation. Passing silvery gellid packets of pure, noble emotion back and forth. At least in my case, inspired by pure and growing love.

Only McCarthy stood apart and pouted, a clear sign he should have been drummed out of the mission. But Irina always said we crystal saviors needed all facets to catch the light.

Though the truth is, a single cracked facet can ruin the view completely.

*****

It was the happiest day of my life.

A massive movement of people swelled the streets of Petrograd, Russia, flowing down every byway in an irresistible human tide. The roar of cheers and song filled the cold October air, the sound of change rising amid the ancient onion-domed towers.

Change that we had brought into being.

Irina's hands slid up over my shoulders. "We've done it," she said. "We've begun the world revolution."

I turned from the window and swept her into my arms. "Yes, *milaya moya*." I called her that for the first time, called her *my sweet*. And then I did something else for the first time, too. "*Ya tebya lyublyu*." *I love you*, I said, and then I kissed her.

She did not push me away.

The moment washed over me, and I reveled in it. My makeshift pseudo-human heart thundered in time with the marching feet outside my window.

I had traveled thousands of light-years from my homeworld to get to this moment. I had toiled five decades on Earth in a myriad of human identities to make this happen, as had all of us. Now here I was, in the Earth year 1917, playing the role of a human named Lenin, calling history's shots from my headquarters in the Smolny Institute in Petrograd.

Kissing the greatest love I'd ever known outside my service to humanity and the universe.

"*Laskovaya moya.*" Irina said it in a whisper. She kissed me again, then leaned back to gaze at me with dancing green eyes. "Your timing is auspicious, my darling. Our greatest work is yet to come."

I caressed the side of her face. "Together, we cannot *help* but succeed."

"Come on." Eyes twinkling, she backed away, pulling me with her. "Let's drink it in. Let's go outside."

Changing our features so we wouldn't be recognized, we slipped out a back door of the Institute. Merging with the vast crowd in front of the building, where people were cheering my name, we laughed and held each other close.

"Don't let it go to your head," said Irina.

"Of course not!" I said it with a grin.

"Not that you'll get the chance." Irina shrugged. "You'll be somebody new in a couple of years, and so will I."

As the crowd continued to cheer and sing around us, I stared at her face. Even disguised, it couldn't conceal her radiance, her passion, her certainty. As ever, she held me mesmerized.

"Who will we be in five years, Irina?" I said. "In ten years? Do you know?"

She tipped her head and smiled. "The plan is fluid, of course, but yes. I have some idea."

"Will we be together?" I took a deep breath. "Can you tell me that much, at least?"

She looked at me for a long moment as the crowd

continued to cheer my name. The currents of history roiled around us like whitewater, churning and seething, overflowing their banks. Thanks to us, the mass of humanity was thrashing closer to a glorious communal destiny among the proletariat of the stars.

"We will not always be together." Irina wrapped her arms around me. "But we will not always be apart."

It wasn't the answer I'd had in mind, but I let it pass as she drew me against her. As she pressed her full lips against mine, and we kissed in the pulsating heart of the revolution.

Both of us knowing we were breaking a fundamental rule of our mission. Not because we were falling in love.

But because we were being selfish.

*****

The next time I saw Irina was nearly four decades later, standing over the dead body of Josef Stalin.

Stalin lay on the floor of his private quarters in Kuntsevo, sprawled at Irina's feet. She stood with her hands on her hips, shaking her head as she looked down at him.

"I'm starting to notice a pattern here." She said it without looking up when I entered the room. She knew it was me, after all; she'd summoned me here from China. "Human gets power. Human abuses power. Human subverts the cause of the workers' revolution."

I crouched beside Stalin's body, letting the mask of my current prime identity--Mao Zhedong, President of the People's Republic of China--melt back into the face I'd worn so long ago as Vladimir Lenin. "I thought he was a great choice, too, Irina. Just like everyone else did."

"Maybe that's the problem." Irina sounded tired. "We make lousy choices."

Placing my hand over Stalin's face, I slid his eyelids shut. "Or it's just going to take longer than we thought, dragging these people into the age of communal civilization."

"There's another possibility, as well," said Irina. "Perhaps we need to modify our strategy."

I got to my feet and shrugged. "That's always a possibility when dealing with complex sentient beings." Face to face with Irina, I gazed into her eyes. They were darker than I remembered and no longer sparkling. "Sentient beings can be highly unpredictable." *Like you*, I thought.

As I watched her stare into space, I wondered why she'd shut me out for forty years. I wondered if she still felt anything for me at all.

"I've been thinking." She turned away and paced across the room. "I've been working on a new approach."

"Tell me," I said. Anything to keep her talking, to spend more time with her.

"I've developed a new identity over the past decades." She stopped pacing and changed shape over Stalin. Until that moment, she'd worn the form of a young woman with long, brown hair. Before my eyes, she became a middle-aged man in a dark suit, stocky and bald. "Meet Nikita Krushchev. I'll be taking the reins now that Stalin is dead."

I folded my arms over my chest. I'd known she was Krushchev, though I hadn't heard it directly from her. I hadn't heard *anything* from her in forty years.

Irina tapped her chin with a forefinger. "Meet the new

face of the revolution. The harbinger of a bold new era."

"So you're following in my footsteps?" I shifted my face to look like my past identity of Vladimir Lenin. "Doing the driving *yourself* instead of trusting a flawed human?"

Irina the bald middle-aged man nodded. "The USSR has been turned inward against itself for too long. Why punish and purge the very workers we need to advance the revolution? Better to secure their allegiance with incentives while working to weaken the outside institutions that seek to oppose the proletariat."

I looked down at the body of Stalin and frowned. "You're talking about reversing the policies of the past thirty-one years."

"I call it De-Stalinization," said Irina. "Let up the pressure at home, increase the pressure abroad. Speed up the timetable of the worldwide revolution."

I listened and nodded. Even in the body of a middle-aged human male, she could sway me. Even after forty years apart, my feelings for her hadn't changed.

"China is coming along nicely." I switched my face back to Chairman Mao's, pear-shaped and heavy-jowled, with a dark fringe of hair around the back and sides of my head. "I think Earth will reach a tipping point soon, and the international proletariat will unify."

"All the more reason to press forward strategically," said Irina.

Reaching over Stalin's body on the floor, I clapped a hand on Irina's shoulder. "Tell me what you need me to do." I gave her shoulder a squeeze and gazed deep into her eyes. "You know I will stand by your side."

Irina held my gaze for a long moment, then laid her hand on my forearm. "Stay the course. That's all."

"I'll have one of the others take my place as Mao," I said. "You'll need my help to consolidate power here."

"I need your help most in China right now," said Irina. "The People's Republic is at a formative, vulnerable stage."

Instead of giving up and letting go, I took hold of her other shoulder. "No." It was the first time I'd ever said that to her. "I'm staying with you."

"That's sweet." Irina lightly touched my face. "But no. You have your orders."

"Orders?" I pulled away from her. "I don't understand. Why did you call me here if you didn't want my help?"

"To warn you," said Irina. "Our own people are working against us."

I was stunned to hear it. "Who?"

"Senator Joe McCarthy, for one. Our U.S. operations are in a shambles thanks to him." Irina sighed. "And there are others. I don't know who yet."

"Unbelievable." I shook my head in amazement. "How could *any* of us turn against the revolution?"

Irina moved closer, shifting back to the form she'd worn earlier, that of a brown-haired woman. Taking hold of my arms, she gazed into my eyes with blazing intensity. "*You* would never betray me, would you?"

I met her gaze with unshakeable steadiness. "Of course not." Her fingers dug painfully into my arms, but I refused to flinch. "How could you even *ask* me that?"

Irina held me a moment longer, then leaned forward and kissed me softly on the lips. "*That* is why I summoned you." Her voice was a whisper in my ear. "Because I had to be sure."

The scent of her mesmerized me. I could barely think straight. "That's it?"

"For now." When she drew away from me, she was Krushchev again.

Standing there, I felt shaky and disoriented. I'd been so *close* to her for the first time in forty years, and now she was moving out of reach again. She'd kissed me, but the kiss had felt empty, intended only as a guarantee of my loyalty.

There was so much I wanted to say to her, so much I *should* have said...but all I managed was this: "When will I see you again?"

"Every time you open a newspaper," said Irina/ Krushchev. "I'm going to take the world by storm."

*****

Nine years later, in October 1962, Irina/Krushchev leaped up from behind her desk as I burst into her office in the Kremlin. She came up with revolver in hand, leveled right at me.

Irina got off two shots without a word. They both missed as I bolted across the office.

Dropping as another shot exploded from the gun, I rolled over the floor and stopped behind a chair with fat red cushions. "Irina! Don't shoot!" I thought hearing that name might make her hold her fire.

But no. She cracked off another shot, straight through the chair, barely missing me.

Taking a breath, I prepared to charge. I'd known this would be the hardest part of my mission. That was really saying something, considering how many times I'd had to change shape and use force to get through security in the heavily fortified inner sanctum of the Kremlin.

But it had to be done. Irina was on the verge of making a horrible mistake, and I had to stop her.

I had to stop her from destroying humanity.

Crouching, I hoisted the chair off the floor and heaved it at her. As it crashed down on her desk, I darted after it.

Irina sidestepped, firing wide. As I dove across the desk at her, though, she got off one more shot.

This time, the bullet struck its target. I caught the lead in the meat of my shoulder, and my body flared with sudden pain.

But I wasn't about to let it stop me. My hands connected, throwing her over backward, sending the gun flying from her grip. We hurtled to the floor, pulling a desktop TV set down with us.

The TV burst to smithereens on the hardwood, spraying us with glass shrapnel. Irina flailed underneath me, using all the mass of her Krushchev disguise to try to throw me.

But I would not be dislodged. I shifted my own form again, changing from an athletic young man to an obese middle-aged one, pressing her down with my greater weight.

"Irina!" Holding her down, I shifted the flesh of my shoulder. Out popped the bullet, ending my pain. "Stop and listen to me!"

She kept thrashing, fighting to break free. "Get off! Let go!"

"You are subverting the cause of the interstellar revolution!" I said. "The community of worlds will not condone your actions!"

Irina bucked and squirmed, scowling with rage. "The situation is under control!"

"You're wrong!" I said. "U.S. forces are at DEFCON 2. Kennedy's about to attack."

"He's bluffing!" said Irina.

"If you don't pull your missiles out of Cuba, there will be worldwide nuclear war tomorrow." I locked eyes with her, dead serious. "Humanity will be exterminated or close to it within days."

Irina shook her head. "You don't understand. We've been negotiating with the Americans through back channels. We're close to a breakthrough!"

"Listen to yourself!" I said. "You're willing to risk the *extinction* of all *humankind*. You'd sacrifice the very proletariat we've come to set free!"

"It won't come to that," said Irina.

"But it *could*. Taking the world to the *brink* like this makes it *possible*."

"It's *always* possible on this throwback planet," said Irina. "We're working to make it *less* possible."

"So it won't bother you?" I said. "Being responsible for the annihilation of an entire *species?*"

"*You* should *talk*. How many millions of humans have you condemned to death in the name of the People's Republic of China?"

"There's a big difference between *purging* and *extinction*."

"Which won't *matter*, because the Americans are about

to *capitulate*," said Irina.

Just then, heavy footsteps marched into the room. "Premier Krushchev!" A thickly built silver-haired man in an olive drab and red uniform gaped in alarm at the wreckage.

Hastily, I took on the shape of an official I'd knocked out on my way to Irina's office. "The Premier tripped and fell," I said as I helped Irina to her feet. "Are you all right now, sir?" said the uniformed man.

"Yes, I'm fine, Boris." Irina dusted herself off. "You're here because of the noise, I suppose?"

"No, sir," said Boris. "I have a message from Intelligence." He stopped talking and stared at me.

"Go ahead." Irina waved dismissively in my direction. "Comrade Sergei is cleared to hear such information."

"Yes, sir." Boris glanced my way once more, then focused on Irina. "Our forces in Cuba have shot down an American U-2 spy plane."

"Oh?" Irina leaned forward on the desk. "The pilot?"

"Dead," said Boris. "And the Americans have shut down the back channel talks."

Irina took a breath and slowly released it. Her whole body stiffened. "Permanently?" she said.

"Unknown at this time," said Boris. "However, Intelligence confirms that the U.S. is about to launch an attack."

"On Cuba," said Irina.

"And the motherland," said Boris. "War is imminent."

"I see." Irina closed her eyes and rubbed her temples.

"Premier." Boris took off his cap and took a step

forward. "The defense ministers agree it is time to exercise the preemptive strike option."

"I understand." Irina cleared her throat. She shot me a look, then sat down on the edge of the desk.

"The ministers await your orders," said Boris.

"Soon enough." Irina waved him off. "I wish to weigh the options first, General."

Boris hung there for a moment, expectant, then saluted. "I'll be just outside, Premier Krushchev."

"Thank you," said Irina.

With that, Boris spun and headed for the door...only to stop midway and turn. "We *will* bury them, sir," he said. "Just as you once promised." Then, he snapped back around and marched out of the office.

When he'd pulled the doors shut behind him, Irina slumped and shook her head. Without a second thought, I put my arm around her shoulders.

"What happened to me?" Her voice was slow and distant. "How did I get like this?"

"We've been away from home a long time," I said. "Maybe we've started to think like the humans."

Irina was silent for a long moment, staring at the shattered TV set on the floor. I wanted to comfort her, make everything better, but I was also acutely aware that time was running out.

"What next?" I said.

She sighed and slid off the edge of the desk. "Try to stop this, if we still can. Give the Americans what they want and hope for the best."

Irina walked around the desk, straightening her jacket

and tie, and I followed. "Let me help," I said.

"You can't," said Irina. "I have to undo my own mistakes."

I headed her off at the door. "Then come with me when it's over." Reaching out, I took her hand. "We'll get away from all this."

"Thank you." Irina squeezed my hand and gazed sadly into my eyes. "But I have more to do now than I ever imagined." With that, she pulled her hand from my grip and reached past me for the door handle.

"You deserve some time away," I said. "You've already done so much."

"Yes." Irina smiled ruefully. Her dark eyes held no trace of happiness. "And I'm starting to think that every last bit of it was wrong."

*****

As soon as the spy slipped me the microfilm, he gasped and crumpled to the sidewalk. A pool of dark crimson spread out around him, radiating from his head.

I didn't wait around to look for the bullethole. Leaping into action, I charged across the street and down an alley, stuffing the microfilm in my pants pocket on the fly. Footsteps clattered on the cobblestones behind me as I ducked into the cheering crowd up ahead.

Heart hammering, I fought my way through the mass of spectators watching the street. No one paid me much attention; all eyes were focused on the men and bulls stampeding down the main drag in the searing July heat.

One thought swirled in my mind as I struggled through the crowd: who had leaked the rendezvous details to the West? Who had known I'd be receiving the microfilm in Pamplona, Spain during the Running of the Bulls?

At least I had a chance of getting away with it. There were plenty of ways to use the crowds and chaos against my pursuer.

Also ways for my pursuer to use them against me. As I plowed forward, a bullet punched through the head of a man in front of me. He dropped dead in my path, knocking me back into a crush of spectators.

As I disentangled myself, another shot whistled past my head and blasted into a woman's chest. People screamed and ducked, giving me my first clear look at the shooter.

And I gasped. The face was unfamiliar--a young woman with long, black hair--but the scent was unmistakable. It was *her*...changed yet again, facing me once more in the heat of the Cold War. In the five years since her defection after the Cuban Missile Crisis, I'd battled her dozens of times in one way or another. She'd gone from communist leader to hands-on field operative fighting for the cause of capitalism and the red, white, and blue. From lover to arch-enemy.

Irina.

With an icy stare locked on her face, she swung up her gun and pulled the trigger twice. I leaped away before the shots could connect and sprinted into the street, joining the rush of runners and bulls.

No time to stop and reason with her; I'd tried that before. Since nearly triggering the annihilation of humanity as leader of the Soviet Union, she'd been steadfast in her new cause. I knew she'd stop at nothing to snatch the microfilm and strike another blow against communism.

As I raced down the street, a dark-haired young man in white t-shirt and pants hurtled past me. Glancing back, I saw why he was running so fast: a monstrous black bull barrelled up behind me, huge horns gleaming white in the afternoon sun.

The bull seemed to decide I was a better target, because it followed me when I veered. Whichever way I went, it galloped after me, heaving and snorting.

As if I didn't have enough trouble to deal with, Irina fired more shots in my direction. A nearby runner cried out and dropped, head bouncing off the cobblestones.

Dashing through the mayhem, I caught up with another bull up ahead. Clapping my hands on its haunches, I vaulted up onto its back and held tight, waiting for impact.

Seconds later, the first bull rammed the second full force from behind. My mount stumbled around and went down hard; I barely sprang off in time to avoid being crushed.

I still made a bad landing, though, twisting my ankle when I hit. Forcing back the flash of pain, I staggered into the crowd on the sidewalk.

I managed to make it into an alley and braced myself against a wall. It took a few seconds to shapeshift away the damage to my ankle.

Which was just enough time for Irina to get me.

"Hello, Comrade." I heard her voice at the same instant I felt the gun barrel touch my left temple.

"Irina." Turning my head, I gazed into the bright green

eyes of her latest face.

For a moment, I felt like we were back in Moscow again, fifty years ago, in 1917. I imagined our love was new and true once more, playing sweetly over the strains of the people's revolution.

Then, she punched me in the stomach. "You have something that belongs to me." Her voice was cold.

"I do," I said. "My heart."

She punched me again, harder. "That microfilm could bring down America. I won't let that happen."

"Stop fighting for the capitalists," I said. "Remember why we came here. Remember the galactic workers' paradise."

"The corrupt communist system drove humanity to the brink of annihilation." Irina punched me again. "We thought a capitalist ideology was aggressive and self-destructive, but *communism* was the more ruthless and ravenous aggressor!"

I shook my head against the barrel of her gun. "What about the interstellar revolution?"

"There's a *new* one." Irina smiled. "An interstellar *counter*-revolution."

"What?" I frowned. "What are you talking about?"

"It's just gotten started," said Irina. "You'll see."

"What kind of counter-revolution?"

"Join us." Irina leaned closer. "Help us change the galaxy for the better. Help *me* change the galaxy, my darling."

I had no idea what she was talking about. I had no reason to believe she felt any kind of affection for me at all.

But as I stared at her, so close, so familiar, I longed to

do what she asked. To do *anything* she asked of me, however insane or impossible it might be.

Because I had *never* lost my love for her, and I never would. No matter how much she hurt me, I knew I could never give up on her.

"Please." She leaned even closer. "We can be together like before. Blazing beacons shining light in the darkness." She drifted closer then, and her lips touched mine. For the first time in fifty years, she kissed me.

In that moment, I nearly went with her. I almost joined the counter-revolution without knowing a thing about it.

But something sparked within my good socialist soul, and I held back. "I cannot oppose the proletariat," I told her. "I am a servant of interstellar communism."

Irina sighed. "Poor thing." She leaned forward once more and whispered in my ear. "Soon, there will *be* no interstellar communism for you to *serve*."

With that, she shot me in the head.

She dug the microfilm from my pocket and left me for dead. Which to our kind, is only dead for a little while. Even as she disappeared in the chaos of Pamplona, I began to reassemble the scattered bits of my human disguise. My shattered mind and senses began to reassert themselves.

But the pain of what she'd done would last much longer than that.

*****

Thirty-seven years later, in the Earth year 2004, I was in the pilot seat of a fighter spacecraft, soaring through the bright blue sky over the Indian Ocean.

Morning sunlight gleamed off my topaz crystalline clusters and multifaceted eyes. I'd reverted to my native form; it was the only way to handle the complex controls of the fighter, which was from my homeworld.

And flying that fighter was the only way I could help win an interstellar war.

Checking the holographic displays in the cockpit, I spotted my target down below. I manipulated controls, and the fighter dropped through the cloud deck.

Emerging from the woolly clouds, I stared in stunned amazement at the tableau before me. Two huge vessels hung in the sky, vast starfaring warships from many light years away. As I watched, they fired enormous cannons, blasting each other with monstrous beams of fiery golden energy.

Tiny fighter craft like my own swarmed all around the warships, spinning and swooping and shooting. One exploded in a burst of orange light, then another; a third tumbled out of control and cracked up against the side of one of the warships.

So this was how civil war looked among the peoples of the interstellar workers' paradise. It was so much different from the hordes of humans hacking each other to bits in the mud with primitive weapons.

And yet, it was so much the same.

The war had been part of my life for years, of course. I'd seen plenty of action on Earth...but this was the first battle of this scope I'd been part of. I'd never seen anything like it in space, either, before coming to Earth. There hadn't been an interstellar war in millions of years, thanks to the lasting peace of the galactic revolution and workers' paradise.

But that was before the counter-revolution. That was before the twisted ideas of Earth had infected the interstellar community.

Suddenly, a flash of light seared across my forward shields, and I knew it was time to take action. Spinning my fighter counter-clockwise, I saw a gunboat coasting toward me like a big silver needle, artillery blazing.

I let loose a few rounds from my fusion guns, then whipped around and hightailed it toward one of the giant warships. The gunboat stayed in pursuit part of the way, until a shockwave picked it up like a toy and hurled it off my tail.

Finessing the controls, I closed in on the warship. I knew it was the enemy from its colors (red and black) and the symbols etched into its hull. It was a ship of the Capitalist Alliance, believers in the wealth of the few at the expense of the many...staunch enemies of the communists of the Interstellar Proletariat.

They were my enemies, though they were no different in appearance than me. I'd come to kill them, though we'd originated from the same homeworld, maybe even the same city or street.

Such was the legacy of the counter-revolution I'd first learned of thirty-seven years ago in Pamplona.

Not that the reasons for the fight much mattered anymore. My mind was focused completely on reaching my goal and doing as much damage as possible to it.

Flying forward, I threaded the maze of enemy fighters with weapons blazing. I banked and dove and twirled, eluding one opponent after another, leaving a trail of smoking and sputtering warcraft in my wake.

Soon, the Capitalist Alliance warship loomed before me, gun batteries blasting in every direction but mine. For that moment, I had a clear path to a gash in the hull amidships, the perfect place to inject a fusion torpedo.

Bearing down, I raced for the gash, calibrating a torpedo firing solution en route. Before I could release the payload, though, the enemy warship suddenly buckled and rolled in my direction.

I pulled up as fast as I could, speeding out of the listing ship's shadow. Just as I cleared the crash zone, the mighty vessel keeled over, barely missing me.

Then, with a series of massive explosions, it split in two. The fore and aft sections scissored apart...and the prow of the Proletariat warship plowed between them. The battered Proletariat ship had brought the capitalists down by ramming them.

But now both warships were heading for the sea.

Instantly grasping the implications, I climbed for the cloud bank as fast as I could. It was time to gain some altitude, time to put as much distance as possible between my fighter and the impending splashdown.

That was when the signal came in over my radio. A familiar voice broke through my furious focus.

It was a distress call. "I'm going down! Help!" It was *her* call, the one call I couldn't refuse. Even after everything that had happened between us, I could never turn my back on her. "My escape pod won't eject! Please help me!"

It was Irina.

Zeroing in on her signal, I whipped around and shot seaward again. Even as the warships plunged toward what I knew would be a catastrophic impact, I dove down after them.

Within seconds, I saw Irina's fighter spinning out of control, spewing plumes of black smoke. The engines were blown to hell, and the nose was mangled, which probably explained the problem with the escape pod.

I had scant seconds to dislodge that pod. Even then, we'd both be doomed if we didn't instantly blast away at maximum speed.

The enormous warships would hit the water soon, throwing out waves of titanic proportions. If we were really unlucky, the impact combined with the battle damage the ships had suffered would blow up one or both of their fusion reactor power plants.

In which case, all bets were off.

Swooping around Irina's fighter, I shot off the nose with an energy pulse from my guns. Then, swinging around, I blew off the tail behind her. The severed pieces of her fighter fell away, leaving the cockpit escape pod in its translucent housing cube.

Just as the cube started to drop, the housing snapped away, blown free from inside by Irina. The propellant ring on the base of her ovoid pod flared to life, burning white hot, and the pod shot suddenly upward with Irina inside.

I rocketed after her without looking back. Over the whine of my fighter's engines, I heard the thundering roar of the warships splashing down.

Irina's pod leaped into the cloud deck, and I followed. We didn't dare slow down on the other side, in the open sky. Our survival depended on gaining as much altitude as possible.

Shockwaves bucked our craft as we punched ever higher. My fighter shook with rising intensity, battling the waves and the g-forces trying to tear it apart.

Irina's pod shivered and spun, then fell away.

My mind swirled with sudden grief. Going back for her would be certain death.

But I was seized by the impulse to try.

The last time she'd truly seemed to love me had been almost a century ago. Since then, she'd used and abused me, betrayed and undermined me, fought and killed me again and again. How could I still feel any love for her?

Or was that what love was about? Pain, upheaval, destruction, the end of the world?

I cut the fighter's acceleration and scanned the skies below me. I made ready to dive down and retrieve her...or accompany her into annihilation.

My scanners were all static. That meant at least one of the warships' fusion drives had ruptured. The Indian Ocean had become ground zero of a nuclear detonation.

But I had to go back for her.

Steeling myself, I toggled controls, ready to swing the fighter around. Ready for anything.

And that was when her glittering crystalline pod came streaking up past me like a shooting star in reverse.

*****

When we'd reached a safe altitude, we stopped climbing. We hung in the stratosphere and looked down at the distant ocean, watching the devastation as it spread.

The battle itself had been cloaked from human technology, unseen by the world, but its effects would be felt by millions. When the warships sank and the fusion drives erupted, the ocean floor heaved from the force of the blast. A monstrous quake wrenched the crust of the Earth, slamming out colossal waves in all directions.

As we watched like satellites from far above, a monumental tsunami crashed down over islands and coastlines, obliterating anything in its path. Snuffing out hundreds of thousands of lives in Indonesia, Sri Lanka, Thailand, India.

We opened a radio channel between our craft, but neither of us said a word for a long time. We just watched as destruction swept that part of the world, destruction that we had helped bring about.

"I only wanted to help," said Irina. "I thought I was doing the right thing."

I didn't say a word. Far below, another tsunami was surging up from the sea, lashing toward shores that had already been laid waste by the first brutal onslaught.

"I wanted to free our people," said Irina. "I wanted to end the oppression of communist totalitarianism."

Still, I said nothing. I wondered how the people in the path of the cataclysm felt, gazing up in horror at the sky-high mountain of water hurtling toward them. Would they care which ideology had done the most to set that mountain in motion? Would any of them agree that the sacrifice would be worth it?

"I'm finished," said Irina. "All my efforts have brought nothing but death and disaster wherever I've gone." She sighed. "No more."

Yet another tsunami cut loose in the Indian Ocean. More people died screaming thousands of feet below us.

"Maybe I should just let myself fall," said Irina. "Drop down in the middle of that nightmare and die. I deserve it."

Finally, I spoke. "Shut up, Irina."

I saw her gape at me from her crystalline escape pod. All six of her multifaceted eyes--two silver, four gold--fixed on me in shocked amazement.

"I've been thinking," I told her. "And I've realized something. I couldn't see it before, because I loved you, but now I see it."

"Because you don't love me anymore?" said Irina.

The sun shone through her green and purple clusters of crystals, glittering within the intricate web of facets. Her fiery parasites zipped around her like schools of flaming fish, weaving in and out of her vent slits.

The sunlight and firelight danced when she moved, and I felt again the way I'd felt so long ago, watching her during the pre-mission briefings in the auditorium on our homeworld. For better and worse, it had been the one constant in my life.

Even now, after everything. Even now.

"I will always love you," I told her.

She gave me a look I couldn't fathom. "What did you

realize?"

"You need me. You always have," I said. "And the galaxy needs a new Lenin."

*****

Five years later, I'm on the terrace of a villa in the heart of the Colombian jungle, sitting across from a fellow extraterrestrial who looks like Senator Joseph McCarthy. He's killed twelve of my men, whose bodies still smolder in the hot sun around us, and now he wants to know where Irina is.

The truth, which I'm not about to tell him, is that I don't know exactly where she is at this moment...but I *do* know she's on her way.

I down another swig of vodka and look at McCarthy through the cut crystal bottle. He's still so blind, so backward, so limited by his all-consuming sociopolitical ideology. I feel like I'm watching a primitive lifeform as it struggles in the mud, wholly unable to comprehend the full potential of the complex landscape around it.

"Where is she, Lenin?" McCarthy's voice is a snarl. "Where's your commie she-devil mistress?"

"She's not a communist anymore," I tell him. "And she's not my mistress. Keep up, Joe."

With an angry roar, McCarthy flips over the glass table, which shatters on the cobblestone terrace. I barely manage to save the vodka bottle, which I was just about to set down on the table's blue-tinted surface.

"No more beating around the bush!" McCarthy springs

from his rattan chair and swats the bottle from my grip. It smashes to bits against a wrought iron light post. "You'll *beg* to tell me by the time I'm done with you!"

I smile as McCarthy lunges forward and wraps his thick hands around my throat. "Wait! I'm prepared to make you an offer!"

He lets up the pressure but doesn't let go. "That was fast." He shrugs. "I would've guessed you had more tolerance for torture, you pinko bastard."

"Join us." I lock eyes with McCarthy, trying to draw him in with sheer force of will. "Forget capitalism. Forget communism. Forget all that."

"A new sales pitch." McCarthy sneers. "How original."

"Help us end the wars on Earth and the war in space," I tell him. "Help us move beyond the hidebound systems of the past. Help us spread a revolutionary new philosophy conceived by a radical new Lenin."

"Would this new Lenin happen to be *you*, comrade?" says McCarthy.

When I look over his shoulder, I smile. "And *her*." My makeshift heart beats faster. She has arrived not a moment too soon, machete in hand.

The love of my life. My guiding light in smooth times and rough. My true partner now, reborn after the battle of the Indian Ocean tsunami, committed to a life of change from a new point of view.

McCarthy starts to turn. Irina draws back and swings the machete, lopping off his head with the graceful elegance of a ballerina.

I leap from my chair and sweep her into my arms. The

machete clatters to the cobblestones as we kiss. As the two halves of the new Lenin bind themselves one to the other once more.

This is the formula that eluded her for so long, the one that was staring her in the face from the start. Again and again, she turned me away, when what she should have done was embrace me. Accept me as an equal and consult me for balance. Go forth driven by love instead of self-righteousness.

Now see what revolution has hatched from this union. We bear a new gospel born not of conflict, but compassion: harmony among peoples by way of shapeshifting. Empathic metamorphosis. Truly love your neighbor as yourself by *becoming* your neighbor. Literally walk a mile in his shoes... and feet, and body, and life.

Yes, human beings can learn this, and we've been teaching it for the past five years. Using shapeshifting as a bridge to understanding instead of a weapon. It's really gone viral, and the movement's about to reach critical mass. Next stop, we take the show back home and end the galactic civil war.

All because of one simple secret it took us a century to figure out.

"Welcome home, darling." Smiling, I touch the side of her face. I run my fingers through her soft red hair.

"I love you." Irina says it with tears in her eyes.

The secret is this: *We are nothing without each other.*

SHROOMS OF BENARES

Father Gavín Obregón lifted the hem of his black shirt, peeled back a flap of skin just below his bottom left rib, and drew out three fresh-baked wafers of communion host from the cavity there, still warm from his flesh.

"The body of Christ, given up for you." Father Obregón said the words softly as he held up one of the round white wafers between his thumb and forefinger.

Piotr Punzak, a squat farmer with shaggy brown hair and beard, stood before him in the dusty farmyard. To one side, the gleaming silver domes of his farmhouse and barn sprawled in the mid-morning light...light cast not from a sun, but from huge fungal sun-blooms drifting across the sky.

In the other direction, the rolling hills were carpeted with fields of morel, boletus, oyster, and matsutake mushrooms, ready for harvest. The fruits of planet Benares, like all native life on the frontier planet, were fungus through and through. In all the world, only the human settlers could claim non-fungal origins.

As a rough breeze shivered the nearby morels and matsutakes, farmer Piotr tipped his head back. "Amen." Just as he opened his mouth for the host, one of the *nube oveja*--the self-propelled fungal "cloud sheep" herding in the sky overhead--slid away, allowing the light from the nearest sun-bloom to cast his face bright gold.

Father Obregón placed the host on Piotr's tongue. Piotr closed his mouth and bowed his head.

Then, it was time for the wine. Father Obregón turned over his right arm and popped the tiny cartilage pour-spout free from his wrist. "Blood of Christ, shed for you," he said.

"Amen." Piotr opened his mouth and closed his eyes.

Father Obregón held his wrist spout over Piotr's mouth, then squeezed the soft, oblong bladder implanted in the underside of his arm. Ruby red wine trickled into Piotr's mouth, sparkling in the light of the sun-bloom overhead.

It was just another Mass for the genetically engineered multi-faith super-chaplain of planet Benares. Just another communion for a human Swiss army knife on the fringe of the farthest frontier in human history.

*****

An hour later, Father Obregón was racing away from the farm in his hoversled, zipping through a forest of giant fungal towers.

He was also speaking without moving his lips.

"I'll be there in three days, Shen." Father Obregón spoke in his mind over the planet-wide Soulnet that kept him in touch with his scattered congregation. "Plenty of time to make your daughter's bat mitzvah."

Shen Ping's words flowed into his brain like warm water. "You're a mensch, Rabbi. I know you won't let us down."

"Have I ever?" Father Obregón chuckled in his head. "*Relax*, Bubbi! Two hundred miles of *wilderness*, and I'll be whipping you at *arm-wrestling* again."

"Doesn't *count!*" said Shen. "You're a *splicer!* How can I *ever* beat a genetically modified rabbi slash preacher slash cleric slash *whatever?*"

Father Obregón's thoughts bubbled with laughter. "You better pump some *iron*, Shen! You *know* I won't *let* you win."

Shen responded with the mental equivalent of a snort. "Maybe *I'm* the one who's been letting *you* win! How *else* am I gonna score points with *God?*"

Just then, another call buzzed for attention in Father Obregón's head. Such was life in the remote wilderness for the clergyman with a switchboard in his brain.

All seven hundred humans on Benares had a direct

telepathic line to the super-chaplain at all times. How else could one man tend the spiritual needs of a flock scattered to the far corners of a huge and untamed world?

Still, sometimes he wished for a respite. Sometimes, he longed for a little peace and quiet in which to commune with no one but God.

The caller buzzed again, and Father Obregón opened the link. Just as he started to say something, a flock of creatures burst out of a stand of morels in front of him. Reflexively, he swerved the hoversled to one side, barely missing the incredible lifeforms as they took flight.

He gazed in stunned wonder as he glided past. Yet again, he'd come across a new species--a flock of what looked like winged pizza shells with a hundred writhing white tendrils underneath. They twirled skyward all at once, twelve of them at least, trailing some kind of neon blue mist. Even as Father Obregón swung his hoversled wide in case the mist was toxic, he marveled at their magnificent strangeness, their utterly alien design. Like every other non-human lifeform on Benares, they were fungus-based, similar to fungi back on Earth yet possessing a multitude of uniquely alien traits.

What a world. How many times a day did that thought run through Father Obregón's mind? *I love this planet.*

"Hello? Can you hear me?" As Father Obregón got his hoversled back on track, he tried to reconnect with the caller he'd cut off because of the pizza shells. But no one answered.

Nothing but silence on the line.

*****

Amazingly, an hour went by without a single call in Father Obregón's head. The constant queue of souls banging on his door was empty and silent.

At first, he passed it off as a fluke. He decided to continue toward his next stop and make the most of the rare quiet by indulging in some meditation amid the stunning sights of Benares.

When he topped a ridge and gazed out over a sprawling valley he'd never seen before, chills raced up his spine. Giant multicolored rills of fungi fanned out over the valley floor, arching like ranks of rainbows under the cloud sheep and luminous sun-blooms in the shifting, golden sky. It looked nothing like the Heaven he'd been taught to expect, but it made him think of Heaven nonetheless.

As Father Obregón crossed a mountain pass under canopies of towering toadstools, glittering silver showers of spores swirled around him like snow. Curtains of lacy lichen hung dancing from the clifftops, making a sound like high-pitched singing as the wind filtered through their fine traceries.

Then there were the creatures in all their multitudes, great and small and every size in between...every one of them *mycozoa,* fungi with the mobility of animals. They flew and crawled and swung and darted through the landscape, screeching and squawking and roaring and croaking.

I need to do this more often. That was what Father Obregón thought as the splendor of Benares continued to unfold around him. As the second hour of peaceful contemplation passed. *I'd almost forgotten what it was like to appreciate God's wonders without constant interruptions.*

But by the middle of the third hour, a knot had formed in the pit of his stomach. The sights of Benares couldn't distract him from what he now knew to be true.

Something was wrong. The Soulnet was malfunctioning, or something was blocking the calls...

Or something had happened to the *callers*.

*****

With the Soulnet apparently down, Father Obregón turned elsewhere for human contact. Parking in a mountain meadow of red and blue puffballs, he switched on the radio in his hoversled, grabbed the microphone from its hook on the dashboard, and called out over the airwaves.

"This is Father Obregón," he said into the mic. "Can anyone hear me? Please respond."

No answer.

"Father Obregón here." As he said it, he watched a pack of pale wolflike creatures with spiked snouts and springs for legs chase what looked like a pink beachball across the far side of the meadow. "Someone, please answer!"

Still nothing. Across the meadow, the beachball turned on the remaining four wolf-things, flung open a huge maw on its face, and bounced after them. It ran down and gobbled up one, then two, then three of them, getting fatter each time.

Yet another new species, thought Father Obregón. *I love this planet.*

*****

One more hour passed before Father Obregón finally heard another human voice.

"I hear you, Father."

For an instant, he thought it was coming in over the radio, but he quickly realized it was inside his head.

"Hello!" He thought the words and said them aloud at the same time. "Thank God, hello!"

The new voice in his head was a woman's. "I was starting to think you were dead, Father." He recognized the low, throaty tone right away: Naima bint Fouad bin Hakim Al-Aziz, an exobiologist. He recognized it though he hadn't heard it for five long years.

She'd refused to call him for five years. Out of all the settlers, she alone had cut herself off from him.

"You thought wrong." Father Obregón chuckled, trying to sound calm, though his heart was suddenly racing. "So how are you, Naima?"

"I've had better days." Naima's voice was stiff and strangely flat. "I'm at the end of my rope, actually."

"Tell me what's happening, Naima."

"Wellll." The slightest quaver crept into Naima's voice. "Everyone's dead up here. Everyone but me."

Father Obregón felt a horrified chill rush through him. "*Everyone?*"

"Yes, Gavín," said Naima.

"*Dios mío.*" Father Obregón shook his head in stunned disbelief. Thirty-six people, counting Naima; that was how many had been stationed at the research camp with her. "What *happened* to them?"

"You know how we hadn't found any signs of sentient life on Benares?" said Naima.

"Yes, of course."

Naima choked back a sob. "We weren't *looking* hard enough."

*****

Father Obregón had first met Naima on the trip from Earth aboard the starship that had brought them to Benares. She'd been a teenager at the time, but the truth of it was, they'd both been 21 years younger. He'd been barely out of his teens himself.

Their personalities had been a perfect match from the start. Not such a shocker maybe, considering the 700 settlers had been selected for general compatibility...but he'd always felt something special with her. Something beyond computer-predicted affinity.

Their reasons for making the trip were much alike. Naima had come for adventure, to witness never-before-seen wonders in the name of science. Father Obregón had also come for adventure, to witness such wonders in the name of God. Both of them were idealists, driven by wanderlust, curiosity, and faith in the power of universal truths and forces.

Drawn together by complementary callings and natures, they'd spent many hours together gazing out at the passing spectacles of space, talking about *everything*. Imagining the great discoveries they would make on the scientific and spiritual frontiers. Dreaming up schemes for turning their brave new colony into utopia.

Dreaming up ways to be together on Benares, too, though their assigned duties would keep them far apart. Because the longer they knew each other, the more they knew they *had* to be together.

Everything between them was perfect, from the meshing of their personalities (they were both thoughtful yet outgoing) to the meshing of their bodies (thankfully, chastity was no longer a mandatory vow for priests in this day and age). They were soulmates, and they had to find a way to stay together even as their work pulled them apart.

Maybe, if Naima found sentient life on Benares, she could get her assignment changed to assistant chaplain; Father Obregón would need an exobiologist to help minister to alien lifeforms, wouldn't he?

Maybe, his genetically-engineered splicer body would have trouble adjusting to the alien environment--with a little help from an undetectable nano-phage tweaked by Naima-- and he'd have to stay put at her lab.

Or, failing either of those, he would figure out a way to always keep her thoughts foremost in his mind. He would scam the Soulnet, whipping up a psychic hideaway for the two of them in the midst of the mental traffic from the other settlers.

One thing alone had been carved in stone: the two of them would find a way to overcome any obstacle the frontier or their fellow settlers threw at them.

*****

Shivering, Father Obregón looked around the mountain meadow, staring at the larger clumps of puffballs, the shadows of the distant toadstool treeline. He wondered if he was being watched by something with intellect and malice.

What troubled him most, though, was the possibility that sentient native lifeforms had taken action all over the world. That the reason no one but Naima had answered his calls was that the lifeforms had murdered them all.

"Are you safe?" Father Obregón said in his mind.

He panicked briefly when no answer came...but then Naima spoke. "I've sealed myself in the lab."

"What do they look like?" said Father Obregón.

"See for yourself," said Naima. "You have my permission."

Father Obregón's pulse quickened. "You mean...you can *see* them? They're *with* you?"

"In the building." Naima said it matter-of-factly. "Come through and I'll show you."

Father Obregón hesitated. It had been a long time since he'd been inside her head. He hadn't gone there in five years, since the two of them had split up.

Though for 16 years before that, he'd visited her mind every day. In spite of their schemes for togetherness on Benares, it was the only way they'd actually managed to be together at all in spite of the miles that were almost always between them. It was the one thing they'd shared that was special to the two of them, the one thing no one else could

432

interrupt.

Because while everyone else could enter *his* mind on a whim, Naima was the only person in the world whose mind *he* could enter.

Father Obregón took a deep breath and steadied himself. This time, he knew, going into her mind was crucial; he had to do it to see what they were up against.

And he had to not let her know how much it meant to him. How much he enjoyed it.

Taking one more deep breath, he dove into the open link, pouring his mind like lightning in Naima's direction.

He felt a thrill as he charged through the crackling darkness of the mental conduit between them. A flare of blinding white light suddenly filled his mind's eye, and he felt himself spinning out of control. A flurry of sensations washed through him, a storm of sounds and smells and tastes and touches, too jumbled to process. The unfiltered input of another human mind.

Then, the sensations faded, and the spinning stopped. Father Obregón blinked his mind's eye, clearing away the afterimage of the blinding flare.

And he found himself looking out through Naima's eyes. He saw her reflection looking back at him from the gleaming silver surface of a metal lab table.

He hadn't seen her in years. Even slightly distorted in the reflection from the table, she looked as beautiful as he remembered.

Long brown hair flowed over her shoulders, wrapping around a small, oval face. Dark-framed eyeglasses perched on a gently sloping nose, setting off eyes of the brightest, most glittering green he'd ever seen. Perfect dimples flanked the soft petals of her rosy lips, curling when she smiled toward a tiny mole on her right cheek...

And a scar on her left. He had to force himself not to recoil at the sight of it. Not because it was ugly, because nothing could make her ugly in his eyes.

But because it was his fault.

"Where are they, Naima?" Better to take his mind off that scar. Better not to think about what had happened between them five years ago.

"I'll show you." Inside the confines of her mind, Naima's voice sounded stronger, less rattled. "Over here."

As Father Obregón watched, the scene shifted, swooping up and away from the reflection on the lab table. He saw stacks of hard-shelled plastic cases, racks of silver lab implements, panels of glowing green controls and readouts.

Finally, there was a clear space, a reinforced glass door a few yards away. The view stopped swooping from east to west and started moving toward the door.

Naima took one step, then two, peering into the twilit space beyond the door. Father Obregón could make out overturned tables, chairs, equipment...

And bodies. He saw the unmistakable shapes of human arms and legs piled in with the wreckage. Then, human *faces* caked with blood, mouths and eyes wide open, unmoving.

His heart sank as Naima took another step, bringing him closer to the corpses. He recognized at least two of them.

Suddenly, something threw itself against the door with

a thunderous crash. Naima stopped in her tracks but didn't look away.

Father Obregón's instinct was to dive back into the link, but he forced himself to stay and watch. It wasn't easy; what he saw as he gaped through Naima's eyes filled him with revulsion.

A human head, a female *child's* head, wobbled atop a mass of mangled human body parts held together by pulsing black foam. The mismatched parts looked like they'd all come from different people: a woman's long leg, a man's hairy arm, another man's torso, a child's hand.

The parts were arranged in roughly the right places for a human body, linked by the black foam instead of tendons and ligaments. They jiggled and slipped around as if the foam were barely holding them together.

As unsteady as the mass of parts looked, they were capable of moving with sudden speed and power. Father Obregón flinched as the patchwork person suddenly lashed out with its male right arm, pumping it into the door so hard, it cracked the outer pane of glass.

Mismatched body parts fell away in the impact, but the black foam stayed attached and snapped them back together. The little girl's head rolled down the torso, then jumped back up into place...but face-down, with the bloody stump of her neck pointing at Father Obregón.

He knew her, of course, as he knew all his congregation on Benares. Her name was Emma, and her parents were Mormons. Good people, all three of them.

He wondered if any of the other patchwork pieces were theirs.

"Dios mío." Father Obregón had to look away. "You say this thing is *sentient?*"

"I *know* it is," said Naima, and then she walked the rest of the way to the door. Father Obregón watched as she pressed the palm of her right hand against the reinforced glass.

Instantly, the child's hand on the patchwork body lunged at the glass, planting itself directly opposite Naima's. Black foam flowed out from its stump, glowing brighter and pulsing faster as it outlined the tiny, pale fingers.

Father Obregón watched, transfixed...and then,

a *third voice* spoke in Naima's head.

It spoke in a kind of hyperfast babble. As Father Obregón listened, images appeared in his mind, somehow triggered by the gibberish. He saw showers of pulsing black foam falling from the sky like rain, covering the ground, clotting and squirming. Looking up, he saw the foam's source: the *nube oveja,* the drifting "cloud sheep," split open from end to end.

Next, he saw a familiar scene--himself, administering communion to Piotr Punzak. He saw the scene from above, looking down from a distance as he drew the host wafer from the cavity in his side and placed it on the tongue of the Catholic farmer.

Then, as if from nowhere, two words shot into his mind, spoken in his own voice: *EAT GOD.*

When the sound of the words faded, Father Obregón saw something else. He saw two more of the patchwork bodies rising from the rubble, picking up tools and guns, and shambling toward the lab in which Naima was sealed.

EAT GOD.

*****

Father Obregón returned to his own body to try to figure out what his next move should be. The Soulnet link to Naima was still open--he didn't dare risk being cut off from her--but he kept her on hold as he pulled himself back together.

What did the patchwork lifeforms want? And how could he stop them?

He knew only one thing for sure: he had to get to the lab in person as soon as he could, whatever the cost. He had to rescue Naima, for what she'd once meant to him... and what she meant to him still, in spite of the mistake that had come between them.

Never mind that she was nearly two hundred miles away. No one else was answering his calls; there might not be another living soul in the whole world who could come to her rescue.

The first thing he did before taking Naima off hold was to start the hoversled moving in her direction. He put it on autopilot and set the speed as fast as he dared, keeping one hand on the steering wheel just in case.

The next thing he did was pull the flask of bourbon from under his seat and take a quick drink. He saved the stuff for especially bad days, and they didn't get much worse than the one he was having.

Then, he put the flask away and took Naima off hold. "Any change?" he said through the link.

Naima sighed. "Three more just showed up outside the lab. That makes six. Not that I'm worried, you understand."

Father Obregón smiled grimly. "Hang tight. I'm on my way."

"Watch for sudden downpours," said Naima. "You don't want to get caught out in *that* rain."

Taking his eyes off the path ahead, Father Obregón looked skyward. A fat, fluffy cloud sheep floated off to one side, well away from his route...but it still made him nervous.

"I can't believe the black foam's responsible," said Naima. "It started turning up recently, but we didn't know it was coming from the cloud sheep...and we *definitely* had no idea it was sentient."

"Have you had a chance to analyze it?" said Father Obregón.

"The foam contains high quantities of an ultra-potent form of *psilocybin*," said Naima. "The hallucinogenic compound produced by certain species of fungi. Otherwise, its structure is a mystery. Nothing to suggest motility, let alone sentience."

Father Obregón kept his eyes on a flock of cloud sheep up ahead, and he shivered. "In the 21 years we've been here, there's never been a sign of danger from the cloud sheep. How is this possible?"

"Cicadas on Earth have a 17-year life cycle," said Naima. "Why not a 21-year cycle for cloud sheep to generate and deposit black foam?"

As his hoversled approached the flock of cloud sheep, Father Obregón pressed buttons on the dashboard, shutting off the outside air vents, switching the blower to recycled air only. He double-checked the cockpit seals and nodded, satisfied the foam couldn't get inside.

Reasonably satisfied.

"So." Naima paused. "When do you think you'll get here?"

He knew she wouldn't like the answer. "Eight hours. Maybe ten."

Naima was silent for a moment. When she spoke again in his head, the tone of her thoughts was dark. "If they...if I'm gone before you get here...please go somewhere else."

"That won't happen," said Father Obregón. "I think maybe they're waiting for me."

Again, Naima was silent. "Then don't come at all. I don't want you to."

"Sorry," said Father Obregón, "but it's not open for discussion. As long as you're alive, I'm coming to get you."

"Then I'm hanging up," said Naima. "You won't *know* if I'm dead or alive."

"Naima, no!" said Father Obregón, but it was too late. She'd already cut the connection.

He pounded the dashboard with his fist, angry that his only link to her had been severed. Desperately worried that she could be dying at that very moment, and he had no way of knowing.

He was also, deep in his heart, overjoyed that she'd hung up on him. Because he guessed that the only reason she'd hung up was that she was worried the patchworks would get him if he tried to save her.

And that meant she still cared. Perhaps, after five years, she'd finally forgiven him for what he'd done.

*****

He'd meant it as a surprise.

One night, five years ago, Father Obregón had decided to do something extra special for Naima's birthday. It didn't matter that he was halfway around the world from her.

What were a few thousand miles to someone who could travel between minds?

He'd parked his hoversled for the night at the base of an enormous toadstool and closed his eyes. Then, he'd done something he could do only with Naima, because of their special two-way link.

He'd sneaked inside her mind. He'd found her through the Soulnet and slipped inside while she was sleeping.

Then, he'd done something even harder, something he'd never done before. Something that took him a few tries before he got it right.

He'd made her *sleepwalk*. He'd taken control of her body, enough to get her up out of bed and make her shuffle down the hall and out the door of the barracks at the research camp.

"What the hell did you think you were *doing?*" That was what Naima said much later...over the link, of course, as she lay in her hospital bed. "What *possessed* you?"

"I wanted to paint a picture with your hands," Father Obregón had told her. "I wanted to give it to you for your birthday, as if I were there with you."

"You can't just crawl into my *mind* without my *knowing* it." Naima's voice in his head had been full of pain and anger.

"But I wanted to *surprise* you," he'd said. "You'd see that painting and wonder how it *got* there. And you'd know how much I *love* you."

"You almost *killed* me!" It was then, when she'd said that in her thoughts, that Father Obregón had known it was over between them. Even before she'd broken it off in so many words, he'd known.

Because she'd been right. He *had* almost killed her.

After she'd shuffled out of the barracks that night, he'd walked her to the main lab, where he'd arranged with other members of his flock to stow some painting supplies. Then, while steering her through the lab to set them up, he'd fumbled his control for an instant.

Naima had tripped over her own feet and crashed through the wall of a plate glass isolation chamber. Dozens of glass shards had pierced her body, barely missing vital organs and blood vessels, ripping open a gash that had left a scar on the side of her face.

That day had left deep scars between Naima and Father Obregón, too. She'd never trusted or forgiven him in the five years since.

But he'd never stopped loving her...and maybe, he thought, she'd held on to her love for him as well.

*****

Two hours passed with no contact from Naima. Against her wishes, Father Obregón stayed the course, charging through the wilderness toward her camp.

As his hoversled glided through the fungiscape, he passed the usual parade of wonders but was only dimly aware of them. He wound his way through a forest of massive chanterelles, their pearlescent scalloped lobes blossoming in spectacular fashion...but he didn't really see them. He skated over a field of waist-high fairy ring mushrooms, their curled skirts uplifted like delicate ivory pinafores...but he couldn't appreciate them, either. Same for the procession of filmy lavender veils rippling through the air like magic carpets over red-orange fungal spires.

All he could think about was Naima and what he could do to save her. He wracked his brain, trying to sort out what had happened, struggling to latch onto a solution.

Suddenly, his head buzzed with an incoming call. He jumped and nearly swerved the sled into a wall of crystalline lattice lichens in his hurry to open the line.

"Naima?" He said it aloud and in his mind at the same time. "Are you all right?"

"You didn't do what I told you." She sounded weary but not angry. "You're still coming, aren't you?"

"I don't think there's anyone else left on Benares," said Father Obregón. "It's down to the two of us."

Naima didn't say anything in response to that.

Father Obregón rubbed his eyes. "Have more of the creatures arrived?"

"I've lost count."

"Have they communicated with you? Have they said anything?"

"No," said Naima, "but I think you were right. I think they're waiting for you."

"What makes you think that?"

"Because they're all facing in your direction," said Naima. "None of them are looking at me anymore."

"I wonder what they want with me." Father Obregón stroked his bearded chin. "'EAT GOD,' they said. Do they think we're actually eating our God during communion? Maybe they want a taste for themselves."

"By eating those of us who've eaten God?" said Naima.

Father Obregón steered out from under a looming cloud sheep. "Attaining divinity by consuming the flesh of those who've tasted the divine. It makes sense."

"Then what about the non-Christian settlers?" said Naima. "*They* didn't take communion."

"The beings don't distinguish between different faiths, maybe? If *one* human takes communion, by extension, they think we *all* do it?"

"Okay," said Naima. "Then why are they waiting for you?"

"I generate the host and wine." Father Obregón gazed out the cockpit canopy as the hoversled swooped over a bubbling lake of yeast. Ever-shifting geometric patterns flowed over the surface, multicolored interlocking shapes dancing like a kaleidoscope. "Maybe they want *all* the God for *themselves*. Every last bite."

*****

When Father Obregón was an hour from Naima's camp, the sun-blooms started to dim. They were the planet's home-grown source of light and heat, enormous fungal disks orbiting high in the stratosphere. Once a day, their luminescence dropped to 25 percent, and night fell over all of Benares at once.

The hoversled's headlamps switched on, lighting up the way forward. Nocturnal mycozoa bounded away from the flare, tails and wings and tentacles flickering.

As Father Obregón gazed into the darkness around him, he felt the same void in his soul. He was at a loss about what he should do when he reached Naima. He felt hopeless, inadequate...and scared.

All he knew for sure was that he had to get there. No other human was left alive on Benares; no one had responded to his repeated psychic or radio calls. No cavalry was coming from the stars, either. Benares was on the farthest fringe of the frontier, months from the nearest settled world by spacecraft.

So it was all up to him. Super-chaplain to the rescue. Time for the splicer to prove there was more to his genetically enhanced superiority than just talk. Time for him to make up for hurting her five years ago.

If only he had a plan. If only he didn't feel so *alone*.

Only now, without the constant calls of his flock buzzing in his head, did he realize how much they'd meant to him. How much he'd depended on them. Only now did he notice how small he felt without them. How weak.

"Father? Imam?" Naima's voice rose suddenly in his quiet mind.

"*Asalam 'Alaykum*." He used the traditional greeting since she'd referred to him by an Islamic title.

"'*Alaykum as-Salaam*," said Naima. "Are you almost

here?"

"Less than an hour away," said Father Obregón.

"That close." Naima sighed. "Perhaps you should slow down a little."

So we can live a little longer. He knew exactly how she felt. "How are you holding up?" he said.

"Second-guessing every decision I've ever made," said Naima, "because they all led me to this moment."

Father Obregón looked around as his sled glided through a thicket of giant, glowing shiitakes and feathery cauliflower mushrooms. "Well, I'm glad you're here," he said. "Not *there,* I mean, but...I'm glad to have you with me. I missed you."

Naima paused for a long moment. When she spoke again, her voice in his mind was soft. "I missed you, too."

"I'm sorry," said Father Obregón. "I'm sorry for what happened before. I'm sorry I hurt you. I shouldn't have done what I did."

"And I shouldn't have pushed you away," said Naima. "We wasted so many years...and now this. Now we're out of time."

"Not out of time yet," said Father Obregón. "Maybe we'll still get a second chance...if we want it."

"That's what I'm praying for," said Naima.

A creature that looked like an upside-down pyramid of blinking violet light floated by in the darkness. *I love this planet.* "That's what I'm praying for, too, Naima."

*****

As Father Obregón pulled into Naima's camp, he realized he was crazy. What was he thinking, rushing to confront a hostile enemy without a plan, a weapon, or backup?

He parked his hoversled in front of the lab shed and switched off the motor. Then, he sat for long moments in the cockpit, knuckles white as he clutched the wheel. Sweat ran down his back and sides as he dug deep for courage.

He found it in his flask of bourbon. Two long pulls calmed his shaking. One more, the longest yet, and he popped the cockpit canopy and stepped out of the hoversled. Stood for a moment in the pool of brightness cast by the lone floodlight atop the lab shed.

Then, heart slamming like a fighter's fist against his rib cage, he walked toward the open door of the shed.

*****

As soon as Father Obregón stepped through the door, they moved toward him. Patchwork assemblages of mismatched human body parts, held together with clots of black foam. All the eyes wide open, all the faces slack and dead.

They looked far more horrifying in person than they had through Naima's eyes--heads lolling, bones protruding, organs dangling. Black foam oozing between joints and out of every orifice. A grinding, sloshing sound as they hobbled and shuffled toward him. A stench of excrement and rot so overwhelming, it made him gag.

And there were so *many* of them. *Dozens*. No wonder

Naima had lost count.

He forced himself to stand with shoulders squared as they surrounded him. As they pressed closer and closer on all sides.

Peering between them, he glimpsed Naima in the sealed lab, gazing out through the reinforced glass door. He heard her in his mind--no words, just breathing. A nervous quaver in each exhalation.

And then something else was in his mind, too.

The familiar presence of the black foam welled up within him, pulsing and pressing against his awareness. Hyperfast gibberish babbled in his head, and images rushed past his mind's eye: black foam falling from drifting cloud sheep to blanket the fungiscape; Father Obregón giving communion to Piotr Punzak and a stream of others, dozens of humans all over the world...all of them dead now.

Suddenly, the creatures grabbed hold of him, snapping his focus back out of his mind. With clumsy power, they wrenched his arms wide and held him spread-eagled. One of them clamped his head between bloody, mismatched hands.

This is it. Eyes wide, heart jackhammering, Father Obregón felt more of the creatures grab hold of him, wrapping him in a solid clinch of rancid flesh and black muck.

"*Stop!*" Naima's voice sounded far away as she screamed in the lab, more distant than when they'd been hundreds of miles apart. "*Please no!*"

The creatures ignored her cries. One of the patchworks wobbled in front of Father Obregón, its head that of a young man with sandy brown hair. Its torso, strung with shreds of green cloth, belonged to a woman; one arm was short and pale, the other long with coal-black skin.

When the dark arm swung up and the tiny pink hand on the end reached for his face, Father Obregón tried to flinch, but the other hands gripping his head wouldn't let him. He cried out, struggling, but the hand moved toward him inexorably.

He shut his eyes and grimaced when the stubby little fingers made contact with his forehead. A fresh wave of gibberish surged through his mind, swirling like a cyclone. More images of communion, more images of black foam showering down.

And then, a new cycle of images coursed through him. Settlers tasting the black foam, putting curds of it in their mouths. Each one dying horribly afterward, convulsing on the ground, then literally falling apart...limbs and heads slumping away from torsos, organs sluicing in the dirt in a flow of black sludge.

Pulled together by tendrils of foam, the body parts became shambling patchworks. The patchworks went after other settlers, feeding them more of the foam, and the cycle repeated.

Through it all, Father Obregón felt the same words rise up in his mind again and again. The same words as before, imparted nonverbally to his fevered mind:

EAT GOD.

His head was spinning as he tried to make sense of what he'd seen. One thing was clear: he knew how the nightmare had started. Settlers had eaten the foam of their own accord...but why? He still didn't understand.

The infant hand on the dark-skinned arm withdrew, then dug its stubby fingers into a bubbling clot between the patchwork's head and torso. The fingers came away smeared with black foam.

Then, they moved toward Father Obregón's mouth.

EAT GOD. Again with the same message. *EAT GOD.*

As the foam-covered fingers slid closer to his mouth, Father Obregón realized how wrong he'd been. The patchworks hadn't been trying to attain divinity by consuming the flesh of humans who'd eaten God in communion. They'd never wanted to reach the God of humans at all.

They'd been trying to do the *opposite*. Trying to get humans to eat *their* god.

But humans couldn't survive it. The black foam sacrament had killed them all. And Father Obregón was next in line.

"Please, no!" Father Obregón fought harder, but he couldn't break the combined grip of the ghoulish patchworks.

"Stop it, you *monsters!*" It was Naima. Father Obregón heard the door to the lab crash open and her footsteps charge into the patchwork mob. "*Leave him alone!*"

But nothing would change the course of events. The tiny fingers jabbed forward, and the black foam touched Father Obregón's lips. He felt it fizzing like a carbonated drink on his lips and then the tip of his tongue.

EAT GOD.

There was a moment as the substance soaked into his

bloodstream, a moment of stillness. The patchworks let go of him, and his arms fell at his sides. Naima pushed through the crowd and stopped in front of him; she looked crushed when she saw the black foam on his lips.

Tears ran down her cheeks. "Don't go. Oh please, don't leave me alone here."

Father Obregón smiled. Just as he was about to say something, the moment of stillness

ended

and everything made sense.

*****

Father Obregón's mind felt as if it had burst. Light poured in from every direction, swirling with color and sweet fragrance. Geometric patterns appeared and shifted before his mind's eye, dancing like the patterns in a kaleidoscope.

Or the patterns on the yeast lakes of Benares.

He felt his mind changing shape, flowing between forms in a dizzying rush of transformations. He melted from a spinning disk to a rippling lavender veil, from a pink beachball to an upside-down pyramid of violet neon light.

Every shape just like the lifeforms he'd seen on Benares.

Waves of textures washed over him, clinging and combining in electric layers of high relief. There was roughness, grittiness, laciness, puffiness, fluffiness, spikiness, foaminess. One after another, from firm smoothness to crystalline latticework.

Just like the multitude of fungal flora thriving on Benares.

All these sensations blossomed and swirled together in his mind, crackling with invisible fire that he felt and saw and swallowed. Structures and instincts from the largest to the most extreme subatomic pulsed and sang within and without him.

And all the while, even as his mind opened and transformed and filled to overflowing, he felt lighter than air. He felt better than he ever had, completely new from tip to toe, from gut to soul.

For an instant, he thought he had died, but then the thoughts of the patchworks, which once had seemed like gibberish, suddenly came into focus. Conveying the truth in a wordless intention, a heartfelt expression.

He has eaten and survived.

He had tasted their god, the collective essence of their world, and not died in doing so. Chalk it up to the splicer physiology of the genetically-enhanced super-chaplain.

The black foam had tuned him in to the psychedelic glory of the life force of Benares. It had expanded his consciousness to encompass the total majesty of the world that had always fascinated him.

And it had done one more thing to him, too.

*****

Father Obregón pulled his hoversled into a misty cove in the heart of a jungle of enokitake. The slender stems of the tall white mushrooms flickered in the breeze, spherical caps bobbing in the morning light from the sun-blooms.

A week had passed since he'd first eaten the black

foam, and he was back on the road again. He was making his rounds again, traversing the wilderness, ministering to believers around the world.

The congregation was different, but the work was the same in the end.

As he popped the cockpit canopy, a call buzzed for attention in his head. He picked it up with a smile. "Good morning, Naima."

"Good morning." Naima, as usual these days, didn't sound happy. She was back at the lab, where she'd been working since the patchworks had evacuated. They'd left her alive and intact at Father Obregón's request after he'd eaten their black foam sacrament. "Where are you this time?"

"Prayer meeting up north." Father Obregón stepped out of the hoversled, his feet sinking in a soft carpet of dewy gray-green mildew. "It's good to hear your voice, Naima."

Naima sent him a thought that was the mental equivalent of clearing her throat. She didn't approve of the new direction his work had taken. She didn't approve of his new calling. "You need to come home, Gavín."

"Not yet, Naima." Father Obregón padded through the mildew carpet toward a cluster of buried lumps in the middle of the cove. "I've got work to do."

"It's not safe, Gavín," said Naima.

Father Obregón chuckled. "God's work is *never* safe."

Naima sighed. "What if the foam kills you? It's *fatal* to non-splicers. What if you're only *temporarily* immune?"

Father Obregón knelt among the buried lumps and

began brushing away layers of mildew and soil from one of the biggest, the size of a basketball. "Naima, please..."

Naima's voice rose in anger and desperation. "You're under the influence of a highly concentrated mind-altering *drug* controlled by a malignant sentient *fungus* that has *killed* everyone else who tried it! How the hell can you be out there *working* for it?"

"It didn't *intend* to kill them, Naima," said Father Obregón. "It wanted the same thing *they* did. To give the settlers the ultimate mind-expanding experience. To help them get closer to *God.*"

"The god of *fungus,*" snapped Naima. "The god of *monsters.*"

Father Obregón felt sorry for her. He loved her as he loved all his flock, but he knew she would never understand. One taste of the black foam was all he'd needed to connect with his new worldwide congregation. One taste, and he'd been able to move on to important new work after the human settlers had died out.

"Can I talk to you later?" Father Obregón finished clearing the largest lump--a giant truffle, the hub of a complex underground network of them. "I'm a little busy just now."

"You've got to listen to me, Imam!" Naima's thoughts burned with wild urgency. "I think I can reverse the effects of the compound! I'm working on a seratonin inhibitor right now..."

Just then, something buzzed in Father Obregón's head, and he smiled. "Naima? I don't have time to talk about this now." Softly, he ran his fingers over the rough scalp of the giant truffle, which was the source of the new buzzing in his mind.

The truffle was signaling for his attention, reaching out to link him with its network. Dozens of other signals were racked up in the queue behind it, clamoring for attention. There were *always* umpteen signals in the queue these days, ever since the black foam, signals from fungal lifeforms all over Benares. Signals from buried truffles and towering toadstools alike, from giant portabellas to microscopic penicillium, from spinning pizza shell flyers to hulking eight-legged shaggy behemoths the size of elephants.

The switchboard in his head was back in business. Father Obregón would never be lonely again. His second chance with Naima might never come to fruition, but his love for his new congregation had to take first place in his heart. Naima might need him, but *they* needed him more. She might love him, but *they* loved him more.

His beloved flock.

"I have another call coming in, Naima," he said. "I'll have to put you on hold."

"Father, wait!" she said, just before he hung up on her.

Then, smiling, he lifted the hem of his black shirt, peeled back a flap of skin just below his bottom right rib, and drew out the fresh-baked communion host from the cavity there, still warm from his flesh.

And he spread that host, the precious black foam, on the tongue of the giant truffle. "The soul of Benares, given up for you," he said. "Amen."

BEWARE THE BLACK
BATTLENAUT

"Looky there," said Swindle, the *leper*chaun on Grist Halcyon's shoulder. He pointed with a crumbling green finger at one of the Battlenaut's cockpit video screens, and Grist looked in that direction.

On the screen, Grist saw the barren, storm-swept surface of the rebel-held moon, Sangre. The latest flare of lightning revealed a towering black figure on the crest of the hill. At that instant, the very first instant he glimpsed it, Grist knew in his heart what it was even as he knew in his head it just wasn't possible.

The flare of light faded, and the black figure faded with it back into the night. When the next lightning struck a moment later, the hilltop was deserted.

"Begorra." One rotting nostril fell away from Swindle's leprous face. "It's *him*, ain't it, boyo?"

Grist blinked hard and shook his head. "Can't say." Just then, his arm burned as the automated hypodermic cuff strapped to his bicep shot a fresh jolt of go-juice into his system. A ring of lights around the forward viewport flashed in a pattern designed to reset his body's circadian rhythms.

Must've been about to nod off. Can't have that, can we? As the go-juice pumped through his arteries, Grist felt himself return to full alertness. The Battlenaut's sensors and computers had done their job again, intervening at just the right moment with just the right dose of meds to keep Grist awake and alert for yet another hour.

Grist licked his dry lips and checked the video monitor again. Lightning spiked nearby, revealing six soldiers in Battlenaut armor facing off on a rocky battlefield...but no sign of the dark figure from the hilltop.

Grist stabbed the comm button and spoke into his mic. "Hey, Freak. Ever hear of the Black Battlenaut?"

When he didn't get a reply, Grist looked at the button he'd just hit and realized it wasn't the comm at all. He was just about to punch the real comm button when the cockpit rocked from a powerful impact. It was enough to crack his helmeted skull against the headrest and snap him back to the reality from which he'd taken a brief vacation.

Fight. That's right. His hands flew back to the steering

456

and weapons controls. *I'm in a firefight.*
I'm fighting a war here.

*****

Sharon "Freak" Freemare laughed like a maniac as she cut loose her Battlenaut's main guns against the oncoming enemy. One slug hit home in a big way, punching through the enemy's armor and leaving a jagged, smoking hole at the top of one leg.

Still shrieking with laughter, Freak swung a laser around and opened up on the damage. Metal and plastic melted before the onslaught, and the enemy Battlenaut's leg gave way within seconds.

The damaged Battlenaut went down hard, flat on its face. The enemy soldier in its cockpit tried in vain to force the smashed war machine to get up and fight, but it was still lying in the mud when Freak marched her own Battlenaut over to meet it.

"Hey, traitor!" shouted Freak, though she knew the downed pilot couldn't hear her. "Special delivery from the *Redeyes* for ya!"

Freak used her lasers to disable the enemy Battlenaut's weapons systems. The whole time, the smell of baking bread was so strong in the cockpit that it made her stomach growl.

Why she smelled baking bread in the cockpit instead of the usual sweat and stink, she had no idea, but she didn't let it trouble her. Better just to soak it in like the smell of roses that had rushed over her moments earlier, or the incredible smooth feeling of silk that had rippled over her skin moments before that.

Better just to enjoy the ride.

Eyeballing the display on her visor, she located the other members of her squad. Lieutenants Grist and Pellucid formed two points of a triangle enclosing the battlefield, with Freak as the third point. Four enemy Battlenauts were trapped inside the triangle, three still standing plus the one she'd just brought down.

Freak cackled as she swung her Battlenaut toward a fresh target. *These bums are no match for the Redeyes.*

That was what Freak's squad called themselves: *Redeyes*, because they fought without rest. Computers monitored the alertness of this experimental squad and administered countermeasures, chemical and otherwise, to keep them awake and fighting. Such sleep deprivation techniques promised to limit downtime for deployed Commonwealth troops, giving them an edge in the ongoing civil war against the Rightfuls.

From Freak's point of view, the experiment was the biggest success of all time. She and the others had been awake for days on end, so long she'd lost count, and still they suffered no ill effects.

If anything, Freak felt better than ever. She'd never fought more fiercely or thought more clearly in her life.

Who knew insomnia could be so much fun?

*****

Lieutenant Robert "Raw" Pellucid was convinced

that the chronometer in the cockpit of his Battlenaut was broken, but he didn't have time to try to fix it.

Even as Raw pounded two enemy Battlenauts with laser fire, he stole another look at the chronometer's readout. He growled like a dog and grimaced at the blinking red numbers.

1805. 1805. 1805.

Seems like it was just 1805 fifteen minutes ago.

Unless the extreme sleep deprivation was affecting his time perception, the chronometer was running ten times slower than reality. What that meant was, the chronometer was definitely running slow, because Raw was running fine, sleep dep and all. He'd been awake for what felt like forever and hadn't needed even a single shot of wake-up juice.

His fellow Redeyes might be running on fumes, but Raw was burning rich. He was just that kind of guy. Even before the program, he'd always kept a lid on, no matter how high the heat.

Nothing but nothing could shake the S.O.B. He was fearless, poisonous, dirty, and smart. Smart enough to wonder if someone was screwing with him.

He went over it again as he raced his Battlenaut, guns blazing, toward his closest opponent. *If the clocks are out, we don't know how long we've been fighting on Sangre. We're on the dark side of this God-forsaken moon, so we can't even count the days by sunrises and sunsets.*

His opponent's Battlenaut stood its ground and sprayed defensive fire that splashed harmlessly off Raw's armor. At the last instant, the enemy leaped out of his path.

But why would someone want us to lose track of time? Why keep us in the field beyond the three-day limit?

Raw growled again, low in his throat. *Because they want to see how far we can go. Because they want to push the redeye tech to the limit.*

Even as he spun the Battlenaut around and threw a missile at the enemy's belly, Raw ran a little mental self-diagnostic to make sure he wasn't being paranoid.

Nope. Don't know the meaning of the word, folks.

He checked the chronometer again.

1805. 1805. 1805.

How long would the researchers leave the Redeyes on Sangre? What had to happen before they pulled the plug?

The answer came to him with a surprising lack of surprise, as if he'd always known it on some level.

The Redeyes had to *die*. Only then would Command pull the plug.

*****

Just as Grist was running his Battlenaut headlong toward a downed rebel, another blast of lightning flared nearby. A burst of static crackled from his comm.

It was followed by music.

The signal was weak, but Grist recognized the music immediately: "Tried and True," an old battle anthem from his homeworld, Tack. At the academy on Ryot, so far from home, he'd sung it to keep up his spirits. He'd sung it during many a night of drinking with fellow cadets who had also come from Tack and missed its jewel-capped mountains and fields of coppery glow-grain.

Cadets like his best friend, Mallet Cray.

Even as the rush of music and memories rocked him, Grist plowed his Battlenaut forward on pure momentum. He slammed it hard against the rebel, which seemed to be undergoing some kind of systems malfunction. As soon as he made contact, Grist wrenched back on the stick, keeping his Battlenaut on its feet while the rebel crashed to the ground.

When Grist had crippled the rebel Battlenaut and disabled its guns, he traced the music signal to a source outside the battle zone. He rotated his Battlenaut's upper body to give him a clear line of sight to the location blinking on his visor display.

Grist saw nothing until another surge of lightning washed over the landscape. In the split-second flare, he spotted exactly what he'd expected to see. What he'd dreaded.

It was at least three times the size of any Battlenaut he'd ever seen. Its gleaming black skin was festooned with weapons but not a single mark of identification. Writhing trails of electrical energy chased over it, as if the lightning had struck it and left a charge.

The Black Battlenaut. And it was playing his song.

Grist's best friend, Mallet Cray, had been singing that same song on the planet Yolanda a year ago, during an earlier battle in the civil war against Rightful forces. He'd always sung it in battle "for protection," and it had worked.

Until the Battle of Enoch on Yolanda, that is.

The song's magic hadn't done him much good when the friendly fire hit...the friendly fire from his best friend *Grist*. Grist's guns had hit a spot already softened up by rebel arms and had blown Cray's power plant. The explosion had caught Cray before he could eject and had not left enough of him behind to fill a shot glass.

All because Grist had lost his head and fired wild during an ambush.

Now, in the midst of another battle, Grist heard the same song his friend had been singing just before his death. Was it a coincidence that it seemed to be coming from the Black Battlenaut?

"It's your turn to die-yi-yi," said the gleaming silver fish wriggling past Grist's visor. "Cray's come b-b-back for the one who killed him-im."

Grist punched the comm button. The music stopped as he switched from "Receive" to "Send." "Freak? Raw? Either of you see the giant black Battlenaut?"

Freak's wild laughter rippled over the comm. "No way, man! Where is it?"

Grist's fingers fluttered over a keypad on the armrest. "I just fired you the coordinates."

"Nothing there," Raw said after a moment. "You have video of this thing?"

Grist spun through recent vid logs from the onboard cameras, cursing as he came up empty. "Missed it," he said, "but I eyeballed it twice. Black armor, heavy ordnance, bigger than our three Battlenauts put together."

Freak stopped laughing. "Whoa! You saw the *Black Battlenaut*?"

"That thought did cross my mind." Grist threw his helmet's optics to maximum magnification and gave the area a hard scan. The only Battlenauts he saw were the four downed rebels and the other two Redeyes.

"Wait a minute," said Raw. "Do you have any telemetry on this thing at all?"

"No." Grist took advantage of a lightning flash to make another scan but still saw nothing.

"Then what if it wasn't there?" said Raw. "What if you're seeing things because of the sleep dep?"

"Not a chance," said the silver fish as it switched past Grist's helmet. Without being told, Grist knew the fish's name was *Lacuna*.

"But what if I'm not seeing things?" said Grist. "You know what the Black Battlenaut means, don't you?"

"The end of the universe!" Freak whooped so loud, the comm filters cut her signal for an instant. "Everyone and everything!"

"It's a legend." Raw's voice was calm. "A bedtime story for children."

"I know I saw something." An orange and black butterfly with the face of a grinning human baby landed on the back of Grist's hand. "Why not look into it?"

"Because we have a job to do," said Raw. "We have to push the Rightfuls off this moon."

Suddenly, the lush green jungle that had sprung up in the cockpit parted over one corner of Grist's forward viewport. In that one open corner, in a fresh burst of lightning, Grist saw the Black Battlenaut walking off in the distance over a rocky plain.

"There it is!" Grist gave one of the vines a tug, and his Battlenaut headed in the direction of the Black Battlenaut. "Hey!" said Raw. "Come back here!"

*****

At that moment, more than anything, Raw wanted to take off his boot and scratch the bottom of his foot. An itch had been growing there for some time, and it was becoming distracting.

Now that Grist had gone charging off, however, with Freak close behind, Raw couldn't stop to scratch the itch. He had to follow the members of his squad and try to keep them from hurtling off the deep end of sleep-deprived insanity.

Up ahead, Grist and Freak raced their Battlenauts across the rock-strewn plain between the wetlands and the foothills of the Prelate Mountains. Raw's instruments and visual inspection both agreed that there was no Black Battlenaut in the distance, that the Redeyes were chasing after nothing.

The itch on the bottom of Raw's foot flared. He ignored it with sheer force of will and punched the comm. "Grist? Freak?" Neither one answered his call.

Raw changed the frequency and called again. "Redeye One to Redeye Base. Over."

Redeye Base ignored him, just like the last dozen times he'd called.

He finished the message anyway. "Request immediate extraction of Redeye Squad. Repeat. Request immediate extraction."

Still, there was no answer.

The only way they'll come for us is when we're dead. All they want's our autopsies and telemetry.

"Redeye One out." Raw punched off the comm and checked the chronometer.

1805. 1805.

He puffed out his breath and shook his head at the obviously incorrect readout. The funny thing was--and it was more funny strange than funny ha-ha--that particular time *meant* something to Raw. It was the exact moment, in fact, five years ago, when he had done the most important thing he'd ever done in his life.

It was the moment when Raw had murdered Braeburn Score.

*****

Freak was halfway across the dry plain when she smelled smoke. She recognized it immediately as the smoke from melting plastic and metal, the smell of a burning Battlenaut. In a panic, she checked the instruments...but her Battlenaut wasn't on fire.

As far as Freak could tell, the burning-Battlenaut smell was coming from the same place as the smells of baking bread and roses that had filled the cockpit earlier...in other words, from thin air.

The burning smell wasn't pleasant like the others had been, though. It turned over a rock and sent things scurrying in her mind.

For example, she thought of the day when Gwen Tuileries had died because of her.

Right after the missile had hit, Gwen's Battlenaut had

465

had that same burning smell. The only difference was, Freak remembered the added smell of frying meat when Gwen had cooked inside the cockpit.

All through Freak's first tour of duty, Gwen had been her guardian angel. She had always been ready to haul Freak's rookie ass out of the fire, even if it meant disobeying orders or bunging up her own Battlenaut. Or losing her life.

One night on Gallop, when their unit was pounding a Rightful garrison, Freak's Battlenaut had been crippled by a land mine. Just as enemy artillery had pumped out a missile to finish her off, Gwen's Battlenaut had leaped in to take the hit and save Freak's life.

Maybe Freak wouldn't have felt so bad about it except for one thing: she'd been working for the other side all along. Even as she'd betrayed the Commonwealth, she'd always planned to save Gwen...and hadn't counted on her own allies being willing to kill her in the bargain.

Freak had worked for the Commonwealth ever since.

As she followed Grist forward, the stench of melting Battlenaut and burning flesh in the cockpit intensified. Finally, it got to the point where it made her gag.

It was then that it occurred to Freak that maybe she'd come across a sign of the Black Battlenaut...and maybe, she had more of a personal interest in the Black Battlenaut than she'd expected.

After all, it couldn't be a coincidence that just as she was searching for the Black Battlenaut, the smell of her dead, betrayed friend rose up to greet her.

Could it?

BEWARE THE BLACK BATTLENAUT

*****

Grist brushed a blob of pink foam from the controls of the spellcaster and programmed it to grant his Battlenaut added speed and virility. He would need every edge the magic beans could give him when he took on the destructive might of the Black Battlenaut.

Pink foam from the cockpit ceiling splattered over his visor, and he wiped it clean. He was glad the foam wasn't quite smart enough to hurt him, but it was definitely more aggressive than the green swirly-gas that had filled the cockpit a moment ago.

When the hot go-juice spurted into his arm again, everything wavered and turned red...then straightened out and became a more soothing pale blue. The ring of circadian lights flickered around the front viewport, only they weren't *lights* anymore but *darks*.

His co-pilot, Broom Thornapple, who lived in Grist's armpit, nudged him and whistled. "Wow," said Broom. "Nice welcoming committee."

Grist looked in the direction where Broom was poking. Through the viewport, he saw a line of Battlenauts lit up by the beam of his searchlight.

The six Battlenauts stood across the mouth of a pass in the foothills, shoulder to shoulder, blocking the way. Each of them was painted red and festooned with bones and skins.

"Best hope your magic hoops have the power to fry those demons," said Broom. "You know what they say about the Black Battlenaut's minions."

"Monsters. Abominations." Grist licked his lips and swallowed hard.

Just then, the line of Battlenauts began to move. Grist lurched to a stop and brought all magic wands and wish-guns to bear on the line.

All at once, the six Battlenauts raised their right knees, then dropped them. Next, in unison, they kicked their right legs in the air, swinging them to chest level.

And dropped them.

They repeated the moves. This time, they hopped a little as they lifted their knees and kicked their legs.

The ground shook whenever they touched it. Wild music skirled over the comm, its punchy rhythm matching the movements of the Battlenaut chorus line.

*****

Freak swore she could feel the hot breath of the Flesh Battlenaut gusting against her own Battlenaut's back.

She quick-checked her visor display and saw the horrible thing still gaining on her. She was running hard, maxing the specs, and she was still going to lose the race.

Just moments ago, she and Grist had been chasing the monstrous Black Battlenaut. Now, she was the prey of something equally monstrous.

"Freak? Come in, Freak." The voice on the comm sounded like Raw's, but Freak wasn't fooled. She recognized the disguised voice of the thing that was hunting her.

All she saw on the video feed from her rear-facing cameras was Raw's Battlenaut racing after her...but she knew that, too, was an illusion. The thing that was back there, reaching for her, could not be caught on video, though the naked eye could see its true form.

Her naked eye had seen it, and she would never *forget* it.

The thing had started out as a single Battlenaut that had stepped into her path. Freak had jammed her Battlenaut to a stop while Grist had continued running onward without her.

The strange Battlenaut had stood motionless for a moment, its gold armor glinting in the beams of Freak's forward running lights. Then, it had raised one arm from its side. It had turned its hand over and opened it, revealing something pink and wet in its golden palm.

Zooming her optics to maximum mag, Freak had gotten a good look at what was in that hand. Just before the mystery Battlenaut had opened its mouth and dumped in what it was holding, Freak had recognized it.

The mangled, naked body of a human being.

As Freak watched, the Battlenaut had chewed up the human remains. It had chewed them with its mouth open, the lower jaw swinging wide to give her a good look at the gruesome mess.

After a long moment, the gold Battlenaut had finished chewing. It had opened its mouth wide once more, showing that the mashed remains were gone, and then its mouth had closed.

Suddenly, streams of pink flesh had boiled up from the seams and joints and vents in the gold Battlenaut's armor. Rolling and twisting and meshing, the flesh had stretched over the metal like a suit of skin, one throbbing layer weaving over another.

It was then that Freak had turned around and started running.

*****

As the squad of Rightful Battlenauts opened fire on Freak, Raw leaped into action. It was either that or let them pound Freak into bits, since she wasn't fighting back.

Based on her recent behavior, Raw thought the odds were good that she didn't even know the enemy was there.

Lasers blazing, Raw charged the nearest rebel and did some damage to its guns. As slugs fired by another Rightful blasted his armor, Raw brought everything he had to bear on the first Battlenaut's midsection...lasers, sonics, missiles. The instant he let it all fly, he swung his Battlenaut hard about and bounded after the other rebel.

As Raw scorched the second rebel Battlenaut with laser fire, he checked his visor display to make sure Freak was okay, which she was: still running, barely staying ahead of the third Rightful Battlenaut. The Rightful was lighting her up with laser fire, but Freak was shrugging it off.

Unlike Raw's Battlenaut, which took a hard shot to the chest from one of his opponent's missiles. Raw's Battlenaut shook and teetered from the explosive impact and started to fall over backward.

Quickly, Raw spun the Battlenaut's upper body around and fired slugs at the ground. The recoil kept the Battlenaut on its feet and ready to continue the fight.

Raw just wished he could deal with the killer itch on the

bottom of his foot so easily.

*****

Grist marched in the Battlenaut Day parade, waving at the throngs of Battlenauts of all shapes and sizes cheering from the stands. The whole time, he searched his surroundings for the Black Battlenaut, who had run off in this direction after Grist's last sighting.

The six dancing Battlenauts at the mouth of the pass, it had turned out, had all been parts of the Black Battlenaut. Right after their big dance number, they had crashed together, cranking and twisting and snapping into one giant Battlenaut with black armor and weapons galore. Then, instead of attacking, the Black Battlenaut had raced off, leaving Grist to try in vain to keep up.

"He's out there somewhere," said High Five, who looked like an oil spill with a mouthful of yellow tongues. His voice sounded like continuous belching. He floated in midair and was Grist's new best friend. "I can feel it, buddy-Joe."

High Five was never wrong, except about women. "I hear ya," said Grist, carefully scanning the crowd. He thought he saw the top of the Black Battlenaut's head peaking out from behind the stands, but the image faded when the hypo cuff poured more go-juice into his arm.

A droning electronic anthem played from speakers along the parade route, and all the spectators hummed along with it. Vendors sold candy-coated humans stuck on sticks, which Battlenaut children licked and crunched.

"You seen one Battlenaut Day, you've seen 'em all, right?" said High Five.

Grist laughed. "You can say that again."

A second later, Grist noticed in an absent-minded way that the cockpit was full of fizzy water, and High Five had been replaced by a word, "GOOD," in bold black letters a foot high.

"What do you say, Word?" Grist slapped in annoyance at his hypo cuff, which had just shot him with more hot go-juice.

Word reshaped itself from "GOOD" to "LOOK," pointing at one of the video screens with the tail of the "K."

Without thinking, Grist looked at the screen Word had indicated. The words "BLACK BATTLENAUT" filled the screen from top to bottom and edge to edge, rapidly flashing bright and dim.

Grist tried for a better view through the forward viewport, and he got it. Just like on the screen, the words "BLACK BATTLENAUT" floated up ahead, blinking on and off.

Grist's heart beat faster. "Is that him?" He pointed at the words "BLACK BATTLENAUT" through the viewport.

Word swirled around and reformed itself from "LOOK" to "CRAY."

And it was at that moment that the comm kicked on again.

The anthem "Tried and True" blared from the speaker. A few bars in, a human voice spoke up over the music. A man's voice.

A familiar voice.

"Hi there, Killer. Time to settle the score."

"*Cray?*" said Grist.

*****

"Hello, Sharon," said the woman's voice over Freak's comm. "Been a while."

Freak kept driving her Battlenaut hard and didn't answer. *That's Gwen Tuileries. Gwen Tuileries is dead.*

The smell of burning Battlenaut and human flesh was so strong in the cockpit, Freak gagged. The hypo cuff was hitting her with go-juice what seemed like every ten seconds. Her head was spinning, her stomach lurching.

And her dead best friend was calling on the comm.

"You're headed straight for me," Gwen said over the comm. "Just a little further, Sharon."

Hearing that, Freak slammed on the brakes. A second later, as her Battlenaut stumbled to a halt, she remembered the Flesh Battlenaut that had been chasing her.

Freak whipped around, expecting the Flesh Battlenaut to pounce on her...but the pounce didn't happen. In fact, she could see no trace of the Flesh Battlenaut in her searchlights.

She did, however, see a towering black figure.

Gwen laughed lightly over the comm. "Oops. I misspoke. Actually, I'm *right here*, Sharon."

*****

Raw had his hands full keeping the attacking Rightfuls at bay, when suddenly his Battlenaut was hit from behind by laser fire.

A glance at his visor display revealed a familiar transponder signal back there, and the feed from the rearward camera confirmed it. Even as Raw fought the rebel Battlenauts who were chasing Freak, Freak had turned around and was shooting at Raw.

So now it was three against one. Not that he was the kind of guy who sweated the odds.

First things first. Set your priorities.

As lasers and slugs hammered his Battlenaut, Raw stormed the closest Rightful. In spite of the heavy fire, Raw drove his Battlenaut up close and shoved the barrel of a laser cannon into a breach in the enemy's armor.

After pumping in a few blasts, Raw darted away. The rebel exploded, throwing out a shock wave that sent his partner reeling.

Even as Raw struggled to keep his Battlenaut on its feet, he growled with delight. *One down, two to go.*

That was before Grist charged up and opened fire on him, too.

*****

"Kill me once, shame on you," Cray said over the comm in Grist's cockpit. "Kill me twice...well, you can't kill the *Black Battlenaut*, can you?"

Grist tried to block out the voice as he fought to keep

up with the Black Battlenaut. The behemoth had grown to colossal size; its walking strides were so vast, Grist had to run at top speed just to stay in weapons range.

He fired his lasers again and watched them skim harmlessly off the Black Battlenaut's ebon armor. The hypo cuff squeezed tight, flooding his arm with blazing go-juice.

That was when the Black Battlenaut stopped and turned. Each footfall made the earth tremble.

Grist cut loose with his Battlenaut's lasers and sonics, but he might as well have been firing feathers. The Black Battlenaut stood unfazed and stared down at him.

"Let me explain," said Cray.

At first, Grist didn't realize Cray's voice wasn't coming from the comm anymore. It took a minute for the truth to sink in.

"We should've done this a long time ago," said Cray, who now was leaning against the cockpit wall, aiming a lopsided grin at the man who had shot him to death.

*****

Raw wasn't sure which bothered him more: fighting off three Battlenauts, two of them piloted by his squadmates, or not being able to scratch his itchy foot.

When Grist suddenly stopped shooting at him, cutting the weapons barrage by a third, Raw's itch moved up to first place. Gritting his teeth, he barely resisted the urge to stop fighting, kick off his boot, and scratch like crazy. In the process, he dropped his guard for an instant and took a laser hit that charred the armor plating on his Battlenaut's left shoulder.

Cursing as a stream of wild shots flared around him, Raw swung around. He charged toward the source of the fire, targeting his own arsenal on what had become the most volatile threat of the moment.

Freak continued to pound him with lasers and missiles as he hurtled toward her.

*****

Freak unleashed the full fury of her weapons, but the Black Battlenaut kept stomping toward her.

Gwen's voice chimed over the comm with no more tension than if the two of them were chatting over coffee. "What do you think I'm going to do to you, Sharon? Burn you alive?"

Freak's heart hammered. *That's exactly what you'll do. Make me die the same way you did.*

"Well, it isn't gonna happen," said Gwen. "Why would I try to kill someone whose life I died to save? Besides which..."

Suddenly, everything changed. Freak was in the cockpit of her old Battlenaut instead of the current one. Looking out the forward viewport, she immediately recognized the steam vents and weird geologic formations of another world.

Laser fire pulsed past her from the fortified walls of a Rightful garrison. Commander Endymion snapped out orders over the comm in the cockpit.

She was back on Gallop, during the battle in which

Gwen had been killed.

"Besides which," Gwen said over the comm, "I don't blame you for what happened."

*****

As soon as Freak's weapons shut down and dropped, Raw doubled back and charged the Rightful behind him.

That was when something unexpected happened. A missile hissed out of his Battlenaut's rack and shot straight toward the enemy. Raw watched as the missile hit the rebel Battlenaut's midsection dead center and detonated, blowing a hole in the heavy armor.

There was just one problem. Raw didn't remember firing the missile.

Suddenly, Raw's Battlenaut lunged forward. Lasers ablaze, the Battlenaut raced at top speed for the Rightful.

As Raw watched through the viewport, his Battlenaut lit up the hole in the enemy's belly, setting off an explosion in its guts. The Rightful danced like a man touching a high voltage power line, then slammed to the ground in a pile of smoking scrap.

Raw quick-checked every status display in the cockpit, scrambling to ferret out the problem. Never in his career had a Battlenaut taken independent action like that.

He only stopped hunting the glitch when he heard a tapping sound in the direction of the forward viewport. He looked toward the noise, and his eyes widened with surprise.

His Battlenaut was pointing one of its own lasers into the cockpit.

The hypo cuff squeezed Raw's bicep and pumped him full of liquid fire. A voice echoed in his head, and he recognized it immediately.

It was the voice of a young man, barely out of his teens. "I'm back. Did you miss me?"

It was the voice of Braeburn Score.

*****

"If you say you're sorry one more time, I'm gonna pop you one," Cray said with a smirk.

"Okay. Sor..." Grist barely caught himself. He was still in a daze, struggling to deal with the fact that a man he'd killed was apparently sitting in the cockpit with him.

"Your apologies are meaningless," said Cray. "What's done is done. Get over it."

"I can't." Grist pulled off his helmet and set it aside. "Not a day goes by that I don't think about it."

"Big baby." Cray snorted and shook his head. "It was *war*, man. *Chaos*. It was *nobody's* fault."

"I panicked." Grist's hands were shaking.

Cray leaned forward. "Okay, look." He rested his elbows on his knees and folded his hands between them. "You're really pissing me off here. All this 'poor me' crap." Cray rolled his eyes. "The not sleeping and the volunteering for suicide duty. How do you think that makes me feel?"

Grist shrugged.

"Makes me feel like kicking your ass," said Cray. "How about getting your shit together, so I can at least feel like my death *meant* something. Like you learned from your mistake and went on to *accomplish* something."

Grist rubbed his chin. "I'll try."

"Just *do* it."

"What about the universe?" said Grist. "Are you going to destroy it?"

"Ask the chicken-fish." Cray hiked a thumb toward one side of the cockpit.

A long, green fish with the head of a chicken bobbed in a bubble of pink water floating in midair. "Redeye Base to Redeye Squad," it said. "Come in Redeye Squad."

*****

Once upon a time, a filthy young beggar decided to ply his trade outside the military academy in Soldier City on Archibald.

(As the hypo cuff pumped go-juice into his arm again and again, Raw listened to the voice in his head tell the story.)

Not surprisingly, the privileged and arrogant young men who passed through the academy's doors proved to be terrible pickings. They spat in his beggar's bowl and ridiculed him. Sometimes, they struck him on their way past.

But one young man was different from the others. Whenever he passed the beggar, this young man always greeted him and put coins in his bowl. Eventually, he even brought the beggar food and clothing.

The beggar was suspicious, as the young man's kindness was so unlike any of the other privileged military students.

The young man, however, assured him that his motives were honorable.

Over time, the two became friends. They were of about the same age, in fact. Each week, the military student took the beggar to a local restaurant for lunch. The student even suggested that there might be a place for the beggar on the estate of his father, a baron.

The student was truly good luck for the beggar... especially after the beggar murdered him.

The beggar did it in a matter-of-fact way, with a strong cord around the throat. He slipped away with enough money to start a new life in another town as another man.

And he never looked back. He never regretted killing Braeburn Score in cold blood. It had simply been a thing that had to be done, a matter of survival.

His name was Flynn Jarvo.

He changed that name to Robert Pellucid. Nickname "Raw."

*****

"You don't know the whole story," said Freak. She had adjusted remarkably well to being thrown back in time and was pumping round after round from her old Battlenaut's guns into the enemy garrison. "That's why you don't blame me."

Gwen sighed over the comm. "Go ahead. Do it."

"Do what?" said Freak.

"This is when you send the signal," said Gwen. "The go-ahead for the rebel ambush."

A chill rippled through Freak's body. "What?"

"You were working for the rebels," said Gwen. "You tipped them off."

"You *knew*?"

"I do now. The Black Battlenaut knows all." Gwen laughed. "I also know you've been beating yourself up about it ever since."

Freak clenched her hands around the joysticks and drove her Battlenaut hard. "You weren't supposed to die."

"Did I or did I not save your life?" said Gwen.

"You did," Freak said through clenched teeth.

"Then I've got no complaints. I'd do the same thing all over again."

Freak pushed the Battlenaut through the forest of close-set, mushroom-like mineral plugs. Geysers erupted right and left, spraying jets of hot steam that misted the viewports and cameras.

The tear that rolled down Freak's cheek felt as hot as the steam outside. "I've missed you so much," she said. "There are so many things I've wanted to say to you."

"I've got something to say to you, too," said Gwen.

Freak continued to manhandle the controls. "What's that?"

"Redeye Base to Redeye Squad," said Gwen. "Come in, Redeye Squad."

*****

"You've never really paid for what you did to me," said the voice in Raw's head, the voice of Braeburn Score. "You

481

feel no guilt whatsoever."

Raw watched the laser cannon outside the forward viewport, the weapon that his own Battlenaut was pointing at itself. "It was nothing personal."

"How do you figure?" said Braeburn. "I reached out to you as a friend, and you *murdered* me. How is that not *personal*?"

The hypo cuff squeezed tight around Raw's arm, shooting in more go-juice. "You would've done the same to me if you were in my shoes."

"You know that's not true," said Braeburn.

"I saw my chance and I took it," said Raw, his upper lip curling in a growl.

"So you think it was *fair*, what you did? You don't feel any remorse for *killing* a man in cold blood so you could *steal* from him?"

"It was *war*!" said Raw. "It was no different from *war*!"

"I have a message for you from the other side," said Braeburn. "You will suffer for all eternity for what you did to me. And that's not all."

"Get out of my head!" said Raw. "I don't want to hear any more!"

"Redeye Base to Redeye Squad. Come in Redeye Squad."

It took an instant for Raw to realize that the male voice he was listening to was no longer Braeburn's. The new voice was coming from the comm.

"Redeye Base to Redeye Squad."

Raw punched the comm button. "Redeye One here."

The voice on the comm sounded urgent. "What is

your status, Redeye One?"

"Request immediate extraction. Repeat. Request immediate extraction."

"Negative," said Redeye Base. "You have new orders."

"No can do," said Raw. "We're falling apart out here."

"Enemy squad is converging on your position." Redeye Base sounded even more urgent. "We're transmitting telemetry now. Prepare to engage."

"Redeye Two and Three are off comms," said Raw.

"Negative," said Redeye Base. "Comms have been restored."

"Redeye Two here," Grist said over the comm.

"Redeye Three responding," said Freak.

"Redeye One is...out of control," said Raw. "I strongly recommend immediate extraction."

There was a pause before Redeye Base spoke again. "Prepare to engage. Repeat, prepare to engage."

The cuff squeezed Raw's arm again. He knew there would be no extraction.

The only way they'll come for us is when we're dead. That was what he'd thought earlier. *All they want's our autopsies and telemetry.*

Only one way out of this, and he'd known it deep down from the beginning.

"Redeye Squad! Form up!" Raw's hands flew over the controls. The Battlenaut responded smoothly, with no hint of rogue action.

At his command, the laser cannon that had been aiming at the cockpit window pointed away from it again.

*****

"Arm weapons!" Raw said over the comm. "Lock and load!"

"Roger that," said Grist, playing the controls with new purpose and alertness. The need for battle readiness had snapped him back to reality.

It didn't hurt that he finally felt at peace with his role in Cray's death. It was a burden he'd been carrying around for years, a burden that had slowly been crushing him.

At last, he felt free of it. So what if his forgiveness had been granted by an hallucination?

Why not use a little insanity to inoculate himself against a greater madness?

*****

"Armed and ready, Lieutenant," Freak said over the comm. "Fit to fight, sir," she added, and she meant it.

She hadn't slept for what must have been days, but she felt fitter than she had in years. She felt like a new woman since her encounter with Gwen.

Freak only wished the visit could have been longer. There was still one thing she'd left unsaid, one thing she'd wanted to say more than anything else.

She switched off her comm just long enough to say it. Gwen was gone, but Freak said it anyway.

"I love you, Gwen. I'll never love anyone the way I love you."

*****

"Here they come," Redeye Base said over the comm. "They're coming right over the ridge."

"Stand by, Redeye Squad," said Raw. He kept his weapons aimed in the direction of the enemy, ready to unleash the Battlenaut's full fury at any moment.

When he checked his visor display, however, his resolve faltered. The telemetry he saw there wasn't at all what he'd expected.

Not for ten seconds anyway.

After ten seconds, the telemetry data completely changed, lining up with Raw's expectations--namely, that a squad of enemy Battlenauts was marching over the ridge.

A squad of enemy Battlenauts instead of a convoy of civilian vehicles.

"Redeye One to Redeye Base." Raw peered out the forward viewport for visual confirmation. Lights glided over the ridge and beamed back at him, the glare washing out his view of whatever was coming. "You sure about that telemetry?"

"One hundred percent," said Redeye Base.

"But first read on the visor was that those are civilian transports, not Battlenauts," said Raw.

"That was a hiccup in the network," said Redeye Base. "Current telemetry is confirmed."

As Raw watched the viewport, the oncoming lights drew closer, and the shapes behind them began to resolve themselves.

There wasn't a single Battlenaut among them.

"Abort!" Raw's hands flew over the controls as he powered down his weapons. "Redeye Squad, abort! Those are civilian transports! Repeat, abort!"

"Really?" Freak said over the comm. "Telemetry says they're hostile Battlenauts."

"Telemetry's wrong," said Raw. "I have visual confirmation."

"Negative, Redeye One," said Redeye Base. "Visual is unreliable. You're hallucinating."

Cold sweat trickled down Raw's back. The itch on the sole of his foot flared up again. "No hallucination! These are civilian transports!"

"Fire when ready," said Redeye Base. "The order is given."

"Abort!" said Raw.

"Redeye Two and Three," said Redeye Base. "Prepare to receive new orders on a secure channel."

*****

"I heard what you said about loving me," Gwen said over the comm in Freak's cockpit. "I want you to know that the feeling was always mutual."

Freak's heart pounded. Tears ran down her face. "G-Gwen?"

"I love you and I want to help you," said Gwen. "I'm going to help you do the right thing."

"What's that?" said Freak.

"Listen," said Gwen, and then she told her what to do.

*****

"I've got some good advice for you," Cray said over the comm. "Consider it a thank-you gift."

Grist wasn't as startled to hear the dead man's voice as the first time Cray had spoken to him. "What's the advice?"

"I'll let the chicken-fish tell you," said Cray.

*****

It was then, in the seconds after he realized what was about to happen and the seconds before it happened, that Raw fully understood.

They're interested in more than our physical limits.

It didn't take a genius to figure out what Redeye Base was telling Grist and Freak on the secure channel. It wasn't hard to predict what was going to happen next.

Redeye Base had ordered the squad to fire on the civilian convoy. Raw, the squad leader, had failed to comply. So Redeye Base was moving down the chain of command to try to get the job done.

They wanted to see if Grist and Freak were so bombed from sleep dep and go-juice that they'd do what Raw wouldn't.

They want to know how far we can be pushed in every way.

It wasn't enough to create Battlenaut jockeys who could fight without rest. They wanted Battlenaut jockeys who doubted the evidence of their own senses.

Battlenaut jockeys who could be completely controlled.

487

*****

"I don't know if I can do that," Grist said after the chicken-fish told him Cray's advice. "Raw said those are civilian transports."

"Raw's a cuckoo, boyo," said Swindle the leperchaun, twirling a green index finger alongside his rotting temple. "Who'd ya rather trust? A nut who's gone without sleep fer who knows how long, or cool-headed authority figures with all that tech at their disposal?"

Grist pinched his eyes shut to try to stop his head from spinning. "They look an awful lot like civilians to me."

"Remember," said Cray's voice over the comm. "The Black Battlenaut wears many faces."

Grist opened his eyes and stared at the forward viewport. What he saw there looked like a cluster of six-wheeled transports, the kind regularly used to carry miners between worksites on Sangre.

Was it possible that what he saw had nothing to do with what was really out there? That his senses were deceiving him?

As the orange and black butterfly with the head of a human baby fluttered past him, Grist knew he had his answer.

*****

"But I don't want to kill him, Gwen," said Freak. "Lieutenant Raw hasn't done anything wrong."

"Oh, honey." Gwen's voice over the comm sounded

loving and sad. "Redeye Base had a good reason for giving that order."

The cuff squeezed in another burst of fiery go-juice. "What reason?"

"I'm alive again, sweetie," said Gwen. "That's right. They grew a clone of me, and we're going to be together... but the lieutenant wants to keep us apart."

Freak felt like she was floating and sinking at the same time. The fog in her head was getting thicker and stickier. "He does?"

"Please, darling," said Gwen. "Please save me this time."

*****

Raw was never sure exactly when he became the Black Battlenaut. Was it before he died? Or after?

He remembered Grist and Freak opening fire on him with everything they had. He remembered thinking

This is the only way it can end and I knew it from the beginning.

That was why

(He remembered the giant golden eyes gazing down from above, gazing down upon him like the golden eyes of God.)

That was why he made no move to defend himself. Maybe, his sacrifice would be enough to satisfy the scientists. Maybe, having learned the limits of one man, they would spare Grist and Freak.

But he doubted it.

Even if they let those two live, the civilians were

doomed, of that he was certain.

(A dark shape huge as a mountain, blocking out the stars, black metal body glinting in the glow of those giant golden eyes.)

The scientists had to know if Redeyes would gun down innocent civilians on a whim from Command, in defiance of the evidence of their own senses and the dictates of their own consciences.

(Was this what Grist and Freak had seen, this gleaming behemoth, this legendary destroyer?)

There would be innocent blood on Grist and Freak's hands. At least Raw himself wouldn't add to it when they finished killing him. His blood was far from innocent.

(He had never expected it to be so beautiful.)

(So terrible.)

The cockpit filled with the sounds of damage...the pockety-pock of slug impacts, the boom-whoom-thoom of missiles exploding one after another, the crackle and screech of metal gashed by lasers. The hiss of air escaping the broken Battlenaut, the whoops and pings and whistles of weapons alerts and systems failure alarms.

(Most beautiful thing he'd ever)

The ear-splitting whine that signalled a breach in the fusion reactor.

(Beautiful and powerful. Reaching down with a hand as big as a building)

Déjà vu.

(Splitting open the shell, the chrysalis, extracting him)

I know you.

(When the halves of the broken Battlenaut fell to

the ground, they exploded in a wave of glittering golden butterflies.)

(He watched from above as Grist and Freak bombarded the civilians in a shower of fire and light.)

Or was he already there by then, inhabiting the leviathan? Or had he always been a part of it?

I am you.

The moon trembled as he turned his eyes from the flurry of smoke and flame and dirt at his feet.

Not tired anymore.

He tipped his head back, each eye the size of a cathedral, and looked up and out at the same flickering membrane of stars that lay reflected on the polished ebon plate of his face.

Good night.

Killer Bod

The servos in my exoskeleton whine. The next thing I know, my fingers are crushing the throat of the waitress who just brought me my drink.

Her face reddens and purples. The choking sounds intensify and fade to nothing.

My hand unclamps. I no more make it do so than I made it clench in the first place. Nor did I instruct it to beat my neighbor's brains in or stab the super in my building or push that stranger off the subway platform in front of the oncoming train.

The exoskel interface in my brain no longer works. I have tried hundreds of times to trigger the system override, but the exoskel ignores me. It's attached to my body, but it acts like I'm not even here.

The networked onboard microprocessor flakes that run this exoskeleton have hacked me out of the loop and developed a mind of their own.

And it's not a nice mind.

Against my will, as always, the exoskel flexes my legs and makes me walk toward the door. When the burly, bald bartender whips out a shotgun, I leap at him. Before he can fire, my hands take hold of the double barrels and pound the gun back into his head. Three times.

The bartender drops dead to the floor. My hands release the gun, and my body turns and keeps walking.

Tears roll down my cheeks. At least I still have control of those.

"Stop it! Please stop it!" I say, but the exoskel does not comply. It kills a bouncer outside and propels me down the street.

Ironically, this out-of-control exoskel I wear is called a Freedom Shell. It was supposed to restore my mobility after the accident that left me paralyzed from the neck down.

What it was not supposed to do is lock me out of the control app and go on a murder spree.

There is a hard-wired kill switch on a pad at the base of my back, but it does me no good. I can't reach for it now that my arms and hands are out of my control.

The Freedom Shell kills three more people on our way down the street. I keep my eyes closed most of the time, but I hear things that make me sick beyond words.

Finally, two cops appear from around a corner and raise their side arms. They shoot me again and again, bullets punching between the gaps in the Freedom Shell's metal framework.

I thank God as my consciousness and life dribble out of me. I pray that I will not be held responsible in the next world for the atrocities committed by the Freedom Shell that encases me.

The last thing I see is the cops as we rush toward them, reaching for their throats. I wonder how many more people will die by my dead hands when I am gone.

ABOUT THE AUTHOR

Robert Jeschonek is an award-winning writer whose fiction, comics, essays, articles, and podcasts have been published around the world. He has written *Star Trek* and *Doctor Who* fiction and *Batman* and *Justice Society* comics. His young adult fantasy novel, *My Favorite Band Does Not Exist*, won the Forward National Literature Award and was named a Top Ten First Novel for Youth by *Booklist*. His cross-genre science fiction thriller, *Day 9*, is an International Book Award winner. He also won the Scribe Award for Best Original Novel from the International Association of Media Tie-in Writers for his alternate history, *Tannhäuser: Rising Sun, Falling Shadows*. He is a member of the Science Fiction and Fantasy Writers of America. Visit him online at www.robertjeschonek.com. You can also find him on Facebook and follow him as @TheFictioneer on Twitter.

MORE GREAT SCIENCE FICTION
NOW AVAILABLE FROM
ROBERT JESCHONEK

BATTLENAUT CRUCIBLE

BY ROBERT JESCHONEK

The Red Battlenauts show no mercy. Roaring out of the darkness of deep space, these ultra-high tech war machines pound the hell out of both sides in a bloody interstellar civil war. No one can even SEE the Reds--no one except Marine Corporal Solomon Scott. Recruited by the hardcore SEAL-like Diamondbacks, Scott becomes a secret weapon in the ultimate struggle for survival. In battle after battle on perilous alien worlds, Scott and the Diamondbacks fight back against the ruthless Reds, desperately holding the line in furious clashes of muscle and metal. But when a face from the past exposes the secrets behind the carnage, a quest for answers becomes a race against time. Because the masters of the Red Battlenauts have more on their minds than a thirst for conquest...and only Solomon Scott can hope to stand against them.

AND NOW, A SPECIAL PREVIEW OF BATTLENAUT CRUCIBLE...

CHAPTER 1

Corporal Solomon Scott held his gray-plated Mark VI Battlenaut armor perfectly still in the thick white mist. Around him lay the broken armor of two opponents, dead pilots who'd fought to the last for the cause of the Rightful rebels. Scott had killed them both just moments ago in a firefight that had left his own armor damaged.

Unfortunately, the larger battle going on around him was nowhere near finished. According to comm traffic and the telemetry displayed on the visor of his helmet, dozens of Battlenauts were still smashing the hell out of each other in all directions. The battle for the Commonwealth outpost on planetoid Chelong III was still raging, the outcome up in the air.

But the big picture wasn't the main thing on Scott's mind at the moment. He was more concerned about where the next attack on his own armor would come from and how he'd survive it with a breach in his belly plating.

1

Tapping buttons on the left armrest keypad, he switched views on the visor, superimposing the telemetry data over feeds from the onboard cameras. As far as he could tell, there was nothing nearby...but the mists of Chelong swirled with crystalline particles that played tricks on sensors as well as eyes.

As he stared at the feed from his aft cameras, the smell of sweat and metal in the cockpit grew sharper, and the hairs on his neck stood up straight. He thought he glimpsed a flicker of movement and gripped the stick tight, ready to fire his rear-mounted guns.

But nothing bounded out of the mist back there, and he didn't shoot. No problem; he was good at keeping a cool head.

Not that anything else in the cockpit of his Mark VI was cool at that point. One of the topside cooling vents had taken a hit, and the whole rig was overheating like crazy. Sweat ran down his sides and soaked every part of him. At least the padded halo mount inside his helmet kept the sweat from running into his eyes and burning the crap out of them.

He was flipping between camera views again when Captain Rollins got on the horn. "Echo Charlie Bravo!" The man's gravelly voice burst from the comm speaker. "Stop standing around, Scott! Dewar and Shen need backup! I just flashed you the stats!"

As promised, Dewar and Shen's telemetry appeared on the visor. They were thirty meters to the right, both taking heavy hits...but from what? It didn't look like there was anyone else in their immediate vicinity. Was the mist screwing with their sensors?

"Damnit, Scott," snapped Rollins. "Get your ass moving!"

Suddenly, something caught his eye on the feed from the rightside camera. He played the armrest keypad, clearing the telemetry data from the visor screen and punching the rightside feed to maximum magnification. "Stand by, sir." He saw nothing...nothing...

Then *something*. A glint, a spark, a flicker in the fog.

"The hell with stand by!" Rollins' voice became a roar. "Shen just went down!"

Scott brought the telemetry back up and saw Shen's specs crashing hard. She was alive, but her armor was fried.

And whatever had fried it was out there somewhere in a rightside direction, exactly where Scott had seen the glint.

Rollins was still roaring over the comm, but Scott blocked him out. His neck hairs were still up, his gut was twisting; telemetry said nothing was out there, but his instincts told him otherwise.

Jaws clenched, he ran spectral overlays on the feed, scanning the full range of infrared and ultraviolet frequencies. Still nothing.

He cut his audio mic so he could talk to himself. "Come on, you piece of *oosh*. I know you're out there."

Scott threw all five feeds on-visor at once--rightside, leftside, frontside, backside, topside--and hit them all with the spectral overlays. Still, he saw no telltale signs of an enemy Battlenaut in any direction.

His instincts were usually good, but maybe they were off this one time. He'd been in battle before; even without actual fog, things could get confusing in the thick of it.

Just then, something Rollins was shouting broke through. "Dewar is down! Get over there *now*, you son of a..."

Grabbing the stick, Scott brought his Battlenaut back to life. He was just about to turn it toward Shen and Dewar when he spotted a blip on the radar. It only lasted a split-second, but it was enough to jolt him into action.

The monitors tracking his vital signs pinged faster across the board. The radar blip had appeared not to the right of him, but the *left*.

Whatever was coming, whatever had taken out Shen and Dewar, it had managed to circle around him.

Instead of turning right, Scott swung his Battlenaut left. At the same time, he played the armrest keypad, jumping all weapons out of standby mode.

That was when he saw the Red Battlenaut for the first time.

It burst out of the mist with guns blazing, marching straight toward him. It was bigger than his own Battlenaut armor--twelve meters tall compared to ten for the Mark VI--with skin that gleamed bright red from tip to toe. And there wasn't a mark on it that Scott could see.

Without thought or hesitation, Scott opened fire with his main guns. At the same time, he threw a half-dozen missiles at the Red. He needed to hit it hard and fast, not give it a chance to get at his damaged belly plating.

Slugs from the Red's guns peppered the Mark VI, pocking the shielding over the cockpit. His own missiles hit the Red's chest in a cluster, exploding with shuddering

4

force.

But they didn't slow it down or leave a scratch.

"What the *flux*?" Scott opened up with his lasers and sonics at the same time, focusing on what he hoped was a weak spot--the backward-flexing knee joint of one leg. The armor narrowed there and lacked any visible shield plating.

Unfortunately, that didn't mean it was any weaker. The searing crimson beam from Scott's laser tagged the joint, accompanied by waves of oscillating vibratory force...but the Red didn't slow down a bit.

Scott clenched his teeth and stepped his Battlenaut back, then leaped forward, propelling his armor's shoulder toward the Red.

He was met by a shower of heavy slugs thudding into his plating, but they didn't stop him. His Mark VI covered the distance in seconds and slammed into the Red with its full weight and momentum.

Collision alarms wailed, and damage reports flashed on his visor. His vital signs spiked, and his head swam from the powerful impact. It had been a hell of a hit.

And apparently, it hadn't done any damage. The Red stood firmly in place; according to Scott's sensors, its armor hadn't buckled or ruptured in the slightest.

But that wasn't the worst of it. As Scott tried to push his Battlenaut back, he quickly realized it was stuck. He couldn't break away from the Red.

Cursing, he summoned new sensor data on the Red Battlenaut. According to the numbers, the Red's skin had become highly magnetized; its grip was more than strong enough to resist the full torque of Scott's armor's fusion-powered servos.

Seconds after he realized this, two panels popped open on the Red's chest, and twin circular blades mounted on extensible arms spun toward him. A heartbeat later, they were biting into the armor plating over Scott's cockpit, sending up showers of sparks.

Scott flipped on the mic and shouted over the grinding screech of the blades. "Mayday! Echo Charlie Bravo! Mayday!"

The blades cut fast, shearing their way through the super-hardened metal of Scott's armor like it was cardboard. Sensors showed the cockpit would be breached in less than a minute.

Scott jabbed the keypad, prepping all weapons to fire at once. It was a desperate move, but he couldn't think of anything else.

Not at first, anyway.

What would Bern do? The question flashed through his mind like a flame running down a trail of lit fuel. Bern was an inspiration to him, the reason he'd become a Commonwealth Marine in the first place. She was his grandmother, and she'd been a hero in an earlier war.

What would Bern do?

Suddenly, an idea flared to life. He would barely have time to try it; the blades were about to penetrate the shell of the cockpit.

Scott's fingers flew over both armrest keypads as he hastily shot commands into the armor's control network. Twice, he had to override fail-safes with pass codes and retinal scans.

"Yeah, I know," he said after jumping the last hurdle. "The armor wasn't built for this. Safety specs exceeded. Blah blah blah."

Just then, the Red's dual blades screamed through the armor, whirling mere inches away from his face. His flesh, skull, and brain were seconds from splattering all over the cockpit.

"Let's see how *you* like it." Scott sneered as he punched the last button. His heart was hammering, adrenaline searing through his bloodstream...and now he'd made his last play.

The lights and displays in the cockpit flickered and went out. The fusion power plant in the bowels of the Mark VI roared, and the armor rumbled violently. All around him, he heard a loud, sizzling crackle and hum.

Suddenly, the Red's blades stopped spinning and shot back toward the slits they'd cut. One popped right out, while the other twisted and caught on the edge of the slit. It pulled hard, working its way free--then snapped off the stem on which it was mounted and clattered down into the bowels of Scott's armor.

"*Now* we're talkin'." Scott braced himself against the cockpit couch and waited for what was coming. He'd fought fire with fire, charging his armor with streams of electrical current from the power plant, turning his Battlenaut into an electromagnet. An electromagnet with the same polarity as the Red Battlenaut.

Since two magnets with the same polarity repel each other, the two Battlenauts could no longer stay locked together. With a loud clang, Scott's armor shot away from the Red and crashed to the dusty ground.

"Yeah!" Scott scrambled in the cockpit, redirecting power from his Battlenaut's skin to the rest of its parts. The lights quickly came back up, and the control system rebooted. His helmet visor flickered back to life in a matter of seconds.

Just in time for him to see the Red stomping toward him.

Scott pounded the keypads and worked the stick, fighting to get his armor back on its feet. Servos hummed as he got the Mark VI to sit up, then roll to one side and brace itself with both gauntlets on the ground.

Meanwhile, the Red kept coming. Scott saw it march closer on his visor's video feed, even as he rolled his own armor onto its knees.

"Come on!" His Battlenaut lurched its upper body erect. Scott hammered buttons, and it drew up one knee, planting its right foot firmly under it.

He felt the ground shake as the Red stormed closer. Why it hadn't already opened fire, he couldn't guess.

Wrenching the stick, he focused the armor's power on the right leg, trying to push up and bring the other foot forward. Once he had both feet flat under him, he'd have the leverage to get the whole unit standing again.

But would he have time to finish the maneuver? The Red's footsteps were getting closer, its image growing larger in the visor video feed.

Scott smelled burning metal and plastic. Servos whined, the armor wobbled...and the legs locked up. The right leg got stuck halfway up, leaving the left foot jammed toe-first in the dirt, unable to flatten and fully extend the leg above it.

Cursing a blue streak, he fought the controls...and then it was too late. Proximity alarms squealed, and the Red Battlenaut suddenly towered over him.

Scott ground his teeth and scowled. Looking past the visor, he saw gleaming red metal fill the blast-tempered glass of the forward viewport.

It wasn't about getting on his feet anymore. The best he thought he could hope for was to take advantage of the Red's close range and unload everything he had.

Is that what Bern would do? Scott took a deep breath, then released it through his teeth. *Hell, yes.*

He counted to three, then played the keypads, quickly bringing every onboard weapon to bear on the Red looming over him. Without pausing, he keyed the system-wide fire command, letting everything loose at once.

Slugs poured up from his guns, bracketed by crimson streams of laser energy. Sonic blasts rippled out of his emitters, and the full complement of missiles leaped from their racks.

The Red took every bit of it without flinching. When the smoke cleared, it was still standing over him, shiny and unmarred as ever.

"Flux *me*." Scott's voice was soft in the cockpit. Sensor data scrolled on the visor before him, displaying the lack of damage in columns of figures that left him stunned.

It didn't seem possible. How could a Battlenaut take that much firepower at close range and not suffer the slightest damage?

No Battlenaut he'd ever seen or fought or heard of could do it, that was for sure. The Red was something new, something completely outside his experience. It was the kind of thing that could win the civil war between the Commonwealth and the Rightfuls.

It was also the kind of thing that could kill him with ease.

Switching to the image from his topside camera, he saw the Red lean down and aim its forward cannons at him. Yellow and red plasma danced in the heart of both barrels as the guns powered up and made ready to fire.

This is it. Even as the words burned in his mind, Scott recalibrated his own lasers, guns, and sonics, bringing them to bear on the Red. He also tripped the self-destruct and started the 60-second countdown; maybe his exploding fusion power plant would finally put a scratch in the Red Battlenaut's hide.

He felt zero fear as the glowing red digits on his visor ticked from 60 seconds to 50 to 40. He wasn't a fearless man, but death itself didn't scare him; it hadn't frightened him since the time he'd died at the age of thirteen. He'd come back a different person...a Marine in the making even then.

The digits read 30...then 20. *Come and get me,* he thought as he opened up hard with all weapons, frying circuits and emptying out his remaining ammo.

Nothing he did seemed to faze the Red Battlenaut at all. When the Red suddenly straightened, it did so with no sign of strain, as if the barrage had nothing to do with its choice of movement.

That's okay, thought Scott. "You'll notice *this.*" He grinned wickedly as he watched the countdown on the visor tick from 20 to 15.

And then to 10.

Scott hooted and howled and kept pouring on the punishment. The timer changed to nine, then eight, then seven, then six...

And that was when the Red Battlenaut abruptly charged away from him.

"*Scudge*!" With the timer at four seconds, Scott put the self-destruct on hold. He threw all camera feeds on the visor at once, looking for the Red that had gotten away.

But it was already gone, vanished into the dense mist.

Suddenly, the voice of Captain Rollins burst out of the speaker. "Echo Charlie Bravo! This is Kilo Papa Zulu, responding to your Mayday!"

"About time," said Scott, and then he flipped on the mic. "Watch your six, Kilo! There's some kind of souped-up Red Battlenaut on the loose!"

"I've got eyes on you, Scott." As Rollins said it, Scott spotted him on his leftside camera. "Looks like you've taken a beating."

No kidding. "Recommend you call additional backup, Kilo Papa." Scott's eyes roamed the feeds, watching for signs of his red-hulled foe. "I threw everything I had at that thing, and it didn't even chip the paint."

"I didn't see it on radar or telemetry," said Rollins as he walked his sand brown Battlenaut toward Scott. "How long ago was it here?"

"Thirty seconds before you arrived," said Scott. "At the most."

"Well, it's gone now," said Rollins. "And no reports of

a Red Battlenaut elsewhere, either."

"Trust me, it's out there," said Scott. "And I'm telling you, the damn thing's a *colossus.*"

Searchlights flared to life on Rollins' armor, combing the mist around him on all sides. "Must be fast, too, if it ran out of sensor range just before I got here."

"Must be." Even as Scott said it, he didn't think it rang true. If the Red had been a speedster, wouldn't it have beaten him a lot faster? Wouldn't it have crushed him before he could get in any shots?

"Wish I could get my hands on this thing." Rollins kept combing the mist with his searchlights. "Sounds like the kind of tech we could put to good use."

Just then, Scott glimpsed a flicker of movement on his frontside feed, in the mist behind Rollins. "Bogie on your six!"

Rollins spun and focused his forward light on the mist. "You sure about that? Sensors read all clear."

There it was again. "Bogie confirmed!"

Rollins aimed his guns at the area in question. "I don't see it, Corporal."

Suddenly, there it was--the same Red Battlenaut, stalking out of the mist...heading straight for Rollins.

"Incoming!" Playing the stick, Scott rocked his armor back and forth, trying to get it unstuck. "Repeat, incoming!"

"What are you talking about? There's nothing out there." As Rollins said it, his forward light shone directly on the red behemoth marching toward him.

"Can't you *see* it?" Scott's heart hammered. Servos whined, then whirred as he regained control of his

Battlenaut's right leg. He straightened it, then pulled the left foot up from where it was wedged and flexed it forward, planting it solidly on the ground. Finally, he was back on his feet.

But he was too late to help his C.O. "All I see is fog," said Rollins, even though the Red Battlenaut was storming toward him in the beam of his own searchlight. "Nothing's there."

It was that exact moment when the Red came to a stop, standing fewer than two meters away. Its forward cannons glowed with roiling energy about to be unleashed.

And then it was unleashed. Twin beams of concentrated golden energy blasted point blank at Rollins' armor.

"No!" Scott couldn't shoot from where he stood for fear of hitting Rollins. He rushed his Battlenaut forward and around until he had an open line of sight.

Rollins' screams over the comm filled his ears...but not for long. Just as Scott started firing, Rollins' Battlenaut exploded. There were no more screams after that.

Then, the Red charged toward Scott with cannons blazing.

The same beams of golden energy that had obliterated Rollins crashed into Scott's armor, stopping him dead in his tracks. The lights in the cockpit flickered, and he knew what he had to do next.

Eject or die.

His armor shrieked as the Red's energy beams blasted it. Sucking in a deep breath, Scott swung his left hand out and smacked the big red button on the cockpit wall.

For a second, nothing happened. The lights dipped,

the control systems shut down, and the ejection sequence was interrupted.

Then, everything flashed back to life. The top of the Mark VI blew off, and the cockpit couch launched upward.

As the couch gained altitude, Scott saw his Battlenaut blow to pieces under the Red's assault far below. If the colossus knew the armor's occupant had escaped, it gave no sign--just stormed through the flames and debris and disappeared into the mist.

Then, Scott went higher and lost sight of the whole scene. As the couch leveled off, following its programmed autopilot coordinates to get him to safety, he found himself staring up at the pale gray sky.

Fighter craft zigged and zagged far above him, firing lasers and missiles at each other. A massive carrier ship hung in the distance, a Commonwealth vessel dispatching fresh fighters and Battlenaut reinforcements. A Rightful destroyer cruised toward it, unleashing a fusillade of missiles.

It would all be over soon. If the Rightfuls had an army of Red Battlenauts at their disposal, they would make short work of the Commonwealth forces on every front. They would tear down the Commonwealth government in nothing flat and institute their own form of domination.

Because nothing he knew could oppose the Red Battlenaut. His own Captain hadn't even been able to *see* it when it had been right in front of him.

Which left Solomon Scott with just one question to consider as the cockpit couch whisked him through the raging battle: why had *he* been able to see it when Rollins hadn't?

ALSO BY ROBERT JESCHONEK

6 SCIFI STORIES VOLUMES 1-4

A GRAIN FROM A BALANCE

DAY 9

HEAVEN BENT

UNIVERSAL LANGUAGE

VENDETTA

"Robert T. Jeschonek is a towering talent." – Mike Resnick, Hugo and Nebula Award-winning author of the *Starship* series

"Robert Jeschonek is the literary love child of Tim Burton and Neil Gaiman—his fiction is cutting edge, original, and pulsing with dark and fantastical life." – Adrian Phoenix, critically acclaimed author of *The Maker's Song* and *Hoodoo* series.

Pie Press